Maggie Makepeace was born in Buckinghamshire and went to school in Devon. She has a BSc in Zoology from Newcastle University and an MSc in Ecology from Aberdeen. She has worked as a TV presenter, for the Scottish Wildlife Trust and in the Wales office of the RSPB. She is married and lives in Somerset. Maggie Makepeace has written three previous novels: *Breaking the Chain, Travelling Hopefully* and, most recently, *The Would-Begetter.*

Praise for Maggie Makepeace's previous novels:

'sparkling comedy… high-value entertainment'
Elizabeth Buchan, *Sunday Times*

'a perceptive black comedy of manners,
morals and emotional muddles'
Living

'a sophisticated, quirkily humorous novel'
Books Magazine

'very witty… a very worthwhile read'
Sussex Life

Also by Maggie Makepeace

Breaking the Chain
Travelling Hopefully
The Would-Begetter

Out of Step

Maggie Makepeace

ARROW

Published by Arrow in 1999

5 7 9 10 8 6 4

First published in the United Kingdom in 1999 by Century

Arrow Books
20 Vauxhall Bridge Road, London, SW1V 2SA

Random House Australia (Pty) Limited
20 Alfred Street, Milsons Point, Sydney,
New South Wales 2061, Australia

Random House New Zealand Limited
18 Poland Road, Glenfield
Auckland 10, New Zealand

Random House South Africa (Pty) Limited
Endulini, 5a Jubilee Road, Parktown 2193, South Africa

The Random House Group Limited Reg. No. 954009

www.randomhouse.co.uk

A CIP catalogue record for this book
is available from the British Library

Papers used by Random House are natural,
recyclable products made from wood grown in
sustainable forests. The manufacturing processes conform to
the environmental regulations of the country of origin

ISBN 0 09 924282 6

Printed and bound in Norway by
AIT Trondheim AS, Trondheim

For MATT and BEN
who turned out so well

Acknowledgements

Thanks to all my Somerset friends for conversation, lateral thinking, insight and laughs: Sue Kay, Laurian Bowring, Hilary Giles, Brigid McConville, Carol Cox, Wendy Mewes, Malgosia Chelminska and Michou Godfrey.

To the Godney Group: Tessa Warburg, Shelley Bovey and Janet Laurence for tremendous help and encouragement.

And to Tim, as ever, for being there, and for building the house around us.

Chapter One

'I dunno what all the fuss is about,' a voice protested on Nell's car radio. 'I mean, if they're that bothered about the drought and the reservoirs getting empty and stuff, then why don't they simply fill them up from the mains?'

Nell gave a shout of derisive laughter and switched off. She concentrated on taking a difficult bend in the road, and when she was back on the straight again, she thought: Water – that's definitely a priority. I want to live in a place where I can watch it flowing past my window, preferably in both directions, so it had better be tidal. I want a little clinker-built dinghy, so that I can potter up and down it and explore the creeks. I also want birds, particularly waders, so I'll need mudflats. I want paintable scenery without crowds. I want privacy and peace. I don't want too difficult a journey into work every day. And I don't just want jam on it; I want quince jelly.

She smiled as she remembered what her mother and father would have chanted, as they used to, to Nell's childish demands: *'I want, I want,' was Fanny's cry!* And then she felt uneasy all over again at wishing to leave their house behind her, and begin again elsewhere. If they were still alive, she thought, I'd have left without a qualm years ago. People of thirty who still live with their parents are definitely sad. But I suppose I've stayed on all this time because it's been my only link with who I am – who I *was*.

The road opened out as it reached the ridge of the hill and Nell, looking to her right, saw a large smug Georgian house serene in its own parkland about halfway down the hillside and overlooking the boat-rich estuary of the River Torrent. A sign by the gates read: 'Thrushton Hall', and below it a smaller one: 'Eely Private Moorings'. She wanted to stop for a better view, but even now the narrowness of the road prevented her until after she had passed the Thrushton estate's Home Farm buildings. Here there was a convenient layby and an uninterrupted view down over the fields, which fell away steeply to the woodland at the bottom by the water's edge. On the other side of the river the precipitous ground was fit only for trees, mostly oak and ash towards the river mouth (proper trees, as Nell always thought) and then increasingly the more commercial sitka spruce the further west she looked, until, at the head of the estuary where the tiny Eel tributary merged with the Torrent, the folds of the hillside were almost entirely submerged in a uniform dark green. The open grasslands beside and below her were now a miserable yellowish brown after a summer almost devoid of rain; not like the lush South West at all. It was rather – Nell searched for the appropriate word – sinister. Would it ever rain again? She vowed never to complain if it did.

She got her binoculars out for a better view, and scrutinised the side of the big house and part of its long formal gardens. Mmm, she thought, I could fancy a place like that – maybe a fraction out of my league though? And I'd have to spend far too much time watering the herbaceous borders. And it's too high above the river. I'd like to be closer. She focused the glasses on the old two-span stone bridge at the upper limit of the estuary, and along the opposite bank to the Eel Creek where there was a spit of land and half a dozen long boats without masts, moored in a line. She followed the flow back down-stream, past a small mid-river islet and eastwards, until the woodland on her left entirely hid the Torrent and its exit to the sea from her view.

She sat on for a while as the September sun warmed the top of her head through the opened car roof, and watched as a couple of tiny bright figures walked the coastal path below her, on the diversion caused by the river mouth which took them inland in a loop. One of these days, she thought, I must do that walk, *all* of it. And then it came to her: Now Martin's gone, I can. I can do *anything*. It was a revolutionary idea.

A movement on the ground nearby caught her eye. A small brown bird flew away from her with an unexpected flash of white from its tail.

'A wheatear!' The first of the autumn migrants. She was delighted. It was high time she migrated too. She took herself, started the car again and moved off. Then almost immediately there was an unexpected sideroad leading down towards the estuary. She overshot it, but backed up for a better look. It was only a rough farm track with a grass strip down the centre and it looked unkempt and rutty, but she decided to risk it anyway. She drove down cautiously in first gear. Trees hung overhead, forming a dappled green tunnel, and then quite soon the track widened on a bend and the wood to her left gave way briefly to open fields and an even better view of the river with its wide curve to the south, the dunes at its mouth, and the grey sea beyond it. Now she could see the well-known sailing club on the north bank, with its plastic tenders neatly arranged down the backbone of the marina walkway, and the multicoloured yachts moored out in the broad stretch of water sheltered behind the head, all pointed the same way by the tide.

She stopped again and scanned the vista with her binoculars. The track ahead of her ran down even more steeply and disappeared amongst trees at its foot, but there surely, just visible through the topmost branches were a pair of chimneys? Yes, and a suggestion of terracotta-coloured roof tiles.

Now, that, Nell thought, driving on downhill, could be more like it!

Robert Hayhoe sat in his office in the upstairs room of Bottom Cottage (in which he also slept) and stared out of the east window at the curve of the river and the nearly empty coastal path. The sun glinted invitingly on the water. In his vegetable patch below he could see his courgettes turning into useless marrows almost before his eyes. It was much too good a day to waste indoors, working. There was firewood to chop and stack before the onset of winter. The garden needed weeding. The hedge wanted cutting . . . He sighed, and addressed himself to his computer, reading the columns of figures on the screen and forcing himself to make sense of them.

He heard a car outside just as he had got his brain back on track again, and frowned. It wouldn't be his milk or the post because both were left in a wooden box in the hedge, up by the top road. It was probably more bloody grockles assuming his lane was a public right of way, and parking in his turning circle whilst they walked down to the sea. He'd always meant to put up a sign, 'Private Road', but hadn't got round to it. He didn't want to call the world's attention to the cottage. He valued its solitude. Anyway, it was now the end of the summer season and he had the whole of the winter ahead of him to have the place to himself. He wasn't going to fuss about it. He didn't have time to spare, anyway. His clients were pressing him to get their accounts sorted out. This one had to be finished today.

His eye was caught nevertheless, a few minutes later, by the sight of a woman standing just beyond his fence, framed by the runner beans on one side and the eight-foot sunflowers he'd grown for Josh and Rosie on the other. She had a pair of binoculars round her neck and she was looking straight at him.

She went on staring so unselfconsciously that he realised she couldn't see him. The sun must be reflecting off the window glass making it one-way only. He indulged himself for a few moments by looking back at her, picking up his own binoculars from the windowsill and examining her face in the same analytical way that he watched the birds on the estuary. She had thick brown hair cut short, broad cheekbones, a wide upturned mouth and a spattering of freckles. An intelligent, sensual sort of face, he decided; rather appealing.

Then she frowned, and turned abruptly away. Had his glasses glinted at her, giving him away? He put them down in some confusion, feeling foolish. Spying on women wasn't something he ever did. What was he thinking of? He made himself concentrate on the job in hand, and was only dimly aware of a car starting up as she drove away.

The following Monday she turned up again. He was sure it must be her, even though she had her back to him. This time she was sitting on a camp stool on the bend of the river, and apparently painting the view. She was further away this time, so Rob felt able to look at her again through binoculars. He could even see some of her picture. It looked pretty good. He hoped she wasn't going to make a habit of driving down his lane. If she did it again, he would have to discourage her. She could always get to the coast path further along by the sailing club like everybody else. But she was probably only a late holidaymaker, so he most likely wouldn't have to bother. Some people have all the luck, he thought. It's going to be years before I'll get the chance again to have a peaceful uninterrupted break where I can please myself. Then he caught himself up. How can I say that, living here!

The next Monday she didn't appear, and Rob (having in an idle moment labelled her *Miss Dowsabell*) was fleetingly disappointed, and then forgot all about her. So when he saw her again, four weeks later, he was unprepared for feeling pleased.

She was drawing this time, and it seemed that his cottage was her subject. The morning light streamed over her shoulders and gleamed in the spikes of her fringe, which were being blown up above her face by the breeze. He couldn't see her expression as it was in shadow, and he didn't like to use his glasses because she was directly facing him. Anyway, he hadn't time for all this. He must get *on*. He worked for a while feeling irritated with himself and then, abruptly, he got to his feet and went downstairs. The back door was the nearest, but he deliberately went through his kitchen and out at the front, so he could see where she had parked her car.

It was a blue Citroën 2CV and it wasn't actually on his turnaround at all, but at the junction of his lane with the coastal path (where it altered course to go behind his garden) tucked carefully out of the way under the trees. She was still trespassing though. He followed the path round to the riverbank, and along it until he reached her. He'd meant to say something pleasant and meaningless, and then lead up to his main purpose gradually, but somehow it all went wrong.

'Hello,' she said, glancing up as he approached. 'I was beginning to wonder whether you had legs.'

'Sorry?'

'Well, I only ever see your top half through the window.'

Embarrassment flooded through him. She must have seen him staring at her like a bloody voyeur! He quite forgot, in his haste to retreat, what he'd planned to say. 'Look,' he said, 'er, sorry, but my lane isn't actually a right of way . . .'

She looked him straight in the eye – she had very fine green ones – and seemed a lot less flustered than he was.

'Oh . . . I do beg your pardon. So, how am I supposed

to get here, then? This is the public path, isn't it?'

'Yes it is. You have to go down the road to the sailing club. It's only about . . .'

'A mile that way?' She gestured with a pencil.

'Yes. Sorry . . . I . . .'

'Fine,' she said. 'Now I know, I won't intrude upon your patch again.' She looked put out.

'It's OK,' Rob said. 'Don't worry about it.' He felt firmly in the wrong, but unable to rectify the situation. 'Um . . . bye, then.'

It was only when he had got back to the steadiness of his empty cottage that he thought, Damn! And I never even looked at her drawing. What a total prat.

Nell usually chose to draw and paint out of doors on Mondays for two reasons: first, she had half of that day in lieu every time she had to work on Saturday mornings, and secondly there were generally fewer people out and about on Mondays, so she suffered less ill-considered appreciation from each passing art critic.

From the day that she discovered the secret cottage, she was loath to go anywhere else. It seemed to her to be the most perfect place imaginable, and there were enough subjects, both landscape and still life, to keep her going for years. The two-storey house itself was very simple: a door in the middle with a window on either side downstairs, three windows upstairs, and a chimney at each end. The roof was clay-tiled, and the walls had not been whitewashed for so long that they'd had plenty of time to accumulate botanical hangers-on: several large patches of a dark fungus and a general wash of green algae. The paint was peeling on the window-frames, and there was a scuff mark on the front door where someone was clearly in the habit of kicking it.

But for all its lack of sophistication it didn't look unloved, and people clearly lived in it. There was a dusty

Land Rover parked outside, and a small child's tricycle and yellow lorry in the centre of the open turning space. On the left of the cottage a vegetable garden flourished; organic, judging by the weeds, the pile of old lorry tyres and the overflowing compost heaps. There were half a dozen huge sunflowers, three of which had faces carved on to their central discs – two eyes and a smiley mouth each – probably done with a spoon! Nell was entranced. Then out of the corner of her eye she caught a movement from an upstairs window and felt as though she'd been caught prying. She turned abruptly and left.

A week later she decided to go back again, taking her painting gear. As she walked past the cottage, she glanced up at the bedroom window and saw a man sitting there, presumably working since he was staring fixedly at something in front of him. She noticed that he looked youngish and had dark curly hair – a Heathcliff type, she thought, but he's probably only five foot nothing when he stands up. Men are usually disappointing.

She went past swiftly so as not to give the appearance of snooping, but she had time to see that the back of the cottage was very close to the water with only a strip of grass and a metre-high stone wall to defend it against flooding. There was a small wooden jetty too, but it looked unused and derelict. It was high tide but today the river was not full. Presumably in the winter it could be a torrent, as its name suggested. She wondered if Heathcliff lived there all the year round. From a buddleia bush a robin sang its intermittent autumn song, dropping the clear notes into the still air. She could hear the distant bumping and crashing of a flail mower as a farmer cut his hedges, but here all was calm. Nell wondered where the children were.

She walked further along the river path leaving the cottage behind her, and kept going past the detour behind the sailing club until she could see the whole of the river mouth. Then she sat herself down on her camp stool and prepared to compose her view of it. On its left were the dunes, piled up by the westerly winds in ridges, ever advancing inland. On its right were grassy slopes, broken at their foot by modest cliffs, on the eminence of which rose the forty-foot tower of the Thrushton folly, greyly self-important and as out of place as a speaker at a Trappist picnic.

Dragonflies hawked overhead as she worked. Puffy white clouds condensed high above and cobbled themselves together into a mackerel sky. Rain in twelve hours, Nell thought. At last. She stayed for as long as the light would allow, and by the time it had changed too drastically, she was confident that she'd got enough on canvas to be able to finish it at home.

The painting eventually turned out well, and she was encouraged to want to do more, but it was a whole month before she managed another Monday by the estuary. Sibyl had been feeling guilty about all the summer Saturdays Nell had volunteered to work, and was insisting that as the proprietor of *ARTFUL^L*, she herself must man the little shop in Boxcombe for the foreseeable future in order to give Nell 'proper' weekends in which to 'take up any good offers that are going'. Sibyl had never liked Martin, but had tactfully kept silent until after he had moved out of Nell's house and taken himself off. Dear Sibyl, Nell thought affectionately. Dear Elly's Ma, what would I do without you?

So it was early October before Nell returned to the cottage, determined this time to do a drawing of the house itself. She hadn't long been there, and was getting on famously with the light behind her illuminating the scene quite perfectly. The wind tousled her hair as she worked and she was glad of her warm sweater, but glad too to be distanced from the unnatural heat and humidity of the preceding summer, which had rendered her exhausted and apathetic. This was the best of English weather, cool but bright – and one of those days when everything went right.

She looked up with narrowed eyes to take a line on the gable end of the cottage, and there he was – Heathcliff himself – walking down the path towards her. Even at this distance, she was sure it was him because this man was wearing a red sweatshirt of the same colour as the one she'd seen him in as she'd passed under his window earlier. It was obvious too that he was considerably more than five feet tall. He'd better be nice, she thought, shading a dark area confidently with a soft pencil, because if he isn't, he's got absolutely *no* business to be living in *my* ideal home . . .

Chapter Two

Now it's mid-October, Nell thought on Saturday morning, I can sit and draw outside at weekends without being pestered by trippers, so I'll go today. But I'll have to carry all my stuff in a rucksack or something, because it's going to be a long walk – nasty possessive *selfish* man!

Looking at the Landranger map that morning, she had decided not to drive as far as the road to the sailing club, but instead to try the track going down by Thrushton Hall leading to Eely private moorings. She expected to find a locked gate barring her way but the one at the bottom was open – maybe because it was out of season – and she was able to drive right down to the river and park there unchallenged. The gardens of the big house, she could now see, ended in a substantial riverside quay but it was empty of boats. In the opposite direction the Torrent was now narrow enough to be crossed by an old bridge in two high stone spans.

I think I want landscape today, Nell thought. I wonder what's across there.

She leant against the stone parapet and looked both ways with binoculars, up river through the spruce forest, and then downstream towards the little tree-filled island and beyond. She could see the wood around Bottom Cottage but not the house itself, and wondered if Heathcliff was in there still staring resolutely forwards, amidst all these wonderfully distracting surroundings. She decided he must be looking at a computer screen and was most probably a teleworker, newly arrived. He's bound to have a totally unrealistic romantic view of the countryside, and after just one lonely, river-lapping, *wuthering* winter, he'll up sticks and leave. Then, she thought – dropping bits of grass into the water and watching them be drawn sluggishly upstream with the rising tide – then *I* shall buy the cottage, and I shall let people use my lane if they want to, and I shall keep all my books upstairs so I shan't panic if the river floods, and I shall live frugally, happily, ever after . . . Mmm. But in the meantime . . .

As she walked on, the spruce woods gave off a musty fungal smell after the recent longed-for rain, and Eely Creek, when she came to it, also smelt autumnal and decaying, but with the sharp, dank odour of anaerobic mud, a whiff that Nell had come to appreciate because to her it was redolent with memories of happy days watching waders, drinking tepid coffee out of a Thermos, and sharing broken chocolate biscuits. Martin had scoffed at birdwatching, so they hadn't done any. This new freedom was intoxicating.

She breathed deeply and loitered beside the half-dozen houseboats moored there – the long boats without masts that she'd seen from the top road. Most were pretty dingy but the last one was a gem: carved and painted like a gypsy caravan in reds and greens, and with all the appearance of a permanent home, with a wide gangplank that had railings like a bridge, and tubs of still-flowering petunias on either side.

How lovely, Nell thought. I must draw that too.

She might once immediately have wished to live in such a whimsical place, but not now. She walked on, across a small wobbly suspension bridge over the thin Eel tributary and found herself on the wooded coastal path that ran downstream above the south bank of the Torrent. If she continued along it, she would be able to look across the river and see Bottom Cottage without having to run the risk of encroaching on anyone's ungenerously defended territory. The thought appealed to her, and she walked briskly until she came to a clearing in the trees where a rough meadow went right down to the water's edge. The sky had clouded over. Nell hoped the rain would hold off until she'd had time to do a decent sketch.

It did. From this direction, right opposite, the cottage looked even more appealing, sheltered as it was on three sides by trees and with the open hill rising behind it, hedged and fenced into fields full of greenly recovering grass. The drought was over, at least for now. Nell made colour notes at the margin of her sketch pad and was concentrating so hard on getting them just right that she was unaware of the arrival of an elderly farmer in an old pick-up, until he stopped it right beside her and leant out of his window.

'All right, that is,' he offered, gesturing.

'Oh.' Nell's instinct was always to hide her drawings, but politeness forbade. 'Thanks.'

'Do a lot of this artistic stuff, do you?'

'Whenever I can, yes. I didn't know you could get a vehicle down here though.'

'Four-wheel drive, see. Collecting up my sheep off the head.' He gestured towards the dog in the back, and the close-cropped headland projecting out of sight into the bend of the river.

'Oh, I see. Not a public right of way, then?'

'No, but you can come down over my yard any time you likes. Don't let the missus see ee though.' He cackled. Nell smiled cautiously.

'Bottom Cottage, that be,' the old man went on. He put out a wide, calloused hand and Nell gave him the pad so he could study her drawing more closely. 'I could tell ee a thing or two 'bout that. Oh yes.'

'What sort of thing?'

'Ooooh, goings-on – shoutings – swearings. Sound of it carries right across the water some days, but I don't reckon they knows that or they wouldn't do it, now would 'em?'

'I suppose not. So who lives there?'

'Oh, she's gone now. Took herself and the two kiddies off to the town, she did. 'Twas either that or have 'em taken off her by the Social.' He shook his head. 'Couldn't stick it even three year. I s'pose 'twasn't so surprising – her with her fancy townie ways and her high heels! Stands to reason, doanit? He'm all right though. Everybody do like him. He must bin there goin on ten year now. He keeps hisself to hisself but he'm no bother to nobody. If you knows what I mean?' Nell reached for her sketchbook and took it back. 'Yes, he'm all right, be Rob Hayhoe.' He had a sudden bright idea, and patted his door as if to emphasise it. 'I reckon he'd buy that picture off you. You wants to give him a try?'

Nell made a point of remembering the name, but waited until after the farmer had driven away, his collie bouncing from side to side in the open back of the pickup, before she carefully wrote it down under her bottom colour notes – *Rob Hayhoe*.

'That's a really unusual name,' Elly said, full length on Nell's sofa. 'Hey! What if he's related to Malachy Hayhoe?'

'Who?'

'Oh, come on, Nell! The sexy actor who plays the senior surgeon in that TV hospital thing.'

'The slimy one?'

'The distinguished, caring, *luscious* father-figure, yes.'

'I hope not, for his sake.' Nell made a face.

'But if he *is*,' Elly said, 'it might be a good career move for me to meet him.'

Nell was sceptical of her friend's recently expressed desire to become an actress, assuming it was just the latest in a long line of short-lived passions, but she said, 'Go ahead. I'll give you a map reference.'

'That's no good. You've got to come too, for moral support.'

'Oh no.' Nell was adamant.

'Please, Nell. This could be really important to me.'

'Why? Why the sudden desire to act?'

'I just know it's for me. I could do it.'

'Then go on your own! You're not exactly shy after all.'

'Can I take your drawing of his cottage to sell, as a pretext?'

'Oh, all right, but he won't want it.'

'Yesss!' Elly punched the air.

Nell regarded her with affection. She couldn't remember a time when she hadn't known her, and her mother. She just wished she could grow to be as fond of Elly's husband . . . 'What would Paul say?'

'Who cares? I shan't tell him until I've landed a leading rôle, and then just watch him lap up the reflected glory!'

Nell privately thought that Paul was too keen on the centre stage himself voluntarily to rejoice in anyone else's success, but she kept quiet.

'Why on earth did we both choose to do Fine Art at university, Nell?' Elly shook her head. 'We must have been loony; *folie à deux*!'

'Not at all. You wanted to do interior design, and I wanted to paint. It was obvious.'

'Yes, but look where it's got us.'

'Well, your business is doing pretty well.'

'Maybe, but I should have done drama. I've wasted *so* much time.'

'Does Paul know how you feel?'

'Nope. He's far too wrapped up in his school and his bloody sailing.'

'And the boys?'

'Oh, Will and Sam know I've been a drama queen all my life.'

15

Nell smiled.

'But what about you, Nell? Isn't it time you reassessed your life too? I know Sibyl would hate to lose you, but she worries about you wasting all your education, working behind her shop counter.'

'I like it there,' Nell said firmly. 'It suits me. I'm not the up-shifting type. I've decided I want a life, not a career. Careers suck people dry and leave them no time to just *be*. But now you mention it, I am thinking of making some changes.'

'Does Sibyl know?'

'No, I mean personal changes. I want to sell my house and live in the country.'

'Where exactly?'

'Funnily enough, exactly where this Hayhoe man lives. Tell you what, if you're determined to make his acquaintance, you couldn't introduce a small neutron bomb into his cottage, could you? You know – the sort that kills people and leaves buildings intact!'

'Nice place to live, eh?' Elly was looking at her curiously.

'The best,' Nell said simply.

Elly did not have time to visit Bottom Cottage that weekend but when she came down from London a fortnight later, she persuaded Nell to go at least part of the way with her to direct her. Elly drove, and when they came to a ridge overlooking a deep valley with a stripe of river at its floor and a gleam of sea on the horizon, Nell made her slow down, and pointed out a cart track on their right.

'OK,' Nell said, 'drive down through the tree tunnel . . . there's a vantage point . . . yes, there on the left. Stop here. The cottage is at the bottom. Now look!' She passed her binoculars to Elly, who obediently peered through them. It had been raining hard all week, making up for past deficiencies, and everywhere this morning looked grey, even the yachts. The grey hills came down to the grey water. The grey trees stopped just short of the grey mud. A few new-fallen grey leaves covered the grey path between wood and river. She looked downstream at the greyly ebbing tide and a few grey birds poking about in the distance. The sky was especially grey.

'Isn't it paradise?' Nell said.

'It's certainly exclusive, but it would be much too secretive and claustrophobic for me.'

'Some people have no soul,' Nell said cheerfully, putting on scarf, gloves and a woolly hat. 'This is where I get out. Don't be long though; it's a bit nippy to be hanging about for ages.'

'Right,' Elly said, restarting the engine. 'I'm not at all sure about the rest of this road though. Sure you won't come?'

Nell shook her head.

'How much d'you want for your drawing?'

'Oh, I hadn't though. Twenty?'

Elly drove slowly on down the track alone, bottoming out twice and having to choose her route with care. No one in their right mind would want to live here! she thought, except of course Nell (and maybe Sibyl?); the unworldly in thrall to the impractical.

At the turning place, she parked by a Land Rover and looked critically at the house. She saw it as a 'Before' photo in a renovation portfolio. She banged on the front door with her knuckles and then brushed flakes of paint off them, holding the picture frame under one arm. No answer. She tried again.

'Can I help you?' a voice said from behind her. A man and two small children were walking up the path from the river. The elder child's wellington boots were making squelch-squelch noises with every step.

'Are you Mr Hayhoe?'

'That's me.'

'Oh good.' He's quite good-looking, Elly thought. Lots of curly brown hair. Mid-thirties, early forties? A bit thin. 'I've brought this to show you.' She held out the drawing.

'Want to see!' The boy with the sodden wellies rushed up and snatched it from her.

'Gently, Josh,' the man said. 'It's breakable, OK?'

'Me, me,' the small girl insisted, letting go of her father's hand and bumbling forward.

'Let Rosie have a look too,' he said, squatting down beside them. 'I'll hold it for both of you.'

'That's my bedroom,' Josh said, jabbing his finger at the window and leaving a smudge on the glass.

'And Rosie's too,' his father reminded him.

'I've got my own room at home!'

'Yes, well, we've only got two bedrooms here, haven't we?' He glanced up at Elly. 'Sorry, these two monsters do rather seem to take things over.' The children swaggered a little. He looked properly at the drawing. 'This is very good. Did you do it?'

'God, no! It's by a friend of mine. She's very talented but she's no good at self-promotion, so I . . .'

'Dad! My feet are cold.'

'Rothie wants to do a weeee . . .'

'Sorry,' Rob said. 'I'd better just deal with . . . Come on . . .' He handed the picture back to Elly and followed his children through the front door. Elly brought up the rear, and waited in the kitchen/living room as the three of them went upstairs, boots and all. She saw that this could be a very stylish room indeed if a great deal of money were to be spent on it. The floor was still covered by its original flagstones. The stove was set in a broad chimney alcove under a thick wooden beam where an open hearth had once been. There was an inglenook – a little seat – on one side of the stove, and an old bread oven on the other. Facing the back door on the opposite wall was a wooden staircase to the first floor, and next to it a large scrubbed pine table, but there all charm ended. There seemed to be no storage cupboards or work surfaces to speak of. The sink under the back window had only one basin and one draining board, and an old plastic drying rack that looked distinctly dirty. A few blackened pans hung on hooks from another beam. There were no curtains or blinds at the window, and any space on the walls which was not obscured by stuck-on children's paintings appeared to be covered in childish scribbles in pencil and felt-tip pen.

A box of toys at the far end had overflowed, and bits of Lego and heads of Play-People crunched underfoot rather like extra large grains of . . . sugar? No, that *was* sugar.

Hmm, Elly thought rather grimly. 'Needs some attention'? Or 'Ripe for development'? How could one put it politely?

'Nice and warm in here,' she said, as Rob came downstairs again with both children.

'Yes, we've got a woodburner. Sit down, Josh, or I can't get these boots of yours off.' He pointed it out.

In Elly's limited experience, woodburning stoves had only three settings – too cold, too hot, and out – but she said, 'Lovely.'

'Pop upstairs and get yourself some dry socks, yes?'

'I want *you* to come.'

'Sorry,' Rob said yet again. 'Back in a mo.'

'Hayhoe,' Elly said as he came downstairs again. 'Are you by any chance related to . . .'

'Yes,' he cut in, rather wearily, it seemed to her. 'But unlike my father, no, I don't act.'

'Oh dear. You're obviously very tired of that question.'

'Just a little.'

'My apologies. Does he ever visit you here?'

'Hardly ever. He has a busy schedule.' He pronounced it 'skedule' with some distaste, as though quoting. 'And

19

'before you ask, he eats wannabe actresses for elevenses.'

'He does not,' Joshua protested. 'He has coffee and shortbread.'

'Hungry!' Rosie piped up, amidst the laughter.

'Forgive me,' Elly said. 'I'm not used to being seen through so speedily.' She waited for a standard compliment, but it didn't come.

'So, do you really want to sell this drawing, or was it just . . .?'

'Oh yes, definitely.' She hastily offered it to him again.

'For how much?' he asked, without taking it.

'Forty pounds.'

He pursed his lips. 'Bit steep.'

'Daddy, Daddy, Rothie's *hungry*.'

'All right, poppet. We'll have something very soon.'

'Pity Nell isn't here,' Elly said. 'As well as being an artist she's also a brilliant cook.'

'Why didn't she come with you?'

'Shy, I suppose. Reluctant to trespass again.'

'Oh . . . is she the woman who's been down here a few times in a blue Citroën?'

'The very one.' A brilliant idea struck Elly, and she acted upon it instantly. 'Actually, I think she rather fancies you, but for God's sake don't tell her I told you so! Look, don't feel obliged to buy the pic. I'm not trying to do a hard sell. I'll just write down her name and phone number, shall I? Then you can take time to decide whether you really want it or not.' She put the drawing under her arm again, opened her shoulder-bag and wrote on a small notepad, tearing the page off and giving it to him.

'Eleanor Chant, eh? Well . . . . thanks.' He stuffed it into a pocket in his faded cords.

'Well, mustn't hold up your . . .' Your what? It was eleven o'clock.

'Breakfast. We're a trifle disorganised this morning.'

'. . . Breakfast, then. Sorry to have bothered you.'

'Not at all.'

'Bye.' She got into her car and drove off up the track, thinking: Well, well, well! I hope I'm right. Could be just what Nell needs after the ghastly Martin – an intelligent, non-macho, well-spoken New Man!

Nell jumped up and down to keep warm. It was far too cold even to do any preliminary sketches as she had planned, and she was cross with herself for having agreed to come at all. When Elly finally drove up and stopped beside her, she saw her drawing was still lying on the passenger seat.

'Told you so!' she said, picking it up as she got in.

'Aha! But it's not the way you think,' Elly countered, raising both eyebrows in an ironic glance.

'What isn't?'

'Well, I may be wrong, but I got the distinct impression that Mr Rob Hayhoe liked your picture so much that he hasn't bought it on purpose.'

'You *what*?'

'Unless I'm very much mistaken, he's going to use it as a ploy to get you to go down there instead of me.'

'Why?'

'I'll bet you ten, no twenty, quid that he phones you within the week.'

'What, to buy the drawing?'

'No, dumbo! To ask you out! The man clearly fancies you. He realised who you were at once. He's probably been fantasising about this beautiful capricious, unknown painter for weeks.'

'What a load of old balls!' Nell said. 'Twenty quid? You're on.' They shook hands.

'Mmm,' Elly said. 'Easy money, that.'

'What d'you mean? How can he phone? He hasn't got my number. He doesn't even know my name.'

'Ah well . . . actually he does.' She grinned triumphantly at Nell. 'Sorry and all that, but I had to write them both down for him. He absolutely *insisted*!'

Chapter Three

As was her habit on at least two mornings a week, Nell dragged herself unwillingly out of bed in order to go swimming. She knew that when she got there she would enjoy every minute of it, but at this early hour, with the day hardly begun and the world outside barely light, it needed considerable willpower. In October there were only the regulars at the leisure centre, so the pool was uncluttered with fair-weather swimmers, and you could do serious lengths and get some real exercise. Today, taking a brief pre-swim shower by the side of the pool, she noticed there was hardly anyone in so far, and then caught sight of a sleek auburn head and thought: Oh good. Anna's here.

Anna Smith had newly arrived in her job teaching biology at Nell and Elly's old school in Boxcombe. She was six years younger than Nell but keen to be friends, and willing to be fearlessly candid to that end. In her first week at swimming she told Nell all about the married man she'd been having an affair with in London, whom she called 'the Boss' to 'protect the guilty'. Last week she'd had an unkind tale about the stupidity of the Boss's wife, also referred to under a nickname.

'So Ermintrude goes to this party,' Anna had said, 'and what does she do? She says to this poor unfortunate woman, "Oh I remember you at X's party last week. You were wearing the same dress as Y." Talk about tactless!'

Nell had felt rather uncomfortable about this, but enjoyed the stories nevertheless.

Today, as was her custom, Nell did ten lengths straight

off before stopping for a chat. When she'd finished, she found Anna lying face upwards, supporting herself with the back of her head on the tiled edge, and with the water lapping at the little pearl earstuds she always wore. She was doing leg exercises.

'Hi,' Anna said. 'How's things?'

'Fine,' Nell said, gliding towards her, smiling.

'Guess what? I've had some really good news. The Boss says he's missed me so much since I moved down here that he's decided to buy a place nearby so we can still meet! Isn't that great?'

'Amazing. So you didn't leave London to end the affair?'

'No way! I just got the chance of a permanent job and felt I had to take it. It was one hell of a wrench.'

'He obviously thought so too.'

'Lovely man,' Anna said contentedly.

'Will his wife know about the new place?'

'Unfortunately yes. He's officially buying it for family holidays, but he'll get down here without Ermintrude and kids whenever he can. So, how about you? Still feeling restless?'

'Even more so, if that's possible.'

'Have you begun looking for your dream house?'

'Worse than that. I've found it, but some wretched man got there before me.'

'On his own?'

'Sort of. I believe his children visit him at weekends. Why?'

'And the house is everything you've always wanted?'

'Absolutely.'

'Easy,' Anna said, breaking into a grin. 'The solution's obvious – seduce the man, and get the house thrown in for free!'

Nell laughed. 'We can't all be like you, you know.'

'Let's swim,' Anna said. 'Watch me scupper one of the selfish squad!' She launched herself on her back and headed off towards a swimmer notorious for hogging his lane, doing a fast crawl and *never* giving way. Nell had to admire her nerve. She swam behind her, doing breaststroke so she could see the outcome, and watched in amusement as the two swimmers powered their way towards each other. Anna, doing backstroke and unable to see ahead, had clear right of way, but the man had his head well down, only breathing every third or fourth stroke . . . Then, at the last minute, he saw her and grudgingly altered course. Anna reached the far end and briefly raised a fist in triumph.

Nell thought, She's the sort of person who always gets what she wants. I'm not like that.

When the telephone rang, and it was Rob Hayhoe, Nell's first impulse was to look at the calendar to see if Elly had won her bet. She had missed by two days! Nell smiled to herself.

'I was wondering if you had anything smaller?' he was saying.

'Oh, well, I'm not sure . . . no, I don't think so. I'm afraid original drawings don't come in a variety of handy sizes like shoes.' Hell! she thought. Why am I being so rude?

'No, of course not. It's just that forty pounds seemed a lo –'

'*Forty*?'

'Yes. That's what your friend said you wanted.'

'Typical Elly! I'm so sorry.' Nell took a breath. 'Look can we start again? I was hoping for about twenty, but since it's of your cottage, and I had no right of way down your lane in the first place, shall we call it fifteen?'

'Fair enough,' his voice sounded amused. 'Including delivery?'

A chance to see inside Bottom Cottage! 'If you want.' Nell was careful to keep her voice casual. 'I could bring it over this evening, if you like.'

'Proper job,' he said. 'See you about six thirtyish?'

'Right.'

Nell decided not to wear make-up. It would make her look as though she thought this was some special deal. But she did brush her hair carefully and put on a clean jersey.

He met her at the door, and stood aside to let her in. 'What a lovely place this is!' she exclaimed, putting her drawing down on the table. 'Do you mind if . . .?'

'By all means. Let me show you round.' He led the way, switching on the lights. 'Sitting room's through here . . .' *Decent size – three windows – oak beams – open fireplace – but no books . . .* 'Then back into the kitchen again, utility room off here, and then the woodburning stove over there, and the back door into the garden . . .' *Sink under window overlooking estuary – cheerful children's clutter – open staircase – photographs of two babies in increasing sizes – still no books.* 'Then up there is a bathroom and two bedrooms, the southern one of which I also use as my study.'

'A room of one's own,' Nell murmured.

'Virginia Woolf? I think I've got *To the Lighthouse*. In case you're wondering, I do have books, in fact I read a lot, but I keep them all upstairs as a precaution against extra high spring tides.'

'Oooohh,' Nell said, before she could stop herself.

'Sorry?'

'No, it's nothing.' She was dying to be shown upstairs as well, but he made no move to take her. Never mind, downstairs was even better than she'd imagined.

'I've written you a cheque,' he said, handing it over in an envelope. 'It's a very good drawing. My son, Josh, insisted I should buy it!'

'Thanks,' taking it rather awkwardly, and putting it straight into her pocket. 'How old is Josh?'

'He's five, and Rosie, my daughter, is three.'

'They must love it here!'

'When they are here.' He made a wry face.

'I'm sorry, I shouldn't have . . .' She stopped in confusion.

He looked impassive. 'You're not a bit like your friend, are you?'

'You mean I'm not beautifully dressed and sophisticated and glamorous?'

'God forbid! No, I meant you're not . . . brittle.'

Nell was uncertain how to take this. 'No, I bounce on impact,' she said flippantly, and then felt stupid. 'Well, best be off, I suppose.'

He saw her to her car, and as she was about to drive away he bent down to the window. 'Feel free to drive down here any time,' he said. 'If you fancy doing any more drawings, that is.'

'Thank you. I might just do that.' She moved off, conscious of his gaze, and didn't stop until she had got up to the top road. Then she undid her seatbelt so that she could fish the envelope out of her jeans pocket. She broke it open and took the cheque out. It was made out to Eleanor Chant in rather spidery writing, and it was for twenty-five pounds.

'Told you so!' Elly said excitedly on the phone that evening. 'I said he fancied you, didn't I?'

'Pretty flimsy evidence,' Nell objected.

'Not at all. Did he pay the full whack?'

'That reminds me – I've a bone to pick with you about that. Who said anything about forty pounds?'

'Why not? I thought it was a bit cheap, actually. People take you at your own valuation, you know. The more you ask, the more they think it's worth!'

'Maybe in London, yes.'

'Everywhere! You're as bad as Sibyl. God knows how you and she ever make any money at all from that shop. So, when are you seeing him again?'

'No idea.'

'He must have asked you?'

'No.'

'Come on, Nell. Didn't he say *anything*?'

'Well, it seems I'm now allowed to drive down his precious lane, but strictly for drawing purposes only.'

'Thought so,' Elly said in tones of satisfaction. 'He's just a bit shy. That type always are. You hate pushy men anyway, don't you? I should just take it as it comes.'

'I've no intention of "taking it" anywhere,' Nell said crisply.

But the following Saturday was one of those unexpectedly warm November days when a late high-pressure system gets blocked in over the British Isles, and hangs there motionless, allowing the inhabitants below it one last chance to sit comfortably out of doors before the sequential lows of winter begin to sweep in from the west. On such a day it was impossible to remain cooped up in Boxcombe.

I'll just drive down the lane to Bottom Cottage and walk along the river a bit, Nell, who wasn't working, told herself. And maybe I'll catch a glimpse of Rob's children. I'd be interested to know what they're like, and see if they're as spoilt as Elly says, but I'm not going to knock at the door or anything. Although perhaps I should return the extra ten pounds he gave me.

But when she arrived at Rob's turnaround, his Land Rover wasn't there. It hadn't occurred to Nell that he might be out and she felt rather foolish, realising that of course she'd intended him to see her all along, and had hoped that he might invite her in again. Instead she set off upstream.

The morning mist had all cleared, and a bright sun shone through the overhead branches of the trees along the river bank, picking out any of the golden foliage that was still attached. Nell shuffled her feet through the bulk of dead leaves on the ground, kicking them up in satisfying puffs and watching them settle again lightly like shoals of tawny flatfish. The tide was going out, and the revealed mudflats were smooth and innocent of footprints. She had the world to herself. Unless Rob was inside all along? She turned abruptly and retraced her steps, going straight up to the cottage and knocking on the front door. Silence. He definitely wasn't there.

Well, if he's not here, she thought, he can't object to my exploring a bit, can he?

She walked round the east side of the cottage, through the dormant vegetable garden, past decaying skeletons of the runner beans and sunflowers, until she came to the back, and the mossy green strip that did service as a lawn. Then she leant against the dry-stone wall just above the river, and examined the flotsam and jetsam displayed along the top of it. There were plastic fishing floats, water-sculpted stones, and bits of gribbled driftwood which (when floating on the sea) had been bored into interesting labyrinths by a species of marine crustacean. She picked them up and turned them over in her hands, examining them. They were exactly the sort of treasures she herself might have collected. She glanced up at the cottage and saw a pair of binoculars hanging by Rob's study window.

'And . . .' she said aloud, 'and he keeps his books upstairs . . .'

'Look,' Cassandra Hayhoe said to her husband on Saturday morning, as he was about to take the children away to spend the weekend with him. 'Look, before you go there's something we've got to discuss.'

'What?' Rob really didn't want to know.

'It's about money.'

'When isn't it?'

'You've got a flaming nerve,' Cassie said sharply. 'You're living on charity, you know. You should be bloody grateful.'

'Get to the point,' Rob said wearily.

'Right, I will. It's this: my parents want their loan repaying. They don't see why they should've paid a hefty deposit on this house when you're going on living in the cottage like a pig in muck as if nothing's happened!'

'You mean *you* don't see why.'

'I *mean*, they lent us the money for this house in good faith, so that you, me and the children could live in a half-decent place *together*. You know perfectly well what the agreement was – that you'd sell the cottage once we'd moved in here.'

'You shouldn't have chucked me out then, should you? Where else was I supposed to go but back to the cottage?'

'That's your problem.'

'I think not. I never wanted to move to Boxcombe in the first place, remember? Now if you'd only made a reasonable effort to acclimatise yourself to the cott –'

'How *dare* you?' Cassie shouted. 'Nobody in their right mind would live in that dump, let alone bring up children down there!'

'Might be a trifle hard to sell then,' Rob pointed out.

'Oh, piss off!' Cassie snapped. 'You think you're so bloody clever. Just you wait until my solicitors get hold of you. We'll have been separated the two years next month, don't forget, and if you think this divorce is going to be *amicable*, you've got another think coming!'

'Never crossed my mind,' Rob said.

As he drove thankfully away with his two children, he knew he would soon have to do something about Bottom Cottage. There was no other way he would be able to repay that poxy loan. Not that Cassie's parents actually *needed* it back . . .

'Daddy?' Josh asked. 'Why do you and Mummy keep shouting?'

Rob was conscience-stricken. 'I'm sorry,' he said. 'I'm afraid we don't like each other very much at the moment.'

'Like Rosie and me, you mean?'

'No, not really. You mustn't worry about it.'

Maybe Cassie's right, he thought. If I could bring myself to put Bottom Cottage on the market (and quite honestly I'd rather lose a leg), then it's entirely possible that no one would want to buy it, and even if they did, it might prove difficult to get a mortgage on it, and how many cash buyers are there about these days? Well, if that turns out to be the case, so much the better! But whatever happens, I'm not having a bloody 'For Sale' sign up. The last thing I want is crowds of sightseers using it as a good excuse for a Sunday snoop.

As he turned the Land Rover on to the top road, he saw a blue Citroën coming towards him. Was it . . .? He took his foot off the accelerator momentarily. Yes it was. Had she been to the cottage to see him? He glanced in his rear-view mirror. She didn't appear to be stopping.

'I want you to go *fast*,' Josh ordered.

'Rothie wants a wee . . .' Rosie said.

'We're nearly home,' Rob said, putting his foot down. 'Just hold on, OK?'

He thought: Pity. If it wasn't for the divorce, and the children, and money worries, and God knows what else, I wouldn't mind . . . Just bad timing, I suppose.

'Hell!' Nell said aloud to herself. 'That was him, surely.' Is he . . .? No, his brake lights aren't on. He probably hasn't seen me. Why did I have to go over there so early? I am *so* stupid. He's probably been collecting his children for the weekend. Why didn't I think of that? I wonder where they live. If only I'd gone an hour later I'd have bumped into them. Oh well, it's too late now. Then she thought, I bet he *did* see me. So maybe the fact that he didn't stop, means something.

It was getting too cold these days to do any sketching out of doors. Nell enrolled in a life class instead, and spent each Thursday evening struggling contentedly with proportions and flesh tones. By December, when she thought she had put Rob Hayhoe and his cottage firmly behind her, she began to go round the estate agents in Boxcombe in her lunch hour, in a tentative search for a second-best house. It was on the third of such forays that she saw it. She recognised the photograph at once, even though it was partly obscured by a 'Sold Subject to Contract' sticker. It was Bottom Cottage. She went inside and asked for the particulars.

'Never known a house move so fast,' the agent said. 'Virtually sold in the first week.'

'So I'm definitely too late?' Nell asked. 'There's absolutely no chance?'

'Well, of course sales do occasionally fall through,' he admitted, 'but I think this one is unlikely to. The client was over the moon about it – made an offer virtually at once. God knows why – I wouldn't be seen dead down there, but it's bread and butter, isn't it? Can't complain.' Nell's eyes filled with tears and she turned away. 'Do you a nice bungalow with a conservatory?' he called after her. She didn't reply. Instead she caught a bus and went home. She looked up Rob's number in the phone book.

'Rob Hayhoe, hello.'

'Hello. This is Nell Chant, the one who drew –'

'Of course. I recognise your voice. Hello, Nell, do you need an accountant?'

'What?' Nell couldn't concentrate on anything but the cottage.

'It's what I do during the day.'

'Oh . . . I see . . . No. I've just found out that you're selling Bottom Cottage; have as good as sold it, in fact.'

'Amazing, isn't it? If I'd been desperate to sell, I'm sure no one would have looked at the place, but since I really do not want to, it goes and sells just like that. Sod's law!'

'But why are you selling it, if you don't want to?'

'Doesn't make sense, does it? I suppose you could call it *force majeure*. My wife's solicitors have been getting heavy.'

'Oh . . .' Nell's voice broke.

'You all right? You sound upset.'

'Sorry,' Nell sniffed. 'It's just that it's exactly what I've always wanted. If only I'd *known* it was on the market . . .'

'What a shame. I'd no idea you were looking for somewhere.'

'D'you think . . .? No, forget it.'

'No, go on.'

'Well, I wondered if I could come and have one last look round, before it goes, but you're probably fed up with people gawping . . .' She wiped away a tear with the back of her hand.

'Not at all. Of course you can. Come tonight. I've got a good bottle of red. We could hold a wake together.'

Chapter Four

'Right then,' Elly said on the telephone. 'Tell me *all*. What did he say to you, and what did you say to him, and what *happened*?'

Nell smiled, remembering the game she used to play with her great-aunts, with strips of paper that you wrote on, folded over, and passed round at each stage, so that your stories became hopelessly garbled.

> *'Miss Painter,'* she began,
> *'met Mr Numbercruncher,*
> *in Paradise.*
> *She said to him, "Please take the extra ten pounds back."*
> *He said to her, "I suppose you could always try gazumping."*
> *And the consequence was – they agreed about divorce.'*

'And I suppose you wouldn't care to translate that gobbledegook?' Elly asked crossly.

'Consequences. You remember? Oh, never mind,' Nell said. 'Actually we talked about his wife quite a bit. She sounds dreadful. That's what I meant about agreeing. It seems to me he's got no choice but to get divorced, but he's worried about the effect it might have on the children. He says they're pretty disturbed already.'

'So, what's wrong with her?' Elly asked, ever alert for gossip.

'Oh, she's totally neurotic; spends far too much money; keeps on being ill; won't do any cooking; has no sense of humour . . . Need I say more?'

'So why did he marry her in the first place?'

'She's good-looking. He showed me a photo of her. She's got blonde hair, and a little belted-in waist. I think she was a TV presenter briefly, some years ago. Anyway, he says she made a dead set at him, and he was dazzled.'

'Does he know why? I mean, they sound an unlikely couple.'

'Apparently she thought she wanted a docile house-husband but then she got bored with country life, and him, it seems.'

'I hope you didn't spend the entire evening talking about his marital problems.'

'Not all of it, no.'

'And so? D'you *like* him?' Elly was getting impatient.

'Oh yes, he's a nice enough bloke, and I think he's had a raw deal, but I really went to see the cottage. It's lovely upstairs, you know, all sloping ceilings and beams, and doors with old-fashioned thumb latches. He's heart-broken at having to sell it, and I can well understand why.'

'He wasn't exactly in romantic mood then?'

'Do shut up, Elly,' Nell said firmly. 'You've got a one-track mind.'

'I'm not the only one, it seems. Sibyl says you weren't back in the shop until three o'clock last Wednesday after-noon!'

'That was the lunch hour I found out about Bottom Cottage,' Nell said. 'I was so upset, still am. Sibyl was brilliant. I can't imagine any other employer being so tolerant.'

'You're right,' Elly agreed. 'She's lovely is my ma, which is more than I can say for my husband. Got to go, Nell. I can hear Paul yelling at someone, probably one of the boys. I think I'll have to intercede. Lovely talking to you. Christmas as usual, yes? Lots of love.'

'And to you too. 'Bye.' Nell put the phone down reflec-tively. She felt unsettled. She worried about Elly and

Paul's marriage, but didn't know how to help. She was reluctant to go to them again for Christmas, but shrank from saying no. She wanted to talk some more to Rob Hayhoe (and less superficially if possible next time) but couldn't think of a plausible excuse to ring him.

She didn't want to do nothing either, but she couldn't decide what *to* do. It's absurd, she thought. It's Sunday. I'm not answerable to anyone. I can please myself, so why am I so wretched? My life isn't going anywhere. I wish I had some purpose. I don't like being so free somehow; it's too selfish an existence. I want to be needed, to matter to someone. I used to get a sense of achievement from my painting, but even that seems too impersonal these days.

These feelings of uneasy discontent stayed with her right through the month. The shop was busy with people buying artist's materials for Christmas presents. The charity cards and the wrapping paper, which Sibyl was experimenting with for the first time, were going well. Nell took money, and gave out change and information. Customers asked her advice about brushes, or the merits of acrylics over watercolours, and some seemed surprised when she knew the answers. Sibyl worked away beside her, pushing up the large blue-framed glasses on her nose, and the odd grey hairs that had escaped from her loose bun, with automatic gestures that made her dangly earrings quiver, and caused the floaty scarf at her neck to slip round at a rakish angle, as if she were some chiffon-clad Biggles.

Yes, they did take Visa. No, they didn't stock candles. Yes, they did do a smaller size sketch pad. No, they didn't do framing, but they could recommend someone who did . . .

'What about Christmas?' Sibyl asked, when the after-lunch lull permitted. 'Will you come to us again?'

'Would you be very offended if I didn't?' Nell asked cautiously.

Sibyl shook her head and gave Nell's arm a squeeze. 'I've been getting the feeling that you need some space to reassess things,' she said. 'Isn't that right?'

Nell nodded and let out a long sigh.

'You please yourself,' Sibyl said comfortingly. 'I'll explain to Elly and the others. And if you change your mind, you know where we are.'

Nell bent and kissed her plump cheek. 'Thank you. You're a true friend.'

The afternoon shoppers came in a reassuringly steady stream. The painting-by-numbers books, which Nell had scorned, were selling briskly. She wrapped pencils, pens, stencils, rubbers. She repacked an easel into its box and stuck it up with tape. She advised on palette knives. She took back a leaking tube of prussian blue oil paint, and replaced it with an undamaged one. She wiped her fingers on a couple of tissues.

'What kind of paints would you recommend for a five-year-old?' a man asked her.

Nell looked up, startled. 'Oh . . . it's you. Are they for Josh?'

'Hello, Nell. Yes, they are. I didn't know you worked here.'

'Let me show you what we've got,' she said, leading the way to the display cabinet. Rob followed her.

'There are these poster colours,' Nell said. 'They're nontoxic and they wash off clothes easily.'

'Sounds good.'

'We've got some lovely paper to wrap them in too.' She indicated it.

'Fine. I'll take a sheet of that as well, thanks.'

There was no opportunity to talk at all. Other customers pressed round, eager to be served. Nell was conscious of an unexpected opportunity slipping away.

'Well, Happy Christmas then,' she said lamely as she handed him his bag of goods.

'Thanks, but I doubt very much if it will be,' he said as he turned to go. 'It's the Mad Cow's turn this year,' and with that, he left.

'Whatever did he mean?' Sibyl asked, eyebrows aloft.

'I *think* he was talking about his children spending Christmas with their mother,' Nell said, looking down at the till drawer and dropping silver into the correct compartments.

'That was *him*, was it not?'

'Yes.' Nell met her gaze. 'And I think *was* is now the operative word.'

Nell had never felt her lack of status before. For her, being a shop assistant had always been as valid a way of earning a living as being a lawyer, and a good deal less parasitic. But how did it compare with being a TV presenter (or an accountant, come to that)? And had she been right in getting the distinct impression that Rob had been disappointed to find her serving behind the counter at ARTFUL [L]?

If he's a snob, she thought, then I don't want to know. But maybe I should give him one final chance . . . Yes definitely. Christmas this year could be an opportunity for experimentation, instead of a season of enforced jollity and other people's family tensions. It was an attractive prospect. Nell thought about it, lying in a deep foamy bath with bubbles popping behind her ears, and a flannel strategically covering her emergent breasts to keep them warm as well.

What would her practical mother have done in similar circumstances? Easy. She would have ignored the Christmas aspect, as being too difficult to do as meals-on-wheels, and would instead have assembled a deliciously nutritious casserole which could easily be transported, and an elegant tart or cakey pud with custard in a jam jar, and she would have taken it all – including tablecloth and napkins – over to Rob's house on Christmas Day to save the poor man from having to spend it miserably alone.

Nell's mum had believed in nurturing her man, devoting herself to him, and taking second place without question, even to the extent of darning his socks. Nell certainly wasn't going to go that far, but she was going to go. The question was, what should she take with her? She sat up and reached for the shampoo, squeezing out a dollop and rubbing it in with enthusiasm. An idea had occurred to her of how she could show off her culinary skills without being thought too mumsy. She had her pride, after all.

Late on Christmas morning, Rob awoke without any feelings of anticipation. He had decided to treat it like any other day, maybe even catch up on some work, the better to ignore it altogether. He tried not to think about Josh and Rosie, and what they might be doing, but couldn't help wondering whether Cassie would take the trouble to cook properly for them. She must surely make an effort today. Much better not to know. He hadn't bothered much for himself at all, just buying a little cut-price smoked salmon at the last minute.

He could tell the stove hadn't stayed on overnight the moment he stepped shivering into the kitchen. There were frost flowers on the *inside* of the windows. Damn thing! He riddled it out, emptied its overflowing ash tray, stuffed kindling and a firelighter inside, struck a match and relit it, adding logs from the basket as it caught. Trickles of smoke escaped round the edges of the hotplate and through the small expansion holes. The chimney was probably all tarred up again and in need of cleaning out. It would draw better once it warmed up, especially in this wind. It sounded rough outside. Rob put the flat-bottomed kettle on to heat up. It was only half full, but it would be some time before he got his mainstay: the first mug of tea of the day. He stamped about a bit to get warm.

An hour later, as he was beginning to thaw out, and whilst eating fried bacon and eggs for breakfast, he told himself firmly that there were obvious disadvantages to living at Bottom Cottage, and he should consider himself lucky that by next Christmas he might well be somewhere centrally heated and comfortable. But where? He was clearly going to have to rent a place. There wouldn't be enough money left over to buy another house. It wasn't much of a prospect. He finished the last mouthful, wrapped both palms around his hot mug, and sighed.

The bang on the door made him jump. He hadn't heard the car outside, and he'd had his back to the front window. Through the condensation he now saw a patch of blue, and a shaft of hope pierced him unexpectedly. He opened the door, and there she was.

'Hello,' Nell said. 'I hope this isn't a bad moment.' She was carrying a large basket, and looked determined.

'On the contrary. Come in.'

The wind was roaring into the cottage, but she hesitated. 'I thought you might have family staying. Maybe your father . . .?'

'No. Bert's had a better offer this year.'

'I thought he was called Malachy?'

'That's his second name. His first is Cuthbert.'

Nell appeared to be suppressing a giggle.

'Feel free to laugh,' Rob said. 'We all do. Come on in then, if you're coming. I can't afford to lose any more of my hard-won heat.'

Nell allowed herself to be ushered inside. 'So, Happy Christmas,' she said, putting her basket down on the table and going to warm her hands at the stove.

Rob smiled. 'It is now.'

Nell had almost lost her nerve, and hesitated at the top of Rob's lane. Visiting someone uninvited on Christmas Day was a decidedly eccentric thing to do. That's good, she thought, driving firmly downhill. I don't want him to think I'm ordinary. At the bottom, she was relieved to find only the usual Land Rover and no other cars, and Rob's expression when he came to the door was entirely reassuring.

His kitchen smelt attractively of bacon and wood-smoke. He had clearly only just finished breakfast. 'Tea?' he suggested. 'Coffee?'

'Coffee would be good. Thanks.' She took off her coat and sat down at the table, resting her chin on her palms and looking over the basket at him.

'So,' Rob said, putting a steaming mug down beside her, 'most people are nailed down and dutiful on this particular day. How did you escape?'

'Special dispensation.' Nell was giving nothing away.

'And can you stay for lunch? I'm afraid it's only sandwiches, although they are smoked salmon.'

'You're sure you haven't anything else on?'

'I'm not much of a cook, I'm afraid.'

'I didn't mean that. I meant, you don't have to go anywhere, or do anything special?'

'I hadn't planned anything, no. What's in the basket?'

'Take a look.'

Rob pulled it towards him and untucked the cloth from the top. 'Good Lord!' he said. 'Do you always carry a pheasant about your person?'

'Never knowingly without one,' Nell said, straight-faced. They stared at one another, and then burst out laughing in unison. Nell thought: It's a long time since I've felt in such complete accord with anyone.

'Seriously,' Rob said, 'you've brought this bird here to cook, for us both?'

'Well, they're horrible raw,' Nell said.

'But that's marvellous.' Broad smile. 'What's this apple for?'

'It's part of the garnish for the chestnut soup, in that jar.'

'And this?'

'Bread sauce. And that's some of my redcurrant jelly, and a packet of game-flavour crisps.'

'And what's in here?'

'Wet cake.'

'Sorry?'

'My father's name for trifle.'

'Nice one. And is it also home-made?'

'Naturally.'

'Incredible,' Rob said. 'You're amazing!'

There was no need to put the pheasant on to cook straight away. It wouldn't take long, and anyway Rob said the stove needed to be stoked up first before the oven would be hot enough. When he suggested a short walk by the river, Nell was pleased in spite of the weather. It is always easier for a shy person to talk to a stranger on the move, without the confusion of enforced eye contact. Nell concealed her shyness well, but she always welcomed help. Rob fetched his binoculars and they went out together, walking side by side along the coast path and having to raise their voices to make themselves heard above the wind.

'Have you had any good presents?' she asked him.

'Not really. My family don't go in for such things.'

She waited for him to reciprocate, but when he didn't she volunteered the information anyway. 'I opened mine first thing. I can never wait. My best one was from Sibyl, my employer – though she's a good friend too. We had some in the shop, and she saw me admiring one.'

'One what?'

'A rucksack-stool, so I can carry my painting gear *and* sit down when I get there. It's brilliant.'

'Neat idea. D'you like working in that shop?'

'Love it. Why?'

'You don't get bored?'

'Not often,' Nell said defensively. 'Do you?'

'Good point. Yes, very often.' He shrugged.

'So, what would you rather do?'

'Something environmental. Nature conservation perhaps? Unfortunately I did the wrong subjects at college.'

'Why?'

'Because my father was determined that I should have a steady dependable job as unlike his as possible.' He turned away from her rather grimly. The subject was not to be pursued.

'I got a brilliant present for Sibyl, although perhaps I shouldn't boast,' Nell said, conscious of chattering on, but continuing anyway. 'You know those racks that go across baths to hold the soap and stuff? Well, this one has holders for two candles and a wineglass. Of course you have to know Sibyl to appreciate how perfect that is.'

The wind was full in their faces now, as they turned towards the sea. It made Nell's eyes water, and her nose run. She was glad she hadn't worn a dress, as Elly certainly would have done, but come instead in her beautiful rainbow cardigan, and her newest, smartest cords. But then Elly wouldn't be out here at all in half a gale. Rob wouldn't have dreamt of asking her. Nell couldn't be sure whether this was good or bad.

'Look!' Rob pointed across to the other bank of the river. 'A roe deer.' He put the glasses up to his eyes. 'Yes, it's a buck. Want a look?' Nell wiped her eyes on her sleeve and took them from him. She found it at once; a small greyish deer with a pronounced white bottom and little pointy horns. 'Winter coat,' Rob said. 'In the summer they're distinctly ginger, and that white patch all but disappears. Got it?'

'Yes.' The animal was beautifully camouflaged amongst the leafless grey trees.

'That didn't take you long.' He sounded impressed.

'Ah well, I'm very used to binoculars,' Nell said. It felt like a major accomplishment.

They walked right down to the dunes on the east bank of the river. The sea was grey and sullen, with irritable white horses further out. Isolated clumps of marram grass were bent double and blew back and forth making semicircular tracks around their bases. On exposed faces the sand rose up in clouds and blasted everything in range. It was not the sort of day to linger, but Nell would happily have done so. She took out a hanky and blew her nose, then she stuffed it and her hands deep into her coat pockets and looked out to sea. A line of black ducks was flying low over the water to the west. Scoters probably, but she didn't feel she knew Rob well enough to volunteer this. She looked at her watch, and reluctantly decided that it was time to return to the cottage and begin cooking.

'Have you got any veg in the house?' she asked.

'Spuds, I think, and maybe some sprouts.' He was scanning the waves. 'There's some sea ducks out there – scoters, I think.'

'Yes. Shall we get back then?'

The kitchen, when they returned, was almost as hot as the oven. Nell stripped off the multicoloured cardigan and hung it carefully on a low hook amongst a jumble of other clothes. Then she began cooking.

Rob went out to chop and bring in firewood, whilst she got on with it, then sometime later, when the meal was all ready he sat opposite her and poured glasses of wine for them both, smiling at her in the confident way of one totally at ease with himself and pleased with life. I could stay all day, Nell thought, (and half the night!) but I won't. I'll leave at about threeish, so he'll have time to miss me. I've no idea what the future holds, but I don't want him *ever* to take me for granted – like Martin did.

She could tell that Rob had enjoyed the food

enormously. He said so. It was good to be appreciated. He was sorry she had to go now. That was good too.

'It's only half-past three,' he protested.

'Yes, but it will be getting dark soon.' She put her coat on hurriedly before she could change her mind, collected the empty containers into her basket and made for the door.

'Nell?'

'Yes?' He came over to her and took her face between his hands. They were firm and warm, and oddly comforting. She felt like a young animal about to be soothed. Then he bent his head and kissed her briefly, but very precisely on the mouth, and she felt anything but calm.

'Thank you,' he said. 'That was so good.'

She got home without any awareness of having driven any distance at all, and then discovered she'd left her cardigan behind by mistake. She wasn't at all surprised. In her experience, people who didn't want to leave, nearly always 'forgot' something. She rang at once to make arrangements to retrieve it.

'I'll drop it into the shop next week,' Rob offered. 'What colour is it?'

'Blue, green, brown, cream, purple, you name it!' she said. She wondered fleetingly how he could not have *noticed* what colour it was. She had been wearing it for at least an hour when she'd first arrived, and it was hardly subtle!

But that was trivial, and she soon forgot it. She was happy.

Chapter Five

Anna was agog to hear the whole story. 'Why didn't you stay the night?' she asked, as they swam side by side down the pool doing breaststroke. 'I would have!'

'I'm not as impetuous as you, that's why.'

'But you do fancy him?'

'Yes, of course.'

'And he is getting divorced?'

'Yes.'

'But he's got two children?'

'Yes. I haven't actually met them, but Elly says they're not shy.'

'Elly?'

'My oldest friend, Eleanor, from schooldays. She lives in London now, but we're always on the phone.'

'And you're an Eleanor too?'

'It's a pretty common name these days, isn't it? Anyway, the children are only three and five, poor little things.' They reached the end of the pool and stopped for a breather.

'Well, when he introduces them to you,' Anna said, 'you'll know.'

'Know what?'

'That he's serious, of course! It's the equivalent of being taken home to meet the parents, but small children are much harder to impress.'

'I wouldn't know,' Nell said. 'I've never had much to do with any.'

'You're an only child?'

'Yes.'

'Me too, and I'm never going to have any kids!'

'But you're a teacher?'

'Yes, and that's quite enough contact for anyone.'

'It must be odd to take on someone else's children,' Nell said thoughtfully. 'Somehow I could never see myself as a wicked stepmother.'

'Huh!' Anna snorted. 'Don't talk to me about wicked stepmothers. I've got one!' And she launched herself into a fast crawl.

When Nell caught up with her again, she asked, 'Why is she wicked?'

'God knows. It seems to come naturally.'

'No, I meant, what does she do?'

'It's what she *did*. My mother had only been dead six months, and I was still in shock. I was five. And what did she do? She only moved in and chucked all my mother's things away – gave her clothes to Oxfam, sold her jewellery, had the whole house redecorated, even burnt her bed! Looking back, it was as though she was trying to blot out all traces of her memory from our lives. It was unbelievable!'

'How could she be so callous?' Nell was horrified.

'Because she wanted *all* of my father, every last bit. She didn't want any history. I think if she'd been able to, she would have thrown me onto the bonfire too, like Guy Fawkes.'

'But what about your father? Why didn't he stand up for you?'

'Oh, he was besotted with her. I don't think he even noticed what she was doing. My mother had been ill for a long time, you see, and I'm pretty sure they'd never got on that well. So when she died, I suppose he felt released. He couldn't wait to make up for lost time.'

'But wasn't he fond of you?'

'No, I was just an inconvenient leftover from a difficult relationship with a long-term invalid, and he *loved* my stepmother, you see, so that made everything all right.'

'Poor you,' Nell said, reaching out and touching her shoulder.

'Yes, well,' Anna said awkwardly. 'Now you see why I'm very suspicious of "love" in any shape or form.'

'But she must be a one-off surely? All stepparents aren't like her. It must work out well sometimes.'

'Not often. But I suppose if I'm fair to the bloody woman – or at least as fair as I can be – it is an impossible position to find yourself in. You can never win. You're always in the wrong, and you can never be a substitute for the real parent. It's not a situation to go into lightly.'

'Good thing I'm not contemplating it then,' Nell smiled.

'Oh yeah?' Anna raised a sceptical eyebrow. 'D'you know what I really like about you, Nell?'

'What?'

Anna held on to the edge, poised. 'How can I phrase this? I know – you're about as Sphinx-like as a pikestaff!' And with that, she sank into a triumphant backstroke.

Paul Tozer prided himself on his inscrutability. He was pretty sure that few would realise how frustrated he had been feeling of late. He'd had very little opportunity to do any of the things he'd really wanted to for weeks; one in particular. The autumn term had been a constant struggle with inadequate funds, his best teachers pushing for early retirement, and constant timetable wars. And now he was nearly halfway through the Christmas holidays, and he still hadn't had time to get things rolling.

He waited until Elly had taken the two boys for their swimming lesson, and then made a series of useful phone calls. It only took him a couple of hours to track down exactly what he wanted. He sat back in his leather, gas-lifted, executive office chair, with his hands behind his broad neck, well pleased with his own efficiency. Of course his wife wouldn't see it his way at all. She never did. He'd wait to tell her until she was in a noncombative mood. Some people are never happy, he thought to himself sourly, Elly in particular. I've thought up this brilliant plan to accommodate everyone in the family (at considerable expense), but just wait for her to rubbish it all . . .

'I'm thinking of moving the boat,' he announced the next morning at breakfast. 'The Hamble is getting much too expensive and far too crowded.'

'Oh yes?' Elly was stirring porridge with her back to him. Their two young sons, Will and Sam, were upstairs in Will's room, watching television.

'Well, don't you want to know what I've got in mind?'

'I'm sure you're going to tell me anyway.'

'Look, Elly, I'm doing this for your sake. You could at least pretend to show a little interest.'

'Since when has anything to do with the boat been of any interest to me?'

'If you'll just listen, you'll find out. Now, Boxcombe isn't far from the River Torrent, yes? And near the mouth of the estuary there's an excellent sailing club. But better still, I've discovered there's an empty quay further up river belonging to Thrushton Hall, you know, that lovely H-shaped Georgian house where Lord Pel –'

'Yes, yes. Get on with it. I was brought up around there.'

'Well, that's the whole point. It turns out that I've recently met a friend of his, and he might be able to swing it for me to keep the boat there.'

'You're surely not going to move your precious boat to the West Country?'

'Just listen, will you? There's more to it. On the other side of the river from Thrushton Quay, there are half a dozen houseboats and . . .'

'House . . .?'

Paul silenced her with an impatient gesture. '. . . and so I reckon this could be the perfect answer. You could stay on the houseboat when I'm sailing mine, and maybe spend more time with your ma – and Nell, come to that – and the boys could please themselves either way, so everyone's happy.' Fat chance of that, but it sounded confidently benevolent.

'It's a long way from London.'

'Not with the new bit of dual carriageway. I can do it in three hours, no sweat.'

'So, what's the catch?'

Why is she so bloody predictable? he thought. 'Do you always have to be so flaming *negative*?' he demanded.

'Maybe it has something to do with eight years of marriage to you.' Elly stretched her mouth sardonically. 'But . . . now I think about it . . . I suppose it could be a good idea. Sibyl would be delighted, and I'd love to see more of Nell. And it would be great to have proper family holidays for a change . . . Yes, OK, I like it. So what's come over you? Why this sudden transformation into model husband?'

'Don't knock it,' Paul said. 'I should grab it while you can.'

'That sounds like a threat.' Elly turned back to the porridge.

'Cobblers,' he said calmly. 'Only to someone paranoid like you.' He put his arms around her from behind, but she moved so he missed her cheek, kissing her ear instead.

'Too loud!' Elly complained. 'Go and call the boys, will you? This is ready.'

Paul went to the bottom of the stairs and bellowed, 'WILL! SAM! BREAKFAST!' Then, suspecting it might be a good few minutes before they bothered to come downstairs, he slipped into his study and dialled a very familiar number. He stood there, keeping an eye on the door and muttering, 'Come on, come *on*,' until she answered. 'Darling? It's me.'

'Oh Paul . . . how did it go?'

'Fine. I've told her and, Lord be praised, she even likes the idea! So I'll be down soon to make sure it's as good as it's cracked up to be.'

'But that's marvellous! I never thought she would. It makes things so much easier for us. You are clever.'

'Got to go, OK? I'll phone again soon. Love you. Bye.'

Rob decided he should do the honourable thing. He didn't regret the outcome of Christmas Day – very much the reverse in fact – but he told himself that he must consider Nell's feelings. What good could he possibly be to her? He counted up his liabilities: he was about to lose his house; any money he had was likely to be bled from him the moment he'd earned it; he was obliged to put Josh and Rosie first (they were a priority he could never disregard). So there wasn't much left. He had nothing, in all conscience, to offer her. He supposed he should ring her up and apologise. Apologise for what? For kissing her? He *liked* Nell, dammit!

He delivered the garish cardigan to ARTFUL[L] as he'd promised, when the shop opened again after the holiday break, but he didn't linger, pretending to be in a tearing hurry. He felt bad about that afterwards, but he fell back upon an enduring habit – when in doubt, do nothing. Things often resolved themselves without one having to commit oneself either way.

Life went on. He sighed a lot. It rained even more. The river rose. Rob kept an eye on it, and filled half a dozen sandbags just in case. The telephone rang regularly. He got on with his work.

When Rob had turned up just before lunchtime on 2nd January, carrying her cardigan in a Tesco bag, Nell

51

greeted him cheerfully and glanced sideways at Sibyl to check that she was on cue with, 'Why don't you take a break? I can manage fine on my own for a while.' Sibyl came forward at once to say it, but Rob beat her to it.

'Sorry,' he said. 'Afraid I've got to rush. Already late for an important appointment. Just wanted to return this.' He thrust the bag at her, made a little gesture of apology with both palms momentarily raised uppermost, and was gone.

Nell found herself standing there stupidly, clutching the bag. Then she closed her mouth firmly and bent her head, not wanting to catch Sibyl's sympathetic eye. Sibyl tactfully said nothing, and went to tidy up one of the display racks.

Nell waited more than two weeks for Rob to phone her. Silence. The telephone sat there inert, unresponsive, useless. Nell felt like throwing it through the window. Rob had definitely fancied her; she knew the signs. So why hadn't he done something about it? She felt more angry than upset, and found herself crashing things about as she prepared a Saturday evening dinner for four.

Paul, Elly and Sibyl arrived all together in Paul's car. Elly and Paul, it appeared, were barely on speaking terms. Sibyl made an 'Oh Gawd!' sort of face at Nell as they came in. Nell wished a lot of things all at once: that she'd been a little more noncommital when on the phone to Elly on Boxing Day; that Elly and Paul would sort out their differences and make a go of their marriage; and, more than anything, that she hadn't asked them all over for a meal that evening. She half smiled at Sibyl and took her cloak to hang up.

'Wuhhh!' Sibyl exclaimed. 'It's horrible cold outside. So much for global warming!'

Nell led them into the sitting room and poured drinks.

'Common misconception, that,' Paul said, taking a careless gulp of whisky. 'Everyone seems to think we're going to end up surrounded by luxuriant growths of vines and lemon trees and olive orchards, and God knows what. But it's a fair chance that it will in fact get *colder* here as global warming takes hold.'

'Why?' Nell asked, welcoming a neutral topic of conversation.

'Oh, don't encourage him,' Elly urged.

'Don't worry,' Paul said testily. 'I won't bore them. I can say it all in a couple of sentences.' He gulped his whisky again.

'You drink too fast,' Elly said.

'Go on then,' Nell said quickly.

'Right, well it goes something like this: extra heat leads to more precipitation, i.e., snow at the poles, which leads to more ice formation and therefore to more icebergs breaking off the glaciers in Greenland, which float southwards into the North Atlantic cooling it down and making the water less salty and therefore less likely to sink. This has a good chance of disrupting the Atlantic conveyor system altogether, and deflecting our Gulf Stream current southwards towards Spain. Don't forget we're on the same latitude as Labrador. Without the Gulf Stream bringing us extra heat from the tropics, we'd be very cold indeed!'

'It's just exaggeration,' Elly said. 'It'll never happen.'

'I certainly hope not,' Sibyl said. There was an awkward silence, and then Elly and Paul both spoke at the same time.

Elly said, 'Just as well you didn't come for Christmas!'

Paul said, 'Christmas wasn't the same without you.'

'Yes ... No ...' Nell said. 'I'm sorry I didn't come, but ...'

'She had better things to do, didn't you, Nell?' Elly looked expectant. 'What's the latest, then?'

'Maybe she doesn't want you to dissect her entire private life in public. Have you even considered that possibility?' Paul demanded.

'Sorry,' Nell said hastily. 'Just got to go and see how the food's coming along.' She retreated to the kitchen. Sibyl got up and followed her, shutting the door behind them. She was wearing gypsy earrings and lots of loose layers of clothes, mostly of navy blue, with a long necklace of bright clashing wooden beads. She looked magnificent. Nell turned to her gratefully.

'Oh dear,' Sibyl said. 'Those two get worse all the time. Just as well the boys stayed in London with their other grandma. Can I do anything useful?'

'You could mash these,' Nell said, offering a pan of drained potatoes. 'What's the problem? D'you know?'

'I've a shrewd idea, but I won't say in case I want to un-say it later.' She mashed away energetically as Nell dished up. 'Perhaps this houseboat of theirs will be a good idea. It'll certainly make family holidays less fraught.'

'What d'you mean?'

'Hasn't Elly told you about it? Oh dear, perhaps it's supposed to be a secret. Pretend you don't know, yes?'

'Right.' They carried in the food, and set it out on the dining-room table.

Paul and Elly came in and sat down. It seemed they had reluctantly made a pact to tone down the conflict.

'Shall I tell her?' Elly asked him.

'If you want.'

'We've got a treat for you tomorrow, Nell, which includes being out for lunch. All right?'

'Great,' Nell said, thinking: Houseboat? One of the Eely creek ones? That would be a happy coincidence.

Sunday morning was sunny. The tide was at its lowest and the river had retreated to a wide stripe of water in the middle, beaching the houseboats and revealing a tatty causeway: Eely Isle's connection to the rest of the world. The Tozers' houseboat turned out to be the red and green one that Nell had admired previously, and she was more than delighted to be shown around it. Inside it was neat and cleverly constructed with wooden panelling, shiny brass, and red velvet cushions. Everything, including the sink and cooker, could be shut away into its own small cupboard. Seats metamorphosed into extra beds. Tables folded up and down. There was even a solid-fuel stove with a long black chimney stack, but it plainly wasn't lit because no warmth emanated from it.

'It's wonderful!' Nell exclaimed. She had expected it to be more like camping, but Elly pointed out facilities at the mooring she hadn't had occasion to notice before: an ablutions block with hot water only yards away, bins for rubbish, electricity lines, and water hoses. 'Does anybody live on these boats all year round?'

'No,' Paul said. 'They're rented out to holidaymakers, so we'll probably never see the same people twice. Suits me very well. I have quite enough of the social scene in London.'

Nell wondered if Elly felt the same.

Elly obviously felt cold. 'Is there any possibility of heat,' she asked, 'or are we all supposed to freeze heroically to death?'

'Give me a chance,' Paul said. 'I'm just about to light the damn stove. All right?'

'How about us two going for a walk while he does that?' Elly said to Nell.

Nell glanced at Paul. He made a '*Please*, get her off my back and out of here before she drives me barking mad' sort of expression with screwed-up nose and pursed mouth. 'Good idea,' she said quickly. 'Upstream or down?'

'Down towards the sea.'

They set off over the Eely bridge and along the path on the south bank of the river.

'Right,' Elly said. 'Ten walking steps, followed by ten

running ones, followed by ten walking ones, and so on. That way, we'll soon get warm. OK?' She set off without waiting for an answer, dodging the puddles nimbly to preserve the shine on her expensive leather boots.

Nell was relieved to be away from the tension that Paul's presence always seemed to generate.

'. . . Nine, ten!' Elly chanted, slowing down.

'It's a lovely houseboat,' Nell said, catching her up. 'Sibyl will adore it too.'

'Good isn't it?' Elly said. 'I can't quite work out why Paul's buying it, but I'm sure there must be an ulterior motive.'

'You don't seem to like each other very much at the moment,' Nell ventured.

'That must be the understatement of the year!' Elly shoved her fists deep into her pockets. 'When the boys are older, I'm definitely going to leave him. I've made up my mind.'

'Oh, Elly!' Nell was distressed. 'I'm so sorry . . .'

'. . . Eight, nine, ten!' Elly counted. 'Come on, run! One, two, three . . .'

After half a mile of this, they stopped and walked normally.

'So, how's Rob?' Elly panted.

'Dunno.'

'Why? Haven't you seen him lately?'

'Not since New Year, no.' The trees around Bottom Cottage were coming into view. In a few minutes the cottage itself would be visible too. Nell wondered whether Rob would be at the window with his binoculars, and whether they should turn round now before he could see them. She didn't want him to think she was mooning after him. But Elly kept going, and it was already too late, so she followed.

'But why ever not?' Elly asked.

'Because he hasn't phoned. Simple.'

56

'The bastard!' Elly said indignantly. 'After all your hard work too.'

'I didn't do it for a quid pro quo.'

'No, of course not. I didn't mean that.'

They walked in silence for a while. Then a high-pitched wailing sound reached their ears. It was travelling across the water from the cottage.

'Listen!' Elly said, stopping and staring across the river. Nell stopped reluctantly beside her. She hadn't got her binoculars with her, but she could see three figures in the garden behind the stone wall, one tall and two small. The taller of the two children appeared to be making the noise, and keeping it up apparently effortlessly in spite of the entreaties and promises the man seemed to be making. Then the smaller child joined in.

'Oh dear,' Nell said. 'Poor things. I wonder what's wrong?'

'Sounds to me,' Elly said, 'as though you're well out of it.'

By the time February came, Nell had hardened her heart and accepted the fact that Rob Hayhoe was not interested in her. Even Elly had stopped pestering her for news of him. It had been a disappointing nonevent and it was now over. Yet somehow she still hadn't had the heart to do any serious house-hunting, nor to burn her boats by putting her own place up for sale. She decided to wait until spring, the season when many people's fancy rashly turns to thoughts of a move.

She sat indoors during the extended winter evenings doing tapestry and watching television. She told herself she would have been better employed in her usual habit of reading intelligent books, but soap operas were unchallenging and provided a necessary distraction from too sharp a consciousness. So when the telephone rang one weekday, just as she was cosily settled on the sofa, she didn't rush to answer it, but got up rather casually, laying her tapestry frame down carefully so as not to lose her needle.

'Hello?' she said.

'Nell? It's Rob Hayhoe.'

'Oh . . . hello.' Only five weeks and three days late! Nell thought resentfully. I hope he isn't expecting enthusiasm.

'Um . . . sorry I haven't been in touch. I don't seem to have had a moment to myself lately.'

'Oh?' Lucky you, she thought.

'But . . . well, something's come up that may interest you. Have you found another house to buy yet?'

'No.'

'Right, well . . .'

He seemed to be finding her monosyllabic replies somewhat unnerving. *Good*, Nell thought.

'Er . . . I don't know why I'm doing this really. It might be considered to be a great stroke of luck for me – well it would be if Cassie weren't on at me all the time about money. I mean, I never wanted to get rid of the place anyway.'

'Sorry?' Nell said, confused.

'No, it's me. I'm not explaining myself very well, am I?'

'Not really, no.'

'Well, I wondered whether you might still be interested. You see, at the very last moment, just when we were on the point of exchanging contracts, my house-buying chain has been broken. It seems my buyer's buyer has unexpectedly lost his job and can't proceed, so my buyer has had to drop out too, at least until he can find another punter to buy his house. So the upshot is – Bottom Cottage is on the market again.'

Chapter Six

The more Nell admitted prospective buyers (PBs) to her old parental home, the more she worried that no one could possibly want it. It was now March, and it had been for sale for a month without even the sniff of a taker. She was beginning to develop an appreciation of house-purchaser-speak, and could now translate most of the comments carelessly dropped by the affectedly casual strangers who trailed round after her estate agent, Mr Block.

Kevin Block was a curious mixture of the pompous and the innocently upbeat, and lavished positive appreciation on every part of the house. 'Spacious kitchen,' he would announce. 'Great potential for modernisation.'

'Oh,' the PB's wife would say. 'Not fitted then?' (*I can't believe people still live like this!*)

'Front dining room,' enthused Mr Block, 'with hatch to kitchen, and gas fire with original period tiled surround. Quite a selling point that!'

PB himself: 'Really? (*That'd be the first thing I'd rip out.*)

PB's wife: 'What a good thing you haven't had it decorated. Much better to let the buyer do it up in their own taste.' (*You naïve fool! You could have covered over all those cracks and that damp patch.*)

Mr Block: 'Lovely views of the garden from the lounge at the back. It's been particularly well maintained, I think you'll agree?'

PB: 'Mmm. You'd need a heavy-duty mower here, that's for sure.' (*No way! More like a concrete mixer.*)

After a while, Nell ceased to follow them upstairs but

stood in the hall mouthing the commonest remarks like a mantra to keep herself amused. 'Only one bathroom then?' 'Is the roof fully lined?' 'Are all the light bulbs included? Ha ha!' 'No fitted carpets? Oh dear, that brings the price down a bit then.' 'Oh well, of course we're used to built-in wardrobes.'

To entertain herself further, she wrote out an honest description of the house – *Large, ugly, detached, unmodernised, 1930s 4-bedroom house, with 3 naff stained-glass windows, ostentatious double garage, and 100ft long high-maintenance garden. Situated in upwardly mobile area, close to local shops (selling 'antiques' but no food). On bus route to centre of boring Boxcombe. Would suit nostalgic, style-challenged Fat Cat, or sad, undiscerning DIY enthusiast with long-suffering partner.*

She gave it to Mr Block who read it through slowly and carefully. 'Just as well you're not in my profession,' he said seriously. 'You'd have a lot to learn.'

'*You'd have a lot to learn!*' Nell mimicked his prissy voice on the phone to Elly, and they both dissolved into giggles. 'How can anybody be so totally humourless?'

'No luck so far then?'

'No. Another couple are coming tomorrow evening. I suppose sooner or later someone is going to be deluded enough to want it.'

'Could take years,' Elly said soberly.

'Thanks! You are so encouraging.'

But the young man and woman who arrived with Mr Block at 6 p.m. the following evening were clearly impressed. 'It's so rare to find a place that hasn't been the victim of *refurbishment*,' the man said, stressing the word as though it were the ultimate crime. 'We've been trying to find a genuine period house like this for far too long, haven't we, darling?'

'Oh, yes,' the woman said eagerly. 'And that fireplace in the dining room is quite marvellous, isn't it? They certainly *knew* about tiles in those days.' Nell stared at them in fascination.

'You see,' the man said, 'we're getting married soon.' He said it with exaggerated modesty, as though he might be going to add, 'although I say so as shouldn't.'

'And we want our first house to be perfect,' the woman said, laying her hand on his arm and smiling up at him girlishly.

'Ah well,' Mr Block said, 'wonderful, wonderful! Look no further!' He rubbed his hands together in a frenzy of enthusiasm that Nell considered a bit over the top, until she realised why. Of course – first-time buyers – no chain! She allowed a modicum of optimism to be released into her bloodstream, and begin to diffuse . . . Maybe the fates were about to be kind.

Cassie Hayhoe felt as though everyone was conspiring against her, especially Rob. She was sure he had sabotaged the sale of the cottage on purpose; his story of a broken chain was too convenient for words.

She wanted the divorce – of course she did. What was the point of being married to someone you despised, a man who never asked you how you were or how you felt; who never noticed anything about you; never *encouraged* you? But she worried about how she would cope. She supposed she would have to get a job, but her secretarial skills were all but forgotten, and the chance opportunity she'd had years ago to present a clothes show on television was very much a thing of the past. If only she hadn't fallen out with that stupid producer woman, she might have been asked back . . . Cassie sighed deeply. At thirty-three she was still young, but . . . She examined herself critically in the bathroom mirror. A cross, pinched face looked back at her. She tried smiling, but it didn't come naturally to her and appeared more like a rictus, so she snapped it off again quickly.

I'm not well, she thought. I can't cope with the children. I can't bear the loneliness. I've lost all my confidence, so how will I ever get a job? And anyway, how can I work with Rosie still at home, and Josh finishing school so early? God! Sometimes I wish they were grown up and off my hands altogether . . . I don't know what to *do*. I need help. I think I must be about to have a nervous breakdown.

She managed to get a cancellation appointment at the health centre for late that afternoon, and trailed off there with both children in tow. Sitting in the waiting room, she tried half-heartedly to keep them from annoying the other patients. She sat Josh on her knee, but Rosie wanted to sit there too and they began, as ever, to whine and hit each other. Cassie thought: Why do I have to have such difficult children? It's so unfair!

'Stop that, Rosie!' she said sharply, knowing that this would precipitate a major sulk, but unable to do anything about it. The child's lower lip trembled. She stumped over to the children's play corner and began throwing the toys about. Josh was fidgeting on Cassie's lap, playing with her silk scarf and pulling it too tight around her neck. 'Don't do that,' she said to him. 'Rosie? That's naughty. You'll break it!'

She looked round rather desperately, hoping that someone else would step in, but most of the people also waiting were elderly and they looked uniformly dis-approving, hitching their feet and handbags stiffly out of Rosie's way as she shuffled round the waiting room on her bottom with a wooden toy train, having as many accidents as possible. Josh wriggled off Cassie's lap apparently to go and interfere, but just at that moment another boy of about his own age came in with his mother. To Cassie's relief, Josh went over to talk to him. The young woman sat down next to Cassie.

'Bin waiting long?' she asked her. She was short and

plump, with cropped pink hair, and dressed entirely in black leather.

Cassie was too exhausted to be critical. 'About ten minutes.'

'It's always bad. Dunno why they bother wif an appointments system. It's a joke, innit?'

'Seems so.'

Cassie saw with relief that the extra child seemed to have diverted her two away from their inveterate squabbling. They even appeared to be playing a game together. Twenty minutes went by. Every now and again the woman beside her went over and sorted her boy out, keeping Josh and Rosie in order at the same time.

'Thanks,' Cassie said, looking up briefly.

'No bovver,' the woman said. 'I'm good wif kids. I'd like to set meself up as a childminder. I know I could make a go of it an' earn enough for meself and Gav to live off, but I haven't got nowhere to do it, so I can't get started. You don't know a place, do you? Trouble is, I can't pay any rent until I've earned enough dosh. Hopeless innit?' Her brief smile was surprisingly endearing. Cassie felt an uncharacteristic urge to confide in her.

'I'm in a difficult position too,' she said. 'I'm not well, and I desperately need a nanny for these two, but my husband's walked out on us, so I can't possibly afford to pay for one.'

'You got a job though?'

'Not now.'

'But you got a house?'

'Oh yes, a large one. Too large really; the children and I rattle about in it, now Rob's gone.' She could hear herself manufacturing a sob story to match the one the woman was telling her. It didn't strike her as dishonest, just polite; a way to reach across the divisions of class and privilege to say: I understand how you feel. We're both wronged women fighting against the odds.

'Well then,' the woman said, hopefully. 'Now c'rect me if I'm wrong, but you've gotta big house and you need a childminder, right? And I've got nowhere to live, and I *am* a childminder, yeah?'

'Well . . . yes.'

'So, you get my drift?'

'Well . . .'

'How about you let me and Gav have a room in your house rent free? Then weekdays when Gav and your boy's at school, I can mind free or four kids (including your youngest for nuffink, of course) and make a bob or two, which wif income support'll pay for our keep. Then we've got a roof and food, and you've got your kids looked after, and the house ain't so big no more! I'd need me weekends off, but that's all. Me name's Mic, by the way. So, what d'you say?'

'Well . . .' It was perfectly logical, Cassie had to admit that . . . 'But I don't know anything about you,' she prevaricated.

'Well, I'm not going to nick the silver if that's what's bovvering you,' Mic said. 'I wouldn't be that stupid. And I don't do drugs or nuffink – well, only ciggies.'

'No, of course not. I didn't mean –'

'Tell you what,' Mic said, 'we're OK where we are for a bit, so you have a fink about it, yeah?'

'Yes . . . all right, I will.'

'Michaela Potton and Gavin,' the receptionist called out. 'To Dr White please.'

'Looks like our doctor's quicker'n yours, dunnit?' Mic said, getting up. 'So, give us your phone number, OK? I'll leave it a week, and then ring you. You can always say no.'

'All right,' Cassie said, delving into her handbag. 'I've got some stickers with my name and address somewhere . . . Yes, here's one.' She gave it to Mic.

'Cheers. Come on then, Gav. Let's get your ears sorted.' And off they went.

When she got home with the prescription she'd gone for, Cassie worried about giving Mic the sticker. *I'm just not thinking straight. My health must be even worse than I thought. I won't tell Rob; he'd say I was mad to have done it. What if she's a thief? She now knows I'm a woman living alone in a big house. She mentioned silver – perhaps she's part of a gang? She's got my phone number too. What if she plagues me with nuisance calls asking for money, or keeps coming round and pestering me? What was I thinking of?*

She knew the answer to that one really. She was desperate to get Josh and Rosie off her back, but also determined that Rob shouldn't have them. *At least Mic would be here with me,* she thought, *if I took her on. I could keep an eye on things. I don't reckon I'm that bad a judge of character either. My instincts tell me she's OK. And we could convert the attic room (the one Rob used to use as a workshop) for her child-minding. It hasn't been lived in since we came here, but it's big enough and light enough, and we could get the heating connected up again. Then she could have the back bedroom for herself and Gavin, and the guest bathroom, so I wouldn't have to meet them first thing in the morning. I suppose if Gavin and Josh got on really well, he could always share Josh's room eventually. I'd have to insist that she only smokes in her own room though. I can't have the whole house stinking of it.*

Rob would strongly disapprove, Cassie knew this, and the knowledge encouraged her to do it just to spite him.

Oh, what the hell! she thought. *Let's give her a try. I could use some company in the evenings. Of course she's not really my sort of person, so we won't have much in common, but she'll be better than nobody.*

When the young couple came again to see Nell's house, this time in daylight, she began to get really optimistic that everything might work out. If they were prepared to approach her asking price, then she would be able to buy Bottom Cottage without the hassle of finding a mortgage. She blessed her parents for having had the foresight and prudence to have paid theirs off before they died. She knew how lucky she was. She said as much to Anna at swimming.

'Jammy bastard,' Ann said. 'I don't think I'll ever be able to get shot of mine, so I'll never be able to give up work. What a treadmill!'

They did a few more lengths, and then Nell stopped and waited for her. 'How's the Boss then?' she asked.

'Lovely,' Anna said. 'When I *see* him, that is, which isn't nearly often enough. It's been a long winter. Thank God it will soon be summer.'

'And the love nest?'

'Brilliant,' Anna said at once. 'It's right out in the country and very small and compact, but everything fits into its own place, and the setting and views are amazing. Mind you, we don't have much time for looking at the scenery!'

Nell raised an eyebrow. 'And you still aren't going to tell me where it is?'

'Sorry,' Anna said. 'Can't. The Boss wants it to be kept a secret from absolutely everybody.'

'That's a bit paranoid, isn't it? Is he afraid of his wife?'

'He's not afraid of *anyone*,' Anna scoffed, 'but he does like a quiet life.'

Nell didn't think much of this, but kept silent. It sounded to her as though the secret hideaway might well be a caravan, and she did wonder whether Anna had banked on a cottage and was disappointed. Perhaps the Boss wasn't as rich as she had hoped. Maybe it would all fall through. She didn't think Anna was the sort who would hang about for long with anyone fiscally challenged.

Nell wondered whether her young couple were well off. It was hard to tell. Presumably they wouldn't have come to see it twice if her house was outside their price range. A week went by, with her keeping her fingers crossed, and then a day later they made a good offer, and her jubilation overflowed.

'Oh,' Sibyl said at work, 'I do so *love* enthusiasm! I can't be doing with people who are never sad and never happy, but always drearily impassive. Emotions are for showing, not suppressing.'

'And for sharing,' Nell agreed, 'or displaying if you're an actress, I suppose. Maybe that's where Elly gets it from?'

'Mmm,' Sibyl said. 'That probably is my fault, yes,' and she looked at Nell sideways, smiling. 'They're talking of having a boat-warming party soon and inviting Hat, Paul's mother, and you too, of course, plus anyone you'd like to bring?' She looked quizzical.

'If you mean Rob Hayhoe,' Nell said, 'you're on the wrong track altogether. I'm hoping to buy his house, not go out with him.'

'I see.' Sibyl was unconvinced. 'Have you made an offer for it?'

'Yes, just. And I've arranged to go down to see it again this evening to do some measurements. I'm going to have to get rid of a lot of my parents' furniture, and I need to find out what will and what won't go in.'

'One collects so much rubbish over a lifetime,' Sibyl agreed.

'Not any longer, for me,' Nell said. 'I've decided to go minimalist.'

'Oh. I like the William Morris philosophy myself: *Have nothing in your houses that you do not know to be useful, or believe to be beautiful.*'

Nell, thinking of Sibyl's cluttered house, caught her eye and snorted rudely.

'Well,' Sibyl said, mock defensive, 'I can't help it if I find so much of life beautiful, can I?'

Nell thought of Sibyl later that day when she arrived at Rob's cottage at sunset. The western sky was magnificent, and she paused at the vantage point to gaze across the river at the distant headland and the tower of the folly redly illuminated against the flat black sea. When she arrived at the bottom, she found Rob out in his garden looking at the same sky.

'Isn't it marvellous?' she called, getting out of her car.

'Certainly is.' She went to join him, and they leant on the back wall and looked across the river in the failing light.

'Still pretty cold though,' Nell said, after a few moments.

'Warm enough inside,' Rob replied, ushering her into the cottage through the back door. As she went in past him, she stubbed her toe on something and stumbled, clutching at the doorframe for support, and looking down to see what had tripped her.

'A *sand*bag?' she said in an exaggeratedly quavering old woman's voice, to cover a sudden attack of shyness.

'Oh,' Rob said at once, 'do come in, Lady Bracknell!'

They smiled at each other in mutual understanding. Nell felt entirely comfortable all at once, but then suddenly annoyed about being charmed in spite of herself.

'Would you like a beer?' he said.

'I think I'd rather have a coffee.'

'Easy.' He slid the kettle over onto the hotplate and it began to sing straightaway. 'I'd much rather you bought this place than that man,' Rob said. 'I'd hate it to be in the wrong hands.'

'How long have you lived here?'

'Let me see . . . I bought it when I was twenty-five, and I'm thirty-five now, so, ten years.'

'Before you were married?'

'Heavens, yes. Three years before. Remind me, do you take sugar?'

'No, thanks. And have there been many floods?'

'Only one bad one. It's not often that heavy rain, a spring tide and a storm surge all coincide, but I take precautions every winter anyway, as you discovered.' He smiled at her. 'Just as well you don't *look* like Dame Edith Evans!' he said, pushing a mug of coffee towards her.

Nell laughed. 'So, where will you go when you leave?'

'That's a tricky one. I may be reduced to living in a caravan. I've been looking round but so far I haven't found a house or flat to rent where I can have the children to stay at weekends. It looks as though I shall have to go back to working in the firm's Boxcombe office too, which will be a pain – definitely a retrograde step. I'll probably have to share one of their poky little offices, so it will be unpopular all round.'

'That's a shame. Have you found a suitable caravan?'

'Not yet.'

'Because I know someone who may be knowledgeable about where to look,' Nell said, thinking of Anna. 'I could ask her.'

'You mean your actress friend?'

'Oh, Elly would love to hear you say that! No, not her, although that reminds me,' Nell said, suddenly abandoning caution, 'They've just bought the best houseboat in Eely Creek, and they're having a boat-warming party at the end of the month. Would you like to come?'

'Oh . . . well . . . what date?' Rob got a calendar off the wall and studied it. 'Oh damn, Bert will be here then. He's paying me a final state visit, before I have to move out.'

'So bring him too. Elly would be in heaven!'

'Well . . . it's a thought. He loves parties, and I'm always at a loss as to how to entertain him, but –'

'Great,' Nell said. 'That's settled then.' She got a steel tape out of her pocket. 'Now, perhaps I should measure a few things.' My dresser will go here, she thought, and my big table over there. My favourite blue curtains might even fit too . . .

When she got home, she phoned Elly with the news.

'Oh my God!' Elly shouted, 'Malachy Hayhoe? You're not serious? I don't believe it! What on earth shall I wear? I've *got* to impress him!' Then she changed tack abruptly. 'Don't tell Paul, OK?' she begged. 'Let it be a surprise or I won't get a look in. I can't have him hogging the man. You do see that? I'll need time to work on him alone. Nell, you are a genius! I'm for ever in your debt.'

'Steady on!' Nell said. 'Try to get this into some sort of perspective, will you? You'll be lucky to be alone with anyone in that confined space, and, anyway, the bunks are a little narrow to be used as casting couches, aren't they?'

'Huh!' Elly exclaimed bitterly. 'In my dreams!'

Chapter Seven

The tide was out when the party began, and the house-boat was firmly supported on its viscous bed of mud. Like a strip of candied angelica on chocolate mousse, Nell thought, remembering how it had looked in daylight the last time she'd seen it. This is a dangerous place in which to get too drunk, she thought, as she stood on the unlit deck getting some air. One slip and I'd be sucked under in no time – I'd rather drown in water . . . She caught herself up; this was supposed to be a party! It was a bit cold. She'd better go back inside.

'Nell?' Rob said, emerging from the companionway and standing in a shaft of light from below. 'What are you doing?'

'Nothing. It was a bit stuffy below. I think Paul's overdone the stove stoking, and the cigar smoke doesn't help. How's it going down there?'

'OK, I think.'

'Does your father know about Elly's ambitions? I don't think she's had the chance to talk to him properly yet.'

'It's all right. I briefed him on the way here, but I doubt whether he'll be much use. In fact it might be wise if you discouraged her.'

'Oh? Why?'

'It just might.'

Nell felt snubbed. 'Are Elly and Paul being polite to each other?' she asked, to keep the conversation going.

'So so.' Rob put out a hand, palm downwards, and inclined it from side to side. 'Who's the energetic woman again, with the short grey hair, talking to Bert? They seem to be getting on famously.'

'That's Paul's mother, Harriet, usually known as Hat.'

'So the boys are her grandsons – what age, about seven and five?'

'I think so, yes. She looks after them quite a lot in London, I think, while Elly and Paul are working. Your father's great at entertaining children, isn't he? Somehow I hadn't imagined he would be.'

'Mmm,' was all Rob said.

'He's very good-looking,' Nell said, still making an effort.

'Isn't he just?'

She gave up. 'I'm going back down. It's cold.'

'I won't be long either,' Rob said, feeling his way past her towards the darkened prow. 'Only came up for a leak.'

'Oh.' Nell turned away, but heard his stream of urine hit the mud below, and thought of an old witticism of her grandmother's – *What a handy gadget to take on a picnic!* – but felt too put out to share it.

In the long cabin below, the party sounded cheerful enough. 'Nice bloke, Rob,' Paul said, passing her on his way on deck, presumably for the same purpose. He patted her arm encouragingly. 'You could do worse.'

I'm doing a *lot* worse! Nell thought. I don't know whether I'm coming or going. I wish I hadn't invited him now.

At the bottom of the stairs she looked about her. The atmosphere was smoky but convivial. Paul had always been generous with drinks, and the plates of open sandwiches, sausage rolls and mini quiches were being emptied with enthusiasm. No one had bothered to draw the curtains, and the windows were all steamed up as the warm breath from many conversations nudged the cold glass and clung there, in tiny beads of moisture. The brass

72

fittings gleamed in the purposely subdued lighting, and in places the red velvet cushions had all but disappeared under the relaxed spread of the partygoers. Everyone had moved away from the heat of the central black stove as if polarised. Hat, Rob's father and the two children had ended up at the sharp end, with the rest of the party nearer the stern by the companionway. Nell could see that Elly wasn't too pleased about this, and knew that sooner or later she would take action.

'All right, Nell?' Sibyl asked her. 'Come and sit here for a bit.' She patted the bunk beside her, and Nell sat down obediently. At the far end, where the pull-down table was, Hat and Malachy Hayhoe were playing I Spy with Will and Sam. Both boys looked creased up with tiredness, but had objected vigorously to any suggestion that they should be put to bed in the fore cabin like babies.

'. . . something beginning with A,' Rob's father was saying (Nell found it difficult to think of him as Bert). He blew a few smoke-rings from a fat cigar and twinkled at his audience. Sam, the younger boy, was resting his cheek on the table, and sweeping an arm back and forth across its polished surface in a bid for inspiration. 'Apple,' he mumbled.

'There aren't any apples in here,' Will said scornfully, putting up a finger to trap a smoke-ring as it drifted past.

'There might be!'

'It has to be something in sight, Sam,' Hat reminded him. 'I mean, if there was an anaconda in that drawer over there, it wouldn't count.'

'What's a nanna . . .?'

Nell turned to Sibyl. 'It's very good of him to play games,' she said. 'I'd rather assumed he'd be busy holding court; being famous.'

'Yes,' Sibyl said, but without much conviction, glancing across at the silent Elly.

Nell turned back to hear Bert saying, 'An anaconda can

swallow a manhole, or do I mean a man whole?'

She leant across to Elly. 'Will and Sam seem to be having a fun time.' She knew Elly was always drawn to people who were nice to children.

'Lovely,' Elly agreed, but she looked unhappy. Sibyl was looking a bit tight-lipped too. Nell frowned.

'Arm?' Hat suggested, guessing the I Spy. 'Or ankle?' Bert shook his head, but his luxuriant silver hair stayed perfectly in place.

'Abdomen?' Paul said, coming down again with Rob, and patting his.

'Antediluvian?' Sibyl said, pointing to herself.

'Anchor?' Will said. 'Since this is supposed to be a boat.'

'There isn't one!' Sam retorted.

'Anorexic?' Paul said, looking pointedly at Elly.

'Autocrat!' she flashed back.

Paul was not to be outdone. 'April fool?'

'It's still March,' Will protested, 'and anyway it's our game, not y –'

'Aphrodisiac?' Elly suggested. Her voice seemed to have gone down an octave. She looked very deliberately down the length of the boat and caught Bert's eye.

'Antipathy?' Paul said at once.

'Rubbish!' Hat said briskly. 'You can't *see* antipathy.'

Sibyl caught Nell's eye, and looked away quickly again.

'Accountant?' Nell said hastily, after an uncomfortable silence.

'Warm,' Bert said, looking at her properly for the first time.

'Artist?' Sibyl suggested, touching Nell's arm.

'Warm again. Do you give up?' He looked smug. 'What about you, Rob? You haven't done one.'

'Just tell them, OK?' Rob said shortly.

'It's an almost actress,' Bert pronounced grandly, giving

74

Elly a long look which fizzed down the boat like a laser.

Nell thought, What's going on? What *is* he playing at? And why is Rob so angry? Some party! She leant against the back of the bunk with her hands behind the cushion, and fiddled with the piping along its edge.

'Nice place, this,' Rob said to Paul, turning his back on his father. 'I don't suppose you know whether any of the other houseboats are for rent?'

'I doubt it very much,' Paul said. 'I have a feeling they're all reserved for holiday letting.'

That's a bit unfriendly, Nell thought. He said he liked Rob! He might at least have agreed to ask around. But it was nothing to do with her, so she kept quiet. She wondered why Rob had accepted this invitation in the first place. He'd barely spoken to her all evening, and he clearly didn't consider himself to be 'with' her. It was almost as though he had turned into another person altogether: an impersonal self-effacing presence, drained of all initiative. Was this his father's influence?

Nell wondered about Bert. Had he been tantalising Elly by deliberately ignoring her whilst monopolising the only two people she couldn't possibly object to? If Rob had really told him about her beforehand, then Bert *must* have known she'd be keen to talk to him. Was this perhaps what all public figures did to keep their fans at a distance, or was Bert being deliberately provocative, even malicious; indulging in a kind of power play? And was Rob's awareness of this the reason for his mood? If so, she supposed she could hardly blame him.

Elly, Sibyl and Paul were now talking about holidays, and Rob was listening. Elly seemed more animated now. Nell was glad of this, and happy to take a back seat. She felt confused.

'. . . Anything for a quiet life!' Paul was saying jovially.

Nell's fingers encountered something hard under the cushion, and she brought it out to examine. It was a pearl earstud in a zigzag gold setting, and it looked surprisingly familiar. She turned it over and over in her hand. Of course! It was exactly like one of the ones Anna always wore. She was about to say, 'Look what I've found!', but the other four were deep in conversation. A verbal coincidence niggled at her from a closed room within her brain. Then the cell door opened a crack, and she remembered Anna saying: *The Boss likes a quiet life*, and she looked across at Paul, frowning . . . No, in all probability the earring belonged to one of the former owners of the houseboat – yes, that must be it. But she slipped it unseen into her pocket anyway, just in case.

The floor moved suddenly, disconcertingly. Nell had forgotten that they were not on terra firma.

'Tide's coming in,' Paul said, steadying himself.

'High time we all went home,' Hat announced. 'These two young men are about dead on their feet, and we're about to lose an hour of sleep on Sunday morning anyway, for the beginning of summer time.' She began organising their departure.

'Well, that's why we had this party on Friday night,' Paul explained, 'to give us all time to recover.' He went to turn on the deck lights.

'Will you be collecting your children tomorrow?' Nell asked Rob.

'As ever,' he said.

'You have them every weekend?'

'Yup.'

'I'm glad I've met your father.'

'Are you?'

'Well, perhaps it might have been better if you hadn't warned him . . .' Nell hesitated, gesturing towards Elly, who was going forward with the coats.

'No,' Rob said, 'it would have been even worse. Believe me, I know.'

'Thanks *so* much for coming,' Elly was saying to Bert.

'It was lovely of you.' She helped him on with his over-coat, all smiles. Then each one in turn climbed the stairs to the deck and crossed the gangplank to the shore, Nell last.

'Bye, then,' Rob called to everyone, 'and thanks.' He waited for his father to get into the Land Rover and then climbed in himself, waving through the open door as he drove off.

'Look!' Elly said to Nell as soon as they had gone, excitedly producing something small and white from a clenched hand. Isn't this great? Brilliant party!'

'What is it?' she bent to look. It was Malachy Hayhoe's business card.

'He says I can phone, and go and talk to him in London,' Elly said. 'Isn't that marvellous? I am *so* excited about it!' She put an arm around Nell's shoulders and squeezed them affectionately. 'And Rob's a sweetie too, isn't he? I'm so glad you brought them both.'

'Bloody hell!' was all Nell could manage.

'You look a bit glum?' Anna said, as Nell came down the steps and joined her in the swimming pool. She'd been hoping that Nell would enliven her.

'It's how I feel,' Nell said. She looked pale too.

'What's the matter?'

'Oh, just Rob Hayhoe. As if you couldn't guess.'

'What's he done?'

'Nothing. That's the problem. I never know where I am with him, and I feel as if I've been making all the running. I've absolutely no idea how he feels.'

'Big mistake,' Anna said. 'You have to let men do all the chasing, or it emasculates them, the poor fragile things.'

'Bit old-fashioned, surely.'

'Basic human nature, I'm afraid.'

'Well, I've decided to give up on Rob anyway. It clearly isn't working.'

'But you'll see him again?'

'I'm bound to, aren't I? I'm buying his cottage.'

'And that's going all right?' Anna rubbed the water out of her eyes.

'Well, it needs some work doing on it, according to the survey, but nothing that can't be fixed. I wish the estate agents and solicitors would get a move on though. I can't see why it has to take so *long*.'

'Always does,' Anna said. She pushed her wet hair off her face with both hands and held it there at the nape of her neck.

'Different earrings?' Nell observed.

'Yes. I seem to have mislaid one of my favourite ones. It'll probably turn up next time I change my bed. Hope so, anyway. I'm not even sure exactly when I lost it, so I don't know where to begin searching.' Anna noticed that Nell was looking peculiar. Embarrassed. 'What have I said?'

'Nothing,' Nell said at once. 'Sorry, I was miles away.'

'Do anything special last weekend?'

'Yes, as it happens. I went to a party.'

'And?' Anna lay back with her head on the tiled edge, kicking her feet lazily.

'And Rob and his father were there, and Paul and Elly, my friends from London.'

Paul and Elly ...? Anna caught her breath, and then put on a carefully casual voice. 'What sort of a party was this, then?' She was conscious that Nell was regarding her steadily.

'A house-warming party on their new houseboat in Eely Creek,' she said. 'It's lovely.'

Shit! Anna thought, pretending to slip underwater by mistake, to escape Nell's look. 'Uhhh!' she spluttered, surfacing. 'What a berk, eh? I need Velcro or something on the back of my neck! Come on, let's swim.' She set off at a fast crawl; anything to keep her face out of sight whilst she gathered her thoughts. Shit, SHIT, *SHIT!* Had

78

Nell guessed? No, why should she? But how on earth did she know Paul Tozer? Perhaps, Anna thought, I should ask her – just come straight out with it. But if she hasn't twigged, that would be stupid, and I did promise Paul . . . No, I'll just deny everything.

'So, where's this Eely Creek then?' she asked Nell when they next stopped.

'On the River Torrent, where my new cottage is, about ten miles east of here. Haven't you ever been there?'

'Not yet,' Anna said, pleased at how firm a gaze she could muster. 'Can you see the houseboats from your windows?'

'No, there's a bend in the river.'

'Oh, right.' Well, that's a relief! Relax – it's OK, she hasn't realised. 'Sounds good,' she said carefully. 'What's the great Malachy Hayhoe like, then?'

Nell drove to work after swimming, in reflective mood. She was now sure that 'the Boss' and Paul were one and the same. It would explain a lot. But she didn't recognise Elly in the catty 'Ermintrude' stories that Anna had told, and she felt thoroughly ashamed of herself now for ever having laughed at them. All her loyalties lay with Elly. Anna was only a recent acquaintance – barely a friend at all. Nell had been astonished at Anna's confident lies, and felt quite unable to challenge them. She needed time for reflection. How should she play this? Should she tell Elly and precipitate a crisis, or should she go on seeing Anna and gather evidence on Elly's behalf? If, as she thought, Anna didn't know she'd been found out, then she, Nell, had the upper hand. It wasn't something that appealed to her; she didn't like that sort of game. Perhaps she should speak to Sibyl. Maybe Sibyl already knew that Paul was having an affair . . . I don't want to upset everyone, Nell thought. Maybe I'll just keep quiet and wait and see.

'You're looking a bit peaky,' Sibyl said. 'I'm afraid the

party was a bit of a strain, wasn't it?'

'You're the second person who's mentioned that today. I do feel browned off actually.'

'Give it time,' Sibyl counselled. 'These things have a habit of working out in their own way, you know.' The telephone rang at the back of the shop, and she went to answer it. Then she came back, looking pleased. 'What did I tell you?' she said. 'It's Rob Hayhoe for you.'

'Oh!' Nell broke into a smile, and walked lightly over to pick up the receiver. 'Hello, Rob.'

'Oh, Nell,' he sounded embarrassed. 'I'm not sure how to say this. My agent is going to phone yours, but I thought I ought to warn you myself.'

'What about?'

'Well, it seems my original buyer is now back with a new purchaser for his place, and he's claiming priority over you and saying the cottage is morally his because he offered for it first.'

'But he backed out!' Nell protested.

'Yes, but through no fault of his own. And now he is in a position to proceed. He's even upped his offer by several thou.'

'But you've accepted *my* offer.'

'Yes, but I'm obliged to "maximise the realisation of my assets", as my solicitor so pompously puts it, in order to pay off my debts and support my children.'

'So where does that leave me?'

'Well . . . I suppose you couldn't match his offer?'

'Oh, come on!' Nell said furiously. 'How underhand can you get? It's supposed to be unethical if I buy the cottage and pay less than him, but if I pay the same, then it magically becomes perfectly above board? What kind of twisted logic is that? It's just extortion!'

'That's life, I'm afraid.'

'Well, if that's your attitude,' Nell shouted, 'then the whole thing stinks, and you can bloody well stuff it!'

Chapter Eight

Cassie sat at the kitchen table, the remains of breakfast strewn before her, and fiddled with her necklace. The cold green stones felt smooth, and steadying. She was getting more and more impatient about the time it was taking for Bottom Cottage to be sold. They needed to have it all settled *now*. Each day's delay was costing her father money, and he didn't hesitate to tell her so. She felt pressured from both sides. Rob didn't seem to have a clue where his own finances were concerned. He never paid his bills until the red one arrived (sometimes not even then), and he was actively antagonistic to her need to sort things out speedily. Anyone less suited to being an accountant . . . Cassie shook her head in wonder.

But, for the moment at least, it was fortuitous that he still had the cottage. It was the first week of April and it would soon be Josh's sixth birthday. Cassie had been busy trying to shame Rob into organising a party for him over the weekend – not that Rob could oversee a blowout in a cream bun factory, but Cassie felt it was about time he made the effort. She would do it herself, but she felt so exhausted all the time these days, and, anyway, it was his turn to do his duty by his son.

'Perhaps Daddy will give you a birthday party at the cottage,' she suggested to Josh.

'I want my party *here*,' he said at once.

'Well, I don't know, darling. It might not be possible.'

Josh burst into tears. 'I want *you* to do it,' he sobbed. 'I don't want –'

'Oh Joshy . . .' Cassie picked him up and held him to

her, patting his back gently. 'Come on, darling, it's all right. We'll work something out.' She felt a tugging at the hem of her skirt. It was Rosie.

'Up!' she demanded.

'Not at the moment, sweetie. Josh is upset. He needs a cuddle more than you do.' Rosie stuck out her bottom lip and stumped off in a sulk. Cassie barely noticed. She was busy wiping Josh's eyes and getting him to blow into a paper handkerchief.

'I've got an idea,' she said to him, sitting down with him on her lap, and stroking the hair out of his eyes.

'What?' His tears had already vanished. He looked guardedly hopeful.

'I've got this friend, but it's a secret, OK?' Josh nodded. 'She's called Mic. You've met her once actually, but you probably don't remember. Anyway, she's going to come and live with us very soon. Now if you're very nice to her, we might be able to do your party here. How's that?'

'Why can't you *and Daddy* do it?'

'Oh, Josh . . . I've explained that to you so many times.' Cassie felt exasperated. 'Daddy and I aren't friends any more. It's sad, but sometimes these things just happen. But you'll like Mic, she's good fun.' Josh wriggled down from her lap without saying anything. 'But she's our secret, remember? Don't say anything to Daddy, right?' Josh made a little shrugging movement with his shoulders and turned away. Cassie sighed. 'Where's Rosie?' she asked him. 'Why don't you go and see what she's doing?' Josh went out.

A few minutes later, Cassie glanced out of the bedroom window with her arms full of dirty linen, and saw both children in the back garden with no coats on. Josh was going round the central flowerbed with a stick, and systematically smashing the heads off her favourite pink daffodils. Rosie was running behind him, cackling with laughter. Cassie dropped the laundry and rushed to open a window.

'Joshua! Stop that, at once!'

Josh defiantly bashed one more head off, and then threw the stick down. Rosie bumbled forwards gleefully and picked it up.

'What were you doing that for?' Cassie cried. 'Spoiling Mummy's lovely flowers! It's a wicked thing to do. Rosie, that means you too. Stop it!' Rosie, in attempting to emulate her big brother, swung the stick, missed the daffodils entirely and hit Josh on the knee. He immediately started howling with hurt and rage and pushed Rosie over, so she bumped her head on the lawn and began screaming too.

'*Oh God!*' Cassie swore, slamming the window shut and rushing downstairs to sort them out. 'Bloody kids. The sooner Mic gets here, the better!'

Once in the garden she picked Rosie up, ticking her off at the same time, and then she crouched down to roll up the leg of Josh's dungarees to inspect his knee. It looked red and swollen.

'Come on,' she said, giving him a kiss and covering the knee up again. She got to her feet and led him indoors by the hand, followed by Rosie. Cassie shut the door behind the three of them, and then turned to her children smiling brightly. 'We'll put some witch hazel on poor Josh's bruise first, OK? And then we'll all have some lovely chocolate, yes?'

She well remembered that she had said, less than an hour before and very firmly, that there would be no sweets before lunchtime because it would spoil their appetites, but with children one had to be pragmatic. Whatever the so-called child-care experts said, it was impossible always to be consistent. After all, rules were made to be broken.

*

In his heart of hearts Rob knew that Nell was right about the ethics of the whole house-buying muddle. She had refused to gazump his first buyer, and now it seemed the man was gazumping her, and *he* was conniving in it. Worse still, Rob didn't even like him! He was a city gent with a dreamy longing for peace, nature and solitude, the sort of ideals a realist must first translate into their equally valid antitheses: boredom, vermin and loneliness, before deciding to opt for them full time. Rob could tell the man hadn't even begun to consider this. Nell, on the other hand, struck him as a thoroughly sensible, practical person. He would like to think of her living there. He knew she would appreciate it.

What am I playing at? he thought. I can sell to whomever I please. What's a few thousand pounds? He lifted the telephone receiver and picked out the number of his estate agent. He knew he was doing the right thing and he felt better at once.

On the tiredly awaited day, Cassie was about to go downstairs with an armful of Rosie's wet sheets, when she glanced through the round window on the landing and saw two figures getting off a bus outside. The woman, in jeans and a bomber jacket, was holding on to a sturdy little ginger-headed boy, and was being handed down a large rucksack and a bulging holdall by another passenger.

Thank Christ for that! Cassie thought. Mic's here.

Mic had come round three weeks before to see the house, leaving Gavin with her mother. She came in the evening when Josh and Rosie were in bed, and was taken upstairs to view them asleep. Josh was lying on his back with his arms up above his head. In the glow from the nightlight his skin looked peachy and perfect, the long eyelashes curling upwards, his breathing regular and even.

'Little angel, in't he?' Mic whispered, and Cassie warmed to her.

In the next room, Rosie was all curled up under her duvet, with only the top of her head showing.

'How old is she?' Mic asked.

'She'll be four on the twenty-sixth,' Cassie whispered back.

'Taurus, eh? I expect she knows her own mind.'

'You can say that again!'

Cassie took Mic upstairs to the attic. 'Rob used to do woodwork and things up here,' she said, 'but I thought we could clear it out, and maybe paint it up a bit when you get here. There's even a loo through there. I think it must have been a separate bedsitter once.'

Mic looked about her. 'Oh yeah, and there's a sink too, where we can wash paintbrushes out, and that big table'd be good too.'

'It belongs to Rob,' Cassie said, 'but he's not getting it back.'

'Could do with more chairs,' Mic said, 'and maybe a sofa or two?'

'We could go to a furniture auction,' Cassie suggested, getting enthusiastic. 'I haven't been to one for ages. It would be fun!'

'Great,' Mic said.

They went down two flights of stairs into the kitchen, and sat at the dining end with one glass of dry white wine and one sweet sherry.

'Cheesy bic?' Cassie offered.

'Oooh, thanks.' Mic took three. She demolished the first in two bites, and then proffered the jar. 'You?'

'No thanks,' Cassie said. 'I don't.'

'That the cooker?' Mic asked, nodding towards it and corralling biscuit crumbs into a neat pile on the table in front of her.

'Yes it is. It's an Aga and it's marvellous.'

''Cos I'd need to give them a hot meal, dinnertime. It's part of the regulations.'

'That's fine,' Cassie said. 'I only cook in the evenings, and then as little as possible. So, what do you think?'

Mic's grin animated her whole body. 'I think I musta died and gone to 'eaven!' she said, and she drained her sherry with a flourish.

And now here they were at last. Cassie dropped the sheets in a heap on the floor, and ran downstairs to open the front door.

'Hi,' Mic said. She looked both hopeful and nervous. 'This is it, then.' She turned to her son, who was dragging the holdall along the ground towards the door. 'Say "Hello, Cassie", Gavin.' The boy ignored her.

'Hello again, Gavin,' Cassie said. He's probably over-awed, she thought. Not used to a house as big as this. She tried an easy question. 'How old are you, then?'

'Go on, Gav,' Mic encouraged him.

'I'm six and I'm reely *reely* strong!' Gavin picked up the holdall and half fell with it into the front hall, crashing into the coatstand and almost upsetting it.

'He's a bit of a bruiser,' Mic apologised, catching it and propping her rucksack against it. 'I reckon he'll be a right little thug, time he's sixteen. Where's your kids, then?'

'I parked them out with a friend for a couple of hours. I couldn't face them going on at each other while you two were trying to get settled in. It's a nightmare sometimes! Now, why don't you dump your bags there for the time being, and come into the kitchen? We could have a cup of something.' As she led the way, Gavin pushed past her legs and got there first, making straight for the toy chest at the far side.

'Well, the kids won't be a problem no more,' Mic said. 'Not now I'm here. Watch yourself with that, Gav!'

'Thank goodness . . .' Cassie began. 'Do be careful, Gavin, that's Josh's best Space Lego. Tea or coffee?'

'Tea, please. Milk, two sugars.'

They sat a little self-consciously together whilst Gavin played heavily on the floor at their feet. I shall be better now, Cassie thought, now I've got help. And the children will have friends to play with, which will be good for developing their sociability. Josh needs to be more assertive with other children; he's a sensitive boy. Gavin could be a great help. He's only about six months older, ideal really, and Josh always said he wanted a brother . . .

Mic put her teacup down with a sigh of contentment. 'It's great to have a proper roof over our 'eads at long last,' she said. 'Know what I mean?'

'It must have been hell,' Cassie said. 'However did you manage?'

'Well, after that sod – not me 'usband, thank Gawd – buggered off, we lived wiv me mum for a while, but that didn't work out. She would keep shovin' her oar in, she were right out of order. I put me name down fer a council flat, but they're like flippin' gold dust – you can wait years. So then we kipped on people's floors for a bit. We was in bed and breakfast when I met you. I've never bin so glad to get out of a place in me life!'

Cassie regarded her curiously. She still wondered whether she had done the right thing, but she couldn't help liking Mic. She looked at her over the rim of her cup, taking in the ridiculous hair, the multiple earrings, the snub nose and crooked teeth and the tough exterior. It was on the cards that she wasn't tough at all. Cassie could identify with that.

And after all, she reassured herself, if Mic isn't paying rent, then she isn't a tenant, so if it all goes wrong then I can always throw her out. And in the meantime, I shall have some personal space – freedom from everlasting childcare – to get myself together again. I'll probably go up to London now and then, maybe even revive my TV career. Why not?

'You divorced then?' Mic ventured. 'If you don't mind me asking, that is?'

'Not yet. We're right in the middle. It's hell, if you want to know. I can't bear to think what it's doing to the children.'

'Is he well off?'

'He says not.' Cassie gave a bitter laugh.

'You wants to take him for all you can get,' Mic counselled. 'All men are crap, in my opinion!'

Cassie laughed. 'I can see we're going to get on well,' she said.

Then the front door opened with a bang, and Rosie and Josh came running in. Cassie went to thank her friend for having them, and then followed them back into the kitchen. 'Josh, Rosie,' she said, 'this is Mic. She's come to stay with us. And this is her little boy, Gavin.'

'Hi, you two,' Mic said. 'Great to see you again.'

But Josh ran straight across to Gavin and snatched the Space Lego rocket out of his hands. 'That's *mine*!' he shouted.

'Come on, Josh,' Cassie said. 'That's no way to talk to Gavin. You three got on so well together last time. Come here and give Mummy a hug, yes?' Josh shook his head vehemently, and turned his back on her and the dispossessed Gavin.

Cassie shrugged. 'Sorry,' she apologised to Mic. 'Not the best of starts.'

It must be fate, Nell thought. After all the stops and starts, and ups and downs, it really is going to happen. In a couple of weeks' time, by mid-April (barring all unforeseen circumstances, and fingers crossed), Bottom Cottage will belong to me! She wasn't sure why Rob had changed his mind, only grateful that he had. Indeed she was so happy that she could even find it in herself to feel a little sorry for the first man who had lost it. I am *meant* to be there, she thought. I knew it from the first time I ever saw it. Thank you, God – whoever you are.

She rang Rob to arrange to go to inspect the points mentioned in the survey as needing attention, but she did it rather nervously, remembering how she had shouted at him the last time they had spoken.

'When would you like to come?' he asked at once.

'This weekend? Look, I'm sorry I was so ratty last time. I –'

'Quite understandable,' Rob said. 'Actually, this weekend is a bit problematical. It's Josh's birthday, and I'm supposed to be doing a party for him and half a dozen of his schoolfriends from Boxcombe.'

'How lovely,' Nell said, thinking of the parties she'd never had.

'Well, I don't know about that. I'm just hoping it won't be an unmitigated disaster. You're a good cook, can you suggest the sort of food I might attempt?'

'Oh . . .' Nell said, considering, 'well, I don't have any experience of cooking for children, but off the top of my head . . . I suppose a special cake, and maybe a hedgehog made from an orange and cheese-on-sticks, and a trifle, or gingerbread people, or –'

'Hang on,' Rob put in. 'I'll just get a pen and jot this down.'

While she waited, Nell imagined him all on his own, and having to cope, and wondered . . .

'OK, got all that. Anything else?'

'Um, pinwheel sandwiches? Celery boats? Maybe a jelly in the shape of something? That sort of thing?'

'Brilliant,' Rob said. 'If I manage half of that I reckon I'll have done well. I don't suppose . . . ?'

'What?'

'No, it would be an imposition. Forget it.'

'No, go on.'

'Well, I was going to invite you to come too,' Rob said.

'Apart from the party, we could kill several birds with one stone. There are various tricks I ought to show you – how to conquer the woodburner, that sort of thing – but perhaps you'd prefer to do that some other day?'

'I'm not sure,' Nell said cautiously. 'You see, I loathe and detest party games of any sort.'

'Oh, there won't be any,' Rob assured her. 'These days I'm afraid one just hires a video. I shall try to get the little toads out for a good walk to the sea and back first, but definitely no games. I hate them too.'

'Well . . . can I think about it?'

'Of course. But I'd like you to meet my children; it's high time.'

Nell put the phone down thoughtfully, remembering what Anna had said: *It's serious – the equivalent of being taken home to meet the parents.* No, she thought, not in this instance. He's just being polite. But then her curiosity got the better of her. She *would* like to see what his children were like, and this time Rob had invited her, rather than the other way around . . . I've had my own way about the cottage, she thought. I can afford to be magnanimous.

After half an hour, she rang him again. 'Have you got a birthday cake for Josh?'

'Not yet,' Rob said. 'I suppose I'll have to buy one.'

'Don't do that. I'll make one for him,' Nell offered. 'Does he have any special interests?'

'At the moment it's penguins,' Rob said. 'He wants to be an explorer like Scott of the Antarctic.'

'Right,' Nell said. 'I'll see what I can do.'

On the following evening she made a standard fruit cake, and then spent her entire free Friday afternoon having fun decorating it. Crisp white icing made good snow. She stood the cake on a board and made it into a snowy island on a thick icing-sugar sea, dyed blue with food colouring and sculpted into rollers and breaking waves. She had bought two small plastic whales to frolic in it, and some sugar penguins, and found the rest of the characters she needed in her old childhood toybox. On the island she built an igloo from glacier mints stuck together with 'snow', clothed several small plastic figures in bits of fake fir to make them into Eskimos, and dotted the island with the penguins and her favourite old model polar bear. Then she finished it off by constructing the up-turned prow of a wreck in the sea at the bottom of the cake cliff, made from two bits of After Eights melted together along their leading edge, with masts and spars of chocolate orange Matchmakers, lashed together with cotton.

Late on Saturday morning she lowered the whole creation carefully into a cardboard box, with a folded towel at the bottom to prevent it sliding about, closed the lid and carried it out to the back seat of her car. Then she set off for Bottom Cottage. Halfway there she began to feel apprehensive. Doing the cake had been the easy bit. But what did one say to children? She had virtually no experience to guide her. She wished Elly were with her. Elly always knew how to amuse; she was good at games and knew heaps of knock-knock jokes and silly rhymes. Nell began to feel more and more inadequate, and by the time she arrived, she had decided just to deliver the cake and leave at once.

Rob met her at the door with a long face. 'I'm sorry,' he said. 'I tried to phone, but you must've already left.' He eyed the box. 'And of course it's far too late as far as the cake is concerned. Shall I carry it?' He took it from her, and led the way.

'Is there a problem?' Nell asked, following him indoors.

'You could say so. The Mad Cow rang me ten minutes ago to say that (a) Josh didn't want to visit me today, and (b) that she and a friend I've never even heard of are taking all the children to some theme park instead, and I'm not to bother telephoning the other parents because she's already done so!'

'Oh no!' Nell exclaimed. 'Talk about a *fait accompli*!'

'Bitch!' Rob said. 'Sorry and all that, but it's the only word for her. She seems to take a malicious delight in doing this sort of thing – messing up my arrangements at a moment's notice. I suppose I should be used to it by now but it gets to me every time.' He looked defeated.

'I'm so sorry,' Nell said gently.

'No. I should be apologising to you for all the effort you've put into this,' Rob said, putting the box down on the only corner of the kitchen table that wasn't already covered in plates of food.

He had obviously tried to do his best for Josh, and what he lacked in finesse, he had made up for in industry. There were thick sandwiches with crusts, sausages on matchsticks, crisps, bought cheese straws, and sausage rolls. There was a bowl of mixed tinned fruit and a turned-out green jelly which had stuck to its mould, so the resulting rabbit was only just recognisable. It brought a lump to Nell's throat.

Rob opened the top of her cardboard box and looked inside. 'Oh Nell!' He lifted the cake out, letting its box fall to the floor, and set it down admiringly. 'This is terrific! It must have taken you hours to do. What a shame. No, more than that – what a bloody awful waste of all your time and effort. I'm so sorry.'

'Never mind,' Nell said. 'It will keep for a week or two, you know. All is not lost.'

'Oh good.' He looked round gloomily. 'But that's more than can be said for the rest of the stuff . . . I hope you like jelly for lunch.'

'Love it.'

'Just as well! Shall we begin at once?'

They ate their way through a quantity of sausages and egg sandwiches. Rob cleared away all the fizzy lemonade and produced beer instead. 'I suppose I could take some of the soft drinks back to the shop,' he said.

'And some of the food would freeze,' Nell suggested.

'Haven't got a freezer.'

'Well, I have. I could store it for you until the next time. When's Rosie's birthday?'

'End of the month.'

'There you are then!'

'Thanks,' Rob shrugged, 'but who knows where I'll be by then.'

'You haven't found anywhere to rent?'

'I'm working on it.' He looked again at the cake. 'This is a work of art, you know. I'm so grateful to you for taking such trouble over it.'

'Have you spotted the deliberate mistake?' Nell asked, pleased.

'Um . . . No, what?'

'Well, you don't get polar bears and penguins at the same pole, do you? Just as well really, or the one would eat all the others!'

'Oh, don't worry. I'm sure Josh won't notice that small detail.'

'No, that's the point, you see. I'd like you to tell him. I believe children love it when adults get things wrong!'

'That's very perspicacious of you.' Rob was smiling warmly at her. 'Clever. I'm so glad it will be you, and not that man living here.'

'Why did you change your mind?' Nell asked.

'Because you were right,' Rob admitted. 'Simple really.'

Nell thought: Martin would never have said that in a million years! At last I've finally met a man big enough to be able to admit that he can be wrong. So, what next?

Chapter Nine

On 19th April, a week after her move, Bottom Cottage began to feel like home for Nell. By then, all the essentials had been unpacked and put into place and she had begun on the inessentials, which are what really matter. As long as her books were in boxes, and her pictures in bubblewrap, then she was in transit. But once the bottom of the bedroom wall was obscured by bulging bookcases, and higher up by familiar paintings, she knew she had finally arrived.

As she looked out of the upstairs window where Rob had sat each day, she saw the first swallow of the year winging its way across the river towards her, and thought, I must make a note of the date! Then it occurred to her to begin keeping a diary every day to record the unfolding, flowering and withering of all the years ahead. Maybe she would also put up a rain gauge to record the monthly totals, so she would know what was really going on, and whether the weather had genuinely begun to change in response to global warming, as people were saying. Of course many decades of data were required for such studies, but she intended to be there for a significant number of years to come. The idea of accumulating a wealth of information about this one place pleased her. The more knowledgeable she became about it, the more she would feel she belonged, and this was important as it was the first time she had ever been able to put down roots of her own choosing.

Nell lay in bed next morning staring dreamily at a shaft of sunlight which shone between the ill-fitting curtains, making a pool of light on the wooden floor. April is the perfect time to begin a new life, she thought, when all of the natural world is also starting afresh. A scratchy sound outside the window alerted her to the presence of some animal, and she got up to investigate. In a new place there were strange noises and unfamiliar things to react to, or to learn to ignore. She pulled the curtain aside and looked out, just in time to see a small unidentifiable bird flying away. In the garden below, the last of the daffodils were heavy with dew. All presented their yellow trumpets to the sun, except for the double ones which were bent right down to the ground and seemed in danger of snapping in half. Design fault, Nell thought. They've been 'improved' so much by hybridising that their heads now hold too much water! Far better to have left well alone.

She sat at her desk, which did service as a dressing table, brushing her hair, and wondering how much of her new garden she would leave to be wild, and how much she would try to impose her will upon. She decided to wait a whole season before doing anything, to find out what was in the soil already, and give it a chance to declare itself. A quicker way, of course, would be to ask Rob, but she had decided to wait for him to telephone her. The last time he had been in touch was the day before she had arrived at the cottage, to say he was in the process of moving out.

'Where are you going?' she'd asked.

'Caravan the other side of Boxcombe,' he said briefly.

'But what about your furniture?'

'In store, what was worth keeping, which wasn't much. I broke up a lot of it for firewood. It's behind the woodshed under some plastic sheeting. You're welcome to use it if you want. Makes good kindling.'

'You could have got a firm in to clear out the things you didn't want,' Nell said. 'That's what I did, and I was amazed at how much money they paid for what I considered to be utter junk. I had a skip too, for the real dross. It's a ghastly hassle, isn't it?'

'Not to be repeated in a hurry,' Rob agreed.

'If you ever want to visit . . .' Nell hesitated, 'do drive down.'

'Thanks. Well, best go. Lots to be done, and all that.'

'Yes of course. Good luck then.'

'And you.'

Nell would have liked to talk for longer, but realised that he was probably being terse in order to remain in control of his feelings. Poor Rob, she thought. It must be hell to have to leave here. I'm sure his children will be upset too.

The scratching noise outside began again, and Nell looking up, saw a long-tailed tit gathering the gossamer threads of spiders' webs from the outside of her window-frame, and flying off with them into the thickest part of her garden hedge. She imagined the new nest in progress, with moss and animal hair being woven together with the cobwebs into the perfect domed shape, and then covered in lichens for camouflage and lined with feathers for comfort. Then she looked at her ancient curtains and the bare floorboards and thought, I could do with a few new rugs underfoot, and the walls do need painting. I suppose a sensible person would have had the place professionally decorated before moving in, but I'd rather it was an evolving process entirely connected with me and my own efforts. I want to do all my nest-building myself.

'You've got terracotta freckles!' Cassie said, coming in and looking up at Mic's face. 'I thought this brand was meant to be non-drip.'

'It's this bloody roller,' Mic said, balancing the paint tray at the top of a step ladder. 'I dunno how else you're s'posed to do flaming ceilings?'

'Looks good,' Cassie encouraged her. 'Keep going!'

'I wouldn't say no to a cuppa,' Mic suggested.

'Nor would I,' Cassie agreed. 'Oh I see, you mean you want me to make it?'

'Well, I'm a bit mucky, like.' Mic displayed painty hands.

'Oh, all right then.'

It's all going pretty well, Cassie thought, as she boiled the kettle. Once Mic has finished the emulsion painting (and that should be later this week, all being well) then there's the woodwork for her to do in yellow gloss . . . and then we can move in the two second-hand sofas we bought from the sale room . . . and maybe my rocking chair as well. I must buy a couple of lampshades – those paper ones that look like hot-air balloons – and maybe see if I can get something to cover that grotty lino . . .

As she made the tea, the idea came to her. The shagpile carpet with the bound edges which had been on the sitting-room floor at Bottom Cottage . . . That was hers by right; she had paid for most of it. It probably wouldn't cover the whole of the floor in the attic room, but it would be good enough. I'll get on to Rob, she thought, and make him bring it back.

She had last spoken to him at work only that morning – well, 'spoken' was hardly the word. She had yelled at him, and with good reason. Her interim maintenance cheque hadn't arrived *yet again*. Rob had refused to get it organised (like any half-reasonable person) by direct debit, preferring instead to write one out when he felt like it, which was invariably long after it was due. I have a right to that money, Cassie thought. 'Your children have a *right* to that money!' she'd screamed at him. 'But I suppose that thought's never crossed your tiny mind.'

'So what happened to the cheque I gave you last month?' Rob had asked. (He must have been using that oh-so-reasonable voice on purpose, because he knew it drove her up the wall.)

'That was then. This is now! We do have to eat *every day*, you know, or had you forgotten that?'

'Why not try inconvenience food then?' Rob had said. 'It's so much cheaper –'

But she'd slammed the receiver down.

That made things awkward now. She was reluctant to put herself in the position of having to make the next move or, worse still, appear to be a supplicant. She always tried to avoid asking Rob outright for (or about) anything; to do so would be an admission of dependency. She usually got her own way simply by reminding him of his duties and her rights. So she was damned if she was going to grovel to him now, but equally determined that he should feel the full weight of his responsibilities as the children's father. If I demand the carpet back, she thought, he'll then want his big table. He's small-minded enough to make it tit for tat, and we need that table.

She voiced her dilemma to Mic as they sat drinking the tea she'd just made.

'Try sending him a solicitor's letter,' Mic suggested. 'That'd sort him out.'

'Just an ordinary letter might do . . .' Cassie considered the idea. 'Yes, why didn't I think of that? Then I can get it all over in one go without him hassling me. You've seen how it is. If I try talking to him on the phone, he just bullies me, and then I get into such a state I can't think what I'm saying. I've got to the stage where I can hardly bring myself to phone him at all, but of course I have to for the children's sake.'

'Yeah,' Mic said. 'That's really tough.'

'Right then,' Cassie said briskly, draining her mug, 'that's what I'll do. You OK carrying on with the painting? I'll go and get this letter off my chest, and then we'll both be advancing the cause.' She thought privately that her task was much the more arduous, but she refrained from saying so. Mic was doing a valiant job, even if she wasn't the world's best painter.

On 22nd April the first orange-tip butterfly of the year appeared in Nell's garden, and on the 28th the first cuckoo. She recorded them both gratefully in her diary. At least some things were still predictable. There was blossom too on the ancient apple tree, and polyanthus and honesty flowering by the back door, but the very idea of an April shower seemed laughable. They'd had only half an inch all month, and the ground was cracking up as though it were high summer. Not for the first time Nell prayed for rain, and marvelled at ever having taken it for granted.

That Saturday she was busy rubbing down the door of her bedroom, preparing it for paint, when she heard the sound of a child's voice outside and went to the window to look. In the garden below was a small boy with dark curly hair, going along her back wall, picking up the *objets trouvés* and stuffing them into the pockets of his coat, counting aloud as he did so. Nell was about to open the window to protest when she realised who he must be. She stopped and watched him instead. He was trying to collect them all up, but some were too big to fit into his pockets, and there seemed to be nowhere else to put them. He compromised by piling them into a heap on the ground, and then he turned to the garden gate and yelled at the top of his voice, '*Dad!*' There was an answering call. 'Dad? I'm having trouble!'

Nell smiled, and waited for help to appear. Then when it did, in the form of Rob and a little girl, she opened the window and leant out.

'Would you like a carrier bag?' she asked.

Both children gaped at her. 'That's my dad's room,' the boy said reprovingly. 'You shouldn't be in there. You'd better come down at once!' It sounded as though he was reciting something recently said to him by an irate adult.

'Hush, Josh!' Rob said. 'She's every right to be there.' He looked up at Nell. 'Sorry about this,' he said. 'I forgot to take the things from the wall. I might have known that Josh here would . . .' He looked round for his son, but he'd disappeared.

There was a bang at the front door, and Nell heard the thunder of wellington-booted feet running upstairs. She dodged out to intercept him.

'Is there something else you've left behind?' she asked him, but he pushed past her without answering and ran into his old room, which was now full of cardboard boxes, with piles of canvases all over her spare bed.

'Where's my bed?'

'I don't know,' Nell said. 'I expect –'

'And where's my chair and my –'

'I had to move them all out,' Rob said, out of breath, appearing at the bedroom door and putting Rosie down. He glanced apologetically at Nell. 'Sorry.' And then back to his son, 'Look, Josh, you can't just burst in here willy-nilly. This place doesn't belong to us any more. It's Nell's house, OK? This is the Nell who made you that lovely birthday cake, remember?'

Josh shook his head. 'Where's my bed?'

'I had to put it in store. Come back downstairs and I'll explain.'

'No,' Josh said stoutly.

'Yes,' Rob said, equally firmly, taking him by the hand. 'Come on now, I'm serious.'

'Willy-nilly,' Rosie began, giggling. 'Willy-nilly, nilly-willy, willy . . .'

'And you too, Miss Silly Nilly,' Rob said, picking her up again and holding her on his hip with one arm.

'Would you like a cup of tea or anything?' Nell asked, following the three of them downstairs.

'Miwk?' Rosie said hopefully.

'Yes, I think I've got enough. You too, Josh?' Josh shook

100

his head vehemently. 'Or orange juice?'

'No!'

'No, thank you,' Rob corrected him. 'Look, I'm sorry about this invasion. We were only really going for a walk. The shelducks are back in the dunes, you know, nesting in the rabbit burrows. I always think when they're first prospecting for their ideal nest hole they look so ridiculously conspic –'

'I don't like this table,' Josh interrupted. 'I want our one back.'

'Milk,' Nell said, putting a mugful down on the table in front of Rosie.

'My cup!' Rosie demanded. 'Want it in my cup!'

'It's not here,' Rob explained patiently. 'None of our things is. We don't live here any more. I know it's hard to accept but we've all got to make a big effort.'

Josh fixed Nell with a baleful look. 'Why's she here?'

'Because it's Nell's cottage now. She's bought it from us.'

'It's *my* house,' Josh insisted, covering his ears and speaking loudly, 'my house, my house, my house . . .'

'Tea,' Nell said, giving Rob a mug. 'So, how's the caravan then?'

'Josh! Please be quiet.' Rob sighed. 'It's perfectly adequate, but fairly cramped, especially at weekends.' He looked across at Rosie. 'Are you drinking that milk then, pudding?' Rosie picked the mug up clumsily and spilt some on to the table. 'Careful!' Rob warned her.

'It's my fault,' Nell said, 'don't worry. I must have filled it too full.'

'It's all *your fault*,' Josh said, sotto voice.

'I'll get something to wipe it up.' Nell went over to the sink, and got the dishcloth from its hook. She understood the children's confusion and felt sorry for them – sorry too for Rob, and almost guilty at her own good fortune. Joshua is a very beautiful child, she thought, looking at his profile – lovely dark eyes and lustrous curly hair. Pity Rosie didn't take after her father too.

'Is the stove behaving itself?' Rob asked her.

'Well, it smokes quite a lot when I first light it.'

'Cold chimney,' Rob explained. 'No proper draught until it heats up.'

'Yes, I suppose so. And it seems to get through mountains of wood. Good thing you left me a decent pile.'

'I reckoned about ten tons a year,' Rob said. 'You want to buy it in the summer as cordwood, and stack it to season for eighteen months or so, otherwise it's too green and the whole system tars up inside.'

'Goodness!' Nell exclaimed. 'It sounds like a full-time job.'

'Don't want this,' Rosie said, slopping her milk again.

'Clumsy!' Rob reproved her. 'Perhaps Josh will finish it for you.'

'I want a bag,' Josh demanded, 'like you said.'

'Oh yes,' Rob said, 'a carrier bag would be very useful if you've got a spare one.'

Nell went into her utility room under the stairs, and came out with several.

'Rosie wanth one!'

'We'd better go,' Rob said, getting to his feet. 'Here you are, Rosie, a bag for you, and one for Josh, and one for me. Let's go and collect up all your treasures, shall we, and then go back to our caravan.'

'I want us all to sleep *here*,' Josh said.

'Well, that would be difficult, wouldn't it?' his father said reasonably. 'Without enough beds?'

'Thilly willy, thilly willy, thilly willy . . .' Rosie mocked him.

'It ISN'T,' Josh retorted furiously. 'And anyway, you haven't got one, so na na-ne NA nah!'

They were still niggling each other as they climbed into

the Land Rover, and didn't even look back at Nell as Rob turned it round and drove off with a brief wave, shutting his door only as they disappeared from view.

'Ah well,' Nell said to the empty air. 'What a surprise, eh? Nice meeting you.'

Cassie reckoned she could talk most people into doing what she wanted, most of the time. Mic had now applied to the local authority to become registered as a child minder, and today a social worker was due to come to inspect both them and the proposed premises. He arrived only ten minutes late, looking, Cassie thought, a bit too smug for her liking.

'Oh, it's Mrs Hayhoe, isn't it? My colleague thought she recognised this address,' he said to her at the door. 'And how are things with you?'

'Fine,' Cassie said rather brusquely, 'but never mind all that. It's Mic you're here to vet, and the wonderful room we've got ready specially. You'll be amazed when you see it.' She led the way upstairs, and stood proudly in the doorway, ushering him and Mic through.

She could tell at once that he was impressed. He looked all around him at the terracotta ceiling, the several-coloured walls: orange, cream, beige and brown, and at the gleaming primrose woodwork. The sofas and chair were grouped together for story-telling. The table had paints and paper and brushes laid out on it. There was a bookcase full of picture books, a box of bricks, another of Lego, and six teddy bears. And discreetly on a corner shelf there was a baby-changing mat with a disposable nappy bin underneath.

'We've made it into a sort of den,' Cassie explained, 'so the children will feel warm and safe. That's why we've used all these lovely earth colours. There's also a carpet coming, and we're planning to get some beanbags for them to loaf around on. The whole ambience is calm and loving and yet stimulating, don't you agree?'

'So, how exactly would *you* be involved with the child-minding?' the social worker asked, frowning.

'Oh, I won't be,' Cassie cried, laughing gaily. 'Perish the thought!'

'So it will just be you, Ms Potton, or may I call you Michaela?'

'Mic's fine.'

'Right. And you're . . . what . . . a tenant here?'

'Oh, no,' Cassie said at once. 'We're friends.' She smiled brilliantly at Mic, who for once didn't respond. Poor little thing! Cassie thought. I hadn't realised she'd be so nervous. You have to stand up to these bloody social workers or they think they're God. I should know. I've had them on my back from the moment Josh was born . . .

'So,' the social worker said to Mic, beginning to jot down notes on a pad, 'you have no security of tenure then, is that right?'

'No it most emphatically isn't!' Cassie said. 'She's going to be minding my daughter, so I'm hardly likely to throw her out, am I? I'm not that capricious!' She thought, I bet he doesn't even know the meaning of that word, and he's sitting in judgment on us!

'It's OK, Cassie,' Mic said. 'I can handle this.'

'That's quite all right,' Cassie assured her. 'I'd like to help. I've got plenty of time this morning, and of course I've had loads of experience with the social services. Yes?' She threw him a challenging glance. He ignored it.

'So where are the children?' he asked. 'I believe you have a little boy, Mic?'

'Yeah, Gavin. He's six. The three of 'em are round my mum's.'

'I thought we could discuss things better with a bit of peace and quiet,' Cassie explained. The social worker looked pained.

'Well, I do need to see you all together,' he said, 'to

assess your interpersonal skills, and the way the children relate to you . . .' He took a deep breath. 'Right,' he said, 'for the time being then let's concentrate on the technicalities, starting with the electric wiring . . .'

'Oh, there are plenty of sockets,' Cassie said. 'I think they're on a different system from the rest of the house, but Rob used to run his heater and his lathe and stuff off them, so I know they work.'

The social worker was bent double, inspecting one. 'Good God! They're the old round-pin sort!' He hauled himself upright again, his face pink with the effort.

He's a bit unfit! Cassie decided, smiling but critical.

'You're right,' she said. 'It's a bore. You can't get the plugs to fit them any more, but if we need to use anything electrical in here, I can always make Rob send us his old ones. I'm sure he won't have thrown them away; he's a dreadful hoarder!'

The social worker again wrote in his notebook. He was shaking his head. 'Must be nearly fifty years old!' he said, partly to himself.

'Is that a problem?' Mic asked.

'I should say! Whatever you do, don't use any of them, OK? They could be lethal!'

'Well, we've turned the radiators back on, so the whole place is centrally heated, so we don't actually need them anyway,' Cassie said. 'Just as well really. We wouldn't want all the mess of a rewiring job, especially now when we've finished doing the decor –'

'Fire exit?' the social worker interrupted. 'Is there one?'

'Well, not exactly,' Mic said. He wrote more in his notebook. 'But there's a toilet through there,' she added quickly. 'Ever so handy, look.'

Cassie thought, I really must remember to ask Mic not to say 'toilet' when she means 'loo'. That's an abomination I absolutely do *not* want the children to pick up.

The social worker finished writing and looked at Mic.

'Right,' he said, 'and how about you? Are you in good health?'

'Oh yeah,' Mic said eagerly. 'Strong as an 'orse, me.'

'Do you smoke?'

Cassie and Mic answered this question at exactly the same time, but Cassie said, 'Yes,' and Mic said, 'No.'

'Sorry?' The social worker looked confused. 'Mic?'

'Well, I do smoke,' she admitted, 'but only in the evenings, like, so it don't count, yeah?'

'We'll have to arrange for you to have a chest X-ray.' He wrote another note.

'There's nuffink wrong wif me chest!' Mic was getting rattled. Cassie put a steadying hand on her shoulder.

'No, I'm sure it's quite all right. It's just regulations. And whilst we're on the subject,' the social worker looked apologetic, 'I'm afraid I'm obliged to ask you whether or not you have a criminal record.'

'Not bleeding likely!'

'Good. And can you provide us with at least two character references?'

'Well, I dunno . . .' Mic looked up at Cassie.

'In this instance,' the social worker said, 'I think one from Mrs Hayhoe would be inappropriate. It needs to be from someone professional; a doctor, a solicitor, or a vicar maybe?'

Mic snorted. Cassie tightened her grip on her shoulder. 'I'm sure we can sort something out,' she said. 'Mic's brilliant with children. She's certainly saved my sanity.'

'Right!' the social worker said, snapping his notebook shut. 'Well, I think that's about all we can accomplish today. I'll come again soon, to see you with the children. Right?'

Cassie and Mic showed him out, and after he'd gone they stood in the hallway staring at each other. Again, they spoke simultaneously.

Cassie said, 'Well, that went off fairly satisfactorily, didn't it?'

Mic said, 'That's it. We've fucking blown it!'

Chapter Ten

Rob read the letter from Cassie and marvelled at the ineptness of her timing. In truth it was not so much a letter, more a statement of demands: a long list of all the household things she had left behind in the cottage and claimed still belonged to her with, at the bottom, orders that the children should no longer be taken anywhere near the cottage because it was causing them psychological damage. Rob curled his lip, and glanced again at the list of things. Eighty per cent of them he had already put into store, and were therefore unreachable. Most of the rest he had thrown away. All that remained was the sitting-room carpet, which he had left behind for Nell to take over.

Could he ask for it back? He had no idea if she particularly liked it or not. He would have to tell Cassie that it had been sold with the house, but would she then immediately demand a new one? He was damned if he was going to buy her one, but he really did not want all the hassle involved in refusing to do so. He wished yet again that he could simply tell her to sod off, but he knew that if he upset her she would inevitably take out her rage on his children – he called it her *Look what you made me do!* syndrome. It seemed that this was the hold she would always have over him; a never-ending form of moral and emotional blackmail.

At the bottom of her letter Cassie had written: 'I'm not going to discuss the above in front of the children, so give me a ring on Friday evening.' *Please*, Rob added sarcastically to himself.

He went to collect the children on Saturday morning, after trying several times the night before to telephone Cassie and then (on finding the line constantly engaged) giving up.

'You never called me!' she accused him, as she opened her front door. 'Was it too much trouble just to lift the phone?'

'If you must know I tried for bloody hours, but all I got was the engaged signal.'

'Well, of course I left it off the hook while the children were going to sleep. I can't have them disturbed. You *must* know that?' Rob raised his eyes to heaven. 'And there's no need to sneer,' Cassie went on, 'or pull stupid faces. I can quite see where Rosie gets it from!'

'Daddy!' Rosie came running out of the kitchen and flung herself at him. Rob hoped she hadn't overheard them.

'Hello, pudding.' He bent and gathered her up in his arms and kissed both of her apple cheeks. 'You look good enough to eat! Which bit shall I begin with?'

'Feet!' Rosie cried, cackling.

'Mmmmmm mmm mmmm . . .' Rob mouthed his way over one sturdy red shoe, and up one thickly trousered leg, smacking his lips and doing a pretend burp on her tummy. Rosie laughed louder.

'There's such a thing as child abuse, remember,' Cassie said sourly. 'The spare things are in that bag over there.'

Rob ignored the implied threat. 'I hope they aren't all Josh's clothes this time.'

'Of course not. Don't forget Rose's medicine, will you? And she's not allowed out in the cold; she's not well.' Cassie turned to go.

'So, where is Josh?'

'Playing wiv Gav,' Rosie said helpfully, pointing to the stairs.

Rob swung her down and steadied her before saying, 'Run up and tell him I'm here, there's a poppet.' When she'd gone, he asked Cassie, 'Who's Gav, presumably Gavin?'

'Just a little friend.'

'Well, he'll have to go home now, won't he?'

'Depends.'

'On what?'

'Josh might rather stay here and go on playing with him.'

'Oh, come on, Cassie. Don't start messing me about again.'

'Don't you threaten me! Josh has a right to make his own decisions.'

'He's only six years old!'

'So?'

'So it's cruel to ask him to decide between us. He'll be so torn.'

'Oh, I think you'll find Josh knows very well where his loyalties lie.'

'That's not true, and it's also not fair, Cassie!'

'Perhaps you should have considered that before you walked out on us.'

Rob controlled himself with difficulty. 'If you remember,' he said, 'it was you who threw me out!'

'Call yourself a man?' Cassie sneered. 'No *real* one would have been so feeble!'

There was a scuffling, bumping noise. Rob turned to see Josh coming downstairs with Rosie and another child behind him. Josh's face looked pale and curiously blank.

'Josh!' Rob cried. 'There you are. That's good. Grab your coat and wellies, yes? It's time we were off.'

But Josh just froze. Then he pushed Rosie out of the way, shouted, 'C'mon, Gav!' and grabbing the other boy's arm, ran off upstairs again and, judging by the hollow sounds, on up the next flight towards the attic.

'See!' Cassie crowed.

'This is ridiculous,' Rob objected. He was very close to shouting.

'Face it, Rob,' Cassie said, 'he just doesn't want to see you.'

'What on earth's going on? What's he doing in the attic? That whole floor is out of bounds to children, you *know* that! There's still some of my tools and stuff up there. It's not safe!'

'Mic'th room,' Rosie piped up. 'Want to go now.'

'Who's Mick?'

'Just a friend of mine,' Cassie said. 'None of your business.'

'So what does Josh want with him?'

'Mic'th not a –' Rosie began.

'Ssssh! Rosie,' Cassie admonished her, 'Daddy and I are talking.' She turned to Rob triumphantly. 'I do believe you're jealous.'

'Oh, go to hell!' Rob said.

'*Pas devant les enfants!*' Cassie warned.

'Want to go, want to go, want to GO!' Rosie cried, breaking into tears and tugging at Rob's sleeve. Cassie was standing, hands on hips, staring him out.

'I wouldn't do that if I were you,' he said. 'Makes you look even more like a fishwife than usual.' Then he picked up the sobbing Rosie in one arm, the bag of spare clothes on the other, and walked out.

Rob drove Rosie to the park in direct disobedience to Cassie's wishes, and managed to dissipate some of his anger in pushing her higher and higher on one of the swings, so that she shrieked in delighted fear. He was furious to have been cheated out of having Josh for the weekend, but equally determined that Rose should not feel second best.

Once the divorce is all settled, Rob thought, there must be proper arrangements about my contact with the children. And let's hope the Mad Cow will find it harder to mess me about then.'

He caught the swing, and kissed the top of Rosie's head. 'More,' she begged. 'Puth more!'

'Hold tight, then.' He wondered why Cassie seemed so indifferent to her daughter, lavishing all her love and affection on Josh instead. He hoped Rosie wasn't aware of the imbalance, but feared she must be. She was certainly not shy of fighting for parental attention, but both she and Josh had developed a worryingly negative strategy for getting it, and Cassie, instead of reacting to it with sensible briskness, positively reinforced the behaviour by rewarding it lavishly so that both children ended up vying with each other as to who could exhibit it the most. Rob had no idea what he could do about it. Weekends were never long enough.

'Puth!' urged Rosie.

'One more time, and then we're going to have one last look at our old house,' Rob said, deciding.

When they arrived at Bottom Cottage, they found Nell outside sniffing one of the long lilac-coloured racemes of the flowering wisteria on the garden fence, and inhaling deeply.

'I'd never realised what a marvellous scent this has,' she said. 'How nice to see you. No Josh?'

'Unfortunately not,' Rob said.

'Geth what I've got,' Rosie said proudly to Nell.

'What's that then?' Nell said, crouching down to her level.

'A really bad cold!'

'Oh.' Nell glanced up at Rob, who shook his head slightly. 'That's hard luck.' She stood up again. 'Are you going for a walk?'

'Why not?' Rob said. 'Want to come?' And they set off along the river path together.

'I can run fatth,' Rosie said.

112

'Go on, then,' Rob encouraged her. 'Run as far as that stile and back, and we'll watch.'

'Sweet thing,' Nell said, laughing as Rosie galumphed ahead. 'Did her birthday party go well?'

'Not at all. She was ill.'

'What a shame!'

'I don't think Rosie thought so. By all accounts, she stayed in bed all day with Cassie dancing attendance, and Josh not getting a look-in.'

'Oh, I see,' Nell said. 'It's like that, is it?'

'It's been one of our main problems,' Rob said sighing, 'arguing about our very different approaches to child-rearing. For instance, Cassie thinks I shouldn't bring them here. She says Josh was so upset after the last time that she had to keep him off school for a week.'

'But that's nonsense!'

'Yes, well . . .' Rob made a face.

'So, why are you here then: defiance?' She looked as though she really wanted to know. Rob was sorry he had an ulterior motive.

'Well, it's a bit awkward . . .'

'Go on.'

'You know the carpet in the sitting room?'

'Don't tell me,' Nell guessed. 'The Mad Cow wants it back? Well, she can have it.'

'Are you sure?' Rob looked at her gratefully.

'Certain. It turns out to be just the wrong colour and, to be honest, I only accepted it in the first place because it seemed churlish not to.'

'Oh, Nell . . .' Rob began, but was distracted by the return of his daughter, out of breath.

'Daddy . . .' Rosie panted reprovingly, 'I runned . . . but you didn't . . . watch!'

'I'm sorry, poppet,' Rob said. 'Why don't you run again, and this time I promise we'll really watch? OK?' And he caught Nell's eye and smiled broadly.

'You haven't done much sailing, then?' Paul asked Anna as he anchored the yacht behind Eely Isle, the most secluded part of the river he could find.

'Not until I met you, no.'

'But you are keen to learn?'

'Of course.' Especially if it takes your mind off incessant bonking, she thought. She looked across at the lush spring vegetation. 'We could take the dinghy and land there,' she suggested, 'and christen the island.'

'Would take too long,' Paul said, smiling meaningfully.

'So why don't we brew up for a coffee, then?'

'Afterwards.' He took her by the hand and led her down into the cabin, taking off his shirt as he went. Anna did not complain. She was all too aware of the bargain she had struck. She wanted Paul because she was lonely and needed a man to bolster her confidence. But Paul, at the moment, just wanted to go to bed with her. She fervently hoped that eventually he would need sex less, and value her companionship more, but on present evidence that might take some time. It's a bore, she thought, taking off her clothes and letting him kiss her, boring to keep on having to go through this undignified, messy process. Worse still, she didn't even *enjoy* it! But if it was the only way to keep him . . . She climbed on to the bunk, and lay there waiting.

A little later she thought, I wonder if other women think philosophical thoughts while they're doing it. Perhaps I'm abnormal. Sometimes people who've had a near-death experience describe being somewhere above, and looking down on themselves as they lie, expired, below. I seem to be like that with sex. It's only when I can be a voyeur on my own life that it means anything at all. Maybe that's why some people have mirrors on their ceilings. She could hear the river quite close to her ear, lapping up and down with each thrust. Eight, nine, ten . . .

she counted. Any minute now. Better switch on the fake ecstasy. She moaned a little, and began to pant. Twelve, thirteen, fourteen . . . I wonder if I'd be less crushed on a water bed, Anna thought, although come to think of it, this *is* a kind of water bed. . . . Seventeen, eighteen, nineteen, GO!

'Aaaaaaaahhh!' She let it out as a strangled scream. Perfect timing yet again.

Paul slumped sideways. 'Bloody wonderful,' he mumbled into her shoulder. 'Never fails, eh?' Then he went to sleep.

Anna dozed too, wondering casually how someone with a Ph.D. in biochemistry could be so easily conned. She was glad of it. The last thing she needed was a nineties man who operated an open-soul policy, and whose pride was hurt if you didn't (really) come. Maybe Rob Hayhoe was like that. Nell had told her last Friday at swimming that she liked Rob because he was gentle and undemanding and nice to his children. Anna had had to restrain herself from putting two fingers down her throat in a *Vomit!* gesture. She liked her men to be masterful and manly; worthy of respect. Paul was ideal.

Of course if she really wanted to know what Rob was like, she could simply ask Paul, but she hadn't yet told him about her connection with Nell, and now she didn't think she would. It was over a month since the boat-warming party, and no one had apparently said anything. Paul was still telling silly Ermintrude stories. His cover still seemed to be intact. And it was now May and the promise of a whole summer of regular illicit meetings loomed excitingly ahead. Anna particularly enjoyed the forbidden aspects of their affair; the excitement without the routine, the possession without the commitment. She eased one arm from beneath his dead weight and turned her back on him, the better to reflect on life in general. It had been a lonely winter, but things were improving:

Paul had finally moved his yacht to Thrushton Quay. Ermintrude was securely tied up in London by her job and her two small boys. Paul would soon be having long school holidays as well as snatched weekends, and he had a well-established habit of regularly going off alone, sailing . . . Things could only get better.

Cassie's letter was bad news. 'I don't believe it,' she complained to Mic, waving the sheet of paper angrily. 'All television these days seems to be run by stupid adolescents!'

'What d'you mean?' Mic asked, stuffing her own letter back into its envelope.

'Well, I thought I'd let them know I might be available again sometime in the near future when everything's settled down, but apparently they've ". . . got no vacancies for a presenter at present".' Cassie read out. 'They say things have "moved on" since I last worked for them. Huh! They've got some little tart (who must be all of sixteen) doing my job now. Have you seen her on *ALL DRESSED UP*? She can't even read the autocue!'

'She's a bit tasty though, in't she?'

'That's hardly the point!' Cassie snapped.

'Sorry, sorry. Don't lose your rag.' Mic put up both hands as if to ward off a blow.

'Who needs them anyway? There are plenty of other programmes or TV companies I could work for.' Cassie looked round crossly. 'Where's Gavin? Shouldn't you be with him? I do hope he isn't filling the loo with lavatory paper?'

'He's all right. He's just –'

'Because I don't want it blocked up again. I really cannot face that gruesome plunger any –'

'Well, at least he can wipe his own arse,' Mic said, flaring up. 'Which is more than your precious Joshua can; sitting there on the toilet and yelling orders, like I was

116

some sort of bloody servant!'

'It's not a toilet!' Cassie shouted. 'It's a lavatory or loo or bog or john – *anything* but a toilet. Why can't you get that into your thick head?'

'Don't worry,' Mic said savagely. 'You won't have to put up wiv me common ways no longer. An' you can clean out your own crapper in future!'

'What d'you mean? What are you talking about?'

'This.' Mic threw her letter over the table at Cassie. 'So, soon's meself an' Gav can find somewhere else to kip, then we're off, awright?'

'But . . .' Cassie took the letter from the County Council Social Services Department out of its envelope and cast her eyes over it speedily. Then by supreme effort of will she changed her whole demeanour. 'Oh, Mic,' she said. 'I'm sorry. I didn't realise.'

'Yeah, well,' Mic looked unappeased.

'Look,' Cassie said, at her most winning, 'just because those sods have refused you as a licensed child minder doesn't mean you have to go. You can still stay on here and mind Rosie unofficially. I should hate to lose you.' I'd fall apart in five minutes!

'So how'm I supposed to make me living, then?'

'You'll still have your state benefits, won't you? And you can go on staying here, rent free. I really need you, Mic.' And I can't have my long overdue nervous break-down without you . . .

'Well, I dunno . . .'

Oh God, Cassie thought, do I really have to grovel? It's all your fault, Rob bloody Hayhoe. Look what you've reduced me to. She put on a bright smile with some difficulty, conscious of it fading at the edges. 'Look, I'm sorry about just now,' she said. 'I shouldn't have gone on at you. Put it down to disappointment and hurt pride, yes?'

'My pride's hurt an' all,' Mic said. 'An' I reckon I'd've got that bloody registration froo if –'

'If what?'

'Oh forget it,' Mic said.

'Look,' Cassie said as consolingly as she could, 'you're upset, of course you are. It's quite understandable. I'm not surprised that social worker turned you down though. They're like that. If one of them happens to take a dislike to you, then you've had it. You could be the best child minder on the planet, but they won't want to know.'

'So I noticed,' Mic said.

It's no good, Cassie thought. She's still not convinced. Let's see if I can . . . She began to breathe fast and shallowly and felt satisfactorily dizzy almost at once. 'Oh no,' she cried, clutching at the table. 'I think I'm going to have one of my . . .' And then she fell off her chair on to the floor in a convincing imitation of a dead faint.

'How are you getting on?' Elly asked Nell over the phone. 'Can I come and help you decide about your interior design?'

'Can't afford you,' Nell said with a laugh, 'and anyway I'm not aiming at fashionable elegance. It's got to be in keeping with what it is – a small, very untrendy country cottage.'

'Don't tell me,' Elly said, feigning despair, 'you're painting all the walls magnolia?'

'But of course,' Nell said cheerfully. 'Makes an excellent background for paintings.'

'You're right. You're a lost cause.'

'So, how's life with you, and when are you next down at the houseboat?'

'End of May. As from now we've decided it's going to be a family tradition for us to spend every half term there.'

'What, even in February?'

'Well, maybe not the spring half term, but definitely the other two.'

'I see. And is everything OK?'

'Fine, in fact better than usual.' Elly broke into a triumphant smile, which it was just as well Nell couldn't see. 'Why d'you ask?'

'Oh, no reason. I just wondered . . .'

'Well, better be off,' Elly said briskly. 'Things to see, people to do.'

'In a manner of speaking!'

Freudian slip, Elly thought, laughing. 'Bye then!'

'Bye, El,' Nell said.

Elly turned to the mirror above the telephone to check for slippage, but her make-up was still intact, and her face glowed back at her with recently renewed self-assurance. She lifted her hair with both hands and watched with satisfaction as it took on a plumped-up, carefully tousled shape. She looked good. She opened her handbag and directed a squirt of scent behind each ear, and on to the gently pulsating area of each wrist. Then she looked in the mirror again and pursed her lips in an ironic kiss, before leaving in her car.

She thought, as she drove, how very kind it was of the fates that Paul should have such a passion for sailing, and that his mother should be such a dutiful grandma. With Hat, one couldn't be sure whether she was keen to have the boys to stay simply because she loved them, or if perhaps she hoped to save them from their father's influence, of which she quite clearly disapproved. Either way, Elly thought, who cares? And she broke into song, smiling at the other motorists, who drew up beside her at traffic lights, with such *joie de vivre* that they too grinned; a positive triumph in surly London.

Who'd have thought it? Elly asked herself. A couple of months ago I was in a deep black hole, but now I'm flying!

She found a parking space in the elegant square at once, as though by right, and walked demurely up the steps to the ornate front door, conscious that he might be watching out for her.

'My darling girl! he exclaimed, as he let her in. 'You look *wonderful*!' He kissed her lightly and led her by the hand up the stairs to his drawing room. 'I've got something for you,' he said, 'and I want to give it to you now, before we exhaust ourselves. A good idea, *n'est-ce pas*?'

Elly stroked his face gently, smiling in agreement. His eyes looked very soft, and the crinkles around them very sweet. She loved the contrast between his large black eyebrows and his silver-grey hair. She noticed suddenly that his nostrils were perfectly symmetrical, and laughed delightedly to have discovered something new about him.

'What?' he asked, beaming at her.

'I'll tell you in bed,' she promised.

'First things first,' he said, sitting on a couch and drawing her down beside him. He gave her a thin oblong parcel wrapped in blue tissue paper, the colour of his eyes, which she tore off quickly and dropped in ragged pieces on the floor. Inside the box, Elly found a necklace of smooth stones, all of the same mineral, but of different swirling patterns and shades from palest eau-de-Nil to almost black, as if deep green water with all its whirlpools and confluences had been captured and fossilised for all time.

'It's *beautiful*,' Elly whispered. 'Oh, darling . . .' He put it round her neck and fastened it, all cold and heavy, and she put up her hands to feel it there.

'Malachite,' he said, 'my all-time favourite, and particularly appropriate too, I think you'll agree.'

Elly gazed at him with love. 'Thank you,' she said. She kissed him on both cheeks and put her arms around his neck. 'You're so good to me. Thank you, darling Malachy.'

Chapter Eleven

The swifts came back from Africa on 6th May and Nell recorded their arrival in her diary, and admired them as they quartered the skies above with effortless agility. By the 14th the ash trees were at last coming into leaf, weeks behind the oak.

If the oak's before the ash, then you'll only get a splash; if the ash precedes the oak, then you may expect a soak.

Nell had her own theory on this, which was retrospective rather than predictive; we've only had a splash of rain this spring, so that explains why they're so late, she decided. In fact ash was always late in coming out, and one of the first to drop its leaves in autumn, like a cautious old maid – exposing her precious foliage to the elements only when she could be absolutely sure that the weather would be clement.

Everywhere else was in full verdure, the lanes pungent with hawthorn blossom and crowded with cow parsley. At night, odd maybugs bumped against Nell's lighted windowpanes. By day the two buzzards, who until recently had been circling and mewing possessively high over her valley, were now nesting somewhere quiet and secret.

In June unexpected delights appeared in her garden; pink and fragrant Albertine roses, white irises, blue delphiniums and orange day lilies which bloomed, and slewed sideways in the summer winds, requiring twine and stakes. By the turnaround where the ground had been disturbed, scarlet field poppies flowered, as brash and beautiful as only high-class weeds can be. Nell took photographs and made plans, and on free hot days at weekends she sat and painted in the garden in the shade of the apple tree and received the envious glances of ramblers on the coast path, with a modest pride. I am where I want to be, she thought. I am *so* lucky.

Later that month she bought tons of cordwood when the weather was dry and the lane surface hard enough to bear a six-wheeler. Then, over several weeks of hard labour, and whilst it was still in four-foot lengths, she stacked it carefully to season in the summer's heat.

'Hubby goin' to cut it up fur 'ee, then?' the lorry driver had enquired, as he'd dumped the load. 'They say as firewood do warm a body three times over, what with the cutting and the carting 'swell's the burning.' He gave her his delivery note to sign.

'He'll most probably hire a chap with a saw bench,' Nell said, writing her name, and taking on an imaginary spouse with practised conviction. She was well accustomed to coping with potentially embarrassing offers of assistance from overconfident strange men.

'Unless he do get thee at it wi' a bowsaw,' the driver chuckled, taking the piece of yellow paper back from her, and making explicit fore and aft gestures with it. 'Good exercise, like.'

'Oh, he wouldn't dream of doing that,' Nell said carefully. 'He does all the heavy work himself.'

'Big bloke, eh?'

'Over six foot.'

'Ar well, best be on me way.' And he put his lorry into low gear and laboured it back up the hill and away.

Nell wondered then, and at regular intervals thereafter, whether she would ever have a genuine flesh-and-blood partner to take cover behind. Rob had been her best bet so far, but now he seemed to be fading out altogether. Months went by without a sighting of him. The drought increased and a hose-pipe ban came into operation. The

River Torrent dwindled, and at low tide took up only a third of its normal channel. Small cracks opened up in the walls of Bottom Cottage as the clay foundations beneath dried up and shrank, and the house subsided into a new summer stance. Nell would have liked to be able to ask Rob if this was its normal behaviour, but didn't want to bother him at Mugglestone, Pudduck and Co., feeling sure that sooner or later he would be down the lane for a walk, and she could mention it then.

But as summer passed and autumn began, with still no sign of him, Nell began to believe that she must have misread him completely. Perhaps he was afraid of the Mad Cow and simply obeying orders; a total wimp. More likely he didn't want to be reminded of a place he'd loved and lost. Nell was aware of feeling disappointed, but her general contentment with her lot stayed intact.

She also saw less of Elly than she had expected to. Paul and Elly did come down, but only for a week at a time in May and again during the summer holidays. Nell sometimes noticed Paul's yacht, with the red parrot motif on its mainsail, sailing past her cottage downriver to the sea, and assumed he must be staying on the houseboat alone (since he had much longer holidays than his wife) but on those occasions he never called on her. Nell worried that he was seeing Anna and wondered what, if anything, she ought to do about it. However, increasingly unsure of her own judgment, she did the easy thing, and said nothing.

As time went on, and during her frequent phone calls to Elly, this self-doubt of Nell's began to escalate. Her friend, who had formerly been determinedly bright but edgy, was now relaxed and funny. Nell, who felt she ought to be celebrating this new zest and sparkle, instead felt confused and uncomfortable. At the October half term, when the Tozer family came down to the houseboat again, Elly and her two boys (and sometimes Sibyl too) came over to Nell's cottage for hours at a time, playing hide and seek, going for walks by the river, and waving to Paul as he slipped past in his sleek white one-off yacht.

'One of these days, when I'm rich, I shall repair my jetty and buy a little dinghy with an outboard motor,' Nell said, as she and Elly sat in the dunes one sunny day, watching the boys searching with buckets and spades along the tideline.

'Didn't Rob have one when he lived there?'

'He told me he had a rowing boat, but Cassie made him get rid of it.'

'Why?'

'Because it would be "dangerous for the children". He assured her he'd teach them to be safe, but she wouldn't have it.'

'Shame.'

'Yes. How about Will and Sam? Don't they want to sail with their dad? I should have thought it would be lovely, pottering down the estuary looking at everything.'

'Don't ever go out with Paul, then,' Elly warned. 'He turns into a speed freak the moment his feet touch the deck. All he wants to do is to get there as fast and as efficiently as possible.'

'Where?'

'Anywhere but where the boys and I want to go, and to hell with scenery or wildlife or anything interesting. We call him Damon Hilltler!'

'So he's put them off sailing? That's a shame.'

'Will just hates being shouted at. I can't say I blame him!'

'And little Sam?'

'Oh, Sam refuses to be tied down. He reckons that a safety harness is for babies years younger than whatever age he happens to be, and he's become expert at unclipping his, which makes me too damned scared to let him go, unless I'm there to keep an eye on him.'

'But Paul would look after him, surely.'

'You're joking! Paul gets so involved with trying to catch every tiny windfart, he'd probably only notice a person had fallen overboard if the bit of rope next to where they'd just been sitting needed pulling round the . . . what d'you call it . . . ? The ratline-gimbal-bilge thing.'

'Wow! I can tell you've got the old nautical jargon well sussed.'

'Oh, yes,' Elly said. 'I feel it's the least I can do,' and she laughed, putting her head back with her eyes closed, to feel the sun on her face.

To Nell's surprise, she now seemed entirely philosophical about her husband's shortcomings. What had changed? As far as Nell could see, Paul was still as chauvinist as ever. Perhaps she'd been quite wrong all along about his affair with Anna, and he and Elly had simply been through a sticky patch. Perhaps Elly had decided to make the best of a bad job at last. Maybe Sibyl had finally convinced her of the benefits of positive thinking. Nell still found it hard to believe.

'What's got into you?' she asked.

'What d'you mean?' Elly still had her eyes closed, but her mouth widened into a broad grin.

'Well . . . you seem different lately . . . lighter . . . younger even. Like you used to be years ago, when we left university.'

'If you must know, I've got these wonderful new pills,' Elly said, sitting up and handing her a tube of the boys' Smarties. 'The secret is in the blue ones!'

'No, seriously.'

'Second childhood perhaps.' Elly opened both hands briefly. 'I dunno, I'm still the same me.' She looked down at her sons, who were now throwing bladderwrack at each other with cries of glee. 'Uh oh, I thought the sealoom hunt wouldn't last for long. It's probably time we made a move.'

'Sealoom?'

'The marine treasure equivalent of heirloom. It's a family joke.'

'I see . . . No I don't!'

'Oh, it's a long boring story,' Elly said, 'but I'll give you the jist of it: valuable jewellery discovered in Uncle Tozer's attic in an *air*line bag, and said to be heirlooms. Therefore anything exciting found in the *sea* must be a . . . and so on.' She got to her feet and began dusting the sand off her clothes.

Nell did the same, looking around her. 'Isn't that Paul's boat coming back now? She pointed at a yacht re-entering the mouth of the estuary.

'So it is.'

'What's the significance of the red parrot?'

'Paul thinks it's part of the boat's name.'

'Which is what?'

Elly made a face. '*Polypeptide*.'

Mic saw the social worker from the landing window upstairs, and thought, Oh, here we go. I might have known! Cassie's parting words to her the week before had been, 'Don't tell Rob or the social services either. Promise?' and then she'd left Mic in charge and (not before time) gone off to get her head sorted at the funny farm. The busybodies there must have interfered. Typical!

Mic was more than happy to be on her own in the house with the three children. She could see an improvement in Josh and Rosie's behaviour already, and she didn't need any 'help' from anyone. The front doorbell rang, and then rang again. She went downstairs feeling defensive, and let the woman in.

'Right, so you're Mrs Hayhoe's nanny?' the social worker asked, fixing her with a penetrating but caring gaze. She had an air of brisk obsequiousness which Mic distrusted instantly.

So what's in a name? Mic thought, shrugging. 'Yeah.'

'And you're employed on a permanent basis?'

'Sort of, yeah.'

'Sorry?'

'Yeah, I am.'

'So, she pays you a salary?'

'Well, not exactly . . .'

'You're not paid *anything*?'

'No, well, we have this, like, arrangement.'

'Are you a relation of hers, is that it?'

'You've gotta be joking!'

'So . . . you have a different sort of relationship with her?'

'Eh?'

'She's your partner, perhaps?'

'For Gawd's sake,' Mic flared up. 'We're *friends*, right?' Friendship made a better story than mutual (hostile) dependency. 'She helps me an' I help her. Not that it's any of your fucking business.'

'We're talking about the children here,' the social worker said emolliently, smoothing her way over Mic's aggression like a snail riding on slime across sharp stones. 'I'm sure you'll agree that their welfare has to be our paramount consideration. And whilst Mrs Hayhoe – Cassie – is under psychiatric care, I have a duty to ensure that they're adequately cared for. How long have you known her?'

'Long enough.'

'And are you perhaps aware of her history of mental ill health?'

'She said she had the baby blues after her kids were born, yeah.'

'Well, it was a little more serious than that. The children were very nearly taken into care, you know.'

'But they wasn't.'

'Well, no, but it was touch and go. Of course, then Mr

127

Hayhoe was around to give her support.'

'An' now she's got me.' Mic stared her out.

'Yes . . .' The social worker looked down at her notes. 'Yes . . . My colleague says that you relate well to both children, but naturally their father is the obvious person to have care of them. You've met him, of course.'

'Well, no,' Mic admitted.

'But, you've been here how long?'

'Since April.'

'But that's . . . nearly seven months! Surely you must have . . . I mean, Mr Hayhoe visits his children regularly, doesn't he?'

'Oh yeah, every weekend, but Cassie don't let 'im past the front hall, and I just keeps out the way.'

'Why is that?'

Mic had a flash of inspiration. 'She's scared, like.'

'Of violence, you mean?' This seemed to strike a chord. Mic nodded, and watched with satisfaction as the woman wrote *?Physical abuse* in her notebook.

'An' he lives in a grotty caravan,' Mic went on, encouraged. 'You couldn't send kids there in November; it'd be too bloody cold. They'd be far better off in their own house wiv me an' Gavin.'

'Continuity is certainly important, yes.'

'So, how long's Cassie going to get banged up for then?'

'Well, I wouldn't put it quite like that. She's gone in entirely voluntarily, you know, until she feels she can cope again. It may be that your advent has precipitated her collapse, in a funny sort of way.'

'You blaming me? I don't fink that's funny.'

'No, no. You misunderstand me. People like Cassie often hold themselves together by sheer willpower and then, when help comes along, they begin to relax their guard and, wham! the floodgates open. I don't anticipate a very long stay, though. I'm sure they'll soon have her stabilised again. Now, if you could just give me Mr Hayhoe's address . . . I'll need to contact him anyway.'

'Haven't gor it.' Mic looked across at the clock on the mantelpiece, and got to her feet. 'I've gotta collect Rosie from nursery school, awright?'

'Right.' The social worker stood up too. 'Well, carry on with the good work for now anyway, and I'll let you know what's decided soon.' She went out, got into her car and drove away.

'Stupid cow!' Mic berated herself aloud. 'If those kids get sent to their dad's, then Gav and me'll get chucked outer here. I was a pillock to get so stroppy; I should've brown-nosed her.'

The winds got up from the south as a deep depression approached the West Country across the Atlantic, and Rob, who had heard the weather outlook, set about battening down the hatches before the worst of the gale should hit. The shipping forecast had predicted *severe gale 9, gusting to violent storm 11* for Wight, Portland and Plymouth, so it wasn't to be ignored. He got his torch and went round the caravan in the dark, checking the stay-legs were firm and tying the tarpaulin more securely over his Calor Gas bottle. Beyond that there was little he could do except hope for the best. He went inside again and hunted through the wall cupboards until he found his collection of half-burnt candles and a box of matches, in case the site electricity should fail. Then he fried a couple of lamb chops for supper, ate them with bread and butter and sat back with a mug of coffee, congratulating himself on his unaccustomed forethought.

By ten o'clock the wind had increased in strength to an uncomfortable degree and the rain had settled into a steady percussion on the thin roof above his head, changing note and amplitude every now and then as squalls of hail went through. A couple of times the lights flickered and the boom of thunder interrupted *The World Tonight* on Radio 4. It's the full works, Rob thought, climbing fully dressed on to his bunk. Could be a bumpy night. He switched off the light and darkness took over.

When he awoke again it was with a start, to find the whole caravan rocking and shivering in the blast. The rain seemed to have stopped, but the wind was screaming around in ever-accelerating strength, and buffeting the sides of the van so that they sucked and bulged spasmodically. The noise was terrific. Rob fought an impulse to bury himself deeper in his bedclothes, and wondered what to do for the best. There were big trees round the edge of the site, but his caravan was out of their range, so with luck he wouldn't be hit by anything from above.

'Just hope the bloody van doesn't overturn –' he began aloud, and as he reached for his torch a ferocious gust roared in and engulfed everything. Rob had a brief sensation of being weightless and upside down, and then there was a huge crash.

Nell lay in bed and worried about her cottage. The tide was low, so there was no need to be anxious about flooding, but the clay tiles on the roof were rattling alarmingly, and she was sure she heard at least one of them sliding downwards. There's nothing I can do, she thought. I'll just have to hope for the best. I do hope the nearest trees have got a grip on things.

She slept fitfully and was tired but relieved when dawn, and the waning of the worst of the storm, came together. At first light Nell got out of bed, put on her fleecy dressing gown and slipper socks, and looked out of the window. It was raining gently. One old and rotten ash tree had fallen across the junction of the coast path with her turning circle, but otherwise all seemed well. She looked round her bedroom – no change – and then went on a damage-inspection tour of the rest of the house.

At the bathroom door she heard the plink plink of falling water and, looking up, saw it was seeping through the hatch from the roof space and pinging into the bath directly below. Handy place for a bath, Nell thought, and then: Damn! I was right. I must have lost a tile, maybe more than one.

She got dressed quickly and went outside in wellies and a parka to have a look. Squinting through the still-falling rain, she saw several tiles had been displaced sideways but there was only one definite hole in the roof, the offending tile having slid down and lodged itself in the gutter apparently unbroken.

It's no big deal, Nell thought, but I'll have to get some-one in to fix it for me. I haven't a ladder high enough, nor a good enough head for heights. In the meantime, it can go on raining into the bath. I may as well go to work and ring for a builder from there.

'Are you all right?' Sibyl enquired as Nell arrived at ARTFUL[L]. 'Only there's been a terrific amount of storm damage, according to the *Today* programme. Apparently it's very bad north of Boxcombe. Did you have any trouble getting in?'

'I had to wait for one fallen yew to be chainsawed out of the way outside the church,' Nell said, 'and of course everywhere's littered with leaves and twigs and rubbish but no, I think I got off relatively lightly.'

'I seem to have missed most of it too. My bit of town is down in a dip and sheltered from the worst of the winds. That's why I was so surprised at the news.'

'Can I phone?' Nell asked. 'I need a builder to put some tiles back.'

'Of course, but I think you'll be lucky. They'll all be gone out by now, sucking their teeth and estimating away; anticipating the fruits of a good disaster!'

Sibyl was right. Nell had no luck.

'You could always phone Rob,' Sibyl suggested. 'He's a practical sort of bloke, isn't he? He would probably do it for you.'

'Well, I suppose . . .'

'Go on! What have you got to lose?'

The secretary at Mugglestone, Puddock & Co. said she was very sorry, but Mr Hayhoe wasn't in today. Nell had a sudden awful thought.

'He's all right though, isn't he? His caravan hasn't been damaged in the storm?'

'I'm sorry. I'm afraid I can't –'

'Look,' Nell said, getting worried. 'You can tell me. I'm a friend of his. Is he all right?'

'If you'd like to leave your name and telephone number, I'll see that Mr Hayhoe gets back to you.'

Fat chance of that if he's lying dead under a squashed caravan! Nell thought, but told the woman her name and the shop's number anyway, and put the phone down, feeling anxious.

At lunchtime, ARTFUL[L] was closed briefly while Nell went out to buy a sandwich, as Sibyl had the afternoon off and had hurried away. Nell skirted round the fallen debris on the pavements, looking down to see where she was going, and at a junction she looked up to cross the road, and saw a pink furry house.

She stopped in amazement and did a double take. It was definitely pink, but the 'fur' was only the still-attached stalks of the Virginia creeper which covered the walls, and whose leaves had all been blown off in the storm, leaving just their pink petioles behind. Nell stared at it smiling, and thought, Sibyl would love this! I must tell her about it. But then she remembered that Sibyl had already left for the afternoon, so there was nobody to tell. I wish I had someone to share things with, she thought, unlocking the shop door again and flipping the 'Open' sign to the front. Maybe even a lodger would be better than no one at all.

The sound of the telephone made her jump. It was Rob. 'I gather you rang,' he said. 'How's the cottage? Any damage?'

'Only a few tiles, and one tree down. How about you?'

'Well, actually it was a bit on the breezy side. My caravan fell over.'

'But . . . are you all right?'

'Oh, you know, bruises, the odd cracked rib, nothing life-threatening.'

'But that's awful. It must have been terrifying. You're not at work, are you?'

'No, I'm at the hospital. I phoned the office and they gave me your message. So, do you need any help with your tiles?'

'Well . . . yes . . . but you won't be fit enough, will you?'

'I'm fine now. I was only in overnight for observation, but there's no concussion or anything, and they've said I can go.'

'That's good.'

'Let's see, it's Saturday tomorrow, isn't it? I could pop round in the morning if you like.'

'That would be great, but what about your children?'

'Long story. Tell you when I see you, yes?'

'Yes,' Nell said. 'Thanks.'

Chapter Twelve

None of the other caravans on Rob's site was occupied during the winter season, which was just as well, as most of them had been wrecked by the storm. The site was covered in pieces of them and their contents, as though a giant rubbish heap had been dropped on it from above. Some vans on the boundary had been crushed by falling trees, and Rob, going over the damage with the site owner, counted his blessings. His Land Rover in the car park was undamaged. He had managed to salvage most of his belongings from his overturned van. And the owner and his wife were willing to put him up in their own house until the area could be cleared and new caravans brought in.

'Thank God we're insured,' the owner said to Rob, shaking his head in wonderment over the mess. 'I've been here over thirty years, you know. Never seen anything like this. Don't you worry though. I'll get you a new van soon's I can. The rest might take a little longer to replace . . .' He blew his cheeks out. 'Never seen anything like it . . .'

'I'll give you a hand with the clearing up later,' Rob offered. 'I've just got to go and help a friend put some tiles back on her roof, but I won't be long.'

'Aye, aye!' The owner raised an eyebrow. '*Her* roof, eh? Sure you wouldn't rather stay with her too?'

'Not at all. I doubt if she'd have me. And anyway, it's not like that.'

As Rob drove towards Bottom Cottage he wondered idly whether in fact Nell would welcome a temporary lodger, but then dismissed the thought out of hand. She might expect more of him, and he couldn't face those sort of complications, not now, whilst he was still disentangling himself from the Mad Cow, and probably not for some time afterwards either.

But, driving along the top road from Boxcombe and looking down at Thrushton Hall and the curve of the River Torrent, he was affected with such emotion that it brought tears to his eyes. It's a great mistake to come back, he thought. Why am I doing this? Maybe it's because *my* cottage needs me!

Nell came out as he was turning the Land Rover by her front door. The big ladder on its roof was attached by orange baler twine, and stuck out over the bonnet and beyond. 'You look as though you've been in a war,' she said, seeing his face. 'Poor you.'

Rob touched his forehead. 'Probably looks worse than it is.'

'Well, it's very kind of you . . . Come in.'

He followed her into the kitchen, and looked about in some surprise. 'Mmm,' he said. 'Poncy.'

'D'you like the new look?'

'Not bad. I should have had the wit to do it myself. Then I could have sold the place for twice the price!'

Nell laughed. 'Coffee first, or afterwards?'

'Now would be good.' He sat down at Nell's kitchen table and took in the transformation all around him. 'Did you do all this yourself?'

'Mostly, yes. I like practical challenges.'

'So I see. Thanks.' He took a mug of coffee and held both hands round it.

Nell sat down opposite him. 'This is very good of you,' she began, 'but why . . .' No, I can't ask that. 'What I mean is, where did you get that long ladder from?'

'Thrushton Home Farm. Tom's an old friend of mine. He's lent me his chainsaw too. His wife's ill apparently, poor thing, so I had to hear all about her health and her forthcoming operation next month, or I would have been here much earlier. He's a lovely man, but a terrible bletherer.'

Nell smiled. 'And will it be difficult to fix the roof?'

'Shouldn't think so. You just have to take off a vertical row of tiles, which exposes a kind of ladder of battens, and then you simply walk up them one by one as you lift the tiles out of the way, to reach the skewwhiff or damaged ones. I've done it plenty of times before. There should be some spare tiles in a pile behind the woodstore, unless of course you've gentrified that area too?'

'Oh no, I haven't begun on the outside. Haven't had time.' *Gentrified?* 'Biscuit?'

'Thanks.'

Nell watched Rob over the top of her mug, still wondering why he had really come, and hoping he would explain without her having to ask. But he seemed more interested in practicalities. 'Shouldn't the roof be lined under the tiles?' she asked eventually, remembering her survey.

'Ideally yes, but it's a pricey job and there isn't usually a problem, except when it snows, which it virtually never does here.'

'That reminds me – I found a sledge in the woodstore. Do you want it back?'

'Not yet,' Rob said. 'I'll wait. The ten-acre over there would be brilliant for sledging.' He gestured to the east. 'I've always thought Josh would love it.'

'What's happened about the children, then?'

'Oh, the Mad Cow's had another of her turns and has booked herself into this hugely expensive private loony bin for a rest-cure. And of course there's no way I can have them living with me now, so the Social Services in their officiousness have decreed they can stay at home with a "friend" of Cassie's to look after them. I even offered to take them to a hotel for the time being, but no, "too disruptive" they said.' He laughed shortly. 'But I've scotched one of Cassie's nastier little schemes.'

'Oh?'

'Yes. The friend is called Mic, and she wanted me to assume it was short for Michael, so I'd be jealous! I did believe it for a week or so too.'

'But you weren't jealous?'

'Do me a favour! It was Rosie who let on, bless her. I'm convinced her mother told them both not to tell me – can you imagine that? – but when I asked her if she liked Mick, she said,' Rob put on a little high voice, ' "Yeth theeth nithe." So then of course I knew.'

'But you haven't met her?'

'Not yet. Once I knew the kids were happy with her, it didn't seem to be so urgent. I may go round tomorrow, if I can.' He put his mug down and got to his feet. 'Right. Point me at the tiles.'

Nell held the bottom of the ladder and watched as Rob sorted out her roof, pushing the errant tiles back into place so that they hung firmly from their battens and overlapped each other properly at their edges. The tile that had slipped down into the gutter had a broken peg at its top, so he threw that one away and used a spare. It was all done very quickly. Then he cut the fallen ash tree in the turnaround into logs and piled up the brash for burning later on. The saw screamed and smoked but did the job very efficiently.

'Can you stay for lunch?' Nell asked when she could hear herself speak. She threw the last branch on to the bonfire.

'Better not. I've arranged to help my site owner clear up, in return for a temporary bed at his house, and the promise of a brand-new caravan with steel guy-ropes.' Rob grinned.

'I was going to ask you where you were staying. I suppose you wouldn't like to . . . lodge here . . .?'

'Sorry?'

'Well, there's a spare room. I just thought . . .'

'I'll be fine,' Rob said. 'But thanks anyway.'

'Right.' She wanted to say something else to cover her discomfiture, but couldn't remember what it was she had been meaning to ask him. 'Do you know where the field poppies came from?' she said instead. 'After all, they're weeds of arable land, and this isn't corn country; yet the cottage was surrounded by them last summer. They were lovely.'

'I'm afraid it's a cheat,' Rob admitted. 'We sowed a packet of wild flower seeds, and they were the only ones that survived.'

'Oh, I see.'

She helped him to tie the ladder back onto his roof rack, and watched as he drove away. She remembered now what it was she had been going to ask him about, and remembered also why she had decided not to bother. The cracks in her walls had all but closed up again; there was no need.

Nell decided to refuse any offers of help from him in future. She could do without feeling like this. She wished above all things that she hadn't weakened, and invited him to stay. She remembered wryly a notice she once saw in a bar – *Please do not ask for credit, as a refusal often offends*. Too right!

Rob drove away, cursing himself for having been so brusque with Nell. Why did he always have to act like that? Anyone would think he was afraid of women. It would actually have been very pleasant to stay with her, and maybe to have helped her with other problems. It would also have provided an ideal place for a day out with his children. She had only invited him to be a short-term lodger, for heaven's sake! He'd been unnecessarily cautious, as ever.

138

The next day, Sunday, he went over to Boxcombe to take Josh and Rosie out for a few hours, possibly for an afternoon walk, but he was unprepared for what he found at Cassie's house. A short woman, with dyed pink hair and too many earrings, opened the door.

'Yeah?'

'You must be Mic,' he said.

'Who wants to know?'

'I'm Rob Hayhoe.'

'Oh, right.' She was staring at his forehead.

'I've come to see my children.' He felt self-conscious about his bruises, but there was no concealing them.

'You should've phoned,' Mic said. 'No . . . wait . . . you got a car?'

'Transport, yes.'

'Great. Then you can take us. We was goin' on the bus, but it's ever such a hassle.'

'Where to?'

'The Odeon. There's some kids' cartoon stuff on, and I promised Gav and the other two.'

'Daddy!' Rosie pushed past Mic and rushed into his arms. 'We're going to thee thome pictures. Want you to come too!'

'Hello, piglet. How are you?' He lifted her high, so that their faces were on a level. 'I thought we'd all go for a walk and see what we can find.'

'No,' said Josh, coming out too with his coat on. 'Me and Gav and Mic's going to a film. You and Rosie can go for a boring walk if you want. You should've come yesterday!'

'Hurt,' Rosie said, reaching out and touching her father's face.

'Yes. My caravan got pushed over in the storm. We could go and see the wreck if you like, Josh.'

'What for?'

'Well . . . just so you can see how powerful the wind can be.'

139

'Can't,' Josh said. 'We're going to this film. I *told* you.'

'You should've phoned,' Mic said again. 'So, you goin' to take us, or what?'

'I don't seem to have much choice.' Rob opened the doors of the Land Rover ungraciously, and they all climbed in. Gavin and Josh scrambled in together and commandeered the bench seats in the back. Rosie sat on the small middle seat in the front, with her hand in Mic's, and seemed entirely at home there. Rob glanced at them from time to time as they drove along – this unknown, clearly unsuitable, female and his precious daughter – and was jealous of their rapport. He tried to talk over his shoulder to Josh, but the boy was too interested in competing with Gavin.

'My feet are bigger'n yours,' he was boasting.

'But I'm taller'n you,' Gavin said.

'My mum says I'll most probly catch up and overtake you.'

'I'll always be older'n you though.'

'Six months is nothing!'

'Oh yes it is.'

'Oh no it isn't!'

'Shut it, you two, awright?' Mic growled, over her shoulder.

Rob's resolve hardened. When they got to the cinema, he stopped on a double yellow line on the opposite side of the road, and they all got out. Rob took Josh and Rosie firmly by the hand as if to cross. Mic was ahead of him with Gavin. 'Right then,' Rob called to Mic. 'Enjoy the film, won't you? I'll bring these two back around six.' Then he opened the rear door and bundled his children back in again, Josh first.

'Hey!' Mic shouted, halfway across the busy road, and already committed. 'You can't do that!'

'Oh, but I can.' Rob nipped smartly round to the driver's side, got in, and drove off without bothering about seatbelts.

'It's not *fair*,' Josh wailed, fighting the child-locked back door without success. 'I *want* to see the FILM!' He began hitting the back of his father's head and shoulders with small fists.

Rosie started to cry too. 'I want Mic. *I want Mic*.'

Rob drove with one hand, fending off the blows with the other. 'Stop it, Josh! You'll get us all killed.'

'I *hate* you,' Josh cried, throwing himself backwards on to one of the seats in despair. 'Everything's *all your fault!*'

I adore snow, Nell thought as she looked out of her window one Sunday morning. I'm glad Rob was wrong!

It was now mid-December and snow had arrived overnight, all six inches of it, without warning. It lay sparkling white under the morning sun, its surface still shifting from time to time in the brisk north wind, as unstable as a sand dune. Nell went out in it, penetrating its virgin purity with her wellies and leaving ugly tracks. There was a four-foot drift right across the door of the woodstore, so she was obliged to dig her way in with a spade to get her fuel for the day ahead. She wished, not for the first time, that the damned stove would stay in overnight and not smoke so much when she first lit it. Getting one's energy from a renewable resource was all very well, and wonderfully PC but it was also self-evidently a health hazard, apart from being bloody hard work . . . She looked across at the river, and saw long sheets of ice by the low-tide channel where the outgoing fresh water had frozen at its edges. The mudflats were covered in snow too. Nell's hands, even in their woolly mittens, felt numb with the cold. She put them under her armpits and hugged them, looking about her at the transformed scenery and deciding which elements of it she would paint, once she was warm again and fed.

She wondered whether the paper shop would have

delivered her *Independent on Sunday* as usual. She would walk up to her box by the top road later on to find out. There were no sounds of distant traffic. Maybe everyone and everything had been snowed up – or should that be down? – to a standstill. Nell smiled gleefully and, gathering up logs, began ferrying them to the basket in her kitchen. The telephone rang as she was finishing her breakfast scrambled eggs. 'Hello?'

'It's Rob Hayhoe. Have you got snow?'

'Masses of it, yes. Oh, I suppose you want your sledge back?'

'Is that a problem?'

'Well, no, I just fancied trying it out first, if that's all right? It's years since I went tobogganing.'

'When I was about twelve,' Rob said, 'I made myself some skis by nailing an old pair of cut-off wellingtons onto a couple of planks.'

Nell had to smile. 'And did they work?'

'Not really. They didn't curve up at the front, you see, so they dug into each passing molehill and I went arse over tit every time. But I persevered, and made a special slide down the field by our house, and that worked a charm. I remember I won a quid from Bert in a bet that I couldn't keep upright all the way down. I've never forgotten it, because the slide turned to ice and lasted for days after all the proper snow had melted.'

'I'd like to have seen that.' Why is it, Nell thought, that every time I get fed up with Rob, he goes and redeems himself by saying something endearing, and then I want to like him all over again? Well, this time I'm definitely not falling for it. 'Do you want to collect your sledge today then?' she asked. 'Are the roads passable?'

'They'll be fine by midday. The gritters and salters are out in force. I'll come straight after lunch, if that's OK? That'll give you the whole morning to use it first.'

But Nell didn't go tobogganing. Somehow she couldn't

142

bring herself to go alone. It would have seemed almost as pathetic as ballroom dancing with a chair. Instead, she sat at her window and did quick pencil sketches of the river before the light changed.

Rob arrived at 1.15, dressed for the Arctic in boots, parka and woolly hat, and with his bruises all but gone. They went together to the woodstore to collect the sledge. 'It's very dusty,' Nell said. 'I'll just get something to brush it down.'

'I thought you were going to try it out.'

'It felt too silly, all by myself,' she confessed.

'Well . . . would you like to have a go with me?'

Nell barely hesitated. The lure of sledging was too strong. 'I'd have to put something on to keep out the cold.'

'Go on then.'

Nell found her red fleece hat with earflaps, her bright blue waterproof jacket, some khaki overtrousers, green wellingtons, and her multicoloured stripey mittens, and donned them all. 'How do I look?'

'Like Noddy,' Rob said, smiling broadly. Then he pulled the sledge up the lane to the top, walking in his Land Rover tracks, which ploughed through several transverse drifts.

'Which is the ten-acre?' Nell asked, puffing behind him.

He led her to the long field which sloped down to the woods by the river on the east side of her lane. Then they sat on the sledge together, Rob at the back using his feet as brakes and digging his boots into the snow until Nell, holding on to the rope and with both feet on the rail, was safely seated.

'Hold tight,' Rob cried, putting both arms around her and letting go of the ground. He fitted his boots next to hers on the rail, and gripped her legs with his knees as though he were riding a charger. Nell felt all too aware of his closeness. The sledge gathered speed on the steepest bit of the hillside and fairly flew downwards. She whooped with delight and felt her steamy breath snatched away in the cold air.

The snow was dry and granular, and thick enough to hide any blemishes on the broad complexion of the great field. The surface grains were still blowing up from time to time in the biggest gusts of wind, and settling at its margins in any available lee, building new flawless curving drifts. The trees at the bottom were white on their windward side and black on the other. From here the river showed black in the middle, and white at its frozen edges. Everything in this monochrome landscape was quiet and motionless, biding its time. No birds flew overhead. No mammals sought shelter behind the leaky hedges. There weren't even any tracks.

What is it about us humans, Nell thought, that we have to put our stamp on everything? We're like children who can't bear to pass a clean blotter in a bank without doodling on it. I suppose it's the remnants of territoriality? Before we arrived just now, there was this smooth white page of a field, all silent and aloof and *complete*, and now here we are, a job lot of noise and colour and frivolity, messing up its perfection, making our mark and loving every min –

'Lean over!' Rob shouted. 'We're going crooked . . . Yee . . . OWWW!' The sledge veered off as it got to the bottom of the slope and ran along parallel to the edge of the wood for twenty yards, before it hit a bump, stopped abruptly, and they both fell off. 'OW!' Mock agony. 'My ribs!'

'That was brilliant!' Nell laughed, lying on her back in the snow. 'More!'

'Race you to the top,' Rob challenged, getting to his feet and gathering up a snowball. It hit Nell on the shoulder before she could even begin to retaliate, and when she did, Rob ducked easily and set off uphill with determination. Nell had to run to catch up, and only just prevented herself from grabbing at his hand for a tow. They trudged together towards the top, pausing every so often to catch their breath and look at the view. There was no sign of the sun now. To the north of them the sky was a dark greyish yellow.

'Looks like more snow,' Rob said, changing hands on the sledge rope. He put the other arm round Nell's shoulders, pretending to lean on her for support. She stood next to him breathing hard and not wanting to catch his eye, in case he realised what he was doing, and stopped. 'Hope so,' she said. 'I'd like to be well and truly snowed in.'

'On up?' He took his arm away.

'Yes.'

After that first time, their ascents of the hill became slower and slower, and each time they stopped longer for breathers.

'I just love it here,' Nell said. 'There's nowhere else I'd rather be.'

'Me too.'

'Oh I'm sorry, I didn't think.'

'It's OK. I'm here now.'

'I don't know about you,' Nell said, 'but I'm starving. Do you fancy some tea?'

'Rob looked at his watch. 'It's three thirty! I'd no idea. It'll be getting dark any minute!'

'Not knowing the time makes me feel marvellously irresponsible,' Nell said happily.

'Do you know R. K. Narayan's description of childhood? That reminds me of it.'

'No. Tell me.'

'He said it was "Letting the day pass without counting the hours".'

'I like that,' Nell said. 'Great to be able to live that way.'

'Maybe it'll be possible at sixty-five,' Rob said. 'You know it's always struck me as odd, that old tradition of ours for presenting people with gold watches when they retire. Wouldn't you suppose that must be the one and only time in their lives when it's precisely what they *don't* need?'

Nell laughed. It's no use, she thought. I like the way his mind works. I like the things he says. I like *him*.

'I suppose I'd best be off,' Rob said. 'I only hope the snow lasts until next weekend, or Josh will kill me.'

'You've been able to see them both while Cassie's away, then?'

'Only with difficulty. The "friend" and I don't exactly hit it off, so it's been a bit of a battle. I meant to get here earlier and take them both out sledging today – another black mark, I'm afraid.'

'I'm sorry.'

'Not your fault. It was good fun, wasn't it?'

It began to snow as they walked towards the lower gate, and back along the river path to Bottom Cottage.

'No tea?' Nell asked.

'No, really. I ought to be going.'

'I hope you'll get back up the lane OK.'

'Four-wheel drive. No sweat.'

'Bye, then.'

He took her mittened hand and squeezed it between both of his own. 'Thanks, Nell. I haven't had such a good shout for ages.'

He set off in low gear, waving from the open window. Nell waved back, and then rushed indoors to keep warm. The snow was falling more thickly by now. She drank tea and watched the wintry scene from her window, and then suddenly remembered her Sunday paper. I'd better collect it today, before it gets dark, she thought, just in case they've forgotten to close the door of the box again; I don't fancy another pile of soggy newsprint.

As she left the cottage, she heard the unmistakable but distant sound of a vehicle revving hard and going nowhere. Someone's stuck, she thought. Surely not Rob?'

But halfway up the lane she came upon his Land Rover. It looked as though it had ploughed into a snowdrift, and then slipped backwards and sideways into the ditch, where it now lay with one of its wheels in the air. The trampled and scraped snow all around it bore witness to Rob's unsuccessful efforts to extricate it. It appeared derelict and decidedly embarrassed. Nell patted its bonnet consolingly, looking round for its owner, but there was no sign of him.

When she got to the top, she found him standing by the road, stamping his feet. He smiled sheepishly when he saw her.

'Hi,' he said. 'I was just debating whether to try to hitch a lift, or walk along to Home Farm and ask Tom if I could kip for the night on their floor.' His hat, shoulders and eyebrows had collected enough snow for an avalanche, Nell noticed, trying not to laugh.

'I came up for my paper,' she said, explaining herself. 'How did it happen?' She wiped her eyes with the backs of her mittens.

'God knows! I've been up and down here in all weathers and never ended up helpless in the ditch before. I think the truth is, we've not had this much snow in the past decade. I'm just not accustomed to it.'

'Well, there's no point hanging around here,' Nell said. 'There may not be any more passing traffic tonight. And anyway, it's freezing.'

Rob nodded. 'I don't particularly want to bother Tom either; not now his wife's in hospital . . .'

'Oh dear,' Nell said, po-faced. 'You're in trouble then.' She went across to her box and extracted the bulky newspaper, stuffing it under her coat. 'I'm afraid I can see only one possible solution to your particular problem.'

'And what's that?'

'You've no other choice.' Nell smiled wickedly. 'You'll just have to swallow your pride, or whatever, and come back down and stay with me.'

Chapter Thirteen

'Tell me about your wife,' Elly said. She was lying in Malachy's four-poster bed with her face against his chest, and playing idly with his fuzz of hair, twisting it into little spirals with her fingers. He shifted the arm under her head, slightly, an unconsciously dismissive action.

'What about her?'

'Everything. How long were you married?'

'Ten years, thereabouts.'

'And were you happy?'

Malachy kept his eyes closed. *'All happy families resemble one another, but each unhappy family is unhappy in its own way,'* he quoted. 'Have you read *Anna Karenina*?'

'Don't change the subject!' She tried to tickle him, but he lay there, controlled, unmoving. 'Don't you want to tell me about her?'

'It's old history,' Malachy said. 'We were very young. We met and fell in love, and then she died. A tragedy for me, of course, but a common enough occurrence in this life, I suppose.' He raised his head to look at her. 'What about that massage you promised me, or have I already worn you out?' The blue eyes challenged her.

'Turn over then,' she said, pushing back the duvet and waiting as he rolled on to his front, resting his head on his crossed arms. Then she sat astride him, and squeezed his hips between her thighs. He had nice slim hips for a middle-aged man.

'How old are you?' she asked him, pressing the muscles of his shoulders in firm circular movements.

'Fifty-five. Why?' His voice was muffled.

'No particular reason. So there's twenty-three years between us. It seems nothing at this age, does it? But in twenty-three years from now, my Will and Sam will be thirty-one and twenty-nine, and that seems unimaginable.'

'Mmm. Don't stop. That feels marvellous.'

She worked her way down his back, pummelling him. His skin was still a little tanned from the summer before – or maybe from a sunlamp? His generation had no sense! She felt superior and loving all at once, and leaning forward, kissed each shoulder blade in turn.

'Is it strange to have a grown-up son?'

'Not really. It just happens.'

Elly was progressing downwards, shuffling herself backwards along his legs as she went. 'Rob's not a bit like you to look at. Is he at all like you in character?'

'No. He takes after his mother.'

'Do I sense some disappointment there?'

Malachy just grunted.

'You're not very forthcoming today,' Elly complained. She leant forwards and blew two raspberries on the soft cheeks of his bottom. They made satisfactorily rude noises. Malachy smiled, turning his head sideways and squinting at her.

Then he closed his eyes again. 'Keep going. That's heaven.'

Elly stroked his back up and down lightly with smooth delicate hands, and then massaged it hard again, making him groan with pleasure. She thought, This may look one-sided, with me doing all the giving, but in fact it isn't. Being a good receiver is just as necessary, and Malachy receives like no one else I've ever known . . . She leant forward again and caressed his back up and down with her pendent breasts, hardening her nipples with the gentle friction. Then she collapsed onto him with her full weight and took the lobe of his right ear in her mouth, nibbling it.

'Is this an erogenous zone?'

'No,' Malachy said, rolling over suddenly and entering her in two fluid movements. 'But this is!'

'The over-fifties can't do this, you know.' She lay on her back with her knees wide apart, laughing at him. 'They need at least two hours for todger-turnaround time.'

'I'm not one of your limp statistics.' He held himself large, but quite still inside her, teasing. Elly began to wriggle, urging him to move, feeling the swelling crescendo of orgasm beginning again, but needing him to drive it for her. 'So, what am I?' he asked, a now familiar game.

'You're amazing.'

Little thrust. 'And?'

'Extraordinary.'

'And?' He began a delicate rhythmic movement. She lifted her pelvis to meet him, holding on to his buttocks, to engulf as much of him as deeply as possible.

'Wonder . . . ful . . . *please . . . now!*'

And only then did he begin to give her what she wanted. She opened her eyes briefly just before the climax and saw that his were wide, and suffused with triumph. He has me just where he wants me, she thought. Then, in amazement: *And I love it!*

Nell cooked Rob an impromptu supper of spaghetti carbonara, using the ham she'd intended for her own meal, and a small tin of mushrooms she had in hand for emergencies. He sat on the other side of the kitchen table from her, looking, she thought, surprisingly shy. She handed him a bottle of cider and, just as he was pouring it, the power failed and all the lights went out.

'Damn!'

'Sit tight,' Nell said. 'I think I can find my torch in the dark.' She felt her way to the wall, and round to her dresser where it was kept. 'I've got candles too,' she said, ferreting through a drawer by torchlight. '. . . Yes, here's some.'

'And matches?'

'Over on the mantelpiece.'

Rob reached for them and, taking the candles from her, lit them one by one and dripped their wax on to a couple of plates to stick them upright. Nell sat down again and began winding spaghetti onto her fork.

'You look as though you belong here,' Rob said.

'I do.' She smiled across at him in the flickering half-light.

'Yes, but I meant . . . Oh I don't know . . . as though you'd always been here.'

'That's exactly how it seems to me.'

'I used to feel that way too.'

Is he hinting? Nell wondered. Does he want me to invite him to stay again? Maybe . . . But I'm not going to risk being turned down a second time. If he's changed his mind and really does want to lodge in my spare room, then he'll have to make the effort and ask me himself.

'Is this all right?' she asked, of the food.

'Delicious. More cider?

'Thanks.'

'There are often power cuts here,' Rob said. 'But they don't usually last long.'

'Well, at least we'll still keep warm,' Nell said. 'Thank goodness the heating isn't electric.'

'How is the woodburner?'

'Difficult,' Nell said. 'It still smokes horribly first thing.'

'Most probably needs its chimney cleaning out. Wood produces a lot of tar as well as soot, you know. You need someone experienced to sort it out for you.' He smiled at her. 'Maybe I could help?'

'Maybe you could,' carefully noncommittal. He's so different on his own from when he's in a crowd of people, Nell thought, remembering the party on the houseboat.

Perhaps Malachy/Bert puts him off his stroke; represses him in some way.

'Tell me about your father,' she invited him.

'Why?' He looked guarded at once.

'No reason. I'm just interested.'

'Everybody is always more interested in him,' he said lightly, but with feeling.

'No, I didn't mean it that way. I don't care about "The Actor" image. I wondered what he was like as a father. Did you inherit your ease with children from him?'

'Not really,' Rob said. 'He's only "easy" in public.'

'You don't like him very much, do you?'

'We've never got on very well, no.'

'That's a shame. What about your mother?'

'She committed suicide when I was nine.'

Nell held his gaze across the table. His face was only half illuminated; black on one side, and unreadable. She dropped her eyes first. 'But that's dreadful. How did you manage?'

'We had an exciting life, travelling about in the States and Europe, wherever Bert happened to be working.'

'But who looked after you?'

'Oh, Bert wasn't alone for long. He attracted a succession of failed actresses, all dying to play the maternal rôle.'

'Did you realise what was going on, then?'

'I had a pretty fair idea. Then years later I learnt to distinguish his favourite mistresses from the overnight stands.'

'How?'

'Easy. After he's got them hooked he always buys them the same egocentric present.'

'What?'

'A green malachite necklace.'

'Mmm,' Nell said appreciatively. 'Well, I suppose it beats a box of chocolates.'

Rob stared into his wine and said nothing.

Nell did a quick mental subject-trawl, but could only come up with small talk. 'So, how's the new caravan coming along? Will the guy ropes be like those on a tent?'

Rob raised his head and made a face of mock despair. 'It's not going to happen at all. It appears the site owner was underinsured so he's decided to sell up in the New Year and call it a day.'

'So what will you do?'

'Find somewhere else. I've got to be out before Christmas, in fact. He's having family to stay.'

But that's in less than a week! Where will you go? Nell thought, No, I'm not asking him that. 'What are you doing for Christmas?'

'Taking the children up to London to stay with Bert. It's my turn to have them this year. They're fond of him for some reason and they love London.'

'Is Cassie home yet?'

'Yes, she is.'

'And will she make a fuss about letting them go?'

'I just don't know. She used to be so desperate to get rid of them, but now it's all "Mic this" and "Mic that". God knows what the two of them get up to together.'

'Really?' Nell raised her eyebrows.

'Who can tell? You'd think with my cosmopolitan background I'd know all there is to know about human behaviour, wouldn't you? The truth is, it confounds me every time.' The lights came on again as he was speaking and, to Nell's disappointment, the intimate atmosphere vanished in the glare of several 100-watt bulbs.

They ate cheese and fruit and talked about the weather, and the likelihood of global warming, and how far up the Torrent valley would become inundated if the polar icecaps were to melt. It's interesting stuff, Nell thought, but too impersonal. I'd like to know more about him and what he's really thinking.

'Coffee?' she offered.

'Yes, please.'

'And then I'd better go and make up the spare bed for you. I'm afraid it will have to be blankets; I've only got one duvet.'

'Fine,' Rob said. 'I prefer blankets anyway.'

Making a bed with someone is an activity usually attended by an easy familiarity, Rob thought as Nell handed him a pillowcase to stuff. Strangers do not make beds together. Not of course that Nell is a stranger, she's a very comfortable person to be with, but it's odd to be spreading bedclothes with her. They folded the top sheet back over the blankets in unison, one on either side of the bed.

'Will you be warm enough?' Nell asked.

'I'm sure I will. In the caravan I used to top up my bedding with an old overcoat my father brought back from Moscow. It's immensely thick and heavy. I think Bert only gave it to me because he got too broad for it, or maybe because it's in a very tatty condition, especially now after the storm. We call it the dead Russian.'

Nell laughed. 'I wouldn't fancy sleeping under one of those.' They tucked in the sides of the bed and stood back.

'Look,' Rob said, suddenly shy again, 'Don't let me mess up your entire evening. Just do what you'd normally be doing, and I'll fit in with that.'

'It's no big deal,' Nell said. 'Some reading of newspapers, a bit of telly – that's about it.'

They sat in her sitting room by an open fire. Nell read the real life section, and Rob the business pages. Then they watched a programme on BBC2 and Nell got out her needlepoint and sewed a bit more of her unicorn design, putting in the shading on its mane with soft brown and beige wool.

'I can't do the background in artificial light,' she said. 'I can't tell the different greens apart.'

155

'What's it for?'

'A cushion cover? I don't know really. I just like doing it.'

Rob put another log on the fire and watched her in amusement as she threaded the ends of wool carefully under previous stitches on the back, before snipping them off with scissors. He thought: I'd like to have had a sister. This could be the nearest I'll ever get to one. I was such a fool to turn down her offer! I do wish I could make fast off-the-cuff decisions, but somehow I never do, and I always live to regret it. Maybe I'll get another chance. I can't very well bring it up now; she's more than likely changed her mind . . . I can still help her with practical things, though. After all, I do know this place better than anybody.

'I've just had a thought,' he said.

'Mmm?' Nell was threading up some ginger-coloured wool.

'Yes. When this snow begins to thaw, any that may have got in under the tiles will start to drip through your ceilings upstairs.'

'Oh stuff!' Nell exclaimed, pursing her lips (nice full lips). 'That's a pain. What's the best thing to do?'

'When it happened to me years ago, I went up into the roof space and rolled the snow into as many snowballs as I could, and chucked them down the hatch into the bath,' Rob said. 'I couldn't get it all out, of course, but enough to prevent the plaster on the ceilings below from collapsing. And it all dried out eventually.'

'Right,' Nell said, considering. 'But not tonight, I think.'

'Not while it's still snowing, no.'

'They're forecasting a freeze for several days, aren't they? So there's no immediate panic. I'll do it before the thaw.'

'Tomorrow,' Rob said, 'I must try to get in to work. I've got a difficult client on my back, and I've got some important figures to sort out. Could I phone Tom now? He'll pull the Rover out for me in the morning, I'm sure.'

And later in the week, after work, he thought, I'll come back and give you a hand with your arctic attic-full. He was pretty sure there would be a lot of snow up there, but he didn't say this to Nell. He wasn't about to alarm her unduly about the unpleasant task ahead.

At 9 p.m. Nell went up to turn on her electric blanket, and offered Rob a hot-water bottle.

'No thanks.'

'I thought you weren't the macho type?' she teased. 'I won't tell anyone, honestly.'

'Oh, go on then.'

Later, lying in the unfamiliar bed with his toes cosily warm on the woolly hot-water bottle cover, he reflected wryly on his fears about staying at the cottage with Nell. What a berk I am, he thought. Why on earth was I worried about 'complications'? Is she after my body? Is she hell!

Next morning at first light he woke with a start to the sound of a working diesel engine outside. He threw on his clothes and looked out of the window. A large yellow tractor with a snowplough on the front had just finished clearing the turning circle as far as Nell's blue Citroën and, on seeing him at the window, the driver reversed over and opened his cab door for a word.

'Mornin',' he said cheerfully, switching off the engine and looking up at Rob. 'Overslept, then?'

'Morning, Tom. Yes. I haven't been used to a decent bed lately.' Rob rubbed his eyes.

'You quite sure you wants diggin' out, or do I leave ee bide a few days more?'

'Today would be ideal thanks.' Rob strove to keep a straight face.

'An' what was you playin' at then, up over? Rally drivin' in reverse, was it?'

'Something like that. I'll come down.'

Rob went downstairs. Nell was in the kitchen, fully dressed, making tea. 'Would he like a mug?' she asked. 'Only I thought I'd let you deal with him in case it was, you know . . . embarrassing.'

'I'll ask him. Thanks.' Rob was unaccustomed to such sensitivity. He put on his parka and boots.

'Tea?' he offered Tom.

'Had some before I came out, thanks.'

'What's the top road like?'

'Handsome. Gritters have bin along. I reckon 'twill all be away come tomorrer.'

'I'll pop back before I get off to work,' Rob called to Nell.

'OK.'

'You'm well in there,' Tom said with a wink. 'Got your old place back an' all!'

Rob climbed into the cab of the tractor. 'I wish,' was all he said.

'I am totally, utterly, *miserably* pissed off!' Anna said, the moment Nell lowered herself into the swimming pool the following morning.

'Oh dear,' Nell said. 'Why?'

She looks genuinely concerned, Anna thought. She's a good person. Perhaps I shouldn't make use of her. But it's a perfect opportunity, so what the hell! 'I just hate the bloody winter,' she said. 'It's dark and cold, and the Boss hardly comes down at all these days. I suppose I'm just plain lonely, but it's at times like Christmas when it really gets to me. Would you believe he's just told me he's taking Ermintrude and the kids skiing on Boxing Day for ten whole days! So just when I most need him, he won't be there. Story of my life! How could he *do* that to me?'

'Well . . . I suppose he has responsibilities . . .'

'So why can't they sodding well ski here? There's been enough snow!'

'It isn't quite the same thing though, is it?'

Anna ignored this. 'I mean, why take crappy Ermintrude anyway? She probably can't even stay upright.' She was pretty sure she could see Nell thinking, *Oh yes she can!* And decided to give her another clue. 'And the brats are too young anyway.'

'Are they boys or girls?'

'Boys.' Anna stared Nell out. She *knows*, Anna thought. I'm sure of it. So why doesn't she just come out with it? I need her to guess, or my plan won't work . . .

'What sort of an age?' Nell asked.

'Sevenish? I dunno. I don't really care. Anyway, I can't go on like this. It's really fucking me up. So I've decided . . .' She put on a determined but defensive expression.

'Decided what?'

'That I'm going to have him. I need him, and I'm fed up always coming second best. And he doesn't love her anyway; he's told me so. So I'm going to reason with him and make him leave her.' *That should do the trick!*

'But you can't do that!' Nell looked horrified.

'Watch me.'

'But it's immoral! You can't just *steal* someone else's husband.'

'Happens all the time. Look around you.' Anna shrugged.

This was clearly too much for Nell. 'Look,' she said. 'I'm going to have to be straight with you. I know who "The Boss" is. I found one of your earrings on his house-boat.' She stared Anna in the face.

Anna pretended to flinch. 'Oh God!' *Good!* 'How long have you known?'

'Since March.'

'So why on earth didn't you say? I thought we were friends.'

'Ermintrude – as you so dismissively call her – is my best friend,' Nell retorted stoutly. 'She and I were at school together.'

'Oh shit!' Anna said. 'I honestly had no idea of that. What can I say? You haven't told her, have you?'

'Not yet.'

'And you won't, will you? Please promise me? I need to be able to choose the right time to talk to Paul. Otherwise the whole thing could just fall apart, and it's my whole life . . .' She put her hand on Nell's shoulder and gazed at her as beseechingly as she could.

Nell shook her off. 'Why should I help you? It's Elly I care about.'

'Look, you're upset. I'm sorry. I had no idea you two were close. But her and Paul's relationship is dead in the water. She must have told you that. She'll probably be relieved to get shot of him. I just don't want it to be . . . messy . . . you know? It would be so much better if he breaks the news to her in his own way. Nell?'

But Nell was already swimming away from her, and Anna could tell by the furiousness of her crawl, that she had taken the bait.

Anna began to swim too, but reflectively, doing a gentle breaststroke. Now, if she had got her human psychology right (much boosted by the unexpected best friend scenario) then Nell would be on the phone to Ermintrude as soon as she could be. Then with luck, the said Ermintrude would flip and demand an immediate divorce and then she, Anna, could step in sweetly and pick up the pieces with no machinations suspected. She really did not want to be involved in anything . . . unpleasant.

As Nell dried herself after swimming, with her mind full of Anna and Elly and Paul, and in a confusion as to what on earth she should do for the best, she discovered to her intense annoyance that she'd forgotten to bring her hairbrush. She had also just towelled her hair into an unmanageable frizz. Then she remembered with even more disgust that Sibyl had arranged to be late at ARTFUL[L] that morning, so she wouldn't be able to borrow hers. There was nothing for it but to go all the way back to the cottage before work. What a damn nuisance.

She had managed to drive up and down her lane without difficulty, after Tom's efforts with the snow-plough. The main roads were already completely clear, with the snow and slush piled high in dirty lumps on the verges. Nell was afraid it was melting faster than expected, and wouldn't last until the next weekend after all. So Rob's children would have to go without their promised sledging. It came to her in passing as she drove that although she'd only met Josh once, she was afraid she didn't actually like him or Rosie very much. But it was an unnatural and unwomanly thought, best swiftly squashed.

It wasn't until Nell had gone upstairs to her bedroom to fetch her hairbrush that she realised how advanced the thaw actually was. On the ceiling above her head was a dark, damp, spreading patch . . .

Bloody hell! Nell thought. This can't wait. I'm going to have to do something now. She pushed her bed out of the way of possible drips, pulled on her gardening clothes, and then turned her attention towards getting up into the roof. By standing her stepladder (unopened) on a towel in the bath, she could just reach high enough, and when she had climbed to the top of it and pushed the hatch cover aside, she shone her torch round the roof space. Above her head glimmers of daylight were visible where the overlaps on the clay tiles were poor or damaged. Parts of the floor were covered in up to two inches of snow, but it wasn't a proper floor. There were a couple of planks laid loosely over the cross-members and some of the gaps in between were half filled with lengths of fibreglass wool. In places the snow was lying directly on the plaster of the ceiling below.

So that's what the survey meant about insufficient insulation, Nell thought. Talk about understatement! No wonder the cottage is so cold. I shall have to do something about it sooner than I'd planned. She put her hands on the sides of the hatchway and heaved herself up through it. There was very little space and the rafters above her head were filthy with dust and bits of old thatch. The cold wetness of the snow soaked through the knees of her jeans at once as she shuffled herself along one of the narrow planks, keeping her balance with difficulty, and conscious that any false move might well result in an expensive replastering job in the rooms below. Then, moving the planks alternately, and using them as thin sliding bridges, she began making snowballs.

The whole operation took an age, and her torch grew dimmer and dimmer as the battery began to give up. By the time she felt she couldn't go on any longer, the bath was three-quarters full of dirty slush and she was chilled to the bone and exhausted. She inched her way along the final plank and climbed wearily down the ladder into the bathroom. The mirror showed her a cobwebbed-haired apparition streaked with dust. She made a heroic face at herself before realising that she would have to get rid of all the icy contents before she could have a bath; and that there wouldn't be enough hot water to do both. She turned on the cold tap, and waited.

Later, she couldn't resist phoning Rob at work to tell him of her triumph.

'Well done indeed!' he said. 'Epic stuff. I'd planned to come back and give you a hand in fact – after going to vet yet another unpromising bedsitter – but you're clearly self-sufficient.'

'I was really worried about putting my foot through the

ceiling,' Nell admitted. 'Those planks were so narrow, and the what-d'you-call-'em cross bits are even worse.'

'They're called joists,' Rob said. 'Which reminds me, have I told you my favourite building joke?'

'Don't think so.'

'Right, well this pompous Englishman asks this Irish Labourer whether he knows the difference between joist and girder. And the Irishman thinks for a moment and then says he reckons he does.' Rob put on a passable Irish accent. '*Oi tink I've got it*, he says. *Joyce wrote* Ulysses *and Goethe wrote* Faust!'

And that was the moment when Nell decided, Oh, what the hell? Why don't I just go for it! 'Nice one,' she said, laughing. 'Look, Rob, what *is* the point of paying for grotty digs somewhere, anywhere, when you could come and be my lodger in comfort here?'

There was a brief silence. Then: 'You're on,' he said. 'Thanks very much. When can I move in?'

Chapter Fourteen

'So, what's it like being a landlady?' Sibyl asked, as Nell drove her towards London on Christmas Eve.

'It's good,' Nell smiled. 'Rob's only been at the cottage for a couple of days, but he's already taken the top off the woodburner and cleaned out the chimney. You should have seen the lumps of tar that came out – all black and shiny, but lightweight like pumice stone.'

'Ah well, at least he's useful.' Sibyl was hoping for more.

'And he's good fun.'

'Can he cook?'

'Dunno. He hasn't yet.' Nell was watching the rainy road ahead.

'Lucky old Rob. What about his children?'

'How d'you mean?'

'Well, is there room for them to visit? And how would you feel about that?'

'Oh, he's getting a couple of bunk beds to go in the spare room with him. It'll be a bit crowded, but they won't be there that often; just odd weekends here and there, he says.'

'Children can be quite invasive,' Sibyl said carefully.

'Yes, I'm sure. I've no experience really, but I suppose one picks it up as one goes along.' Nell pulled out to overtake a slow caravan, and her whole being looked rigid with concentration as if she were willing the Citroën to risk a stab at 70 mph. Sibyl wondered how she would react to two children who, from what Nell had already told her, were clearly disturbed.

'Anyway,' Nell went on, 'you can always give me good advice, can't you?' She glanced briefly sideways and smiled.

'I wish Elly would take my advice,' Sibyl said soberly. 'Has she told you about her latest damn-fool idea?'

'Of selling up her business and going to drama college? Yes.'

'And do you believe that Hayhoe character will really mastermind her transformation into a working actress?'

'Well, Rob doesn't think much of him,' Nell admitted. 'It is a bit worrying, isn't it?'

'I do hope we won't have constant rows this Christmas,' Sibyl sighed. 'Last year was quite awful – probably because you weren't with us to act as a buffer.'

'A buffer,' Nell said lightly. 'I suppose that's marginally better than being called a fogey.'

Sibyl didn't reply. 'I may be mistaken,' she said slowly, 'but I sense trouble ahead. I have a nasty feeling that Paul . . . No, I'd better not say. Let's hope I'm wrong.' She looked at Nell's profile and saw a frown crease her forehead and noticed her catch her lower lip between her teeth. She's anxious too, Sibyl thought, but like me she's keeping shtoom and hoping it will pass.

Nell was tired when they arrived, but Elly was on a high. Oh Lord, Nell thought, how am I going to tell her about Anna? I don't want to ruin her Christmas, but I do have to say something.

'Guess who or what can blow the biggest smoke-rings in the world?' Will challenged at supper, kicking his younger brother under the table to prevent him from jumping in with the answer.

'That *hurt*!' Sam said, aggrieved.

'Red Indians?' Sibyl suggested.

'You mean Native Americans,' Will corrected her. 'Wrong!'

'Malachy,' Elly said with a silly grin.

'Wrong again.'

'Go on then,' his father said cheerfully. 'Get it over with.'

'Mount Etna.' Will looked pleased with himself.

'Really?' Nell asked.

'Yeah. It's a volcano, right? An' every so often it goes POP! and blows a perfect smoke-ring. I've got a photo in this book to prove it.'

'I'd like to see that,' Nell said.

'I'll get it,' Will said, slipping down from his chair. 'It's cool.'

'Not now, Will, OK?' Paul said. 'In fact it's time you two boys went to bed. No doubt you'll both be awake at sparrowfart tomorrow, so we adults could do with a little peace over our coffee now. All right?'

I've never liked Paul very much, Nell thought, watching him shepherding his sons upstairs, but he is competent with his children. He's a disciplinarian too (unlike Rob) but they apparently don't resent him for it. She wondered how Rob was getting on at his father's house on the other side of London, and whether Bert was blowing cigar smoke-rings for Rosie and Josh.

'Penny for them?' Sibyl asked her.

'I was just wondering what Rob was doing.'

'How's it working out between you?' Elly asked.

'Fine so far,' Nell shrugged. 'I didn't intend to invite him to Bottom Cottage at all, but he made me laugh.'

'Fatal mistake,' Elly said. 'I know just how easy that is. Malachy creases me up sometimes.' Sibyl turned to her daughter, frowning and was opening her mouth to say something, when Paul came back into the dining room.

'Well, that's the boys sorted,' he said. 'I think they're even more excited about going skiing than they are about Christmas!'

'I've got something to say about that, actually,' Elly

said. She looked determined.

'You've always got something to say!' Paul was flippant. 'More coffee anyone?'

'Just *listen* for a change!' Elly's hands were two fists on the table in front of her. 'I'm not going skiing with you after all. Malachy says there's someone I should meet who's over from the States for only three days, who could be the vital catalyst for my career as an act –'

'Stuff that!' Paul exploded. 'Of course you're coming skiing. It's all arranged. The boys are depending on it.'

Elly ignored this. '. . . And that's not all.' She took a gulp of black coffee. 'I'm sorry if this spoils Christmas, but it can't wait. Malachy thinks I've got a big chance here, and I'm not about to blow it.'

'*Malachy thinks this: Malachy thinks that!*' Paul mocked. 'Why should he bother himself with someone like you? Just answer me that?'

'You really want to know?' Nell saw Elly bracing herself, turning her profile towards an imaginary camera – the powerful heroine about to deliver the *coup de grâce*.

'Oh, give us a break,' Paul snapped. 'Do you think you could just stop bloody acting for one moment? We're not impressed, OK? We know you too well.' Nell found her head swinging back and forth between them like a spectator at Wimbledon. She sensed Sibyl doing the same, but couldn't look at her.

'You may think you do,' Elly retorted triumphantly, 'but Malachy might have something to say about that.'

'*Fuck* sodding Malachy! What the hell's it got to do with him?'

'Everything.' Elly raised her chin proudly. 'You see, he loves me.'

'That old poseur? Don't make me laugh.'

'And I'm leaving you.'

Paul stared at her.

'B – B – But . . .' Sibyl stammered, breaking the sudden

silence, 'I thought it was the other way aroun –'

'You can't!' Paul interrupted. His face was flushed. He reached across the table, grabbed Elly's wrists and held on to them hard. 'What about me? What about the boys? You're my *wife.*'

'Oh God, Nell thought, no wonder she's been so elated lately. But why did she have to do this today of all days? And why the hell didn't I tell her about Anna months ago? Now she's put herself irrevocably in the wrong, and it's all my fault.

'Let go,' Elly said, dangerously quietly, 'or I'll do you for assault.'

'Come on, Nell,' Sibyl said briskly, scraping her chair backwards on the polished floor. 'Washing up.' And the two of them went out into the kitchen without a backward glance.

'Happy Christmas,' Anna said aloud with heavy irony. She raised a glass of buck's fizz and toasted her reflection in the mirror. Then she put the special spring-cap back on the half-bottle of champagne to keep the rest for later, and stood at the window of her flat, sipping the alcoholic orange juice and watching the rain dripping from the bus stop and backing up round the blocked drain in the street outside.

What have I ever done, she thought, that I should be alone today? It's so unfair. I can just imagine Paul all cosy with wife and kids having a happy traditional time with booze and a massive turkey and mountains of presents. Alternatively, of course, Nell might have done the decent thing and told Ermintrude about me, so Paul might well be coping with a hysterical wife and desperate to escape to the peace of the houseboat – and me!

She looked at the special gold-wrapped parcel he'd given her weeks ago and wondered whether to open it now, or if she should wait and discover what he'd chosen as his idea gift for her whilst she was actually talking to him on the telephone. 'I'll phone you as soon as I'm able,' he'd promised, 'but it could be tricky to find time alone. I'm sure you understand.'

She understood all right, but that didn't make it any easier. She wondered how Paul would feel, being by himself on such a day: the one day when all your friends desert you, when everything is shut, and when even the weather is sulky. I could go for a walk in the rain, she thought. I used to love sloshing about in mac and wellies when I was little. But then she thought: No, I can't go out. Paul might phone, and I can't risk missing him. I could read. I've got piles of books I've been dying to have time for . . . No, I won't be able to concentrate if I'm waiting for the phone to ring. Maybe I could at least call up somebody for a chat. But who? God! I hate Christmas.

She opened the champagne bottle again and poured herself a refill. Then she turned on the television and slumped in front of it. The morning passed with the help of her clock on the mantelpiece, which ticked loudly and gave due weight to each lengthy minute. The television programmes were rubbish, but there was nothing else. The canned laughter etched out her *amour propre* like acid. She looked at the gold parcel longingly. It couldn't all be bad. She was sure his present would be worth waiting for. But still he didn't phone.

She drank the rest of the champagne and got maudlin, curling herself up with a cushion to hug, and snivelling into paper handkerchiefs until she had filled her waste-paper basket with pulpy crumpled tissues. Then she ate a virtuous cheese sandwich for lunch and thought, well, anyway I won't be pigging out today and feeling gross like ninety per cent of the population. But she still felt hungry so she scoffed a creamy yoghurt . . . and then another one . . . and a Tesco custard tart . . . and a whole bar of fruit and nut chocolate. And then she wanted to be sick, and couldn't. And still he didn't phone.

The flat needed hoovering. The bath needed cleaning. There were even cobwebs hanging from the ceiling above her head. She might as well do housework if she was trapped there for the day, but the noise of the hoover might drown the phone bell, and anyway, why should she do horrible chores on Christmas Day. Wasn't it bad enough being alone?

Finally at half-past three in the afternoon when daylight was fading, there was at last an intelligent programme to watch on Channel 4. Anna settled back with a tall glass of water and a sigh, and prepared to be entertained. And it was then that the telephone rang.

'Hello?'

'It's me,' Paul said. 'Look, I'm sorry, this has to be quick. They're all out for some stupid rain-walk but they'll be back any moment now it's getting dark.'

'And a happy Christmas to you too!' Anna said tartly.

'Oh, don't you start,' Paul said wearily. 'I was counting on you at least to be understanding today.'

'Why?' Nell's done it, and they're all having a miserable Christmas too! Anna thought gleefully. Brilliant! Now we'll be able to commiserate with each other, and then he'll realise how much better it would be with me! 'What's wrong?' she asked.

'Only every bloody thing.'

'Poor Paul,' Anna said, putting on her most caressing voice. 'Tell me all about it.'

'You're not going to believe this.'

'Try me.'

'Elly has chosen today of all days to announce that she's leaving me for another man.'

'WHAT?!' Conflicting thoughts surged through Anna's mind: *Yes!* and *Wonderful!* and *Damn! Why did I go blathering to Nell?* and *Who would have thought it?* and *YES!* 'You don't mean it?'

'I'm afraid I do.'

Afraid? 'But who?'

'Oh, she's deluding herself that the great Malachy (I'm-so-divine) Hayhoe wants to marry her! It seems she's prepared to throw it all away; marriage, children, the lot, to shack up with him. Can you credit it? Of course it's doomed from the outset, but then what? And how shall I tell the boys? I just don't know . . .' He sounded desperate.

'You're kidding?' Anna was astonished.

'I'll kill him! To think I entertained the gutless bastard on my houseboat, and all the time he was . . .' He stopped.

'*Our* special hideaway houseboat, darling,' Anna reminded him gently.

'Anyway,' Paul said shortly, 'sorry and all that, but you can imagine how I feel, and it certainly isn't festive.'

'But, Paul, can't you see? This is our big chance. You've always said your marriage to Ermintrude was a sham. This could be the perfect solution. Now you and I can –'

'Eleanor is my *wife*,' Paul shouted. 'Surely you can appreciate what that means to me. I'm sorry . . . I'm too upset . . . *too* angry . . . I'll call again when things have calmed down.'

'You can't mean –' Anna began, but he'd put the phone down. She felt mortally wounded, and at the same time outraged by his double standards. She didn't know what to think. In a daze she saw his present still lying in its golden Christmas paper on the table. She unwrapped it. It was a box of chocolates.

Mic had been looking forward to having Christmas in a proper house with all the trimmings. She was well aware that she would be expected to do most of the cooking, but accepted it as the price she had to pay for comfort and security. She had however reckoned without Josh and Rosie being there too. This was the year they were supposed to go with their dad to London for Christmas

171

with their flash granddad (and bloody good luck to them). But at the last minute, Josh had refused to go, and Rosie couldn't be persuaded to go without him – understandable really. So there Mic was, lumbered again.

Mornings were always her best time; Gavin, half asleep, would climb into bed with her and they'd have a cuddle and discuss the day ahead, and she would privately wonder what sort of mood Cassie would turn out to be in – better these days, since her four weeks of intensive therapy. Today it had all begun much too early, inevitably so. Gavin had woken in high excitement at five o'clock and had roused her by trying to pull her eyelids up.

'*Mum!*' he'd said urgently. 'Open your eyes! 'SChristmas!'

'Gerrof!' Mic groaned, burying her face in the pillow. 'Too early.'

'But I want ter open me presents.' He pulled the bulging sock up the bed towards her.

Mic squinted blearily at the clock. ' 'Snot morning for a nuvver two hours yet. Ger in, and we'll have the rest of our kip together, yeah?'

'Oh, Mum . . .'

'Come on. I mean it.' Gavin climbed into bed and settled down with reasonable grace, with his back to her. Mic rested her chin on his tousled ginger head, and was just about to drop off again when the door burst open and an ear-splitting cacophony of football rattle and over-blown penny whistle blasted her into total wakefulness.

'Yoo hoo!' Josh cried. 'Look what I've got!'

'An' me, an' me!' Rosie was right behind him and together they bounced onto Mic's bed, waving their instruments.

''Snot fair,' Gavin protested, struggling out from Mic's embrace and sitting up. 'They've 'ad their presents and I 'aven't.'

'Not all of them,' Josh boasted. 'I've got loads more. I bet I've got squillions more than you have!'

'That's enough,' Mic said sternly. 'It's way too early. Back to bed the pair of you, and don't come in 'ere till seven. Right?'

'But it's Christmas,' Josh complained. 'We always get up early.'

'Well, I don't,' Mic said. 'I needs me beauty sleep. Off you go. You too, Rosie. An' settle down, Gav.' She watched through half-closed eyes as they trailed out again. Gawd, she thought, it ain't half hard work disciplining those two, but I reckon I could still win. All I need is a bit of backup from you know who . . .

The bedroom door burst open again. 'What did I say?' Mic demanded furiously, sitting bolt upright in bed. 'I said don't come back until seven o'clock!'

'When the little hand'th on theven and the big hand'th on twelve,' Rosie supplied helpfully.

'Right.'

'Well, it is,' Josh said, holding up the battered nursery clock with its front glass missing, and showing her his handiwork with pride.

Mic was torn between sighing and wanting to laugh. 'You have to wait for it to 'appen, dumbo! Just pushing the hands round don't make the time pass, do it? An' it wrecks the clock an' all! So, go away, yeah?'

'Mum told us to come in here,' Josh said sulkily. 'She says she's got a headache and mustn't be disturbed. She said we could open some more presents with you.' He was pulling a loaded pillowcase behind him.

Oh terrific! Mic thought. Thank you, Cassie! A compromise seemed to be the only way out. 'Well, not in here, right? You two take 'em downstairs, and me and Gav'll get dressed and get down quick's we can. Off wiv yer.'

Gavin raised a clenched fist. 'Yeah!'

'An' you can leave that out an' all,' said his mother.

173

Cassie did not appear downstairs until eleven o'clock, by which time Josh was tearful in his thwarted desire to show her his presents and get her to help him play with them. They were, in Mic's opinion, too pricey, too breakable, needing too many batteries, and would most likely run out of power before their owner could yell, 'Hey! Give us that back!' She had tried hard to be as equitable as possible, giving all three children similar toys, but Cassie hadn't attempted to disguise her favouritism, and her presents were all too obviously ranked in the order of her affections: big for Josh, middling for Rosie, and tiny for Gavin.

Mic's heart went out to her son. She was torn between trying to pretend that everything was fair, in order to bolster his self-esteem, or sympathising with him, which was more honest but which might make him feel even worse.

'Knock knock,' Gavin said stoically, toughing it out.

'Who'th there?' Rosie chanted obediently.

'Scott.'

'Thcott who?'

'Sgot nothing to do with you!'

Cassie put on her Lady Bountiful act at lunchtime, and produced an expensive confection awash with fruit and cream, from a box Mic had overlooked. 'Marks & Spark's best,' she said proudly. 'And so much lighter and easier to eat than the usual figgy stodge, don't you think? That stuff lies like lead on your stomach for hours, not that I ever have room for it, of course.'

'So how do you know, then?' Mic muttered sotto voice, moving the steamer containing the pudding she had bought as a contribution off the heat.

What am I doing here? she asked herself, not for the first time. Being taken for a ride, that's what!

After lunch she had planned to take Gavin to see her mother, just the two of them, and had deliberately not mentioned this to Cassie, knowing from experience how she tended to hijack such plans. Mic now decided to be assertive. After all, it was Christmas Day.

But Cassie got in first. 'Oh dear,' she sighed, within moments of her last mouthful, 'I think I can feel my migraine coming on again. I'm afraid I'll have to desert you all once more. I'm so sorry.' She got up.

'Hang on a minute,' Mic objected. 'Gav and me are off to me mum's for a bit. I promised her we'd go today.'

'But of course,' Cassie said generously, at once. 'Then you must see her. I expect Josh and Rosie would love to go along too, wouldn't you? I'm sure she'll have one of her little presents for you both.' She smiled bravely at her children and then at Mic. 'That's a lovely idea of yours, Mic. They're always telling me how fond they are of Granny Potton.'

Nell hadn't reckoned on having Elly with her as well as Sibyl on their journey home on Boxing Day; an Elly moreover who had become seriously deflated since the previous day. They had all gone to Heathrow to see Paul and the two boys off to Switzerland, and after the plane had taken off, Elly went all weepy and announced that she was leaving Paul's car in the long-stay car park, and coming home with them both.

'I can't bear to be alone,' she wept in Nell's car.

'Here,' Sibyl said, leaning forward and offering her a lacy handkerchief.

'I've never left Paul in charge of the boys before,' Elly sniffed, taking it and clutching it to her mouth with one hand. 'How can I be sure they'll be safe?'

'Well, he takes his pupils on school trips,' Nell said reasonably. 'He's very responsible.' When he's not sailing.

'I didn't mean it to happen like this,' Elly said, 'I really didn't. I was going to go on the skiing holiday and then break it to him in the New Year, but then Malachy told me he's going abroad, filming for most of January, and I suddenly couldn't bear . . .' She was crying again. 'I'm so . . . sorry . . . if I ruined your Christmas.'

'You did rather,' Sibyl observed from the back seat. 'How about stopping for a coffee at the next opportunity, Nell?'

'Good idea,' Nell said, but she was thinking: I can't put it off any longer. It would be much too cowardly to break it to her over the phone.

At the service station they carried coffee for three, and Bath buns for two on a tray to a window table and sat down. Nell and Sibyl ate the buns and had milk in their coffee. Elly sat, tragic but dry-eyed, sipping hers black and without eating. 'You both blame me, don't you?' she asked.

'No, darling,' Sibyl said. 'I've seen this coming for quite some time, but I must confess it isn't turning out quite as I'd imagined.'

'Actually, I think it is,' Nell said. Sibyl raised her eyebrows. Nell braced herself. 'Would you be surprised if Paul was having an affair too?' she asked Elly.

'Amazed!' Elly snorted. 'Who'd have him?' Then she saw Nell's expression and frowned. 'D'you know something that I don't?'

'Well, I suspect something, yes,' Nell said, fudging and despising herself for it.

'Paul? Having an affair?' Elly seemed mildly amused.
'Yes.'
'Who with?'

'Strangely enough a woman who swims at the same pool as me. She's called Anna Smith.'

Elly frowned again. 'The name seems familiar. Didn't she used to teach at Paul's school?'

'She is a teacher, yes.'

'Thought so,' Sibyl muttered. 'Explains so much.'

176

'Hang on a minute,' Elly said. 'How long has this been going on?'

'I'm not sure.' Nell blushed.

'It started well before Malachy and me, didn't it?' Elly was staring at her.

'Probably,' Nell said feebly.

'But don't you see,' Elly said, getting heated. 'Don't you see where this leaves me? Paul is going to feel fully justified in blaming me for our break-up now, when all along he's been screwing some slag. The incredible hypocrite! No wonder I was driven into Malachy's arms.'

'But you didn't know then,' Nell protested, confused.

'No, you should have told me!' Elly flashed back. 'Both of you. Look at the position you've put me in now. Even my boys think it's all my fault. How could you do that to me?'

'We were hoping it wasn't true,' Sibyl said.

'You've talked about it behind my back?'

'No,' Nell said. 'Honestly, we haven't.'

'Oh well,' Elly said sighing, and then disconcertingly upbeat: 'at least I won't have to feel guilty now. Damn! I do wonder where Malachy is. I assumed that he and Rob and the kids would have been at his house yesterday and I was going to give him a nice surprise, but I rang and rang and all I got was his bloody answerphone.'

'Aren't you supposed to be meeting some American friend at his house this week?' Nell asked. 'I mean, that was the reason you didn't go ski –'

'So I lied,' Elly interrupted irritably. 'I'm not proud of that, OK? The friend's coming over at the beginning of February.'

'But why –' Sibyl began.

'Because I needed some space. Because I was fed up with Paul. Because I wanted to see Malachy. Why d'you think? How was I to know he'd do a disappearing act?'

'Maybe because he thinks you're in Switzerland,' Nell pointed out reasonably.

'I'll get in touch with him soon,' Elly said. 'Oh hell! I shouldn't be going home with you at all today. I should be staying in London. But after Paul and the boys left, somehow I just couldn't face you two going as well . . .' She began to cry again.

'It's all right,' Sibyl said, patting her shoulder comfortingly. 'You need a day or two with no pressure to sort yourself out. Perhaps when they get back from skiing –'

'No.' Elly said, blowing her nose fiercely. 'It's finished. I've made up my mind.'

'And Malachy?' Nell asked.

'He really loves me, Nell, and he's great with the boys.' She managed a tremulous smile. 'It'll all work out, you see.'

After the coffee break, they journeyed doggedly westward and Nell, who was beginning to feel worn out, was grateful that it was a neutral grey day; ideal for driving. After several hours she dropped her passengers off at Sibyl's house and headed thankfully for Bottom Cottage.

Rob was there before her. She saw his Land Rover as she got to the end of her lane. Then the front door opened and he was standing there, smiling.

'Oh, Rob,' she cried. 'I can't tell you how glad I am to be home!' She got stiffly out of her car and walked towards him.

'Was it rough?' he asked.

'Ghastly. How about you?'

'A complete washout,' he admitted.

'Oh! I'm so sorry. God, I'm absolutely exhausted.'

Rob came forward and put both arms around her in a bear hug.

'Better now?' he asked.

Chapter Fifteen

Over the last weekend in January, when Josh and Rosie visited Bottom Cottage, Rob made boats for them out of odds and ends of wood nailed together, and quarter-filled the bath with tepid water for them to float on. Nell was downstairs in the kitchen washing up the lunch things when there was a crash, the sound of thudding feet and Rosie's voice raised in protest. Nell looked up from the dishwater, expecting to hear Rob's voice, but then saw him outside the window, fetching firewood, and thought perhaps she should go and see what they were up to. She met Rosie on the stairs, carrying two small damp contraptions which were both dripping water freely. The front of her red dungarees was sopping wet, and she looked sulky.

'Joth keepth thinking my boat. Not playing.'

Nell could hear Rob downstairs, filling up the log basket. 'Why don't you go down and see your daddy?' she suggested. Rosie stumped on down. Nell put her head round the bathroom door to find out what Josh was doing. He had a handful of glass marbles and he was standing up and balancing on top of the bath with his feet beside the taps, and throwing them one at a time onto the remaining boats below him. The bath was very nearly full of water and at each hit, more of it splashed over the edge on to the swimming floor.

'Att-att att-att att-att!' Josh cried, 'BOOM!' He threw another marble. It missed, and hit the edge of the bath a glancing blow, quite hard enough to chip its white enamel surface.

'Oh, Josh . . .' Nell began, hesitating to reprimand him so early on. 'That isn't a very good idea.'

'It's a raid,' Josh explained. 'I'm a bomber, and this is the enemy fleet, and I'm winning and they're all going to get sunk. Watch!' He threw two marbles at once and scored a direct hit, which turned one of the boats over on to its side. 'Yesss!' Josh crowed. 'See that. You can be a used bomb collector if you like. You can get them out of the water and re . . . re . . . something them.'

'Recycle?'

'Yes, recycle them. You'll have to roll your sleeves up though. It's pretty deep. It's got to be miles down there. It's a bottomless ocean!'

Nell was quite touched at his concern, but unsure as to how to proceed. Perhaps she should have said 'Stop it, Josh!' at the beginning. But she didn't like to be so immediately authoritarian to a comparative stranger. 'No, I don't think so. You see the bath is likely to get damaged if you go on,' she tried to explain, 'and you're making an awful mess, so I wouldn't do it if I were you.'

'Oh, *I* would,' Josh said with satisfaction. 'And anyway my dad doesn't mind. He *made* these boats.'

Nell strode forward and pulled the plug out. 'I mean I don't want you to do it,' she said firmly (perhaps too firmly?).

Josh let out an injured wail. 'Hey, you're spoiling it all. It's not *fair*. And anyway, it's nothing to do with you. *We were here first!*'

'Let's go downstairs, mmm?' Nell said lamely. Josh jumped off the bath and stamped out ahead, shrugging off any attempt at contact with her. Then he ran straight downstairs and out of the back door.

When Nell got down to the kitchen she found Rob giving Rosie a shoulder ride. The child seemed to have forgotten her upset feelings already, and was seeing how many wet hand-prints she could make on the newly decorated ceiling just above her head, and gurgling with laughter. Nell frowned.

'Shouldn't we be changing her clothes?' she asked. 'We don't want her catching a chill.'

'Good thinking,' Rob said. 'Spare clothes in that bag over there. OW! Stop pulling my ears, you monster!'

Nell searched through the spare things Cassie had sent and held them up in turn for Rosie's approval. 'This one?'

'That's Joth's,' Rosie said witheringly.

'Oh well, what about this then?'

'Joth's.'

'And this?'

'Joth's.'

'Well, that's all there are,' Nell said. 'It doesn't look as though your mum's sent us any of your clothes. You'll have to borrow something of his just for now, until yours are dry again.'

'Don't want –' Rosie began, but Rob distracted her by swinging her down from his shoulders and tickling her under her arms. Rosie screamed with mirth, and Rob expertly stripped off her dungarees and the woolly pullover underneath them, and stuffed her into a jersey of Josh's, rolling up the sleeves to expose her podgy little fists. It was far too long but it, plus her still-dry tights underneath, would have to do.

'Guess what Auntie Nell made yesterday for us to eat,' Rob asked.

'Apple cumble,' Rosie said hopefully.

Rob laughed. 'No, marmalade. She made it all herself. Isn't it a lovely orange colour?' He took one of the jars from the shelf and held it up to the light.

'That's my sweater,' Josh protested, coming in again and leaving muddy footprints on the floor. 'I didn't say *she* could have it.'

'No,' Rob said, 'I did. OK? We haven't got any of her clothes here, so we haven't got much choice. Sorry.'

Nicely said, Nell thought. She felt much more comfortable when Rob was there.

The rest of the afternoon passed. Nell mopped up the bathroom floor and put all the marbles back in their box. She made toast-and-Marmite soldiers for Rosie, and honey slices for Josh at 4.30, and at five o'clock Rob helped Rosie back into her newly dry dungarees and then put both children into the Land Rover to take home. Rosie left, clutching one of the jars of Nell's marmalade, and wouldn't put it down even when Rob was strapping her in. 'Marmlade,' she crooned softly to herself. 'Olinge marmlade.'

'Bye, Rosie. Bye, Josh,' Nell said, looking in through the passenger door. 'See you again soon, I hope.'

'Anyway,' Josh said stoutly, as though completing an argument of long-standing, 'anyway, my mummy doesn't make jam. She's on TV.'

I think I'll aim for television work, Elly thought to herself as she wrapped the silk scarf artistically round her throat to keep out the penetrating February wind. 'Whaaa!' she exclaimed aloud as she got out of her car and into the northerly blast. 'I hope my nose won't go all red with cold. Today I've got to look my absolute best.' She glanced around to check whether anyone had observed her talking to herself, but the few people walking or driving through the square were in their own bubbles, self-absorbed and apparently remote from the communal atmosphere. That's why I like living in London, Elly thought. Only here, where you're surrounded by strangers, can you be truly free of other people's expectations. I'm going to shed all those labels that categorise me: no more 'Headmaster's wife'; no more 'businesswoman.' I need to get a life – no, *lots* of lives. I shall be someone different every week! A man passed her, pushing twins in a pram. I shall always be a mother though, Elly thought.

That's something I can't escape – even if I'd quite like to some of the time. And I'm very happy to be a lover, or even a mistress . . .

She skipped up the steps and rang Malachy's front doorbell. Six whole weeks, she thought, with only a measly couple of postcards signed 'Best wishes'. He's got some explaining to do! I shan't tell him I didn't go skiing though. She pushed her hair into place whilst she waited for him. I must get him to give me a key, she thought. Could I live here, or would I be better being independent to begin with?

'A belated happy New Year,' he said, opening the door and embracing her. 'I've missed you. Mmm, you smell delicious! Good festive season?'

'Actually, no,' Elly said.

'Me neither. Never mind, you're here now.' He stood aside for her to go up the stairs before him. 'Would you like a drink first?'

'Isn't your mysterious American friend here? I thought we were going to talk about my career?'

'Darling girl, I'm so sorry. He couldn't make it after all. Pressure of work. You know how it is.'

'What?' Elly stopped abruptly halfway up.

'He said to promise you he'd see you next time he's over here. He's a dear man, I'm sure he'll keep his word.'

'But . . . I was relying on meeting him,' Elly began. 'You prom –'

'It's a damned shame,' Malachy agreed, patting her bottom. 'On you go. We've got a lot of catching up to do.'

Elly frowned but went up, and along the landing into the drawing room, where she stood in the large bay window with her back to him.

'Don't be vexed, sweeting,' Malachy said. 'There'll be other times.'

'But I'm selling my business!' Elly protested. 'I can't just enjoy myself. I have to have some way to earn my living.'

'Relax,' he said. 'A calm interlude as a kept woman wouldn't do you any harm at all. You're all tense and stressed out. You've even got a little pink quivering nose!' He came forward and kissed the end of it gently and then stood back, regarding her gravely.

'Would you really?'

'Would I really what?'

'Keep me?'

Malachy made a little deprecatory gesture with his hands. 'Well, naturally I meant Paul, but yes I'll certainly help pamper you, you know I will. I'm having a Campari and soda, how about you?'

'White wine,' Elly said automatically. He's got no idea what I've done, she thought. How shall I tell him? What if he isn't overjoyed? She didn't know why she suddenly had doubts. She had been so confident. She stood in the window and hugged her arms around herself.

'Poor love, you're freezing,' Malachy said, coming in with a tall half-filled wineglass and giving it to her. 'Isn't the climate just bloody these days?'

Oh God, Elly thought, he's talking about the *weather*! He surely can't be bored with me already.

'This time of year is always a letdown, don't you think?' he said. Worse and worse.

'I tried to phone you before you left,' she said, 'but you were never in, and you didn't answer any of my messages.'

'Damned machine,' Malachy apologised, sitting down. 'Somehow I can never bring myself to get to grips with it. Rob set it up for me, but all it does is to double the number of people I don't want to speak to.'

'Including me?'

'Of course not, darling. Whatever's the matter? You've been as perverse as a porcupine ever since you arrived! Come and sit down.' He patted the couch next to him.

'Something happened over Christmas,' Elly said. She

184

rested against the button-backed leather and closed her eyes.

'Something bad?'

'Yes and no.' She opened her eyes again and took a gulp of wine. 'Paul's got some woman.'

'I see.' He looked for the first time like an actor playing for time, having forgotten his lines. He's a fake, Elly suddenly realised. He never says what he truly thinks; even now, when he's supposed to be in love with me! Her resentment made her strong. She thought, I'm not going to help him out. This is the ultimate test. If he tries to get some clues from me about what I want him to say, then I'll know for sure that his attachment to me isn't real . . .

'So, how do you feel about that?' Malachy put a sympathetic hand on her knee. Elly shook it off.

'I thought you'd be pleased!' she cried. 'Paul's *leaving me*. We could be together all the time. How do *you* feel?'

He rose to his feet and walked deliberately over to the fireplace, where he poked at the glowing coals unnecessarily. Then he leant against it elegantly. 'Startled,' he said. He waved his hands expressively. 'Concerned for you . . . This isn't something one can react to instantaneously in some sort of slick sound bite, you know. It needs considerable thought.'

'No,' Elly said, getting up to leave. 'That's just where you're wrong. It just needs a spontaneous response from the heart. But maybe, as I'm discovering, you aren't any good without a script.'

Living with Rob seems entirely natural, Nell thought. Our lives fit together almost effortlessly on a practical level. Rob's taken command of the woodburner and supplies it with regular firewood, and I do the cooking and . . . most other things, now I think about it. But if I put some of his dirty clothes into the washing machine with my stuff, it's simply because it would seem petty-minded only to do half a load. I iron the odd thing of his too when doing my own, but then I quite like ironing.

'Wonderful,' he said, coming downstairs wearing a freshly laundered shirt. 'The Mad Cow never ironed *anything*.'

Nell had felt obscurely from the very beginning that she was in some sort of contest with the aftertaste of Cassie, and only if she could win hands down would she feel even adequate. At the moment she was clearly doing all right on the domestic front, but the very fact that he was comparing her with his wife made her wonder whether he actually saw her in those terms. She began to feel a little put out that he hadn't shown any interest in sleeping with her. She wasn't that unattractive, was she?

She began to wear a little make-up at home to see if he would notice. Then she wasn't sure if he had or not, because he didn't mention it. She dabbed a spot or two of Anaïs Anaïs behind her ears. Still no comment. She thought of Martin and how, in Rob's place, she would have had to fight him off, and smiled wryly to herself. But if Rob had been equally as keen, would she then have accused him of taking advantage of the situation? Perhaps he couldn't win. She tried to see it from his point of view. Maybe he was unsure of himself; crushed by his experience with Cassie. Nell decided he needed some unambiguous encouragement.

An opportunity presented itself the following Saturday when Rob was sitting at the kitchen table opening his post. Nell had already discarded hers as being junk mail, and was about to put some soup on for lunch.

'At last!' Rob muttered under his breath.

'What?'

'My decree nisi has arrived. Only another two or three months and I'll be shot of the bloody woman for ever.'

'That's great,' Nell said with enthusiasm.

'Of course, it won't actually be like that,' Rob said,

making a face. 'To be realistic, I shall still have to co-operate with her for the next God knows how many years, until the children are grown up and off our hands.'

'But at least you won't be married to her.'

'No, thank the Lord.'

That evening Nell prepared a special meal, and set it out on the table with wine and candles and a background of Beethoven. Rob came in in his stockinged feet, having taken his boots off, and switched the lights on.

'What's all this?'

'Turn them off again,' Nell said. 'I'm recreating that evening when we had a power cut. D'you remember?'

'I remember being bothered about the Land Rover stuck in the snow,' Rob said. 'I was worried I'd buckled the axle.'

'Sit down anyway. I'm just dishing up.'

'Looks good.'

'I hope it's one of your favourites.' Nell handed him a plateful, and he helped himself to sprouts.

'So, what's all this in aid of?'

'I thought we'd celebrate the beginning of your life as a free man.'

'That's nice. I'm pleased about it naturally, but I didn't think . . . it would be any big deal for you.'

'Well, that's up to you.' She said it deliberately.

Rob actually blushed. Even in the half-light she could see the colour rise in his cheeks. 'Really?' he said. 'I had no idea.'

I'm out of practice at this sort of thing, Rob thought. Haven't chatted up anyone for years. Makes me feel about seventeen again, and . . . flustered. Didn't think she fancied me. Have there been other signs I've simply missed? I've been so preoccupied with the divorce and the kids . . . But it could be dodgy, with us living in the same place – what if it all goes wrong? Oh, to hell with all my puritan prudence. She's lovely! I'd be crazy to pass up a chance like this. He finished his food and sat back, smiling at her.

'More wine?' Nell asked.

'No,' he said, holding her glance. 'I want to be totally *compos mentis* tonight.' He put a hand out across the table and took one of hers.

'Why?' Her eyes looked darker than usual. Was it only because of the subdued light?

'Because I want to know exactly what I'm doing.'

'What did you have in mind?' She took her hand back.

'I'm not sure. What grabs you most: spontaneity or strategy?'

'Mmm,' Nell regarded him steadily. 'Well, strategy can be a bit too inflexible maybe . . . but on the other hand, too much spontaneity can be disconcerting.'

'What about honesty?'

'Oh, honesty is absolutely essential.'

'I'm glad about that.'

'So, maybe an honest happy medium?'

'Right.' Rob took a breath. 'Shall we go to bed?'

To his relief, Nell broke into a broad smile. 'We didn't mention finesse, did we?'

'Never touch the stuff.'

'So I see.'

'Well then . . .' Rob leant across the table and kissed her on the mouth. There was a sharp fizzing noise and the acrid smell of burning hair. 'Shit!' he exclaimed, slapping the side of his head. 'Bloody candles!'

Nell burst out laughing and getting to her feet, switched on the lights. Then she blew out the candles, came round to his side of the table and took his hand.

'Come on,' she said, 'it's safer upstairs.'

Chapter Sixteen

Mic was coming to appreciate that she had finally met someone even more manipulative than herself, and she felt stumped. She now realised that whatever she did, Cassie would somehow top it. But she's *dependent* on me, Mic thought, so how the fuck can she?

One incident in particular still rankled. She hadn't wanted to hurt the children's feelings way back on Christmas Day by saying, 'No you can't come. Me and Gav's goin' to me mum's on our tod,' which certainly was what she should have done, but which Cassie, of course, had banked upon her not saying . . . It had simply not occurred to her that Cassie would want to get rid of her own children on such a day. She, Mic Potton, was losing the plot! I've got to get out, she thought. It's a nice warm house and everything, but it's not worth selling my soul for. I could go back to Mum's for a bit. I could maybe even get that council flat? I've been on the list long enough.

'Mic?' Cassie called from the front hall. 'Did you do that ironing I asked you to?'

Right! Mic thought. Perfect opportunity. She walked to the top of the stairs and leant on the banister rail. 'Nope,' she said.

'Oh, that's too bad,' Cassie said crossly. 'I need that dress this afternoon. I thought you knew that.'

'Ironing,' Mic said, 'is not part of me job. I fought *you* knew that.'

'Oh, Mic,' Cassie sighed, 'you're not having one of your moods again, are you? Is it the time of the month? It's like trying to deal with a primitive trade union, negotiating with you these days. I thought we agreed we wouldn't have who-does-what disputes.'

'Fine 'slong's it's fifty-fifty,' Mic said, 'but it ain't, is it?'

'Well, you're so much better at doing –' Cassie began, but was interrupted by a quarrel breaking out on the landing behind Mic.

'That's mine!' Gavin complained.

'No it's not. Everything in this house belongs to us!' Josh shouted. 'You don't really live here.'

'Stop it!' Mic cried, whipping round and nearly clouting Josh on the back of the head. 'Don't you never let me hear you say that again, Josh Hayhoe. You got that?'

Cassie ran up the stairs. 'Did she hit you?' she demanded of her son. 'I saw that!' She rounded on Mic.

'Course I bleedin' didn't,' Mic retorted. 'Not that he wasn't askin' for a slap.'

'How *dare* you?' Cassie shouted. 'He's absolutely right. Everything in this house is *ours*. You're only here on sufferance.'

Mic clenched her teeth. 'Right,' she said, 'that's it. Pack up your things, Gav, we're off.' She went into their room and began stuffing her clothes into her rucksack.

'You can't do that,' Cassie sneered, leaning against the doorframe. 'You've got nowhere to go.'

'Anywhere's better'n here.'

'You were grateful enough for my charity at the beginning.'

'Charity be buggered!' Mic almost laughed. 'Slaves have done less than what I've done fer you. Anyway, you'll be rubbish wivout me. Who's goin' ter pick up the pieces the next time you frow a wobbly? Eh?'

'Please don't concern yourself,' Cassie said icily. 'I'm not entirely without resources, you know.'

'You must need ter make a lot of friends,' Mic observed. 'You certainly get froo 'em and spit 'em out again quick enough.'

'What would you know about friends, a sponger like you?' Cassie snorted.

'You askin' fer a fat lip or what?' Mic advanced on her.

'Oh, that's right. Violence – the last resort of the incoherent.'

'What, you mean like sarcasm – the last resort of the mental case?'

'I'm not going to waste my time bandying words with someone like you,' Cassie said wearily. 'I've got better things to do,' and she marched off, ushering an astonished Josh and Rosie before her.

'Yeah, like the ironing fr'instance,' Mic called after her.

'Mum?' Gavin asked, wide-eyed. 'Where we goin'?'

'To yer gran's.'

'Bu there isn't r –'

'Not anuvver word, right? I've had it up to 'ere.'

It didn't take long to pack. Neither of them owned much. Mic took pleasure in leaving Cassie's Christmas presents ostentatiously behind. She didn't bother making the beds either, or unblocking the toilet. When they humped their luggage downstairs, Cassie was nowhere to be seen.

'Good riddance!' Mic shouted as they opened the front door. There was a howl and a scuffle. The kitchen door burst open, and Rosie came running out, crying noisily.

'Don't go . . . Mic!' She clasped her round her knees and held on tightly.

'Oh, Rosie . . .' Mic very nearly wept too. 'I'm sorry. I love you very much, yeah? This is nuffink to do wif you. It's just your mum and me don't get on.'

'Don't go, don't go, don't go,' Rosie wailed.

Mic picked her up and kissed her on both cheeks. 'I'll see you again soon,' she promised. 'Straight up.'

'Put her down!' Cassie ordered, out of sight in the kitchen. 'And leave your key on the hall front table.'

'Bye, love,' Mic said to Rosie. 'Gotta go, OK?' Then she

set the child on her feet again, shouldered her rucksack, and gave Rosie her front door key. 'Tell you what,' she said, 'see how far you can sling that, eh?'

She and Gavin were halfway to the front gate by the time Rosie had stopped swinging her arm, and by the time the key had landed somewhere in a fallow flower-bed, they were walking side by side along the frosty pavement towards the town.

'Knock, knock,' Gavin said, after a while.

'Who's there?'

'Ewan.'

'Ewan who?'

'You and me's well outta there.'

Nell and Rob sat side by side in Nell's big bed, propped up on pillows and drinking tea. It was Saturday morning and late, judging by the full daylight beyond the iced-up windows. Rob had on an old jersey to keep warm; Nell, the top of a pair of brushed cotton pyjamas.

'You look like a cherub.' He leant over to kiss her cheek.

'I feel positively devilish,' Nell said, 'after last night!'

'Was it all right?'

'It was lovely.' A little overemphatic?

'But?'

'Well, it was strange, wasn't it? I suppose it always is, the first time you sleep with someone, especially if you've got into a routine with the person before. It takes time to adjust, to mesh . . . if that's the word.'

'To bed in?' Rob suggested.

Nell smiled. 'Mmm. I'm sure we will though, aren't you?'

'You haven't had second thoughts?'

'Certainly not! Why, have you?'

'No,' Rob said. 'More tea?'

'I'd love some, but you'll have to get out of bed.'

'Easy.' He pushed back the duvet and went across to

the table where he'd left the teapot and milk on a tray. Nell admired the shape of his naked legs, and neat bum half hidden by the loose hem of the jersey. As a lover he'd been a fraction tentative, and she'd been obliged to assist him by saying 'down a bit' or 'up a bit' at times, when he'd seemed unsure of the topography. But Nell was convinced she could train him up; the potential was there. He was gentle and considerate and sweet, and she felt entirely at home with him. Who could ask for more?

He came back with the tea. 'This "person before" . . .' he began carefully, '. . . is he still around?'

Nell laughed. 'Heavens no! He's long gone. His name was Martin and he was a disaster – nothing like you.'

'Well, that's a relief.'

'What about you?'

'Me? Well, only Cassie as it happens.'

'And . . . was that a success?'

'Define your terms? We got the children, so yes . . . I suppose.'

No, Nell though, that wasn't what I meant but now isn't the time to pursue it. 'I only wish we hadn't wasted so much time,' she said.

'Well, it's best not to rush these things.' Rob put his mug down on the bedside table. 'Look!'

A green woodpecker was flying past the window and away downstream in characteristic undulating flight, and calling loudly like an excited punter on a switchback ride: *Look at me! – whoops – look at me – whoops! – look . . .*

'Yaffle,' Nell said, identifying it. 'I've just thought. You know some people keep a tally of birds and other animals seen from their gardens? Why don't we make a list of everything seen from our bed?'

'Haven't we got better things to do?' Rob raised an eyebrow.

Nell grinned. 'So we have.' She took her pyjama top off, and snuggled down. Rob was just pulling his sweater over his head when the telephone beside the bed rang.

'Hello?' Nell said.

'Mr Hayhoe please,' a sharp woman's voice said.

'Oh, hang on, I'll just see if I can find him.' Nell winked at Rob. 'Who's speaking?'

'Mrs Hayhoe.'

'Oh . . . is that Cassie? This is Nell here. I was wonder –'

'Just tell him to phone me,' the voice interrupted. There was a crash.

Nell held the receiver away from her ear. 'Terrific,' she said. 'The Mad Cow isn't exactly sweetness and light, is she?'

'What did she want?'

'You to phone her.'

'Oh Gawd,' Rob groaned, 'what's she after now?'

'She didn't say. She was amazingly rude.'

'That figures.' Rob leant on one elbow and traced a finger round her mouth. 'Lovely lips,' he said. Nell held out her arms and pulled him down to join her. He sucked each of her nipples in turn, until they became pink and erect. Then he slid his hand over the curve of her stomach and down between her thighs. 'There?'

'Up a bit.'

Cassie waited impatiently for Rob to phone her back. The house was already in chaos: beds not made, washing-up not done, toys underfoot . . . Rosie had wet the bed again and the smelly sheets were still in a heap on the kitchen floor in front of the washing machine. Rosie herself was being even more bloody-minded than usual, and deliberately winding Josh up. She's doing it on purpose to spite me, Cassie thought. How could a daughter of mine be so malicious? The answer was clear – she took after her father.

'Why don't you ring me, you bastard?' she muttered. 'Here I am, all on my own, trying to cope with two

194

hyperactive children, and there you are shacked-up with some totty and living the life of Riley! It's time you bloody well took your responsibilities seriously.'

Then she discovered that the lavatory was blocked. This was the final straw. Everyone is conspiring against me, she thought. Why? And why should I put up with it? 'Shut up, Rosie!'

This won't do, she told herself. It'll push me over the edge again. She made herself sit down with a cup of coffee and a Prozac. 'Go away,' she said to Rosie. 'You're making me ill. You too, Josh. Go and play in your rooms. I need some peace and quiet.'

'But, Mum –'

'GO AWAY!'

After half an hour she felt calmer. She knew exactly what she had to do. She stood at the bottom of the stairs and called, 'Josh? Rosie? Get your coats on. We're going for a ride.'

Elly phoned Nell late on the Saturday morning. They hadn't been in touch since Boxing Day, and a lot had happened in the last month and a half. She was surprised Nell hadn't already rung her. It was out of character for her to be silent for so long.

'Nell? It's me. How's things?'

'Elly! Lovely to hear you. Everything's fine. How about you? Where are you?'

'I'm at Ma's, but I'm about to go down to the houseboat to live on my own for a while. I can't take any more of Paul.'

'It'll be a bit cold and uncomfortable, won't it?'

'No, I've bought loads of fuel for the stove. I'll be snug as a bug.'

'Look, Elly, Rob and I have been talking. He's told me to warn you about Bert.'

'Too late,' Elly said briskly. 'I found out the hard way.'

'Oh dear. What happened?'

'It's all off. I must have been stark raving mad. I've gone off the idea of acting too.'

'So . . . what will you do?'

'Live off the proceeds of the business for a while. Think of something else. I really don't know.'

'What about the boys?'

'They're fine. They're being very adult about the whole mess, now they know it wasn't my fault. And to be fair to Paul, it seems he handled them brilliantly in Switzerland so I feel a lot more relaxed on that front. The only problem is, Paul's now saying he wants to take early retirement. It seems he can't stand the stress at school any longer. Typical midlife crisis! So everything's up in the air.'

'But you're not leaving the boys with him? I thought –'

'Oh no, not entirely. Hat will be there for them, and they love being with her. Anyway, they'll be down here most weekends as soon as the weather gets warmer, staying with me while their dad goes sailing. It'll work out, you see.'

'Well . . . yes, but you won't live away from them for long, will you?'

'Who knows? We've got to sell this house and divide the proceeds. Could take some time.'

'So you're still going ahead with the divorce then?'

'Of course. The way Paul's behaved leaves me no option.'

'Oh.'

'So, how's life with you, Nellykins? How's Roger the lodger?'

'Wonderful.'

'Hey oop! Do I detect nookie down t'cottage?'

'Rob's lovely. He's just what I need.'

'But that's great! I never thought he'd actually get round to it. How did you swing it?'

'That's not the sort of thing you ask.' Nell was indignant.

'Sorry, sorry. I'm getting too cynical. Look, I'm really pleased for you. It's terrific news. How are his children reacting?'

'They don't know yet. We're going to wait a bit before we tell them. They're very young, after all.'

'It's a good age,' Elly said, thinking of her two. 'They're so easy to please at this stage, and it's so rewarding. You want to make the most of Rosie and Josh, you know, whilst they're still only babies, before the teenage horrors begin.'

'Mmm.' Nell sounded unconvinced.

'Anyway, must dash. Pop over to the boat whenever you want.'

'Right. I'll look forward to that.'

Nell put the phone down. 'It's all right,' she said to Rob, 'that was Elly. She's seen the light.'

'Just as well,' Rob said. 'No broken heart?'

'Apparently not, although you can never tell with Elly; she puts on a good act. She's pretty resilient, though.'

I wish I was too, Nell thought, but when people like Elly talk that way about children, I feel like some sort of alien being. Am I totally lacking in normal female maternal feelings, or what? Or am I just scared of the responsibility of someone else's children? Most people seem to be able to cope instinctively, so why do I feel that I can't? Thank goodness Josh and Rosie don't live with Rob full-time. I couldn't survive that.

'Hadn't you better phone Cassie back?' she reminded him.

'I suppose so, but it's bound to be trouble.' He sighed, and picked up the phone. After a few moments he put it down again. 'Well, that's a relief,' he said. 'No reply.'

'Oh good,' Nell said. 'I was looking forward to a nice

uncomplicated self-indulgent day.' Two car doors banged outside as she spoke. 'Oh no! Who's that?'

Then they heard the sound of a car driving away up the hill, and almost immediately the front door was kicked open and Rob's children burst into the kitchen, hitting each other.

'What's going on?' Rob demanded. 'Josh?'

'Mic's walked out on us and Mum's ill,' he said. 'I didn't want to come, but she says it's your turn now.'

Chapter Seventeen

'She just dumped them and ran!' Nell said to Elly. 'What if we'd been out?'

'Well, I suppose both your vehicles were there, so it was unlikely.'

'Or in bed?'

'Now that could have been awkward.' Elly sat back against a red velvet cushion and grinned at her broadly. 'How's it going then?'

'It was bliss – until the children arrived.'

'Well, they're only staying for the weekend, aren't they?'

'Yes, and then for the whole of half-term the week after next! Rob's having to take leave from work. And then they're coming every weekend after that for the fore-seeable future.'

'But why?'

'It seems the Mad Cow needs "a rest". Her live-in skivvy has done a runner.'

'Don't blame her! Never mind, you can do what you're doing now: escape here from time to time, to me.'

Nell looked out of the small windows of the houseboat to Eely Isle and the grey river beyond the creek. The tide was on the ebb, and the first mud was coming into view at its edges; a gradually expanding buffet for the waiting curlews and other birds with long probing beaks.

'I suppose I ought to be at the cottage getting their lunch,' she said.

'There's no "ought" about it!' Elly exclaimed. 'Rob can manage baked beans on toast, surely?'

'Maybe, but he isn't much good at discipline.'

'I expect he feels guilty, having left them in the first place. He's probably, unconsciously, trying to make it up to them all the time.'

'That's more than likely true,' Nell said, 'And I'm sure it's selfish of me, but I don't want my lovely cottage all grottified by flying food, sticky fingers and muddy boots.'

'Don't blame you. You'll just have to set some rules and get Rob to enforce them too. At least that's one thing Paul and I did manage to do together – bloody man! I hate all men at the moment.'

'So what happened with Ber – Malachy?' Nell was dying to know.

'Oh, him. He just wanted a compliant female to flaunt. There was nothing in it for me. He never had the least intention of helping me with my career. It was a total con. Great shame – he was brilliant in bed – really knew what he was at.' Elly smiled ruefully.

'Well, you always did go for masterful types, didn't you, even at school?'

'Much good it did me. Is a liberal nineties man less of a disappointment then?'

Nell blushed. 'Most certainly.'

'I'm so glad for you, Nellie.' Elly put out a hand and patted the knee of her jeans. 'But someone like Rob would never do for me. If I get my own way too often with a man, I begin to despise him or walk all over him, or both. Either way it's a disaster. Let's face it – I *am* a disaster with men!'

'No, you're not. You're sometimes not a very good chooser, that's all.'

'Let's go to a pub for lunch,' Elly suggested. 'Preferably somewhere high up with good reception for my mobile. It's useless trying to call the boys in this valley. It's like being inside a railway tunnel.'

'You must miss them.'

'Oh Nell . . .' Elly collapsed into tears. 'What on earth am I doing here?'

Anna made up her double bed with great care, using the best duvet cover and matching pillowcases. She put coasters on the bedside tables so that any glasses wouldn't leave ugly rings on the polished wood if they were to be put down too sloppily in the heat of the moment. She tried to think of all the places she didn't normally clean, that he might notice – under the loo seat, that high shelf in the kitchen, where else? She was pretty confident he'd be too busy to be critical, but she didn't want to take any risks.

She wondered how much sex it was going to take to seal their relationship once and for all. She would have to be careful not to let her reluctance show; she'd so nearly lost him altogether at Christmas, and to be without him was unthinkable . . .

He'd rung the day after Boxing Day to apologise. 'I'm sorry,' he'd said. 'Just a quickie to say I haven't been myself lately.'

'Of course not.' Anna said, managing heroically to conceal her accumulated rage, disappointment and pique. 'I quite understand.'

'Bless you,' Paul said. 'I knew you would. Look, love, I've still got to take the boys skiing, but we'll meet soon, I promise. Love you. 'Bye.'

Soon? It was now mid-February! But at least he is coming, Anna thought, and for the whole half-term week too. So if I want him, then I've got to forget how angry I sometimes feel, and just grab him while the going's good. And I do want him. I need a man to belong to me. It may well be trendy to be twenty-five and unattached, but then I never was a slave to fashion.

'Aaaaaah,' Paul said when he finally arrived, sinking

into her sofa. 'It's so good to be here. I am totally knackered.'

'That's no good,' Anna said. 'I need you to be on full power. We've got a lot of talking to do.'

'Cup of tea,' Paul said, 'then I'll be fine.' Anna went to make a pot, and put out some biscuits on a plate as well.

'So,' she said, handing him a full cup. 'What's happening then?'

'Where do I start?' He opened his hands expressively.

'The divorce?'

'Well, there is that, yes, but it's not what's occupying my mind at the moment.'

'So what is?'

Paul sighed deeply. 'I've had enough of being a head teacher. I simply can't recruit any decent staff, let alone keep them. Anyone who's any good isn't going to subject themselves to the bloody awful conditions and the pitiful pay. Absolutely no one with a grain of sense would want to teach these days.'

'I do,' Anna said. Had he forgotten that?

'Well, of course there are shining exceptions,' Paul said hastily, 'but in general it's a thankless task. I nearly got beaten up by a bloody parent last week! No, I've had enough.'

'But, what will you do?'

'Take early retirement.'

'But Ermintrude will take half your money when you divorce, won't she? How will you manage?'

'Oh, I'm not sinking into pipe and slippers quite yet. I've got some part-time consultancy work lined up, and there's always Uncle Tozer's heirlooms. Anyway, Elly has some money of her own.'

'Oh I see.' Anna was reassured. 'So,' she said, settling back into the sofa and looking at him expectantly, 'what shall we do for one whole glorious week? I thought we could spend some of it at the houseboat. We could get the stove going, and it would be really cozy.'

'Sorry,' Paul said. 'I've just dropped the boys off there.'

'Why? What d'you mean?'

'Elly's living there. I think she's off her trolley, but there you are. If she wants to freeze to death, I suppose it's up to her. I only hope the boys will be warm enough. I've sent their warmest clothe –'

'But it's *our* special love-nest houseboat!' Anna interrupted furiously. 'She's no *right* –'

'I'm afraid there's one difficult concept you are going to have to grasp at the outset, my darling,' Paul said firmly, 'if this week is going to be a success.'

'And what's that?'

'It's this: Elly – for the moment at least – is still my wife, and the mother of my children and therefore has more "rights" than you do. Sorry.'

Land Rover doors banged and raised voices sounded outside the cottage, and Nell, within it, experienced a guilty sinking feeling. They had arrived. I must remember, she thought, they're only *children*. It's not their fault.

Josh came in first, kicking the door as usual and bursting into the kitchen. Nell saw that his mother still hadn't bothered to get his hair cut.

'Hello, Josh,' she said. No answer. Rob came in then with Rosie, who was clearly having a sulk, judging by the way her bottom lip was sticking out.

'How old are you?' Josh suddenly demanded of Nell.

'Thirty-two,' she smiled at him.

'My mummy's thirty-*four*, so she's older than you,' he said triumphantly. 'So there!'

Nell glanced across at Rob, hoping for an amused raising of the eyebrows but he was busy trying to jolly Rosie out of her sulk.

'Come on, pudding, it's not that bad.'

'Is!' Rosie said.

'Hello, Rosie?' Nell said experimentally.

'Go 'way,' Rosie shouted. 'Talking to my daddy, not you.'

Oh wonderful, Nell thought. I apologise for existing. She turned her attention to the stove where lunch was nearly ready.

'What is it?' Josh asked.

'Spaghetti bolognese.'

'Oh no,' he complained, 'we had that yesterday.'

Nell turned to him with a determined smile. 'I'm so sorry. My telepathy line must be on the blink.' Josh stared back at her, uncomprehendingly scornful. God! Nell thought turning away, does it have to be such hard work? She hoiked out a length of spaghetti to test whether it was done, and glanced round, chewing. It was ready, but Rob was putting his boots on. 'Don't disappear,' she said. 'I'm dishing up.'

'Just getting some firewood in,' Rob said easily. 'Won't be a moment.'

'Me too,' Rosie said at once.

'Sorry poppet,' Rob said. 'No wellies today, remember? And it's muddy by the woodshed.'

'Oh no! Why?' Nell asked, vexed that Cassie's deliberate withholding of boots would mean no possibility of good walks for any of them that week.

'Rosie's not very well,' Rob explained as he went out of the back door. 'There's the usual pink stuff she's got to take. I've left it in the 'Rover. Cassie wants her to stay indoors and keep out of the cold.' Rosie swung her legs, looking smug.

She's always 'ill', Nell thought. What nonsense. She looks perfectly all right to me. It's not that cold, anyway, and I'm sure fresh air would perk her up no end. She's a tough little person, not a hot-house flower.

Nell wondered as she drained the spaghetti, whether pink medicine was Cassie's substitute for love. Then Rob came in with an armful of logs just as she was carrying the hot bowl of bolognese sauce to the table and she had to wait until he was out of the way before she could set it down on the mat. She managed it just in time, before the heat penetrated the tired oven glove and burnt her fingers. Josh was already sitting in his place.

'Yuk,' he said, peering suspiciously at the sauce.

'Yuk nothing! Come on, Rosie.'

'Daddy isn't thitting down.'

'Well, he's just about to, aren't you, Rob?'

'Just washing my hands. Have you two washed yours?'

'No.'

Nell divided up the spaghetti as fairly as she could on to four dinner plates, while the two children argued over who should have the soap first. Then they squabbled over who had the most food, and then who had been the illest the week before.

'The most ill,' Rob corrected them. 'Not the illest.' Nell wondered why anyone would want to be more ill than the next person. There must surely be better ways of getting attention.

Then Josh began singing, to the tune of 'Frère Jacques', a round he had learnt at school:

'Life is but a, Life is but a,' he began.

'Collyfl –' Rosie joined in lustily.

'No!' interrupted Josh irritably. 'That's *wrong*! You've gone and spoilt it. Now I'll have to start all over again. So shut up this time.' He continued:

> 'Life is but a,
> Life is but a,
> Melancholy flower,
> Melancholy flower,
> Life is but a melon,
> Life is but a melon,
> Cauliflower! Cauliflower!'

'I thang that!' Rosie retorted.

'No you didn't!'

'Yeth I –'

'That's enough,' Nell said. 'Stop it.'

'*Life is but a* . . .' Josh began again.

'Josh,' Rob said mildly, 'no singing at mealtimes, right?'

'Thang that, thang that, thang that . . .' Rosie muttered provocatively.

'That means you too, Rosie,' Nell said. She felt her tummy muscles tighten involuntarily. She had never experienced sibling rivalry herself, and so felt ill-equipped to deal with it. Rob was little help. He barely seemed to notice, and was now bending over his plate and concentrating on enjoying his lunch. At one point he botched his aim and ended up with only part of a forkful of spaghetti in his mouth. Then he glanced across at her with a rueful expression, and bit off the trailing ends so that they fell back messily on to his plate. Nell realised it was the first time he had actually caught her eye since he had brought the children home for the week.

'Ooooh, Dad!' Rosie said reprovingly.

'I never bite mine,' Josh said virtuously. 'I hoover them. Watch!' He sucked mightily, so the strands of spaghetti disappeared upwards at speed and were whipped out of sight through rosebud lips, flicking gobbets of sauce far and wide.

'Careful!' Nell warned him. She wondered whether real parents ever found children as *boring* as she did . . . 'Look!' she said, hoping to distract them. 'There's the hummingbird robin again.' She pointed to the bird table outside, where a robin was hovering furiously below a bell full of fat, darting up from time to time to snatch a beakful. 'Robins don't usually do that,' she explained. 'This one seems to have invented a completely new trick.'

'P'raps he caught it off a hummingbird?' Josh said. He grinned, displaying newly gappy teeth.

'No, we don't get them here. They only live in the tropics.'

'But you said it was one?'

'Tropicth, hopicth, bopicth, mopicth, thopicth . . .' Rosie began.

'*Shut up!*' Josh hissed at her.

Nell sighed. 'Ice cream for pud?' she suggested.

'Nell?' Rosie asked. 'Will you thtay here for ever and ever?'

'But, how long are they staying?' Anna demanded. 'I thought we were having the whole week together.'

'Be reasonable, darling,' Paul said. 'I'll only be gone for a few hours. I can't just abandon my boys, can I? Especially when their mother is in such an emotional state.'

'So why isn't she hamming it up in London with her flashy actor? Couldn't he cope with children? That type never can – too selfish.'

'Oh, didn't I tell you?' Paul said casually. 'That's all off.'

'What?'

'I knew it wouldn't last.' Paul looked pleased with himself.

'But . . . you are going to . . .?'

'Oh, we're still getting divorced, yes.'

'But . . . doesn't she want you back?'

'Very probably, but it's too late now.'

'I'd better go and see her,' Anna said, making up her mind. 'We need to talk.'

'Absolutely not!' Paul said. 'Don't interfere, Anna. This is nothing to do with you. I'm serious, right?'

'Ooooh, isn't he masterful!' Anna mocked, high camp.

'I know,' Paul smiled, 'I'm so handsome when I'm angry.'

Anna put both arms around his neck. 'Kiss me goodbye, then. Mmm.'

Paul broke away from her with some difficulty. 'Nice try,' he said, kissing her forehead. 'I'm sorely tempted, but I really do have to go.'

'I expect you were glad to get away,' Sibyl suggested the following Monday morning at ARTFUL[L].

'Too right,' Nell said. 'I've come to work for a rest.'

'It's been very difficult?'

'At times, yes. It's so disconcerting though. The children fight all the time, and they're badly behaved and negative and horrible and then, just when you're despairing of them, they come up with something lovely which completely disarms you.'

'Instinctive self-preservation,' Sibyl smiled, 'evolved over millennia so that parents stop just short of murder!'

'Survival by brinkmanship,' Nell agreed. 'It certainly works. I just wish it didn't have to be so exhausting. Actually, I wish I was more like Elly. She manages Will and Sam almost effortlessly, it seems to me.'

'Well, of course up to now they've had a much more stable upbringing,' Sibyl said soberly. 'To tell you the truth, I'm a bit worried about Elly.' She stopped to serve a customer with some sheets of mounting board, and to give advice about getting oval frames with bevelled edges cut in them.

'I'm worried too,' Nell said, when there was an opportunity. 'She's always been impulsive, but now she seems slightly . . .'

'Hysterical?'

'Yes, that's it. What d'you think she'll do?'

'I doubt whether she'll stay long at the houseboat after half term.'

'Me neither. No, what I really meant was, what will she do for a job?'

'Oh, I expect she'll be all right,' Sibyl said, pushing a wisp of hair back, 'in the long run. She's had crises before.

She's very resourceful, after all. And how about you, Nell? Will you be OK?'

'Me?' Nell asked, pulling herself together. 'Heavens, yes. Life couldn't be better for me now I've got Rob. We just seem to belong together – it's amazing. You know, I really do believe I've fallen on my feet this time.'

Chapter Eighteen

Josh stood upright amongst the groceries in the super-market trolley and held out his hand for the change.

'Me too. Me too!' Rosie demanded, twisting round from her position in the baby seat.

The checkout lady smiled, and handed them half each. 'There you go,' she said. 'Now you can give it to your mummy and she can put it in her purse.' Nell held out her hand, smiling too.

'*She's* not my mummy,' Josh said loudly. 'She's just one of daddy's friends.' Nell looked quickly away.

'Come on,' Rob said, 'let's have it – and yours, Rosie – and stop jiggling about, Josh. You'll break the eggs.' He pushed the trolley out of the aisle towards the exit. Nell followed feeling foolishly that the checkout lady must be following her every movement with a knowing look. She wanted Rob to reprimand Josh on her behalf, but the rational part of her thought: What for? You can't expect tact from a six-year-old.

She remembered her grandmother always used to say, *Who's she? The cat's mother?* in such circumstances, and Nell remembered being quelled by it, but had to admit that in Josh's case it was unlikely to work. She made a face at the thought, and caught up with Rob as they emerged into the car park. He didn't seem to have noticed her discomfiture.

'Right,' he said, 'we'll just load this little lot, and then it's off to the houseboat for lunch with Will and Sam and Elly.'

'When are we going home?' Josh asked.

'After lunch.'

'No, I mean real home, to Mum's?'

'Tomorrow evening.'

'Why can't we go today?'

Yes, please! Nell pleaded silently.

'Your mum might be away. I don't know.'

'Well, you could phone her.'

'We'll see,' Rob said. 'Come on, all aboard the *Skylark*. Let's get you strapped in, Rosie.'

They drove the ten miles from Boxcombe in relative peace. Rosie even nodded off briefly. Nell wanted to talk to Rob about Elly's problems, but couldn't because of Josh's alert presence. When the children are with us, she thought, I feel as though my life is on hold. I'm not myself. I'm a sort of pretend 'responsible adult'; acting a part. I suppose I'll get used to it.

They turned downhill through the Thrushton Hall parkland, through the open gate at the bottom, and bumped over the high stone bridge at the top of the estuary. The tide was well out, and the smell of stranded debris and exposed weed was heavy on the cold air.

'Look,' Nell said without thinking, 'you could do a mud walk from here all the way to Eely Isle.'

'Ooooh, could we?' Josh looked enthusiastic for the first time that week.

'No, I didn't mean it literally,' Nell said, cross with herself.

'Just a figure of speech,' Rob explained. 'Come on.'

'But you said we could.'

'Come *on*.'

'But why can't we ever do what *I* want?'

That's rich, Nell thought, since that's exactly what Rob's been doing with you all week!

On the boat and with other people in charge, Nell began to relax. Elly's boys were sensible enough, and a calming influence on Rob's two. Will organised Josh and

Sam into a game at the far end of the cabin, and Rob sat at the table with Rosie, drawing pictures. Nell joined Elly in the small galley, glad of the opportunity to talk to another adult without interruption.

'How's it going?' Elly asked, making sandwiches.

Nell screwed up her face. 'It's hard work, I have to say, and it's not very rewarding either.'

'They're basically nice kids though?'

'Yes, of course.' Loyalty to Rob demanded this.

'How are the sleeping arrangements?'

'Oh, why not stop prevaricating, and get straight to the point?' Nell gave her an old-fashioned look.

'OK, are you going to try for a baby?' Elly grinned.

'For God's sake!' Nell protested. 'A child is the last thing I want just at the moment.' Elly raised her eyebrows. 'If you must know,' Nell said, 'I'm on the pill again, but we've gone back to separate beds whilst the children are with us.'

'Why? They have to know sooner or later.'

'Yes, but if they know, then so will Cassie.'

'Does that matter?'

'Oh, it would just be another stick for her to beat Rob with. But it's actually more than that. Everything we do gets relayed back to her, and I really don't want her to know anything at all about our life together. You can't believe how undermining such a lack of privacy is.'

'But she must suspect anyway.'

'That's fine. It's not the same as *knowing*.' Nell sensed that Elly didn't understand what she meant. She didn't know anyone who did, and it was a very isolating feeling. 'Anyway, how are you coping?' she asked.

'I'm fine when the boys are here, and desperate when they're not. But I'm hoping to be able to hang on to the London house now. It seems that Uncle Tozer's treasures were worth more than we'd thought.'

'That's good. But where will Paul go?'

'He can go and live with his tart for all I care! What sort of a house does she have?'

'I think it's a flat, but I've never been there. We only meet at swimming.'

'Do you still?'

'Not since before Christmas. I wouldn't know what to say to her now.'

'Oh, that's a shame. I was hoping you'd be able to keep me up to speed on what's going on.'

'Well, I was intending to swim again next week . . .' Nell said doubtfully.

'Good! You can pump her for information for me.'

'She probably won't speak at all. She knows you and I are close friends now.'

'Well, if she does, you can mislead her accidentally on purpose, can't you?' Elly grinned wickedly. 'I do like a good intrigue.'

'Mmm . . . This soup seems to be boiling. Shall I turn it down?'

At lunch, Nell saw that Will and Sam's table manners were noticeably better than Josh and Rosie's, and wondered why Cassie – or Rob for that matter – hadn't taught them how to behave properly.

'In the summer,' Will said, cutting an apple into quarters and removing the core with some dexterity, 'we eat lunch on deck and throw these bits in the river.'

'Biodegradable,' Elly murmured.

'We can do that now,' Josh said eagerly.

'Too cold today,' Rob said.

'And the tide's out,' Sam put in.

'Looks messy,' Elly explained.

'This mud underneath us is hundreds of metres deep,' Sam announced proudly.

'No it isn't,' Will corrected him. 'It's just deep enough to drown you and fill all your lungs up with thick brown goo, so you choke to de –'

'Stop it, Will!' Elly protested good-humouredly. 'We don't want to know. We're trying to eat our lunch.'

The thought made Nell shiver involuntarily, and wonder whether in fact this was a safe place for children at all.

After lunch they played snap with Rosie and Rob working together, and fierce competition between Elly and Will. The stove pumped out heat, the windows steamed up, the daylight began to fade early, and Nell – released from responsibility – began to enjoy herself and wonder why she had been so up-tight before.

Rob looked at his watch. 'Well,' he said, 'I suppose we'd best be going home. Can we help with the washing-up first?'

'No, no,' Elly said automatically. 'That's all right. What d'you want, Josh?' He had pushed past her into the galley.

'These,' he said, grabbing something.

'Come on then,' Nell said reluctantly. 'Coats on, and let's be off.'

Josh struggled into his, keeping one fist tightly closed and trying to stuff it like that down the arm of his anorak. It finally went with a rush, and Nell zipped him up. Rob did Rosie, and the four of them emerged on to the deck, their breath condensing in clouds in the frosty air. Josh made a sudden dive for the front of the boat, running as fast as he could away from the gangplank towards the bows.

Nell was gripped by a sudden horror. '*Josh!*' she screamed, 'Stop!'

'Oh, Cassie, don't be so melodramatic,' Rob muttered, embarrassed.

Josh skidded to a halt by the bow rail, and threw a handful of apple peelings overboard. Then he came back, looking pleased with himself. Nell put her hand to her mouth, breathing hard.

Elly came up on deck looking startled. 'What's up?'

Nell shook her head. Rob said nothing.

'Well, thanks for coming,' Elly said cheerfully. 'We enjoyed having you, didn't we, boys?'

'Yeah,' Will said, putting his head out briefly.

'Not!' said Sam cheekily from below.

Both Josh and Rosie fell asleep on the way back to the cottage, but Nell and Rob drove in silence, Nell containing herself with difficulty until much later that evening, when the children had gone to bed and were reliably dead to the world. Then she confronted him.

'You called me Cassie!'

'I did? When?'

'On the houseboat, when Josh ran –'

'Oh, then. Well, it was probably because you were behaving like her.'

'What d'you mean?' Nell was outraged.

'Being absurdly overprotective. There was no need to shout at him like that, was there? He was perfectly safe.'

'Gav!' Mic shouted. 'C'mon, hurry up in there or we'll be late down the doctor's.'

She looked out of the window of her new flat to check on the weather. No one in the pedestrian precinct below had umbrellas up, so it wasn't raining. Mic's eyes lingered on the scene below her, taking in Woolworth's, the building society, the burger bar and W. H. Smith. It was all so gobsmackingly handy! She couldn't get over it. From the launderette below them to the papershop (for fags) two doors up, she had everything she could possibly want within hobbling distance. I can stay here till I'm ninety and totally crippled, she thought, and I'll still be able to manage on my own.

'Gavin?'

She was becoming accustomed to the rhythm of the week in this new habitat. Yesterday, being Sunday, was pretty quiet, but today the Monday morning workers had all arrived and a smattering of shoppers were already wandering up and down. As she watched, the regular beggar plus mongrel walked up to his usual pitch, put down his dog blanket and collecting plate and began to play his guitar and sing. He wasn't half bad, but he only knew five or six songs, so it could get on your nerves a bit. Still, Mic thought benevolently, it's not a problem. Look at me – I've got a two-bedroom flat all to myself, with no one telling me what to do or where to go!

She went and beat on the bathroom door, smiling to herself at her good fortune. 'Gav! What you doin' in there?'

'I'm comin'.' The door opened and Gavin emerged reluctantly. 'Why do we 'ave ter go?'

' 'Cos we do.' She gave him a hug and helped him on with his coat.

As they began to walk along the street to the surgery, Mic felt buoyant with hope. At last she was beholden to nobody. She didn't have much to live on, but there was a good charity shop for clothes just round the corner, and the chip shop in the next street was ever so cheap. And best of all, her boy was much happier. They'd survive. In a sudden fit of generosity she gave Gavin ten pence.

'Go on,' she said. 'Give it to 'im, poor sod. Least we're not that bad off. Don't touch 'is dog, mind. Could be dodgy.'

Cassie sat in the waiting room with Rosie uncomfortably on her knee. 'Don't fidget,' she said. There was no denying she had enjoyed her week without the children. She'd *needed* it. But now she felt resentfully that Rob and his bit-on-the-side had unfairly stolen a march on her. Both children were going on and on about what they did at the cottage, what they'd eaten and who they'd seen, but this morning was the last straw. Josh, fresh from a good night's sleep had yawned and smiled . . . and called her 'Nell'! Cassie wasn't having that. If the woman thought she could steal her children . . . well . . . quite clearly a different strategy was called for.

Cassie examined the pictures on the surgery walls with ill-disguised contempt. She suppressed a yawn. People came and went, or sat and coughed unhygienically. She didn't know any of them. She read the headlines on the noticeboard again, and looked at the clock one more time. *Come on!*

Rosie suddenly struggled off her lap and began running towards the door, crying, 'Mic!'

'Well, if it isn't my Rosie!' Mic picked her up and kissed her soundly on both cheeks. 'How you doin' then?' She glanced across at Cassie. 'Hi.'

'Good morning,' Cassie said without enthusiasm.

Rosie dragged Mic and Gavin over to chairs next to where she and Cassie were sitting.

'We've gotta stop meetin' like this,' Mic observed cheerfully. Cassie didn't reply. 'Everyfink awl right?' Mic enquired.

'Well, clearly not, or we wouldn't be here,' Cassie said. 'Rosie's chest is bad again.'

'Poor little old you,' Mic tickled the child under her arms, making her burst into delighted giggles. 'Missed you,' Mic said to her.

In spite of herself Cassie was intrigued to discover why Mic was so jaunty. 'And you?' she asked.

'Oh, we're great, fanks. Gav's still 'avin' trouble wif 'is ear, aren't you, love? But 'part from that, we're bofe good, ain't we?' She ruffled her son's hair and turned back, smiling, to Cassie.

The grin was a challenge which Cassie couldn't ignore. 'We're fine too,' she said. 'And having the extra space is a tremendous help.'

'Couldn't agree more,' Mic said. 'It's great havin' a place to yerself, in't it?'

'Oh,' Cassie was considerably taken aback. 'You found somewhere to live, then?'

'Yeah, no sweat. We've got a flat all of our own, ain't we, Gav? Kitchen, barfroom, lounge, the lot.'

'But I understand the Council had a long waiting list?'

'Well, we did wait more'n a year, didn't we? An' then one come up just when we was needin' it. Couldn't be better!'

'That was handy.' Cassie thought: Typical! People like her always fall on their feet – there's no justice in this life. Then she thought: Wait a moment . . . 'So,' she enquired, 'are you doing child-minding now?'

'I've applied again, yeah. Looks like I'll get me licence this time an' all.'

'So Rosie could come and spend some time with you?'

'Yeth!' Rosie said, climbing on to Mic's knee.

'Love to 'ave 'er,' Mic said, squeezing her. 'Cost you, though!'

'Well, naturally I'd pay the going rate,' Cassie said stiffly, but she was thinking: Wonderful! Well that settles that!

Nell ventured out of her changing cubicle to the pool-side showers, feeling uneasy. There was no sign of Anna yet, but she was worried as to what she would say when she did turn up. She had decided she wouldn't be rude to her, but she couldn't be unduly friendly either.

'Nell!' Anna's voice behind her. 'Long time no see!' She was smiling at her as though nothing had happened.

'Oh,' Nell said, 'hello.'

'I was beginning to think you'd given up swimming altogether.'

'No.'

'So what's the news?' She climbed down the ladder into the water, and Nell followed her. 'Tell you what, let's do our usual ten lengths first before we catch up with each other.'

'Fine,' Nell said, launching herself into a leisurely breaststroke. She was out of practice; her arms began to ache after only five lengths, but she kept going. Whatever Anna says or does, she thought, I'm not giving up swimming. I need the exercise. She wondered why she was being so friendly and felt suspicious. What did she want? She swam on, nodding and smiling to the other regulars as she passed each one, and at the end of ten lengths Anna was standing at the shallow end, waiting for her.

'How's things?'

'Fine,' Nell said. 'You?'

'I've just been spending a week with the B – with Paul,' Anna said happily. 'We've had a wonderful time – with notable exceptions.'

'Oh?'

'Yes,' Anna said, 'he had to keep on visiting his boys. They're at the houseboat with their mother, but I expect you know that.'

'Yes.'

'I don't know about you, but I'm finding it really difficult coping with the reality of his kids. Somehow they're an invasion even when they aren't there. And the lack of privacy is a nightmare, isn't it?'

'Certainly is,' Nell reluctantly agreed.

'I mean, don't get me wrong,' Anna said, 'they're nice enough little boys. I just wish they didn't exist. Awful of me, isn't it?'

'But,' Nell began, 'I would have thought you of all people would understand – having a stepmother yourself, I mean.'

'God!' Anna exclaimed. 'What are you saying? I'm never going to be a *stepmother* to them. I've told Paul that right from the start. It's part of our deal.'

'So you managed to "get" him then?' Nell was quite shocked by her own acidity.

'Not at all,' Anna seemed surprised. 'He practically ran into my arms.' She looked shrewdly at Nell. 'Oh, you're probably thinking about the last conversation we had. Yes?'

'Something like that.'

'But you do realise I never meant it? I was just upset at the time; talking nonsense. It was just a bit of luck for me that his wife went off with that actor. But there you go, lose some, win some.'

'Or in your case win some, then win some more.'

'Mmm,' Anna said mockingly. 'We're a bit sharp today, aren't we?'

'Well, what do you expect?'

'Look, Nell, I know you're that woman's best friend, but have I hurt her? Have I hell! She's happier without Paul and I'm happier with him, so what's the problem? We're all winners.'

'Maybe.'

'And you and I are both involved with men who've got children, so we've even more in common these days. We should support each other.'

Nell took a breath. 'It's like this, Anna. I can't pretend to be friends with you, but I'm not going to be an enemy either. So let's just keep it neutral, shall we?'

'Fine,' Anna said lightly, 'but I think you'll find I could be very supportive. There aren't many people around who are willing to acknowledge the problems people like us have.' Then she swam off doing backstroke and cutting a swathe through all the other swimmers.

People like us? Nell thought, insulted. I'm not like you at all. Even our circumstances aren't alike. But later, driving to work, she went over the conversation in her head and acknowledged there were a few (a very few) similarities.

'Anna's acting as though everything's hunky-dory,' Nell reported to Sibyl when she arrived at ARTFUL[L].

'Of course she is.'

'Why, of course?'

'Because she probably needs some solidarity.'

'How do you mean?'

'Someone to moan to, who really understands. A sort of second wives' club?'

Nell laughed. 'No, you're way off beam. Anna's never going to marry Paul, and Rob and I probably won't marry either.'

'Don't you want to?' Sibyl looked surprised.

'Oh, it's not that,' Nell said. 'I've just got this niggling feeling that he'll never ask.'

Chapter Nineteen

Nell opened the bedroom curtains and surprised a roebuck outside in her garden, in the act of thrashing her magnolia with its head to clean its newly grown horns. She went to the window to wave her arms in protest but it was already aware of her; neck upright, staring straight towards her with pricked ears and, she noticed, a strip of velvet hanging off one of its points. Then it ran away in a series of vertical leaps like an antelope, melting through her garden hedge as though it had no substance.

Oh no! Nell thought before she had time to resent its choice of shrub or appreciate its grace, I'm going to be sick again! She rushed to the bathroom and vomited into the lavatory, and then whipped round just in time and sat on the seat, wiping the strings of saliva from her mouth with scrunched-up toilet roll and reaching for her flannel to mop the sweat from her face.

'You all right?' Rob enquired from the landing. 'You seem to have been up and down all night.'

'Don't come in,' Nell said hastily, 'the smell's terrible.'

'Got to you at both ends, eh?'

'And how,' Nell agreed. 'I feel like death.'

'Poor you. What can have caused it, d'you know?'

'Might have been that noodle thing I bought for lunch yesterday. It's something I *never* do.'

'And now you remember why.' He made sympathetic noises. Nell groaned. 'You'd better stay in bed,' Rob said kindly. 'I'll phone Sibyl. You'll just have to drink lots of fluids and hope it soon passes.'

'I daren't leave the loo,' Nell complained. 'Every time I

think it's stopped, I explode again!'

'I'll get you a drink of water,' Rob said, making for the basin.

'No!' Nell cried, 'don't come in. You'll be sick too!'

'I doubt that very much,' Rob said calmly. 'I've dealt with much worse with my children. Here.' He handed her a glass of water and Nell drank it. It tasted curiously sweet after the sour acidity of the vomit. Rob stroked her hair back off her forehead as though she were a favourite dog, and she was touched in spite of her embarrassment. If he can cope with this without going off me, she thought, then I reckon I'm lucky.

'I wouldn't mind a clean nightie,' she said. 'Could you . . . ?'

Rob fetched one from the airing cupboard and helped her to take the old one off, pulling it up over her head. Nell shivered and held her arms up to receive the new one.

'You could do with a warm bath,' Rob suggested.

'I daren't,' she said. 'It might happen again. You go on downstairs. I'll be OK soon. And thanks.'

'Sure?'

'Yes, really.'

Then after a while when she felt confident enough to move, she wobbled back to bed taking a sick bowl to keep beside her, just in case. Once there, she slept a lot and drank water whenever she could, if only to prevent the pain of dry retching. Rob was unexpectedly solicitous, coming home for lunch to make sure she was all right and bringing her some Dioralyte to compensate for dehydration. In the evening he was home promptly with a bottle of lemon barley water and a new box of tissues. She lay there feeling weak but increasingly content. It was a long time since she had been looked after by anyone, and never before by Rob.

Outside the sky was a cold clear blue. Nell could see a

223

pair of buzzards high-circling above the cottage and hear a wren singing lustily. It was nearly the end of March and officially spring. Only a year ago, Nell thought, there was that unsatisfactory party on the houseboat. I didn't have Rob then. I even thought I'd lost his cottage too. Life may not be perfect sometimes, but it's a damn sight better than it was.

The phone rang, and she let Rob answer it downstairs. His tone of voice sounded agitated and then angry. The Mad Cow, Nell thought sinkingly. Now what?

'Hello?' Rob said, holding the phone between jaw and shoulder as he tightened the top of a hot-water bottle for Nell.

'It's me,' Cassie said wearily. 'Bad news.'

'What?' Rob could hear his voice sharpen with apprehension.

'I've been having such a terrible time, you wouldn't believe. Josh is in hospital.'

'Josh? Why?' Rob's heart beat uncomfortably.

'Well, they've done tests for meningitis. I can't tell you how frightening it was, waiting. I've been frantic. I had to wait hour –'

'So has he got it or not?' Rob interrupted, dropping the bottle, and gripping the receiver fiercely as if it were Cassie's neck.

'They don't know what it is. I don't think they have a clue what they're doing. They keep changing their minds. First meningitis, then glandular fever. God knows what they'll come up with next.'

'But is he all right?'

'Well, he wouldn't be in hospital if he wasn't pretty poorly, would he? These last three days have been a nightmare. You have no idea!'

'But . . . when did this begin?'

'Oh, we came in on Thursday. I've had to stay here the

whole time. I haven't even been able to get a change of clo –'

'*Thursday?* But, where's Rosie?'

'Oh, she's all right. Don't you worry.'

'*Don't worry?* Why the hell didn't you tell me this at once?'

'I'm not going to speak to you at all if you're going to bully me,' Cassie said in a tiny voice. 'You should be more considerate after all I've been through.'

'Sod that!' Rob cried furiously. 'You've no right . . .' He stopped himself with difficulty. 'Where is he? I want to see him.'

'Got to go,' Cassie said. 'The money's running . . .' The line went dead.

Rob dialled 192 for Boxcombe Hospital's number, and finally got through to the ward and asked how Joshua Hayhoe was.

'I'm his father,' he said. 'I've only just heard.'

'Josh is fine,' a cheerful nurse said, 'much better. I expect he'll be fit to go home in a day or so.'

'So, is it glandular fever?'

'Oh no, just acute tonsillitis. He does love his ice cream, doesn't he?'

'I'll come in and see him,' Rob decided.

'That's nice. We'll see you soon, then.'

Rob put the receiver down with a flood of relief. 'Bitch!' he said. Then he went upstairs to tell Nell.

'Where've you been?' Anna asked. 'I haven't seen you for over a week.'

'I had sickness and diarrhoea,' Nell said. 'So coming swimming wouldn't have been very public-spirited of me.'

'Oh, you got it too, did you? Apparently there's a tummy bug going round Boxcombe, but luckily I haven't caught it yet. Did Rob look after you?' She leant against the side of the swimming pool and pushed the hair out of her eyes.

'Yes, he did,' Nell paused beside her. 'Well, at first, that is.'

'Then he got fed up with it?'

'Oh, no. Then Josh was in hospital, so he had to keep going to see him.'

'Oh, and of course if it's a contest, the kids always come first?'

'Well, naturally.' Nell hadn't expected anything else, but felt obliged to defend him. 'Rob was very upset. The Mad Cow's been treating him abominably. She didn't even tell him Josh was ill, and then when he wanted Rosie to come and stay with us, she told him she was at Mic's but wouldn't give him Mic's new address. I don't understand how she can be like that.'

'Oh I do.' Anna laughed shortly. 'They just want to get their own back on us, any way they can.'

In your situation, yes, Nell thought. I can well understand that. But we've got two kinds of quasi-stepmother here, haven't we – one like you, who's stolen someone else's husband: and the other like me, who's simply stepped in to pick up the pieces. The two cases are not comparable. But she didn't point this out to Anna.

'Cassie seems to want to mess us about as much as possible,' she said instead. 'She's got some crazy idea that I'm trying to suborn her children and take her place as their mother, when in fact nothing could be further from my mind! The upshot is that she won't let them stay overnight at the cottage now, so Rob has to keep taking them home and collecting them again next morning. It's a ridiculous waste of time and energy.'

'Well, at least you get rid of them.'

'Yes, but it's so disruptive. They get no chance to settle in and adapt to us and to our different ways of doing things.'

'I expect that's the idea. Have you got to have them at Easter?'

'For a week, yes.'

'Paul's having his too, on the houseboat after he's been with me for a week on our own – bliss! – Erm . . . Elly's probably told you she's going back to London for a fortnight.'

Nell nodded.

'It's like bloody musical chairs. She's not bad-looking, is she?'

'You've met Elly?'

'Only in passing when Paul was collecting the boys. Not for long enough to make an informed judgment.' Anna pushed her hair back again, and held her hands on her head for a while. It looked like a deliberate gesture, to Nell, and then she realised why. On the third finger of her left hand was a thin gold wedding ring. Nell frowned.

'Good, isn't it?' Anna said, smiling proudly and holding her hand out for Nell to examine.

'Did Paul buy it for you?'

'Yes, we went and chose it together. And then I simply had to wear it straight away. Didn't see any point in waiting.'

'But he isn't divorced yet?'

'No, but as soon as he is, we're getting married. He proposed last week. That's why I was so impatient to see you.'

'But I thought . . .' Nell hesitated. 'Why?'

'He wants to make sure of me,' Anna said contentedly. 'He's always afraid I'll go off with someone my own age. D'you know what he said?'

'What?'

'That I'm the sexiest woman he's ever had!'

'Congratulations,' Nell said mechanically.

'And he says he's fed up with urban squalor, so he's

going to move permanently to the country and live half his life on *Polypeptide*. He even talks of sailing round the world!'

'But what about you?'

'Oh, I'll go too, of course. It'll be the trip of a lifetime.'

'No, I mean, what do you think about getting married? I thought you were dead against it.'

'Whatever gave you that idea? I think it's great.'

'But I thought you said . . .'

'It's like this,' Anna explained, 'I've been discovering recently that I really need the status of marriage. If it were just him and me on our own, it would be fine the way it is, but the moment his boys are around, I seem to be demoted into being a kind of optional extra; you know what I mean – dependent upon their every whim. But when I'm his *wife* I'll have equal call on him, won't I, maybe even priority?'

'Well, I doubt that . . .' Nell began, but found she couldn't go on. She felt sick, not food-poisoning sort of sick, but queasy and a little faint.

'What's the matter?' Anna asked. 'You look rather pale.'

'I'm OK,' Nell said. 'It's time I got out though.'

But as she stood under a warm shower shampooing her hair, she still felt odd, and wondered if this was perhaps what was meant by the phrase 'sick with jealousy'.

'I don't understand Josh,' Nell confided to Elly over the phone on 10th April. 'We sang "Happy Birthday" to him and he got all embarrassed and cross as though we'd been getting at him or calling him names!'

'Poor child,' Elly said. 'He must be very insecure.'

'And he keeps on twitching his shoulders about. I don't think he even realises he's doing it.'

'Nervous tic?'

'Yes, I suppose so.'

228

'What a shame. He's obviously in a state. Have you got them for long?'

'Just this week, but days only.'

'Ah well,' Elly said, 'so it looks as though we'll both be childless again next week. We must phone regularly and console each other.'

This is silly, Nell thought uncomfortably. Elly's making me feel as though Anna of all people understands me better than she does, and she's my oldest friend! 'Mmm,' she said.

'So, what's the gossip from the pool?'

'Anna's wearing a ring,' Nell reported carefully.

'A curtain ring? A makes-your-finger-green ring, or a proper one?'

'Looked like gold to me, but it wasn't an engagement ring.' Nell wasn't sure why she said that.

'Ah well, that's all right then. One doesn't want to feel instantly replaceable, does one? Not that I really understand what Paul sees in her anyway. Tell me, Nell, what do you think is her big attraction?'

'Well, she's got nice auburn hair . . . but I gather it's mostly sex.'

'Oh that's a relief,' Elly said.

'Why?'

'I was afraid you were going to say brains!'

Nell laughed. 'You sound good,' she said. 'Is life getting better?'

'You could say so. Three things: one – both my boys have told me independently that they want to live with me, not Paul. Two – I've been promised some good freelance design work again, and three – Hat is firmly on my side; says Paul is acting just like his father did before their divorce. So I've got lots of support. I even feel quite sorry for Paul and whatshername.'

'Why?'

'Because if it's just sex it won't survive for long. I know

Paul. He'll get jaded. He's fine in short bursts, but he hasn't got the stamina. That reminds me, have I ever told you my sure-fire way of telling whether a bloke's good in bed or not – before you get there, that is?'

'No, but I sense you're about to.'

'You want to look for a good belly laugh. Even if a man is quiet and shy, if he's uninhibited when he laughs, then I guarantee he'll be a performer!'

Nell was silent. Rob didn't exactly guffaw, but she didn't think that proved anything.

'Nell? You still there?'

'Yes, sorry, I was miles away.'

'Anyway, time I went. Happy Easter and have fun with the little ones. Are you giving Josh a birthday party?'

'Not this year. He's fine, but Cassie doesn't want him exposed to any germs.' *Thank goodness!*

'Oh, that's a shame. Must go. See you in a week or so.'

'Bye,' Nell said.

'Why can't Mum and you and me and Rosie and Nell all live in the same house?' Josh asked from the back of the Land Rover as Rob was driving him and Rosie to Bottom Cottage on the third morning of the Easter holiday. 'It'd save all this travelling.'

Rob smiled wryly. 'I don't think that would work out,' he said. 'We wouldn't all get on.'

'But Rosie and me don't get on anyway.'

'Rosie and I,' Rob corrected him.

'Yeth we do!'

'No we *don't*.'

'OK, OK,' Rob said, 'that's enough.'

'What's for lunch?' Josh asked.

'I'm not sure. Something delicious, I expect.'

'Delithuth,' Rosie said. 'Delithuth, delithuth, delithuth, del . . . OW!'

'Stop it, Josh,' Rob said, without turning his head.

'I'm bored.'

'Well, after lunch you can help me plant potatoes. We could get some peas in too.'

'An' me, an' me,' Rosie insisted.

'Yes of course, you too.'

Nell came to meet them at the door as they arrived. 'Cassie rang,' she said. She looked cross. 'She told me to give you a message – although why she couldn't have said it to your face while you were there I don't know. Apparently she's going to London for a few days. Mic isn't working over Easter, so the children are to stay here, nights and all, until the sixteenth.'

'Excellent!' Rob said. 'Good news. There you are then, Josh, less travelling at a stroke.'

Nell felt exhausted. Was it just having the children, or something more profound? She was glad the day was over, and ready for bed.

'Well, that's that,' Rob said, coming downstairs. 'They've both gone off soundly. I don't know why Cassie has such trouble; they always sleep well enough here.'

'Until six o'clock if we're lucky, yes,' Nell yawned.

'I always used to wake at crack of dawn when I was their age,' Rob said.

'Is that supposed to be encouraging?'

'Fancy a coffee?'

'No thanks. I've gone right off it for some reason. Rob?'

'Mmm?'

'Where are you sleeping tonight?'

'I don't know. I hadn't thought.'

'Will you sleep with me?'

'I thought you didn't want the children to know?'

'Well, now that your decree absolute's arrived, I've changed my mind.' It was something that Nell remembered Anna had said about status. It had touched a nerve, and now she found she wanted her relationship with Rob to be properly acknowledged. She was determined not to feel like a bit on the side.

'I don't see why not,' Rob said.

'You don't think it will upset them?'

'Why should it? I'll bribe Josh tomorrow with the promise of my grown-up bed. Then Rosie can sleep on the top bunk and they'll both be happy.'

Next morning Nell was dragged unwillingly from the depths of sleep by Josh, bouncing on their bed and calling to his father.

'Dad! *Dad!* Why are you in here? I want you to sleep in *my* room. Dad! *Dad!*' Nell looked blearily at the clock. It was only half-past five.

'Go back to bed,' she said to him. 'It's much too early.'

He ignored her and pulled the duvet off Rob, who sat up, blinking. 'What's the matter?'

'You're in the wrong bed!' Josh accused him.

'Well . . . things change,' Rob said, gathering his wits with obvious difficulty.

'But I don't want them to!'

'Look, Josh, you remember I used to sleep in the big bed with Mummy?'

'Yes.'

'Now I've decided to sleep in this bed with Nell.'

'So . . . is Nell a mummy now?'

'No,' Nell said quickly. 'Cassie is still your mum, but Daddy and I are . . . special friends.'

'Cassie and I have decided we don't want to be married to each other any more,' Rob explained. 'So we've got divorced.'

'But we'll all still look after you,' Nell put in, feeling that this was too bald a statement, and sitting up as well. 'It's not your fault at all.'

'So whose is it?' Josh looked belligerent.

'Mine and Cassie's,' Rob said. 'We're not nice to each other, in fact we make each other very unhappy, so it seems sensible to live in different places.'

'But if you sleep in her bed,' Josh said, pointing scornfully at Nell, 'and my mum has to sleep all by herself, it's not fair!'

'Cassie will probably find herself a new man soon,' Nell said consolingly.

'*No she won't!*' Josh cried passionately. He turned his back on Nell, sitting on Rob's lap. 'Why can't you sleep in my room, then Rosie can sleep with her,' he protested to his father. 'I think men ought to be together and girls ought to be somewhere else.'

'It doesn't work like that when you're grown up,' Rob explained smiling. 'Men and women like to be together.'

'Well, I don't like it.'

'I'm sorry about that, Josh. Look, it's far too early in the day to be having important conversations like this. I'll take you back to bed, yes? And we can continue it when it's proper morning.'

'Only if you'll stay with me.'

'Yes, all right.' He turned to Nell. 'See you later.'

'Right,' she said. She snuggled down again and closed her eyes, but by now she felt far too wide awake to go back to sleep. She wondered how they would pass the day, and whether it would seem as long as the previous ones. Josh would ride his new bike on the turnaround at the front of the cottage for ten minutes, if they were lucky, before demanding attention. Rosie would execute splashy paintings on the kitchen table. Maybe Rob would cut their fingernails, since Cassie had singularly failed to do so. Josh might be persuaded to draw too, but his pictures were mostly of tiny stick figures and lots of black explosions, like those of a child brought up in a war zone. Children don't seem to draw what's around them, Nell thought, but what's inside. They were making progress though. They were managing knives and forks better, and they really did seem to have grasped the no-welly-boots-upstairs rule. It does help, Nell acknowledged, to have them here for more than just a couple of days at a time . . .

She jumped. She must have dozed off in spite of herself. 'Hello, hello, hello!' Rosie was saying joyfully, clambering on top of her. 'Play the hair game!'

'Oh, Rosie . . .' Nell rubbed her eyes. The clock said seven o'clock. 'Is it that time already?'

'Yeth.' Rosie was carrying a small hand mirror and looked expectant.

'Where's Daddy?'

'Making tea with Joth. Play the hair game?'

Nell pulled herself up and sat back against the headboard. Rosie snuggled in with her back to her, sitting on top of her outstretched legs under the duvet, and holding up the mirror. Nell stroked her hair.

'Now what have we here?' she said. 'My goodness, it's a devil. Look at those horns!' She gathered Rosie's hair up into two bunches on top of her head and waggled them. Rosie giggled delightedly. 'No, I'm wrong. It's an Old English sheepdog.' She pulled the hair forward and made a long fringe covering her eyes. 'Or maybe it's a pussycat, all soft and sleek.' She smoothed the hair off Rosie's forehead and stroked her head. 'I can't hear purring.'

Rosie snorted and began blowing through her lips.

'Sounds more like a camel,' Nell teased. 'Oh yes, look, it's got a hump on top! What a strange creat –'

'Move over!' cried Josh, rushing in ahead of Rob with the tea tray. 'We're all getting in!'

They sat in a row: Nell, Rosie, Rob and Josh. Nell and Rob drank their tea very carefully, making warning noises about the necessity for sitting still.

'I'm your baby,' Rosie said to Nell.

'My pretend baby,' she agreed.

'So you have to kith me.'

'Mmmmmmwah!' Nell planted a smacker on her forehead.

234

'I want to live here all the time,' Rosie announced rapturously.

Elly telephoned Nell the following week.

'Are you all right?' Nell asked her.

'I'm missing the boys, but otherwise I'm OK. I've actually got some work this week, so that takes my mind off things. How did your Easter go?'

'Pretty well. It got better as time went on, and we all got used to each other.'

'Oh good. I thought it would.'

'And the best thing was that Rob's decree absolute has come through, so he's finally divorced.'

'Marvellous. How did you celebrate?'

'He moved back into my bed.'

'About time.' She sounded as though she was smiling.

'But then at the very end, just as they were leaving, Josh said something that really upset me,' Nell confessed. 'They were all in the Land Rover and actually driving off at the time, so I couldn't do anything about it except feel bad.'

'Oh dear. What did he say?'

'You'll laugh. It sounds so trivial now.'

'Go on.'

'He said, "Fuck off, Nell." '

'You're not being sick again, are you?' Rob asked, putting his head round the bathroom door a few mornings later. 'If I didn't know any better, I might suspect you were pregnant!'

Nell flushed the lavatory and turned to him, blotting her mouth with a ball of toilet paper. 'I can't be!' she protested. 'I haven't missed a single pill.'

'But you did have the shits, didn't you?' Rob pointed out. 'What if several of the pills went straight through you without doing their job?'

235

'But . . . can that happen?'

'I'm not sure.'

Nell put the seat down and sat heavily on it. 'Oh God!' she said. 'What if I am?'

'No problem,' Rob said cheerfully. 'After all, what's one more?'

'You mean, you wouldn't mind?'

'Not at all. I like children.'

Chapter Twenty

For the first three months of her pregnancy Nell felt tired all the time. The children visited them every weekend, and for some reason best known to herself, Cassie now decided that they should again stay overnight. Nell could have used the respite, and done without the disturbed sleep that this new regime occasioned, but didn't like to complain as Rob was so openly delighted to have them.

'I knew she'd never stick to it,' he said triumphantly. 'Too much like hard work.'

One Saturday afternoon towards the end of June he took Josh and Rosie to their school open day. Nell debated whether to go too, but fearing that Cassie would be there and not wanting a confrontation, she decided against it. Now, standing at the edge of the vegetable garden hoeing a row of peas, she felt, as ever, ambivalent. As Rob's partner maybe she should have gone with him for moral support? It was much more pleasant not to have to. But on the other hand was she, by her absence, indicating to his children that she was a person of little importance? No, she thought, I'm much better off here doing something useful. If Rob is obliged to live his other life occasionally, then I should be relaxed enough to stand back and let him get on with it.

Later, sitting on the seat under the apple tree in the shade, she drank a glass of orange juice and was grateful for the rest. The afternoon was heavy with the sweet smell of the mock orange blossom. In the evening the nicotiana she had grown from seed would scent the air as well, attracting the dusk-flying moths. Nell breathed deeply.

All too soon there was the sound of the Land Rover coming back down the hill, and she braced herself for the onslaught. But when it stopped, there were no high voices raised in argument or competition, and Nell realised with a lift of the heart that the children had not returned with him.

'What happened?' she asked, going to greet him. He looked harassed.

'You were right, Cassie was there,' he said, 'and she deliberately enticed Josh to go home with her. It was flagrant!'

'What about Rosie?'

'Oh, she was all for leaving her with me.'

'Divide and rule, eh?'

Rob snorted. 'Well, I'm not having it. If she thinks she can dump Rosie on me whenever she feels like it and hang on to Josh, then I'll more than likely end up barely seeing Josh at all. So I said it was both or neither.'

'So you got neither. Tomorrow too?'

'Yes.' He looked fed up. 'Stupid of me.'

'It might be easier having them one at a time, in fact,' Nell suggested gently.

'Very possibly. But if so, I want it agreed at the outset.' He slammed the door angrily and stumped off towards the cottage.

Nell thought, A free Sunday! and then felt guilty. These days she and Rob's best interests seemed always to be at odds with each other, just at the time when they ought to be pulling together. And now I'm three months pregnant, Nell thought. The die is cast. Soon it won't only be me who's out of step, but the baby too. What should I do?

She tried to explain her feelings in the most general terms to Elly over the phone, when Rob was out in the garden turning the compost heap.

'I don't feel comfortable with the children,' she confessed, 'even now. I suppose your own are different because they have your genes, and behave in much the same way as you do. But other people's are foreign and unpredictable. I feel I can't trust them, and it upsets me.'

'Sometimes one's own feel like that too,' Elly pointed out.

'Mine wouldn't.' Nell was sure of it. 'When you have a baby right from the beginning, it's got to be different, surely?'

'You're not getting broody all of a sudden?'

'Maybe.' Nell was glad she couldn't see her blush. She had decided not to tell anyone about her pregnancy just yet, not even Elly.

'Not before time!' Elly said cheerfully. 'Well, best be off. I'm working again tomorrow so I've got to clean the house today. I'll be down on the houseboat in the second week in July.'

'Look forward to it,' Nell said. 'Bye.'

I'll tell Elly about the baby when I see her, she thought. I do hope it's a girl. I'm glad Rob doesn't mind either way. I'm really very lucky. I shouldn't let minor irritants build up into major difficulties. I should be *happy*.

'This is bliss,' Elly said, eyes closed, settling her back into the slope of the dune and angling her face to catch the sun. She was beginning to feel truly calm for the first time in months.

'You'll cook to a crisp in no time,' Nell said, pulling her cotton hat down to shade her eyes.

'No. Factor 15 is the answer. Put some on your legs and you'll be fine too.'

Nell obediently applied suncream to her knees, and smoothed it down her calves. 'How long will they be sailing?' she asked, looking out over the mouth of the river to the open sea.

'I'm not sure. I expect the boys will soon get fed up if Paul's his usual dictatorial self. Maybe that Anna woman will see the light too!'

'How's he getting on living with her, d'you know?'

Elly shrugged. 'Dunno. He wouldn't tell me even if it was hell. We only meet to discuss the boys these days.'

'Cassie wants to meet me,' Nell said. 'She sent a royal command via Rob.'

'Good idea.'

'I suppose so.'

'Well, why not?'

'Oh, I don't know. I sort of feel she's too much in our lives as it is. It's all intrusion and power play with her.'

'But you must be curious.' Elly wouldn't have been able to restrain herself from having a peek at the Mad Cow by now.

'Yes I am . . . Elly?'

'What?'

'I'm pregnant.'

Elly opened her eyes wide and sat up abruptly. 'Brilliant! You are pleased?' She felt a surge of affection for her friend.

Nell smiled. 'Yes.'

'And Rob?'

'Oh he rushed out straight away and bought me oranges for extra vitamin C. He was so sweet. He's all for it.' She looked happy, but somehow reserved.

'I sense a "but".'

'No, not really. Rob is very keen on children. I'm so lucky in that respect. But I suppose I didn't expect to have one so soon.'

Elly brushed that aside. 'Time marches on. Why wait?'

'True.'

'So that's what you were on about the other week, on the phone! How far gone are you?'

'Fourteen weeks.'

'Fourteen weeks and you never let on?' Elly feigned indignation.

'I wanted to be sure.'

'Oh,' Elly said sighing, 'I remember so well how I felt when I was pregnant with Sam. The first three months I was totally knackered *all* the time. The next three, I was all twitchy and randy. Paul didn't know what had hit him! Then the last three, I was peeing all the time and so uncomfortable . . . But how are you? You look good.'

'I'm fine,' Nell said. 'I feel much better lately.'

'Due at Christmas,' Elly said, counting on her fingers. 'Promise me you won't call it Noel?'

Nell laughed. 'Promise.'

'Horatio Hayhoe,' Elly said, trying it out. 'Or Hiram, Hercules or Humphrey . . .'

'It's a girl,' Nell said, crossing her fingers.

'Oh well, then, Hortensia? Hedwig? Hermione?'

'I want to call her Charlotte,' Nell said. 'Lottie for short.'

'Not bad. What does Rob think?'

'He wants Lesley after his mother.' Nell made a face.

'Lesley Lottie Hayhoe!' Elly chanted. 'Sounds like Milly Molly Mandy. Oh, Nell, I'm so pleased for you. You'll be a proper family when you've got your own.'

'I only hope Rosie and Josh will take to it.'

'Of course they will. It'll bring you all together.'

The sun was unrelenting. Elly put on a sunhat and turned over to give her back a grilling. Nell sat and dreamily contemplated the sea. It was flat calm and nibbling only gently at the base of the cliffs on the other side of the estuary. To the north of them the sky had turned black, and rumblings of thunder could be heard from the hills.

'Perhaps it will rain,' Nell said.

'No chance,' Elly said. 'Have you got a hosepipe ban here too?'

'Yes. We've been siphoning the bathwater out of the bathroom window to water the vegetable garden. The ground's all cracked and . . .'

'And what?'

Nell didn't answer. A thirtyish couple with a young girl were walking through the dunes and passing close by. Elly rolled over to look. The man and woman had their arms around each other and were giggling and gazing into each other's eyes, stumbling over the uneven sandhills as they went, and laughing anew each time they nearly fell over. The little girl, who looked about nine, trailed slowly after them, kicking at tufts of marram grass.

'Come *on!*' the woman called irritably to her. The man was oblivious of her, digging his lover in the ribs and sprinting away across the beach. The woman hesitated, glanced crossly at the child again, and then bounded after him. The child followed, dragging her feet in the sand and making long skid marks.

Nell and Elly watched her walking away from them in silence until she was out of earshot. 'Poor little thing,' Elly said then. 'Did that look like a new relationship to you?'

'With an unwanted leftover from the previous one,' Nell agreed. 'Yes.'

'How can people do that to children?' Elly demanded passionately. 'Thank God that's one thing I don't have to worry about with Paul. He'd never neglect Will and Sam for any fancy woman.'

'Rob's the same. In fact he's so conscientious about his two that sometimes I wish he'd be a little less single-minded, and pay me more attention,' Nell said honestly.

'Not like that, though,' Elly objected. 'That was actual mental cruelty. I wish I'd said something now.'

'What can you say?' Nell stared out to sea. Elly made a small dismissive gesture and turned back to her sunbathing. After a moment, Nell said, 'I think I can see

Paul's boat coming back.'

'Already?' Elly sat up again and peered past her pointing finger.

'You're right. That was quick. Damn, I suppose that means I'll have to get back too. I don't want him commandeering the boys this afternoon.'

'Let's both walk back,' Nell suggested. 'It's a bit too hot for me here anyway.'

They folded up the rug they were sitting on, and strolled back along the north bank of the Torrent, climbing the two stiles on the way and glimpsing the sledging field through the trees on their right. Like all the adjacent fields it was a very pale green, having recently been cut for silage. *Polypeptide*, with Paul at the helm, motored past them as the river narrowed. Elly waved to Will, who was standing on the foredeck.

'Hi, Mum.' His voice carried clearly over the intervening water. 'Guess what. Sam fell overboard and nearly drowned!'

'Look, there's no need to carry on sulking,' Anna complained the following day when she and Paul were alone again. 'It was a shame that Sam fell into the sea. I've said so, haven't I?'

'That's not the same as apologising,' Paul said.

'Why is it *my* fault all of a sudden? Will was there. *You* were there.'

'We were both busy going about,' Paul said. 'You were the only one on the same side of the sail as Sam, and you *know* the boom swings across very suddenly.'

'I also know that he's your son; your responsibility. You might well have married Ermintrude so's you'd have someone to blame, but don't expect me to take that on board.'

'God forbid,' Paul said fervently.

'And anyway, Sam's perfectly all right so it was no

great crisis, was it? He was wearing his life jacket, and you fished him out straight away. He hasn't suffered any after effects, has he? It might even have taught him a useful lesson.' She stuffed both hands into the pockets of her denim shorts as far as her thumbs, and rocked slightly on the balls of her feet. She could see that Paul was looking at her breasts, so she pushed them forward subtly to stretch the thin cotton T-shirt as tightly as possible across them.

'Oh well . . .' he said, distracted by the challenge. 'I suppose there's no harm done. Come here.' He came round the back of the sofa and stood behind her, undoing her bra and the button at her waistband.

'It's too hot,' she protested automatically.

'It's never too hot for this.' He thrust the flat of his hand down the front of her shorts, and slid it through her pubic hair, searching delicately for the way through. She opened her legs fractionally to let him in and stretched backwards against him as he found the right place.

'Juicy,' he murmured in her ear, sliding his fingers in and out. 'My little knickerless juicy Anna . . .' After a while he withdrew his hand and began unzipping the front of her shorts. She bent forwards to take them off, but whilst they were still round her ankles, he entered her from behind, picking her up bodily and draping her over the low back of the sofa.

'The blood's all running to my head!'

'Mine's not,' he said cockily, holding her hips firmly between strong hands. 'Mine's . . . in *exactly* . . . the *place* . . . where it's *most* . . . *needed!*'

Anna cradled her head in her arms and let him get on with it. It was a small price to pay for winning one battle in the war against his unreasonable expectations of her. Whatever happens, she thought, he's going to have to learn one thing. I am not going to be a stepmother!

*

244

Nell had put on eye make-up to give herself confidence and a façade to hide behind in her first meeting with Cassie. She was determined to avoid any hostility, but felt absurdly nervous as she rang her front doorbell. What am I anticipating, she asked herself crossly, some sort of gorgon?

The woman who opened the door was smaller than she had expected, and older-looking. She had large bags under her eyes and petulant creases on her forehead, but she was smiling after a fashion.

'Come in,' she said. She was wearing a pale summer dress and little high-heeled sandals which clicked on the lino of the hallway as she led the way to her sitting room. Nell's flat canvas shoes made no sound as she followed her, stepping carefully past several overflowing cardboard boxes on the floor, and dodging a set of wooden wind chimes hanging from the ceiling, which tinkled melodiously as she passed.

'You look just like Rob's mother!' Cassie said, in surprised tones.

'Oh?' Nell wasn't sure what to say. 'Did you know her?'

'Heavens, no,' Cassie said. 'She died when he was a child. He must have told you that?'

'Well, yes. But . . .'

'I've got photos of her.'

Nell glanced around the room curiously. Every flat surface was covered with things: paperweights, little porcelain bowls, candles, vases, ornaments, bits of paper, children's toys . . . and framed photographs.

'Rob took those,' Cassie said, following her gaze. 'He started when Joshua was born. I've got albums and albums of him in every conceivable situation and expression: awake, asleep, yawning, crying, smiling, serious, crawling, walking, you name it.' She let out a little high-pitched laugh.

She's as nervous as I am! Nell realised, and felt better.

'And Rosie?' she asked, failing to locate more than a few pictures of her.

'Oh well, by the time she came along I expect the novelty had worn off a bit. Would you like a coffee?'

'Could I just have hot water?' Nell sat herself down whilst Cassie went to put the kettle on. The house was shabbier than she had expected, but more interesting. There were ornate mirrors and tapestry hangings on the walls, and small terracotta plaques with mottoes. The floor was covered in brightly coloured rugs and, high up where the ceiling met the wall, there were several floaty cobwebs. It felt surprisingly friendly. She sat back and waited.

'Just water on its own?' Cassie asked, coming back in.

'Yes, please,' Nell said.

'I thought it was important to meet without Rob,' Cassie said, sitting down. 'He always seems to put a block on things. I can't imagine how long it's going to take to get the money side of the divorce settled, if he sticks to that attitude.'

Nell took a sip, but found her drink too hot.

Cassie tried another tack. 'I'm so worried about Josh,' she said. 'I think I'm going to have to get professional help for him. He's just so difficult these days, and he has the attention span of a goldfish! I can't seem to settle him to anything.'

'Yes,' Nell said. 'I've found that too.'

'I've been trying to arrange some activities for him,' Cassie said, 'but it's all so expensive, and we're permanently short of money. I'm even having to cut Rosie's hair myself because it's prohibitively expensive at the hairdresser's!'

'Rob's paying interim maintenance,' Nell pointed out. 'He is doing his best. And we aren't all that well off either.'

'But you've got a job?'

'Not a very well-paid one.'

'Oh, I'd love the luxury of being able to work again,' Cassie said, closing her eyes at the thought and then opening them very wide. 'I used to be a television presenter, you know. That was *so* rewarding – socially as well as financially. I do intend to get back to it when the children need me less, but just at the moment I really don't have the time, and of course I've been ill.' She put on a brave expression.

'I'm sorry,' Nell said.

She's got a pleasant face, Cassie decided. She's a bit fatter than I imagined; not much of a waist. Pity her job is so low grade. Rob really needs someone with a bit more of an up-market career if he's going to be able to support his children properly. But then again, maybe a homely sort is better for Josh and Rosie – a nanny figure. At least they get well fed when they go over there. She looks the type who actually likes to cook. Can't understand that myself; life's too short for daily slavery in the bloody kitchen! 'So, do you like being buried all down there in the valley bottom?' she asked her.

'I love it,' Nell said, looking animated for the first time. 'It's my ideal home.'

'It's certainly very different from here. Frankly I'm concerned about how both children are adapting to the two different regimes,' Cassie said. 'Josh often comes home in a highly excited state, and then won't sleep all night.'

'Well, we don't let him run riot, you know,' Nell said defensively. 'We do have rules.'

Cassie laughed. 'I tried that at first,' she said kindly, 'but I soon discovered it's a mistake to be too rigid. It never works and it just causes bad feeling. No, I was thinking, maybe if you were to keep him indoors on Sunday afternoons, doing something calming? You might make toffee together.'

247

'Well, I don't know about that,' Nell frowned. 'I always encourage them to spend most of the time with Rob. I mean, that's the whole point of having them, so they can be with their father, isn't it?'

'Officially, I suppose, but I sometimes feel that Rob doesn't always know what's best for them. Men aren't as sensitive to emotional signals as we women, are they?'

'Rob's absolutely devoted to both of them,' Nell said firmly.

She's not as biddable as she looks, Cassie thought. Pity.

'Oh, and one other thing,' she said, swiftly changing the subject. 'I've discovered that if you get Rosie up at about four a.m. and pot her, she's much less likely to be wet in the morning.'

Chapter Twenty-One

Nell walked a little way along the river path early on the Saturday morning before the children arrived for a fortnight's summer holiday. It's all a question of mental attitude, she told herself. I'm going to take everything as it comes, and not get myself all worked up about things I can't alter. She climbed the first stile and paused on top of it to look around her. The fields were yellow with drought. It was said to be the hottest July of the century so far, but so many weather records seemed to be being broken all the time these days. Nell wondered if it was a genuine phenomenon, or whether it was simply being studied more intensively; a preoccupation with climate reflecting the new *Zeitgeist*. I'll walk as far as the next stile, she thought and then I'd better get back. She already felt ungainly even though the bump in her belly was very small. She patted it encouragingly. She was longing to feel the baby move inside her – incontrovertible proof that it really existed as a separate being.

At the next stile she heard raucous cries and came upon two pairs of magpies grappling with each other; all beaks and wings and claws in a mêlée of black and white feathers. They saw her at once and flew off raggedly in two directions.

'*One for sorrow, two for joy, three for a girl and four for a boy,*' she quoted. 'Oh dear, and fighting too. I do hope that isn't a bad omen.'

'I didn't realise you were so superstitious,' Rob teased her when she got back.

'I'm not usually,' Nell said. 'But then, I'm not usually

pregnant.' She looked at the clock. 'Isn't it time you went to Boxcombe?'

'In a minute.'

Rob still hadn't asked her how she had got on at her meeting with Cassie. Nell found his lack of curiosity peculiar. 'The Mad Cow told me she's really hard up,' she now volunteered.

'When isn't she?'

'But apparently she's swanning off for two weeks' holiday abroad.'

'Poverty is always relative for Cassie,' Rob said sourly. 'And by that I mean that her relatives are anything but poor. Her parents are always bailing her out. You have to take all her sob stuff with a hefty pinch of salt.'

'Oh, I see.'

'Right then, I'll be off to collect my two monsters.'

When he had gone, Nell busied herself putting away all the things she didn't want the children to appropriate or fiddle with, and everything that might be dangerous or cause disagreement. Anything for peace, she thought, closing her bedroom door on her own life and preparing to survive in enemy territory for the next two weeks.

When they arrived, Josh was back to his pre-tonsillitis bumptious self, but Rosie looked like poor little Orphan Annie. Her hair was a disaster with long strands falling the wrong way, and her dress had a large Ribena stain all down the front.

'Nell!' she exclaimed at once. 'Look what mith did!' She showed her half a bar of chocolate with tiny tooth marks all round the edge.

'It's been in the 'Rover for a week or so,' Rob said, smiling and putting it back. 'We've obviously got travelling mice.'

'Well, I wouldn't leave it there,' Nell said. 'It'll just encourage them, and it's not exactly hygienic.' She went to retrieve the chocolate, intending to throw it away.

'It's fine. OK?' Rob stood in her way. 'We'll cut the tooth marks off later.'

'Well, I still don't think that's a good –' Nell hesitated.

'I want it to stay there,' Josh said grandly, delivering the last word on the subject.

'I *like* mith,' Rosie said, capping it. Nell retired as gracefully as she could, feeling irritated.

When she thought about it later, dispassionately, there definitely were rewarding times to be had with both children: the morning when she recut Rosie's hair and washed it for her, and Rosie said, 'It looks much more nithe now than when my other mummy did it.' Or the time when Josh fell and cut his knees and came running to her for Elastoplast and comfort. Or when he bet her ten pence he could catch a grasshopper, and actually managed it. But these were more than counterbalanced by the occasions when Josh woke them at five in the morning to have his bottom wiped, and the night when he cried for his mother – to such an extent that Rob felt obliged to try to ring her – and Josh was inconsolable when she wasn't there. Or the day when he deliberately made holes in a new bag of potting compost, snapped the spout off the watering can, broke a pane of glass in the kitchen window with a stick, trying to attract their attention, and then fell flat in the mud at the edge of the river *again*, and needed a complete change of clothes. All these things are only trivial, Nell reminded herself, but she still felt depressed. She had hoped by now to have become accustomed to the children, and to be able to be as comfortably capable with them as Elly was with hers.

Then there was the afternoon when Rob accidentally knocked Rosie over and, as he picked her up again, Nell heard her say indignantly, 'I didn't hear a "thorry".' She smiled at the recollection, but even that amusement was tempered with unease. Rosie was so clearly repeating something her mother had said to her. Shades of Cassie had been there all the time in the background, trying to catch Nell out, but now she had actually met the woman, she could see her in her children too; her expressions, her mannerisms, her attitudes. And because Cassie had known Rob for many more years than she had, and had had two children by him, her relationship with him appeared to Nell to be far more significant than her own. She was jealous.

Ten days into the so-called holiday, Cassie phoned unexpectedly in the evening and demanded the children back. Nell heard Rob's half of the conversation and deduced the rest.

'They're fine,' Rob said, 'absolutely fine . . . Well, how should I know if they're missing you? . . . No, of course I haven't asked them . . . Look, we agreed fourteen days, so a fortnight it is . . . No, actually they're not at all bored . . . Well, I can't help that . . . Oh, Cassie, there's no need for hysteria. Just calm down! . . . Oh, for heaven's sake. I . . .' He put the receiver down with a crash. 'She hung up on me.'

'Bloody woman,' Nell said. 'Ignore her. Tell you what, why don't we go out tomorrow to the proper seaside where there are ice creams and donkey rides and other children yours can play with?'

It was a good idea. Both children welcomed it with uncustomary enthusiasm, and were still in good spirits the next day when they all four walked along the crowded beach to find an open patch of sand to bag for themselves. They dumped their bundles of towels and swimming costumes, their buckets and spades and frisbee, the cool-bag full of food and cold drinks, Rob's camera and a couple of optimistically included books. Nell rubbed suncream on everyone and then on herself and finally settled down to watch Rob and Josh in a sandcastle-building competition.

'I want an ith cream,' Rosie announced.

'Good idea,' Rob said.

'I'll get them,' Nell offered. 'You stay with Daddy and Josh.'

She walked back along the beach alone, glad of the brief freedom. It was thronged with people all enjoying themselves. I'm a freak, Nell thought. Why do I have to be different from *everybody* else? She imagined idly how good it would be just to keep on walking, and not to have to feel responsible for anybody but herself. Then she came to the ice-cream van and bought four large cornets with chocolate flakes stuck in them, and was obliged to turn back again.

She walked for some time before she realised she'd lost Rob and the children. She hadn't taken note of how far she'd come and the beach was featureless and more crowded by the minute. She scanned the tideline in case they were paddling, and then the sea of faces. All were unfamiliar. She couldn't have overshot, could she? She walked on uncertainly. The sky above was a brash hot blue. A heat haze shimmered over the dunes. Something cold hit one hand. The ice creams were melting, running down their cones and dripping wastefully on to the sand. There was a splash of sticky white on her new polo shirt, and she didn't have a spare hand to wipe it off. She looked all round helplessly. Still no Rob.

Then her chest constricted suddenly, and her eyes filled with tears which poured down her face. She felt as desolate as a lost child, and stupid at the same time. She stumbled on blindly for what seemed an age and unexpectedly there they were – two familiar dark heads and one fair, with two sandcastles now twice as big as before. Nell sniffed determinedly and went to join them.

'My ith's all melted,' Rosie complained, taking one from her.

'So's mine,' Josh said, making sure he got the biggest.

'I'm sorry,' Nell said, 'they all are. I got a bit lost and it's hot.'

'What d'you think of our castles?' Rob asked, taking his without really looking at her.

'Good,' she said.

Later that night when the children were asleep, and Rob was breathing deeply beside her, Nell found that her eyes were leaking again. She cried as silently as possible, making the pillow all wet, but finally had to sit up in bed to blow her nose.

'What's the matter?' Rob asked, turning over blearily and switching on the bedside light.

'I was just remembering getting lost on the beach today.' Nell managed a tremulous smile. She badly needed a hug.

'Were you? When?'

'When I got the ice creams.'

'Oh then,' Rob said not unkindly, patting her through the duvet. 'That's nothing to cry about, you silly sausage!'

The inevitable day arrived when the children had to be taken back to their mother. Rob woke with feelings of gloom even before he was fully conscious, and then lay there staring at the ceiling, worrying about whether he and Cassie would ever be able to sort out the problems of residency and contact for their children amicably, or whether it would have to go to court to be at the mercy of a welfare report and a judge's decision. He worried too whether the financial settlement would be achieved with any degree of dignity and without any more trauma to Rosie and Josh.

Josh was awake early too, and in a state of high excitement, twitching his shoulders and bolting his breakfast, asking all the time, 'When are we going home? Can we go now?' At eleven o'clock just as they were preparing to leave for Boxcombe, the phone rang. It was Cassie.

'We're just setting off,' Rob said.

'What, now?'

'Yes. Why not? Today's the day we agreed.'

'Oh, it's not at all convenient at the moment. You'll have to give them lunch and bring them home later this afternoon.'

'And there's me thinking you were desperate to see them.'

'Oh go to hell!' She slammed the receiver down.

When he told the children, Rosie danced on one leg and chortled, but Josh burst into tears. 'I want to go home *now*!' he wailed, hunching his shoulders convulsively.

Nell didn't seem overly pleased either, but she waited until the children were out of earshot before saying. 'But I haven't got anything for them for a proper lunch. I didn't think they'd still be here.' She sighed heavily. 'Have you noticed how the Mad Cow invariably arranges things so she does the minimum amount of cooking and Muggins here always has to step in?'

Rob made an impatient gesture. 'Bread and something will be fine,' he said.

Later that afternoon he drove them home in a sudden isolated thunderstorm, feeling it had been a pretty good holiday, all things considered. Josh was still clutching the painting that he and Nell had spent most of the morning doing, and Rosie was still very taken with the pretend menu that she and Nell had thought up for supper.

'Thtewed gnu and cuthtard, wathed down with python cruth,' she intoned. 'Thtewed gnu and cuth . . .'

'You can't even *say* it properly,' Josh jeered. 'It's stewed gnu and custard, washed down with python crush.'

'. . . tard, wathed down with python cruth. St . . .'

'Oh, shut *up*!'

'Hush, Josh.'

'Thtewed gnu a –'

'And that's quite enough, Rosie. Repetition ruins the joke. Here we are.' He slowed the Land Rover down and brought it to a stop outside Cassie's house. The front door opened and she stood there. Her face looked pinched and disagreeable in spite of the fine features.

'You're late!' she accused him. Josh suddenly burst into floods of tears and rushed at her. 'What is it, Joshy?' she crooned, bending down to encircle him in her arms. 'What's up with my best boy?' She glanced at Rob venomously.

'He's been fine all fortnight,' Rob protested. 'We've had a good –'

'Inside, Rosie!' Cassie interrupted sharply, pulling at her daughter's sleeve.

'But I want to kith Daddy goodbye.'

'Not today.' Cassie yanked her indoors. 'You might get struck by lightning.' Then she slammed the door to within an inch of Rob's face, and all he was left with was the sound of both his children crying.

He stood there for a moment in the rain in furious indecision, but then feeling that if he made a fuss it would only upset the children more, he turned on his heel and squelched back to the Land Rover. Once there, he turned back to look at the house, hoping to see at least one of them at the window so he could blow a kiss, but there was no one there. Cassie would have made sure of that. He climbed in, dripping, and discovered that his feet were resting on Josh's precious painting.

All the way home he worried about him. What on earth had upset him? Wasn't seven a bit old for this cry-baby stuff? How could Cassie undermine him so? What did she think she was *doing*?

I've done my absolute best not to argue with her in front of the children, he thought bitterly. I've behaved 'properly' and look where it's got me! It feels as though I'm trying to fight an unending war armed only with a popgun. Cassie always has the advantage – Cassie has the children. I've tried to be accommodating and civilised and she just takes advantage of me. I try to be polite and she mocks me and alienates Josh. I try to discuss things sensibly and she gets hysterical. What more *can* I do?

He drove badly, causing a lorry to brake suddenly and blast him with its horn. When he finally turned in at the entrance to his lane, he felt totally done in. 'They should be here,' he said aloud, bumping over the ruts with practised negligence. 'This is their home.'

Nell met him at the door, smiling a welcome. She was invariably cheerful; a quality that had endeared her to him right from the outset. How could he ever have fancied Cassie?

'Hello, love,' she said, hugging him. 'Everything OK?'

'Not really.' He kissed her cheek absently and went through into the kitchen, where he got himself a bottle of beer and a glass. 'Drink?'

'No thanks.' She sat down opposite him at the kitchen table. 'What's wrong?' She ran her fingers through her fringe, making it stick up rakishly. Her hair was not her best point. Rob didn't answer. 'Well?'

'Oh, just the usual.' He felt almost too tired to explain. 'Josh sobbed his heart out the moment he saw his mother. I can't think why. He was fine here, wasn't he? I thought we'd had a good holiday.'

'Maybe it's just a conflict of loyalties, plus some emotional blackmail from Cassie?' Nell suggested, reaching across for his hand. 'Poor you. You can't win, can you?'

'Certainly seems like that.'

Nell stroked his hand, and then squeezed it as though she'd come to some conclusion. She often did this when attempting to distract him from gloom. Rob recognised it as an unspoken signal which said, 'Right, now let's change the subject.'

'I heard a lovely new adjective on the radio just now,' she said.

'Oh?'

'Yes – retortful. Good isn't it?'

'It isn't a real word, is it?'

'So what? I think it's got a definite future. It would describe Josh beautifully, don't you think? As in – Josh was in trouble at school today for being retortful!' She grinned at him.

Rob didn't respond. He couldn't. He was unable to bear any criticism of his children at all. If they behaved badly, it was because they were being brought up incompetently; because Cassie was useless as a mother; because he had abandoned them and was thus a cruel and unfeeling father; because *she* had them, and he didn't. The least disapproval, even from Nell, pointed up his own inadequacy and his own loss. It was all too much.

'Come on, Rob,' Nell encouraged him. 'Don't let the Mad Cow get to you.'

'Too late,' Rob said bitterly. 'Whatever happens, it seems I can do nothing about it. *Nothing!*'

'Sorry,' Nell said. 'I didn't mean to upset you.' She squeezed his hand again. Rob made a noncommittal noise, and slipped his hand from hers to pour more beer for himself.

'Little sip?' Nell suggested.

'You said you didn't want any.'

'Just a smidgen of yours.' She wrinkled her small elegant nose at him and pursed her lips hopefully. She had nice lips.

Rob smiled at last. 'Oh, go on then.'

Nell looked encouraged. 'I went up and got the post whilst you were out,' she said, taking a good gulp of beer, 'and there's something that should interest you.'

'What?'

'A booklet about the problems of step-parenting. I sent away for it. I haven't had a chance to read it properly, but it looks as though it might be useful.' She handed it to him.

'Oh, right.' He took it from her, glanced at it and then put it down again. He had no intention of actually reading it. What was the point? He wasn't a step-parent.

By the time she went to bed that night, Nell was tired too. It was exhausting trying to cheer Rob up and jolly him along all the time. There were times when she almost despised him for being so wimpish where Cassie was concerned, and yet of course she did understand. It was difficult for him. What more could he do? He was a nice man, and nice men don't break down their ex-wives' doors, beat them up, and liberate their children – well, only in their wildest dreams.

It's all very well, Nell thought resentfully, but where do *I* come in? I get the brunt of everything. When Cassie is horrible to Rob, he disappears inside himself and leaves me out. I do my best, but it's hopeless if it's all one-sided. I need Rob to make big efforts for me too. Then she thought, I'm being selfish. I'm an adult; I ought to be able to manage. And anyway, I know a sure-fire way to make him forget his troubles . . .

She lay in bed smiling in anticipation as Rob undressed, watching him reach up to the back of his collar, yank off his shirt in one easy movement, and drop it on the floor. He eased his feet out of his shoes one against the other, lowered his trousers and his underpants and kicked them aside too. Nell was about to protest, but thought better of it. One thing at a time. She pulled back the duvet invitingly as Rob climbed in. He lay down on his back.

'Mmm,' Nell said, snuggling up.

'Lost your nightie?' Rob asked, surprised.

'No.'

'Oh, I thought . . .'

'And *I* thought this would be nice,' Nell said, kissing the shoulder nearest to her, and sliding an arm over him to stroke his chest and stomach. His skin felt hot. 'It's a great defuser of tensions, I always think.' She was glad he hadn't got a hairy chest. She loved its smooth hardness, and the good spicy smell of him. She shuffled herself up on to one elbow and, bending over him, nibbled an ear lobe. He turned towards her abruptly. His expression was not encouraging.

'Sorry,' he said. 'It's been a bad day, and I'm totally knackered. Maybe tomorrow, eh?' Then he turned away, pummelled his pillow irritably, and settled down with a long sigh.

It seemed to Nell that he was asleep in moments. She envied him this facility of instant shut-down. It always took her much longer, especially when she was all hopeful and receptive . . . Two tears of frustration slid down her cheeks. Bloody kids, she thought furiously. *I hate you both!*

Chapter Twenty-Two

'You mustn't worry about Rob's two,' Sibyl said during a slack period at ARTFUL[L]. 'Children nearly always come through these things all right. It's the parents who crack up!' She caught a stray strand of hair and pushed it back into place, raising an eyebrow as she did so.

Nell laughed ruefully. 'You're not wrong there.' Thank goodness for Sibyl, she thought. At least I can really open up to her. I never seem to talk to Rob at all these days, and when I try to discuss my problems with Elly, I end up feeling even more incompetent. I don't want to share things with Anna either – although she's very keen to do so – because I can't trust her, but with Sibyl I'm fine.

'It's the total lack of privacy that I find so hard to bear,' she confessed.

'How often are you having them these days?' Sibyl asked.

'Every weekend, and all Rob's annual holiday allowance. Of course we get weekday evenings on our own, but that's not exactly quality time.'

'No, I can see that.'

'I just feel I'm under a kind of critical scrutiny all the time. They see everything I'd rather keep to myself: the things I buy on impulse, the food I throw away, the under-clothes I wear, the housework I don't do, my moods, my habits, and worst of all, my interactions with Rob.'

'Mmm?' Sibyl said, inviting more.

'I mean, we can't argue or even discuss trivial things when they're around, because they always have to be included and they're always on his side, against me.

They're like spies in the camp; I end up feeling as though my life isn't my own.' Nell ran her fingers through her fringe. 'And it's horrible being permanently in the wrong. Am I paranoid d'you think?'

'No, no,' Sibyl said comfortingly, 'of course you aren't. You're in a very difficult position.'

'But real mothers don't feel like this?'

'I think "real" mothers, as you put it, are a lot less assured and confident than you might suppose. But they don't have a full-time rival to contend with, so they aren't challenged all the time.'

'I seem to be so unsure of myself lately,' Nell went on. 'I never used to feel this insecure, but now I keep agonising about why we're together. Is it something Rob actively chose, or did he just find himself persuaded into it because of his devotion to the cottage? I really doubt sometimes whether it's *me* he wants to be with at all.'

'Oh, I'm sure he does! Isn't he at all demonstrative?'

'Very rarely, and never when the children are around. It's as though he's embarrassed to show me any affection in front of them.'

'He's probably trying to prevent them from being jealous,' Sibyl suggested.

'Yes, I'm sure that's true, but I would like them to know that I matter a bit to him. I feel taken for granted.'

'I'm sure they've worked out how important you are. Children pick these things up very quickly. Do they know about the baby?'

'No . . . I don't want Cassie told yet. That's one bit of privacy I can hang on to.' Nell sighed. 'I suppose if I'm honest, I feel trapped. I didn't plan it to happen like this. I wanted to settle down and get fond of Rob's children first, before I had any of my own, so that by the time mine came along, I'd feel established and secure. Instead I seem to need constant reassurance. I'm not usually so feeble.' Nell made a dismissive gesture.

Sibyl patted her shoulder. 'You're not feeble at all. Can't you discuss this with Rob?'

'Not really. He's all upset and preoccupied about the divorce settlement and the wrangling about residence and contact, and Cassie isn't helping.'

'She's being obstructive?'

'Deliberately, so it seems.'

'So it's never the right moment?'

'That's about it.'

'But it isn't all gloom and doom with the children?'

'Oh, by no means,' Nell smiled. 'They can be very funny. Rosie went round the house the other day looking for "presents" for us all, and wrapping them up in pretty paper. She obviously chose things very carefully to reflect her view of our proper stations in life. Josh got a plastic dinosaur and Rob got a book.'

'And what did you get?'

Nell made a face. 'A bottle of Fairy Liquid!'

Cassie finished her bottle of duty-free gin regretfully, and felt it was already high time for another ten days in the Algarve. She had enjoyed her holiday enormously – it was real life that was proving so impossible. I need to do something different, she thought. It isn't working out as things are. If I could just persuade Mic to mind the children every other weekend, then that Nell female wouldn't be able to get her claws so firmly into them, and I'd still have some peace. Cassie had an uneasy feeling, now that she had met her, that Nell just might be a natural when it came to child care. She would have to make damned sure her authority wasn't undermined.

So far, Mic had been resistant to all her pleas. She was already taking Rosie every afternoon (and sometimes Josh too) until five o'clock, which was a big help – Cassie was forced to acknowledge – but it wasn't enough. She had been brought up by her parents to buy her way out of trouble, and was frustrated not to be able to do just that. The kids need structured activities, *distractions*, she thought, and I simply can't be expected to provide that, day in day out. At least I've sorted out violin lessons for Josh on Saturday mornings, but if Mic would have them after that . . . She could take them swimming, or playing in the park, or to the cinema, or to any of the 101 things that come so easily to her. It would solve all my problems.

'Meself and Gav needs our weekends free,' Mic insisted over the telephone. 'So's we can spend time tergevver an' I can clean the flat, get the washin' done, buy food an' that.'

'I'll pay you double,' Cassie suggested recklessly.

'No can do.' Mic was adamant. 'Not on a regular occurrence, no way.'

'But now and then?' Cassie persisted.

'Well . . .' Mic weakened, 'maybe, but I'm not promising nothing, mind?'

'You're an angel, Mic!' Cassie put the receiver down, smiling, and then picked it up again.

'Hello?' Nell said, answering the phone.

'I need to speak to Rob.' It was Cassie using her I'm-so-exhausted-look-what-I-have-to-put-up-with voice. Nell had just got back from an antenatal checkup, and felt tired herself. She was now twenty weeks into her pregnancy and putting on weight.

'I'll see if I can find him,' she said, knowing by now not to say, 'Oh, is that you, Cassie? How are you?' as one would to any normal person.

'Rob?' she called up the stairs.

'Yep.'

'Cassie for you, on the phone.'

'I'll take it up here.'

She went back to the telephone to replace the receiver as soon as she heard his voice, and as she did so, she felt it – a quiver inside her as the baby kicked its legs for the first time. She sat down clutching her stomach, entranced by this long-awaited sign of life. She was still sitting there beaming from ear to ear when Rob came downstairs.

'It kicked!' she said. 'I've just this minute felt it kick.' She reached out and put his hand over her bulge and held it there, to see if he too could feel it.

'That's terrific,' he said, but he didn't smile.

'Is something the matter?'

'Oh, just Cassie. She says the children get bored visiting us, so they only want to come every other weekend from now on.' He took his hand away.

Nell felt a treacherous lurch of relief but strove to conceal it. 'How can they be bored?' she asked. 'We have Lego and drawing and water games and bike rides and walks, and heaven knows what!'

'Search me.' He looked unhappy. 'What can I do?' he asked. 'If I entice them to come and see me with nonstop treats and no discipline, they'll end up as spoilt brats, but if I give them a bit of discipline and try to get them to amuse themselves and use some imagination, I apparently end up with unwilling visitors. I can't win.'

It's 'We', Nell thought, not 'I', and it's *me* that has to supply the discipline more often than not . . . But she let that go. 'Well, maybe they'll discover that weekends with Cassie can be just as boring,' she suggested.

'I'm not happy,' Rob said, 'not happy at all.'

I was, Nell thought, until a minute or two ago.

Anna saw Nell lowering her increasingly large bulk into the swimming pool and swam towards her, eager for a chat. 'I hate August,' she said. 'Summer's jaded, autumn hasn't begun, and everything's airless and exhausted and endlessly bloody hot.'

'I like spring best,' Nell said.

'Yes, you would. Optimists always do.'

Nell remembered a joke Rob had told her, in what now seemed to her to be another age. 'Optimist says to pessimist, "Guess what? Optimists live longer than pessimists,"' she offered. 'Pessimist replies, "Serves them right!"'

Anna laughed. 'That's better,' she said. 'You have been a bit down in the dumps lately, haven't you?'

'Not really.' Nell clearly wasn't going to admit it.

'Are you and Rob going to get married?' Anna tried tactlessness to see whether the unexpected approach would break down Nell's frustrating reticence.

'No.'

'Why not?'

'There's no need. We're fine as we are.'

Anna understood then that Nell had decided to shut her out, and that was that. 'Probably just as well,' she said. 'Apparently seventy per cent of second marriages fail within the first ten years.'

'So what about you and Paul?'

'Oh, we'll be in the thirty per cent success band. Did I tell you he's finally negotiated his early retirement?'

'Elly did.'

'Yes, she would. So I suppose you know it's not as good as he'd hoped, but he's just so over the moon he doesn't have to go back to that school in September. He says he didn't fully appreciate before how much he hated the job!'

'That must be grim,' Nell said. 'I'm very lucky. Sibyl's more my friend than my employer. Let's swim.' They swam side by side, doing breaststroke.

'So, will you go on working after the baby?'

'Sibyl says I shouldn't, and I must say I agree with her, but she says she'll always have me back if I decide I want to. I'll probably have to eventually anyway. We need the money.'

'Oh God, don't talk to me about money!' Anna

266

exclaimed. '*All* Paul's money runs down his first family's drain . . .' She stopped, not wishing to antagonise Nell. She was her friend . . . maybe her only friend. I'm not good at friendship, Anna thought with a pang. That's why I need a man.

They reached the far end of the pool and stopped again. 'Enough of that,' she said. 'How are you?'

'You know women's brains are supposed to shrink during pregnancy?' Nell said with a little shrug.

'Really?'

'Yes, well that's how I feel, pea-brained! And my back hurts, my new maternity bras are getting tight, and I keep needing to go to the loo, but at least in here I'm almost weightless and blissfully cool.'

'And the two little angels?'

Nell sighed. 'Don't ask. I spend ages teaching them basic things, like good manners, then they go home, and by the time they come to us again, they've forgotten the lot. It's disheartening to say the least.'

'Seems to me it's the ultimate responsibility without power,' Anna said. 'I feel for you. Thank the Lord I won't be saddled with it.'

'How d'you mean?'

'I mentioned our round the world trip on *Polypeptide*, didn't I? Well, it's on. We're leaving at the end of October.'

On 3rd September, two days before the children's school term began, Cassie went round to Mic's with a light heart, to collect Rosie. Tomorrow she would go and meet the new form teachers at a special start-of-year parents' day, and from then on both Josh and Rosie would be safely contained at school all morning, to Mic's later in the afternoon, and only home in the evenings. Her days would be blessedly free once more, and she would be able truly to find herself again. She rang Mic's bell and stood there smiling.

'Wotcher,' Mic said, opening the door. She was holding someone else's baby, and had a toddler clutching the hem of her shorts. 'Rosie's just coming.' She turned her head. '*Rosie?* Yer mum's 'ere.'

It's a good sign, Cassie thought, that Rosie isn't over-eager to come home. It shows I've found the right place for her, and that she's happy here. 'All right for next weekend then?' she said lightly. It wasn't really a question. 'I'm off to London to see some old friends I worked with a few years ago. In television, you know.'

'Eh?'

'Next . . . weekend . . .' Cassie said patiently, as if to a halfwit.

'Come off it,' Mic objected. 'What you on abaht? I done two weekends out of the kindness of me 'eart, an' that's enough fer anyone.'

'But you can't let me down now!' Cassie objected. 'I've made arrangements!'

'Well, stuff . . .' Mic shifted the baby to her other hip and ruffled the toddler's hair. 'Sorry, Cassie, I told you I wasn't doin' it regular, and I ain't.'

'But, Mic, I absolutely *rely* on you. You know that.' She put on a pleading look that should have melted the stoniest heart.

Rosie came to the door at that moment, carrying a brown pill bottle and eating something from it.

'What's that?' Cassie was in a panic at once.

'I'm a nurth,' Rosie said proudly, 'and I'm making all the babith better.'

'But how did you get the top off?' Cassie almost shouted. 'It's child-proof!'

'Mic thowed me,' Rosie said sulkily. Cassie whirled round on her.

'Keep yer 'air on,' Mic said. 'It's only sweets. It's just a game, right?'

'Ohhhh . . . of all the irresponsible, stupid, *brain-dead*

things to do . . .' Words almost failed her.

'Look,' Mic said confidentially, ignoring the outburst. 'I knows just what you oughter do.'

'What?' Cassie felt hope despite her rage.

'You wants ter put your money where your mouf is, right? So go back to bloody London and effing well get yourself a job in sodding telly . . . if you've got the bottle for it, that is!'

Nell decided to go to the school parents' day with Rob. It was time to come out, both about her status as Rob's partner, and about her pregnancy. She put on her best maternity smock and some make-up and summoned up some of her old determination.

When they arrived, they found both children rushing about with their friends, and Cassie deep in discussion with a bored-looking Headmistress. Nell noticed that the Mad Cow was wearing a necklace of green beads. Surely not? she thought, frowning, but later on when she and Rob went over to talk to her, Nell saw that they were indeed made of malachite.

'. . . I'm taking Josh to a psychiatrist,' Cassie was informing Rob. 'I'm worried about his nervous tic and I'm convinced he's got ADD.'

'ADD?'

'Attention Deficit Disorder, surely even you must know about that?'

'Well, why don't you try giving him some more attention?'

'Are you trying to be thick, or does it just come naturally? It's nothing to do with *giving* him attention – it's that he can't *pay* attention for the normal length of time. He needs professional help. I was just telling Mrs Whatsit . . .' She looked around for the Head, but she was now some distance away talking animatedly to someone else. 'Oh, and I've arranged music lessons for him on

Saturday mornings,' Cassie said, 'so he won't be able to go to the cottage until just before lunch.' Then she noticed Nell in detail for the first time, and her eyes widened. Nell smiled at her with a slight lift to one eyebrow.

'Good God!' Cassie exclaimed. 'Some people don't waste much time! I do hope you aren't thinking of giving up work? There's little enough money in this so-called extended family as it is.'

'I'm sure we'll manage,' Nell said, steely.

'Oh, and while we're on the subject of work,' Cassie said offhandedly to Rob, 'I've decided it's nonsense to expect to get any worthwhile employment down here in the sticks, so in the New Year the children and I are moving house.'

'Where to?' Rob caught her arm.

'Why, London, of course. Where else?' She shook him off.

'You can't do that!' They glared at each other.

'I'm not prepared to discuss it here,' Cassie said, closing her eyes very deliberately, head back, and then opening them again languidly. 'All right?'

Nell glanced at Rob's horrified face and felt sorry for him, but she couldn't prevent her heart from lightening.

'But before we move,' Cassie said, 'there's things of mine you've still got, and I want them back.'

Rob was clearly averse to making a scene in public. His voice was studiedly neutral. 'You got the carpet, didn't you? What more?'

'They were on that list I gave you over a year ago, but I suppose you've conveniently lost it?'

'Write it out again,' Rob said, 'give me back my photographs, and you've got a deal.'

'Typical!' Cassie snapped. 'Why do I bother?' and she went off in a huff to collar another member of staff.

Rob and Nell found Josh and Rosie and got them to introduce them to their form teachers. Sitting at low tables in rooms with walls covered in childish writings and drawings, Nell found it hard to concentrate, and equally difficult to stop smiling dreamily.

When they finally got home again, Rob was scratchy and irritable. 'Trust the Mad Cow to drop a bombshell on me in front of everybody, where I couldn't have it out with her,' he complained. 'She can't just take my children away like that. How would I ever see them? It'd cost a fortune in petrol to be up and down to flaming London all the time!' He stopped and glanced at Nell. 'What's so funny?'

'Sorry,' Nell composed her face. 'You just reminded me of something I heard on the radio this morning. This man was talking about some crisis about to hit the government and he said, "This is a ticking time bomb, which we have got to get a grip of" . . .'

'This is serious, Nell,' Rob said, with a dismissive gesture. 'I shall have to find out whether I can legally stop her from going, but whatever happens it will cause no end of a fuss.' He ran a hand through his hair, and took a handful of it as if to tear it out.

'I'm sorry,' Nell said hastily, touching his arm. She felt genuinely sorry for him, but an unwonted sensation kept creeping in and overtaking everything as she contemplated a future with Rob and the baby – and no one else. She welcomed that feeling like a long-lost friend. It was deliverance.

Chapter Twenty-Three

August had been uncharacteristically dry, and as uncomfortable as the previous months. September so far appeared to be no better. Nell was philosophical about her misfortune to be pregnant during the hottest summer for three hundred years, and grateful to Sibyl for suggesting that she work mornings only at ARTFUL[L] for one more month, before stopping altogether. So now, thankfully, she spent a lot of her time indoors with an electric fan for company, only venturing out of the cottage in the blessed cool of the evening to wander by the river and wonder about the baby. She had taken to referring to it as 'him' whenever she discussed it with Rob, in order to hoodwink the contrary fates. And because she had begun to feel more hopeful about the future, she came to appreciate that Rob was as excited as she was about their forthcoming child. He started to accompany her on her evening walks, helping her over the stiles and being generally attentive. And now that there was a real prospect of his children moving away, Nell felt much more relaxed when they visited at weekends. It was as though a life sentence had been commuted.

She felt less disturbed by Cassie as well, since she would soon be removing her malign influence to another sphere. Nell looked forward to being able to walk around the whole of Boxcombe without having to look over her shoulder in case the Mad Cow was observing her. I really have been paranoid about her, she thought shamefacedly. How silly!

She asked Rob about Cassie's malachite necklace, when

they were on a walk together. 'She wears it on purpose,' he said, 'to annoy me.'

'So Bert did give it to her?'

'Oh yes.'

'But not for the usual reason?'

'Who knows? He gave it to her when Josh was born, but I wouldn't put anything past her.'

'You're joking! But presumably she wouldn't have had the opportunity to sleep with him anyway?'

'On the contrary,' Rob said, 'when we were first married she was still working for television. She used to go up to London regularly to record the programmes, and she always stayed overnight at Bert's house.'

'So she knows him well then? You never said.'

'Well, you never asked.'

Nell felt unreasonably jealous, considering that she didn't even *like* Rob's father. 'And is Bert fond of her?' Why was she asking this?

'Oh, yes. He thinks she's wonderful.'

'Oh.' Nell was silenced.

'I think I may have thought of one way to scupper the bloody woman's plans for moving,' Rob said, stooping down and picking up a smooth stone from the river bank.

'How?'

'Well, she's clearly hoping the financial settlement will be through by the New Year, so she can make a clean break and start afresh in London.'

'Ye . . . es?'

'So it's obvious,' Rob said, throwing the stone with a flick of the wrist so that it skimmed the surface of the water, bouncing four times before sinking from view. 'I can just stall and stall so she doesn't get the money she wants, at the time she wants it!' He picked up another stone, crouched, and got five bounces. 'Why on earth is this called ducks and drakes?' he asked, smiling up at her.

*

On 15th September the rain began in earnest, and looked to be settled in for a season. Josh and Rosie arrived for the weekend, Josh in new pale beige suede shoes which were already soaked through and stained.

Very practical! Nell thought, glancing down from the stove where she was preparing lunch. 'Right,' she said, 'this is ready. Time to wash your hands.'

'We always have sandwiches for lunch,' Josh said, squishing the soap between his hands so that it skittered across the draining board and landed on the floor.

'So, what d'you have for supper?'

'Thandwiches,' Rosie giggled, giving it a kick. 'That thoaps all furry!'

Nell bent, picked it up and washed the dust off under the tap. 'You must have proper meals sometimes,' she said, and thought, I sound just like my my mother!

Rob came in with an armful of firewood and dropped it into the basket, brushing the sawdust off his jumper. 'Ah,' he said, 'food! That smells good. Come on, you two.' He sat down at the table looking expectant.

'Smells like poo,' Josh said, looking sideways at Nell as she put his lunch in front of him.

'Sssshhh,' Rob said. 'You know that's not true.'

'Pooh, pooh, pooh, pooh . . .' Rosie chanted in an undertone.

'That means you too, Rosie.'

'What's this?' Josh asked, prodding a boiled potato disdainfully with the prongs of his fork. 'And why are we having soup all over it?'

Nell looked hard at him. It appeared to be a genuine question. 'It's not soup,' she said patiently. 'It's gravy, and it's what you have on meat and potatoes to make them tasty.' *What does Cassie feed them on?* She glanced interrogatively at Rob across the table and he made a *God knows!* sort of face.

'What's for pud?' Rosie mumbled with her mouth full.

'Blackberry and apple crumble. I picked the black-berries this morning.'

'Yummy.'

'My mum says you shouldn't eat wild blackberries because the flies spit all over them,' Josh said, 'and they get full of maggots.'

'No, that's much later in the season. They're all new and fresh and delicious now.' Horrible child!

'How are your music lessons going, Josh?' Rob asked.

'Great. Mrs thing says I'm a natural.' He swung the top half of his body from side to side as though acknowledging the applause of an enthusiastic audience. 'Bet you can't play the violin?' he challenged Nell.

'I don't know,' she said, remembering an old joke. 'I've never tried.' But it was lost on Josh.

'Reasonable weekend?' Sibyl asked as she arrived at ARTFUL[L] on Monday morning.

'So, so,' Nell said. 'It's been wonderfully cool and wet at long last, hasn't it? We stayed indoors all Saturday and were reduced to playing Happy Families.'

'Good fun?'

'Yes, except that Josh just has to win, so he cheats quite blatantly! I was always brought up to be strictly truthful, so it's off-putting to say the least. Then on Sunday we went out for a walk in the rain and looked for conkers, so that was better, except that Rosie has taken to holding her nose every time she passes a cowpat.'

Sibyl smiled. 'You sound more relaxed about things.'

'Yes, we had some laughs. You should have seen Josh trying to eat sweetcorn with half his baby teeth missing!'

'I knew you'd settle down to it in time,' Sibyl said comfortably, opening the till and emptying bags of small change into it.

'Well, I'm sure I will, when Cassie moves,' Nell said. 'I hope to God she does, though. That's the trouble.'

'What is?'

'Well, I want them to go, but Rob is desperate for them to stay, so it doesn't make for a very united front. I wish I could get him to see it from my point of view, but I haven't even tried. For some reason I feel I don't have the right . . .'

Sibyl went to change the sign on the shop door to 'Open'. 'I know what you mean,' she said. 'It's a ticklish subject.'

Nell was encouraged to unburden herself. 'I suppose I feel that now I've taken Rob and the children on, I have a duty to see it through. But I just wish he'd be more open to discussing things with me. He takes it for granted that I think the same way he does. He doesn't seem to have come across *empathy* as a necessary accomplishment – pity I can't get him to go to evening classes on the subject!'

'Ah, well . . . you know what they say,' Sibyl warned. 'You shouldn't try to teach a pig to sing. It never works, and it annoys the pig.'

Nell laughed. 'You mean it's useless to try and change people?'

'That's about it.'

'So what *do* you do?'

'Well, I suppose you have to keep attempting to talk everything through as much as possible, and eventually when you come up against the immutable, you just have to learn not to mind.'

The rains continued and Nell observed with fascination the speed at which the countryside greened over again. Grass seemed to have supernatural powers of recuperation. She was glad not to have to keep on watering her precious plants by hand, now that God had taken over and seemed to be doing a much better job of it. She lay in bed after Rob had got up, listening to the raindrops beating against the windows, and smiling to herself. The news was full of the *'Is this really the end of the drought?'* story, with reports of a fleet of tankers still attempting to fill up one spectacularly empty reservoir from another in a more favoured part of the country.

Nell remembered the time she had driven along the top road – almost exactly two years ago – and had first seen the two chimneys of Bottom Cottage emerging through the trees. She had felt as parched and brittle inside as the surrounding fields were then. She had wanted so much that seemed unattainable . . . And now she had got it all – or nearly all.

And the rain was coming down steadily, and all the latent fecundity of a hot summer was now realising its potential by swelling into fruits. The Bramley in the garden was bent double with flushed green apples. The oaks were dotted all over with acorns, and coiled ropes of ripening black bryony berries now decorated the hedgerows. Nell felt at one with the world around her, and content. The distant bellowing of a recently calved cow, dispossessed and calling for her lost bull-calf, was the only sadness. It caused her a pang of understanding for Rob, and reminded her again of how fortunate she was.

With the new-found luxury of free afternoons, she had time to watch the season slide irrevocably into autumn; the swallows collecting, twittering, on the telegraph wires one week, and then mysteriously gone the next; the harsh chattering *Tchak tchak tchak!* calls of the fieldfares in the tallest trees, signalling their passage from Scandinavia to winter in softer climes; and the sun slipping ever southwards behind the hill, so that eventually on the shortest day it would rise from the sea behind the dunes.

In the fresh lulls between showers, Nell went out and knelt awkwardly in the garden, planting bulbs for the spring. Her bulge got in the way, and her back hurt, but she felt full of hope and driven by a desire to propagate as much life as she could.

The children, briefed by Cassie, commented on how fat she looked, so she let them feel the baby kicking and explained, as well as she was able, how it came to be there in the first place.

'I know all about sex,' Josh said loftily, 'but what I want to know is, *who* did you have sex *with*?'

Nell blushed. 'Well, with Rob of course. Who else?'

'Oh no,' Josh was positive. 'My dad wouldn't do anything like *that*.'

She and Rob laughed about it afterwards. 'You will explain to Josh, won't you?' Nell urged him. 'I want him to know that this baby belongs to you in exactly the same way he does.'

'Of course I will, Miss . . .' He stopped. 'I can hardly call you Miss Dowsabel nowadays, can I? And Mrs D. sounds all wrong. What does he think?' He rubbed her stomach proprietorially.

'He likes it. What does it mean anyway? I've always meant to ask.'

'I believe it's the English form of the Latin name Dulcibella. It means sweetheart.'

'That's nice.' Nell reached to kiss his cheek. 'And you called me that right from the beginning?'

'Before I knew your real name, yes.'

'I called you Heathcliff!' Nell grinned.

'Oh, so you did notice me?'

'Of course.'

'Oh dear, that must be a bit of a letdown.'

'Why?'

'Well, I'm not exactly the rugged type, am I?'

'You'll do,' Nell said, taking his hand and squeezing it.

It was obvious to her now that Cassie had been responsible for at least ninety per cent of the trouble in their marriage. Nell was convinced that, given a proper chance, she and Rob would do much better. Soon, when the children were settled in their new home, he would get accustomed to the fact of their removal and ease into a regular routine for visiting them. It would be expensive, yes, but not prohibitive, and Nell vowed never to make a fuss about it. Then their relationship would settle down too, into comfortable familiarity. Maybe they would even get married. She wouldn't hold her breath on that one though.

'I think I'll make green tomato and apple chutney,' Rob volunteered unexpectedly one weekend.

'Yes, do.' Nell was amused and grateful, and remained so, even when the whole house stank of vinegar and spices.

The 17th November brought the first frost of autumn, and Rob began making porridge every morning for their breakfast. The cherry tree went golden yellow all over, and there were crowds of redwings close to the cottage, eating the hawthorn berries under cover of the morning mists. A pair of buzzards soared and dived over the valley, and Nell found forty ladybirds all hibernating together in a crevice outside her bedroom window. Life was gentle and full of discoveries.

'Do you understand how I feel about Rosie and Josh?' Nell asked Rob one evening, meaning to explain herself at last.

'Well, naturally you don't feel as strongly as I do. That's quite understandable.'

'No, you're right.'

'You're good with them though.'

'Am I? You've never said that before.' Nell was surprised.

'Oh yes, and they're very fond of you.'

'That's nice.' She felt pleased but perfidious.

'So?'

'Oh, it's nothing.' She couldn't say it. It would only upset and antagonise him, and what good could it do?

The telephone rang. It was Elly.

'Have a word with Nell,' Rob said to her, passing over the receiver.

'How's it going?' Elly asked.

'Backache, constipation, *anticipation*,' Nell said cheerfully.

'Not all bad then? Good for you.'

'Not at all. Rob's being a great help.' She smiled at him as she spoke, and he responded by looking suitably modest. 'How's life with you? We missed you at half term.'

'Yes, the boys had things to do in London – shame really. But we're fine. I've been getting quite a lot of work, in fact, and Hat's still a treasure.'

'Have you heard from Paul?'

'That's what I'm ringing to tell you. He got in touch to speak to the boys and he's in great form. Says he feels genuinely free for the first time in his life!'

'And . . . you don't mind that? I should have thought . . .'

Elly laughed, a deep-throated chuckle. 'Wait, she said. 'I haven't told you the best bit yet.'

'Go on then.'

'It's Anna. Paul says she's driven him completely up the wall – or should that be up the hull? Honestly, I haven't laughed so much in ages.' Nell began to smile too, such was the infectiousness of Elly's tone of voice. 'But you'll never guess what he's finally gone and done?' Elly said, exploding with mirth.

'What?'

'Dumped the stupid woman in the Azores!'

Chapter Twenty-Four

Rob's father told him over the phone on 22nd December that he would be visiting Bottom Cottage for Christmas.

'But why?' Nell was horrified.

'Well, we usually see each other sometime about then,' Rob said. 'It's what families do.'

'But where will he sleep? The children will be in the spare room.'

'On the sitting-room floor. On the sofa cushions in a sleeping bag. It's very comfortable, in fact. I've done it myself.'

'Oh, Rob . . .'

'What's the problem?'

'Well, it's bad enough having to have Rosie and Josh when I'm feeling so huge and so tired, but Bert as well . . .'

'He'll help,' Rob said. 'He'll take them off our hands some of the time. It'll be easier, you'll see.'

'And what about food?'

'We've got a turkey ordered, haven't we? It'll stretch to one more easily. You worry too much.'

But I'll have to clean the house, Nell thought. He'll be super-critical of everything, and I haven't the energy . . . and we'll need heaps more booze . . . and a gift for him . . . She felt defeated before she'd even begun. 'I thought you didn't like your father?' she objected. 'Especially after last year.'

'I never said that.' Rob was indignant. 'It was Cassie who messed things up.'

'Oh well, I expect we'll manage.' After all, Nell

admonished herself, if my parents were alive, I'd want them to come, wouldn't I?

Bert arrived late on Christmas Eve, later than he had said he would. He was driving a flashy car, which turned out to have a boot full of fancily-wrapped presents. Nell went out with Rob to greet him and, seeing them in the light from the porch, was pleasantly surprised.

'Clementines,' he said, handing her a carrier bag. 'And Rob, take this wine, would you. No kids?'

'Asleep upstairs,' Rob said. 'Don't bang the doors, eh?'

They helped him in with his things, and put his presents on top of the others under the Christmas tree in the sitting room.

'I hope you'll be all right on that?' Nell asked, indicating the makeshift bed on the floor. 'I've put a hot bottle in it.'

'Positive luxury,' Bert beamed. 'You should see some of the places I've slept in my time. I think the worst was in a desert full of scorpions in North Africa! Freezing cold, it was. Did I ever tell you abut that, Rob?'

'Once or twice.' Rob smiled at Nell. 'Have you eaten?'

'Oh, don't go to any trouble,' Bert said cheerfully. 'A light omelette would do just fine. Cheese and tomato for preference.'

Nell sighed audibly without really meaning to.

'When's it due?' Bert asked, as though coming upon her condition unexpectedly.

'Fortnight,' Nell yawned. She could barely keep her eyes open.

'Oh, it'll be late,' Bert said confidently. 'First ones always are.'

God! Nell thought, I do hope not. But she smiled politely.

'You get off to bed,' Rob said to her unexpectedly. 'We'll manage.'

She went upstairs thankfully, cleaned her teeth,

undressed, and manoeuvred her large bulk into bed without washing. And she was just lapsing into blissful unconsciousness when Rob popped his head round the bedroom door. 'Sorry,' he said, 'do we have any cheese?'

The children woke unnecessarily early on Christmas morning as always. Nell came to to the sound of Josh chanting, *Fat head, wet the bed! Fat head, wet the bed!* and knew that Rosie would be goaded into retaliation at any moment. She nudged Rob. He had a happy knack of sleeping through mayhem, which Nell wished she could emulate.

'Happy Christmas,' she said into his ear. 'Can you get up to prevent a murder?'

'Whaaa . . .?'

'In the children's room. They're awake and –' The bedroom door burst open and someone came in. Nell switched on the bedside light. Josh was dragging a sheet behind him.

'She's done it again,' he said, 'and it's Christmas Day!' He sounded exactly like Cassie.

'That's unkind, Josh,' Nell protested. 'She can't help it.' Rosie stood sulkily in the doorway knuckling her eyes.

'Guess what?' Nell said, on sudden inspiration. 'Your granddad's down in the sitting room.'

'Yeah!' Josh dumped the smelly sheet, pushed Rosie aside and ran. Rosie bounced off the doorpost and clattered downstairs after him. Nell breathed a sigh of relief and closed her eyes again.

'That was a bit inconsiderate, wasn't it?' Rob protested. So Nell began Christmas in the wrong, and her inner bells felt jangled not jingled.

'There ought to be snow,' Josh complained at breakfast in the kitchen, glowering through the window at the driving rain. ' 'Snot fair!'

'Life isn't fair,' Bert said, 'but then again, why should it

283

be? There will always be some people better off than others.' He smoothed his thick white hair, and put a lot of butter on his toast.

'I want prethents,' Rosie announced.

'Go on then,' Nell encouraged her. 'Pop and get one for each of us, and we'll open them now.' Rosie disappeared into the next room with alacrity and was gone for some time. Scrabbling noises could be heard and mutterings as she read the labels, but when she reappeared she was carrying only one parcel. 'Can't find any.' Her lower lip trembled.

'Go and help her, Josh,' Rob urged.

'She can't read!' Josh taunted his sister. But he was gone for some time too, and when he came back he looked bewildered.

'What's up?' Rob asked.

'The presents,' Josh said, 'they're all for *him*.' He pointed accusingly at his grandfather. Everyone turned to stare at him.

Bert looked entirely unabashed. 'I get given so many,' he explained modestly. 'It would have been a waste to leave them all in London.' He shrugged charmingly. 'What's a man to do?'

By lunchtime the family presents had been unearthed from beneath Bert's pile, and the children were busy eating chocolate money from the tree, picking off the realistic gold wrappers and dropping them all over the floor. Nell, occupied in the kitchen, had detailed Rob to make sure they didn't spoil their appetites for lunch, but he was deep in conversation with his father and, as she came into the sitting room to call them in to eat, she saw the evidence and sighed. She wondered whether Rosie or Josh had yet discovered the two real pound coins that she had slipped in amongst the chocolate ones, but so far neither of them had come running up to announce a happy find.

'. . . I'll have a word,' Bert was saying to Rob. 'I'm sure I can talk some sense into her. Unfortunately she hasn't a cat's chance in hell of getting back into television these days. She's just too long in the tooth and too out of touch.'

'And you're going to tell her that?' Rob snorted. 'Rather you than me!'

'Is this Cassie you're discussing?' Nell enquired, wiping her hands on her pinny.

'Yes,' Rob said, smiling. 'Bert thinks he can persuade her to stay.'

'Sadly, I've had a lot of experience of having to warn people off attempting to be actors or television presenters,' Bert said, affecting weariness. 'They come to me in droves expecting instant fame, and I just have to tell them life's not like that.'

Except for you, of course, Nell thought, recognising the all-too-common scenario – successful people like Malachy/Bert trying their damnedest to prevent anyone else from sharing their good fortune: *I'm in, Jack. Pull up the drawbridge!* She hoped Cassie would have the wit to see through him too.

'Would you come and get the turkey out of the oven?' she asked Rob. 'I'm about to dish up.'

'Right then, kids,' Bert said, clapping his hands. 'Grub up! Get those paws washed pronto!' and he swept the children before him into the kitchen.

Nell was relieved to find that the Christmas lunch looked fine. Everything had cooked properly and was ready at the right moment. She brushed the sweat from her brow with the hem of her apron and sank into a chair as Rob carried the crisp browned turkey to the table, and Bert prepared with a flourish of knife and steel to carve it. Bowls of vegetables steamed invitingly. Rich gravy, cranberry and bread sauces waited in a huddle with ladles at the ready. Bert lifted slices of turkey, spoonfuls of stuffing and charred chipolatas on to warm plates and passed them round.

'I don't want any,' Josh announced.

'What on earth d'you mean?' Nell asked, upset.

'I don't want this. I want sandwiches.'

'Oh, Josh . . .' Nell began.

'Well, I suppose I could make you a turkey sandwich,' Rob said. 'If that's what –'

'What nonsense!' Bert interrupted. 'This is terrific food! And it's all there is, so eat it or go without!'

He's right, Nell thought with reluctant admiration, but he doesn't understand what a bind Rob's in. If children live with you all the time you can afford to be tough. But if they've got another home to go to, and you're hard on them, then there's always the fear that they might go there and never come back. I can see it so clearly from Rob's point of view, so why can't his father?

Josh held out for ten minutes, watching furiously as everyone ate.

'Roast parsnips!' Bert said rapturously. 'Manna from heaven!'

'Rob grew them,' Nell said. 'And they've been well frosted, which makes them sweet.'

'Is that so?' Bert queried. 'I've never heard of that.'

'Oh, yes,' Rob assured him.

'Why?' Bert challenged. 'How could frost affect the physiology of a parsnip?'

'Well, it obviously breaks down the cell walls and causes the starch . . .'

Oh no, Nell thought. Don't let's have one of those discussions where no one knows what they're talking about, and as a result argues even more fiercely. She heaved herself up and went over to the stove to check the pudding.

'Have we got any brandy?' she interrupted them.

'Miniature in the cupboard, I think,' Rob answered after her third try.

'Come on, young Josh,' Bert said heartily. 'Let's set fire to it, eh?'

Josh could not resist, and as his grandfather poured the warmed spirit over the pudding, he struck a match and ignited it, crowing over the fleeting blue flames. Then, having forgotten about the necessity to sulk, he ate a huge bowlful of it with cream and brandy butter, and found more hidden five-pence pieces in his than anyone else.

'It's no good being afraid of your children,' Bert said confidentially to Nell later on over the washing-up – which he was doing with great flamboyance and too much foam. 'You have to show them who's boss.'

Nell retired to a stool to dry a handful of cutlery with the teatowel, feeling resentful. Rob had taken the children for another rainwalk to dissipate some of their energy, and Bert had stayed behind rather obviously to help her. She got the impression that he didn't like her very much. Perhaps she wasn't beautiful enough. Perhaps he was influenced by the fact that she'd worked in a shop. Nell knew by now that Rob was not a snob, but suspected his father might well be.

'I'm glad to have this time on our own.' Bert said to her conspiratorially. 'I've got a little present for you. It's really to celebrate the birth of your first child, but now seems an appropriate moment.' He dried his hands and went to fetch a small package.

Oh no! Nell thought. What if it's . . . She tore off the blue tissue paper nervously and opened the box. In the virgin white interior lay a beautiful malachite necklace. 'No,' she said at once. 'It's very kind of you, but I couldn't possibly accept it.'

'Why ever not?' Bert's eyes were wide with ersatz affront.

'I just couldn't.' She wanted to say, 'You know very well why not!' but was afraid to do so.

'You're being illogical,' Bert said quite gently. 'You like

it, I can see you do, and I want you to have it. Surely those are good enough reasons?'

'It would upset Rob,' Nell said stubbornly without looking at him.

'Oh, I see . . . That old canard!' He put out a hand and raised her chin so that she could not avoid looking at him. 'You don't believe that nonsense surely?'

'Yes,' Nell said stoutly. 'I think I do.'

He dropped his hand abruptly. 'I'm disappointed in you,' he said, closing the box and slipping it into his pocket. 'And to think I was so glad when Rob found himself someone after Cassie . . .' He sighed. 'I suppose I shouldn't have expected you to be alike.' He made for the back door, shrugging himself into an immaculate Barbour jacket and pulling on a fisherman's cap at a rakish angle. 'Fresh air,' he said. 'That's what's needed.' And he went out into the weather. Nell took herself into the sitting room to recover her composure, and saw him through the window, striding out along the coast path all boldness and self-confidence; a man unburdened by insight.

Poor Rob, she thought. No wonder.

Ten minutes later Rob and the children came back with Bert, and there was a great disrobing and shaking of waterproofs and pulling off of muddy boots. Nell let them get on with it. She had cleared up most of the torn wrapping paper and the empty nets which had held the chocolate money. She felt she had done enough for the day.

They came into the sitting room with faces pink with cold and glowing with exercise. Josh's feet were bare. 'Not another welly-full?' she asked.

'It was an accident.' He grinned cheerfully.

'It always is!'

'Look what I've got, Nell!' Rosie pranced in joyfully. She was wearing the malachite necklace, and it hung down her flat little chest like an oversized garland of green pebbles. Nell glanced straight at Rob, but his face was expressionless. She cast about for something neutral to say.

'Rosie and Josh,' she said, 'did you find the real pound coins we put in amongst your chocolate ones?'

'Yeah,' Josh answered for both of them. He looked cautious.

'So why didn't you say so?'

Now he looked shifty. 'I thought they might belong to someone else.'

It went on raining solidly all Christmas Day and Nell was glad when it got dark so she could draw the curtains and no longer have to look out at the brown river and the brown trees and the brownish leaden sky. At least indoors there were bright lights and cheerful decorations. By eight o'clock in the evening the children were tired and peevish, and only staying awake to spite each other. Nell didn't want always to be the one to send them to bed, and wished Rob would be more decisive and take charge. He didn't notice, of course, and seemed quite happy lolling on the sofa, occasionally administering a mild reproof to one or other of them.

'Right!' Bert said, looking at his watch. 'Bedtime for kids. Who's going to be up the stairs first?'

'I don't want –' Josh began, but Bert, rising from his chair and bent double, rushed at him, grabbed him in a fireman's lift and bore him aloft laughing and complaining all at the same time.

'Me too, me too, me too!' Rosie shouted joyfully.

'I'll come back for you,' Bert promised, disappearing. They heard the clump of his feet on the wooden stairs and Josh's squeaks and giggles. Then he was down again for Rosie. 'Which way up is this parcel?' he teased, standing her on her head. 'Ah, that's right.'

'No, it ithn't!' Squeals of joy.

'This better?'

'No!'

'Or this?'

'*No!*'

Nell and Rob exchanged glances as he went up with her too, and as the bedroom door closed and the noises diminished, Nell said, 'It'll never work. He'll get them so hyped up that they won't sleep for a week!'

'Mmm,' Rob agreed.

'There's a programme about painting on BBC2 that I wouldn't mind watching,' Nell said. 'D'you think Bert would mind?'

'Shouldn't think so.'

'Or you?'

'Fine by me.'

Bert came back a quarter of an hour later, looking tousled but pleased with himself. 'Out like lights,' he reported.

'Asleep?' Nell was astonished.

'Yep. Now then . . .' He walked across to the television, switched it on and pressed the button for ITV. 'Good, he said. 'Just in time.'

It was his own programme and there he was in his surgeon's mask, saving lives, making impossible decisions, seducing nurses and fighting the hospital management committee. Nell looked anxiously at Rob. He never watched the programme on purpose. She waited for him to protest, but he just sat there. For her own part she was intrigued to see Malachy in action, so she made no move to dissent either.

Bert sat back on the sofa with legs crossed widely, ankle on knee. 'Now she,' he said, pointing to the actress playing the theatre sister, 'is actually a lesbian. Never know it, would you? Looks a real doll. And he, with the red hair, has done time for actual bodily harm, but he's as mild as baby food, bless him. And watch this bit coming up . . . you can just see the overhead mike, that fuzzy bit of grey . . . got it? It took us a ridiculous amount of time to shoot that scene because the bloody casualty kept on corpsing. Look, you can see him trying not to laugh . . . there!'

Even Rob was smiling. Nell couldn't help but be amused, and was flattered by his indiscretion. During the ad breaks she got Rob to fetch drinks; beer for himself, orange juice for her, and malt whisky for Bert. The three of them sat comfortably in front of the log fire, totally relaxed. This is more like it! Nell thought. This is what Christmas should be like. She didn't even feel annoyed about her missed art programme since everyone was enjoying themselves so much.

At ten o'clock Elly phoned, and Nell went into the kitchen to speak to her. 'Happy Christmas!' She sounded cheerfully tipsy.

'And to you. Have you had a good day?' Nell asked.

'Very good. We're all at Sibyl's and Hat is taking the boys out for a treat tomorrow, so I wondered if you'd meet us in the Wheatsheaf for lunch?'

'Oh, I'd love to,' Nell said, 'but we've got the children, and Bert's here . . . and I don't suppose you want to see him . . .'

'He's not my favourite person, no!'

'So I'm afraid . . .'

'Well, why don't you leave the kids with Bert, and you and Rob come?'

'Wouldn't that be rather selfish?' Nell said, thinking (as always) of the awful example set by Anna's step-mother.

'What, escaping for a couple of hours? What d'you want to be, feminist or doormat?'

'Something in between for preference!'

'Well then, you do have to put your foot down some-times and do what *you* want for a change. Get a life!' Elly urged. 'Go on, we haven't met for ages, and I'm dying to see you.'

'I'd like to . . .' Nell hesitated.

'Tell you what,' Elly said, 'we'll be there between twelve thirty and two, so if you can come, do.'

Rob was awoken in the middle of the night by Nell shaking him and turning on the light. 'Whassermatter . . .?'

'Your father's shouting downstairs. Go and see what's wrong.'

'Probably . . . nightmare . . . go back . . . sleep.'

'No! I'm sure it's more than that. Please wake up!'

Rob groaned and sat up, peering at the clock. It was 3.40 a.m. 'God . . .' he grumbled. 'This had better be worth it.' He pulled on his dressing gown and was just about to go downstairs, when he met Bert coming up. 'What's the matter?'

'You might at least have given me a boat to sleep in,' Bert said, turning round to show him the back of his silk pyjamas, which were soaking wet.

'Oh Christ!' Rob elbowed him aside and rushed downstairs, thinking: All that rain . . . the river . . . high tide . . . Why the fuck didn't I put out the sandbags? . . . Distracted by booze and talk, and bloody Bert!

The damage was not as great as he had feared. The flood was only a few inches high across the floors of the cottage – too low to have buggered up the electric power circuit, thank God, but enough to have soaked up through Bert's makeshift mattress and muddied the carpets and the legs of the furniture. Rob splashed through it in bare feet to the corner by the back door, where he kept the sandbags. He had no idea whether the tide was yet at its height, and he didn't fancy trying to sweep the river out of the cottage if more were to pile in than he could get rid of. So, for the moment at least, he would wall up both doors and try to stop things getting any worse.

He was furious with himself for not taking precautions. He *knew* this was likely to happen after such rain, especially during a period of spring tides.

'Rob?' Nell called from upstairs. 'What's happening? Can I do anything?'

'No,' he shouted back, dragging sandbags about. 'It's all . . . under . . . control. Stay where you are.'

'Is it a flood?'

'Yes, but it's not . . . very . . . bad.'

At least, he thought, the lights still work so I can see what I'm doing, and I've got the wherewithal to contain the water. I'm not totally stuffed. He completed the sandbag barrier inside front and back doors and watched it tensely to see if it would do the job. He made a pencil mark on the skirting board and inspected it every few seconds to check it was still on the waterline, not below. It was. He began to breathe more easily.

'Dad?' Josh splashed across the floor towards him. 'What's all the shouting for, and why's Granddad having a bath in the middle of the night?'

'See for yourself.'

'Is it the river or the sea?'

'A bit of both, probably.'

'And will we all be washed away and drowned?' Josh hunched his shoulders anxiously.

'Oh, no. Everything's all right now. The sandbags will stop it.'

'What about the windows?'

'Oh, it won't get that high.'

'But why didn't you put the sandbags out *before* the water came in?'

'Good question.' Rob ruffled his hair affectionately. 'Some people have no foresight.'

Nell was unable to sleep for the rest of the night. It was difficult enough at the best of times in her condition to get comfortable, but now they had Bert all warmed up again from his bath and snoring loudly on a heap of blankets on their bedroom floor. All right for some! she thought crossly.

She worried about the mess there must be downstairs, and how she would ever be able to clean it all up, and how she would prevent the first floor from getting covered in mud and water as well, with everyone going up and down the stairs . . . Then she thought of Elly and about putting one's foot down, and she made a decision.

'The children will have to go home to Cassie,' she said in the morning. It was the first time she had ever interfered in an arrangement made between Rob and the Mad Cow about their children.

'Oh, we'll manage,' Rob said at once, brushing the idea aside. 'They can help in the clearing up. Rosie's absolutely furious that she slept through the whole drama last night!'

'No, Rob, I mean it.' This was also the first time she had asked for something important for herself, and it felt dangerously egocentric. If she hadn't had the obvious excuse of late pregnancy, she might have found it impossible, but exhaustion spurred her on. 'I can't cope with them here. It's all too much.'

'Well . . . I'd have to see whether Cassie's there,' Rob said doubtfully. 'She might well be away.'

'Yes,' Nell said, 'you do that.'

Bert announced that he would be leaving early too. 'Best get out of your way,' he said. 'I never sleep properly on the floor anyway. I was built for luxury not utility.' He offered to return the children to Cassie and to have a word with her at the same time. Rob was obviously torn between the possible benefits of this intervention, and the disappointment of sending his children away. Nell was worried too, but for just the opposite reason. She heard

Bert on the phone to Cassie, joking and teasing her. 'At least she is there,' she said to him as he put the receiver down.

'Oh, she's there all right. Sounds to be in good form too.'

'Lucky old her,' Nell muttered.

'Don't worry,' Bert said, patting her on the top of her head. 'It's a very minor flood. You'll get it cleared up in no time.'

No thanks to you, Nell thought sourly.

Elly kept an eye out for Nell and Rob as she and Sibyl sat in the Wheatsheaf having a Boxing Day drink. She had also seen the man she'd hoped would be there. He was sitting with a few of his mates, and he'd waved at once and invited them over to join the group, but she hadn't done so. She'd chosen instead to sit in a position where she could catch his eye from time to time.

'Who's that?' Sibyl asked, antennae fully deployed.

'Old school friend,' Elly said carelessly. 'Nice chap. Wife's just left him. Stupid woman!'

'I *see*,' Sibyl smiled.

'Did I show you Paul's card from Tenerife?' Elly said, getting it out of her handbag.

'You did,' Sibyl said, 'and now you can show it to Nell.'

Elly looked round. Nell was negotiating her way towards them through the lounge bar. She looked enormous.

'You made it!' Elly cried, getting up to give her a hug. 'I'm so glad. You look as though you're about to pop at any moment!'

'Can't be too soon for me,' Nell said, giving Sibyl a kiss. 'I feel grotesque.'

'No Rob?'

'No. I've left him at home mopping up.' Elly raised an eyebrow. 'The river paid us a visit last night,' Nell explained. 'Only a little flood, thank goodness, but still very messy. I feel a bit mean actually. I should have persuaded him to take a break and come too.'

'And the monsters, not to mention the luvvie?'

'Gone home, thank the Lord. Bert went off of his own accord, but I had to insist that the children should go too. I felt really selfish.'

'What's with this "selfish" caper?' Elly demanded. 'It was an entirely reasonable request, wasn't it, under the circumstances?'

'Well, yes.'

'Well then!'

'Have you got heat and light still?' Sibyl asked.

'Oh, yes. The woodburner's on a plinth, so it was above the water, and so were all the electric sockets.'

'Seriously, Nell,' Elly said, 'it's very important to be able to ask for what you need, and to say no sometimes. Rob will take you at your own valuation of yourself, so if you hold out for the things you want, he'll take you less for granted and be more thoughtful. And then you'll feel a lot less resentful. It's basic survival, honestly.'

'She's just joined a women's group, you know,' Sibyl said behind her hand to Nell, and they laughed.

'Paul's in Tenerife,' Elly said, handing Nell the postcard. 'Or he was when he wrote this. He's probably on the high seas off Africa as we speak.'

'You don't regret the divorce, do you?' Nell asked.

'God no, not at all. I couldn't stand that macho laddishness for a moment longer.'

'It's strange,' Sibyl said, gazing into her gin, 'but it seems to me that people often get divorced for exactly the same reasons as they got married.'

'You're right!' Elly said. 'How ridiculous we all are.' There was a shout of mirth from the table she'd been watching. She saw Nell glance across and identify the man laughing the most uproariously.

'Hey!' Nell said. 'That's Kipper Jarvis from school, isn't it?'

'Certainly is,' Elly said, 'and he's on his own again, like me.'

'Really?' Nell gave her a knowing look. 'And have you tested out your theory of belly laughs yet?'

But Elly just smiled enigmatically.

Nell was tired when she got home from the pub, and rather guilty for having enjoyed herself so much. Rob had taken advantage of the low tide and had dragged the ruined sitting room carpet out into the garden and draped it over the back wall. He was now busy on his hands and knees scrubbing the kitchen floor.

'Oh, well done, love,' she said. 'Good effort.'

Rob looked up, smiling all over his face. 'Easy,' he said. 'I've been buoyed up by excellent news. Bert phoned.'

'Oh?' Nell felt suddenly empty.

'Yes. He says he did have a word with Cassie, but in fact she'd already made up her mind. She knows she would never have got a job in television, but was too proud at first to admit it.'

'You mean . . .?'

'Yep, she and the children are staying in Boxcombe after all! Isn't that *great*?'

Chapter Twenty-Five

At thirty-nine weeks Nell felt she couldn't bear to wait a moment longer for her baby to be born. She could hardly walk or bend, or even eat. The pressure on her bladder was unrelenting and her back hurt almost all the time. She had stopped going swimming some time before, but had frequent warm baths instead to ease the discomfort. She, who never normally went to the doctor, was now seeing her twice a week, and was grateful for the care and attention. Rob was helpful too, simply by being there and by being calm because he had done all this before. Nell felt ambivalent about this; reassured that he would know what to do when the time came, but sad that they wouldn't be sharing their first birth together.

One night she dreamed that the pregnancy was all a mistake. She looked down at herself and found that her stomach was back where it used to be, and she'd zipped up a tight pair of jeans to prove it. She'd realised with joy that she had got her old life back again and then had woken up, feeling confused and guilty. 'I want this baby,' she said aloud to break the hold of the dream. Then she felt positive and hopeful as usual.

A week later, when she was having another bath, she lay back watching her huge bulge and the little sticking out bump that undulated from one side to the other as the baby moved. Was it an elbow or a foot or perhaps a knee? It was certainly active. People had told her that a child's personality was there right from the beginning. She could believe it. She thought about the little person inside her and wondered how and what it would be. Would it have hair, and what colour? Would it look like her, or Rob? Would it be all right? If it turned out to be a boy she wanted to call him William, but she hoped so much that it would be a girl. Tonight she had an extra niggly ache that came and went, and a specially heavy feeling. 'You're due,' she told her bump. 'You can come out now.'

Getting out of the bath wasn't easy. She heaved herself forward and got a good grip of one of the taps before easing herself up and putting one foot cautiously onto the bathmat. She dried herself slowly and then became aware that the towel was sticky. When she looked down, it was mucus streaked with blood.

'Rob!' she cried, arriving breathless downstairs in the sitting room without slippers, and with her naked stomach protruding beyond the inadequate dressing gown. 'I think it's begun!'

Rob zapped the sound off on the television and inspected the towel. 'Yes,' he said. 'That's called a "show". Good.'

'So what shall I do? I've got my bag all ready. I just need to put in my toothbrush and my flannel . . . and . . .'

'Relax,' Rob said. 'Remember what they taught you at antenatal. It'll be hours. You haven't got any contractions yet, have you?'

'Well, not proper ones, no.'

'It might be days even before your labour starts, and you'll catch your death going about like that. Best thing would be to go to bed and get some sleep. You'll get precious little once it's born.'

'*Sleep?*' Nell was incredulous.

'Why not? We don't need to go to the hospital for ages yet.'

'Will you come up too?'

'In a while. I just want to see the end of this programme.' He stroked her back affectionately and turned up the sound again.

Nell went up to bed and lay there with her hands on her stomach, collecting her thoughts. She went through the breathing exercises she had been taught, and reminded herself of what she should expect to happen. An hour later she looked at the clock. She was feeling mild contractions every so often. She was sure it was beginning. She wanted Rob to be with her for reassurance, but she didn't want to make a fuss.

'If he's born tomorrow,' Rob said, coming to bed eventually, 'it will be the seventh of January, which was my mother's birthday.'

'That's nice,' Nell said. 'It's definitely started.'

'So we should certainly call it Lesley; ending in ie if it's a boy, or ey if it's a girl.'

Dreadful name! Nell thought. 'Tell you what,' she compromised, 'if it's a boy he can be Leslie – maybe William Leslie – but if it's a girl she'll be Lottie. Yes?'

'If you like,' Rob said, yawning. 'We'll wait until the contractions are about ten minutes apart and regular, right? Then we'll nip into Boxcombe, no sweat. Don't worry about a thing.' He yawned again, kissed her cheek, turned over and went to sleep.

Neil lay beside him wide awake, unsure whether to feel reassured or cheated. She was far too keyed up to sleep. After another couple of hours her pains were becoming more businesslike. This is going to hurt like hell, she thought, but I shall just have to bear it. She waited for an age, dozing a little between contractions and watching the clock, until they were coming about every quarter of an hour, and then she felt a sudden urge and had to rush to the lavatory. Sitting there, she began to feel anxious. What if she had more diarrhoea when she was actually producing the baby? What if she was late in getting to hospital? What if the roads were icy? What if they were blocked by roadworks or a crash? What if the Land Rover wouldn't start? What if she couldn't wake Rob up? *Silly!*

She wrapped herself in a tartan rug ard crept downstairs as silently as possible. Then she made herself a cup of Horlicks and ate a Mars bar. Sitting in the cold kitchen with the dark January night outside, and swathed in prickly Dress Stuart, she looked about her and thought: This is the last time I shall be alone and absolutely free . . .

She timed the pains again. They were coming every ten minutes. She gathered herself mentally and physically and climbed the stairs again.

'Rob!' she shook him awake. 'It's time to go.'

Rob found himself comparing this birth with his two previous ones. Cassie had had to be induced, and had forceps deliveries and an episiotomy both times, which required large amounts of stitches. And, as he remembered it, she had played it for all it was worth and made sure of the sympathy vote. The whole procedure had been far too messy for her; bodily fluids everywhere. She was unnecessarily fastidious, overdependent upon painkillers, and just plain terrified.

Nell will be different, he thought fondly, standing beside the head of the delivery table and wiping the sweat off her forehead with a cool damp flannel, as she gritted her teeth and didn't yell. He remembered that Cassie had shrieked from the outset and demanded pethidine. Nell had good wide hips, had declined the offer of an epidural and was determined to have a drug-free birth. He felt inordinately proud of her.

They had come into hospital far too early, of course, and had waited around for hours and hours, but he had understood Nell's sense of urgency. He felt comfortable, having done all this before, and glad he was so well equipped to reassure her. He'd had plenty of time to slip home again for a flask of coffee, some sandwiches and the newspaper, and as an afterthought had brought along Nell's hand-mirror for use later on. He considered bringing his camera as well, but there would be plenty of time for photographs later. He didn't want to be distracted from his main purpose – that of looking after her.

He glanced at the clock on the wall. It was now seven o'clock in the morning, but still dark outside. Nell's blood pressure was good. Her contractions were being recorded on the monitor (along with the baby's heart rate) and they were coming about every minute, some double-peaked and clearly excruciating.

The midwife did an examination. 'You're four fingers dilated and going into transition,' she reported encouragingly. 'You're doing fine. Not long now. I think it's time we broke your waters.'

'All right?' Rob asked Nell, as they gushed out.

'No, it's bloody agony,' Nell muttered through clenched teeth. 'I'm not sure I can . . .' But she declined the offered pethidine.

'Breathe in time with me,' Rob said, reminding her. 'OK?'

'I've *got* to PUSH!' Nell cried, gripping both of his hands painfully hard. 'I can't help it!'

'Not yet dear,' the midwife cautioned. 'Have some gas and air.'

'Breathe,' Rob said, 'and slow, and breathe.' He had never felt more needed, or more capable of helping her. She was responding to him like someone drowning. 'You can do it,' he told her.

Then after what seemed a long time, 'Push!' instructed the midwife. Three more contractions. 'The head's coming. One more nice big push.'

'All right?' Rob asked again.

'No!' Nell shouted. 'Have you ever tried shitting a bloody melon?'

Just as Nell thought she wouldn't be able to bear the

torture a moment longer, and would be forced to give in and ask for some pain relief, the midwife said, 'Nearly there. I can see lots of black hair.'

Incredible! Nell thought wearily. It's a real person with hair just like Rob's! And tears of joy came into her eyes. She gave one last hugely painful push and the head was born.

'Rest,' the midwife said encouragingly, 'and then one more push for the shoulders.'

'I want to see!' Nell cried. Rob supported her as she leant forwards over her collapsed abdomen, and held up the mirror. The baby's head was slowly rotating and one shoulder was becoming visible. As she watched, it opened its mouth, eyes still tightly shut, and let out a small high-pitched cry. Nell braced herself for the last contraction and then opened her eyes just in time to see the little wet dark red body with flailing arms and puckered face, slithering out of her into the midwife's waiting hands.

Rob wiped his own eyes. 'It's a Lottie!' he said.

'Congratulations!' Elly said over the phone as soon as Nell was home again. 'What was the best bit?'

'When they put her on my stomach and I could touch her for the first time, and she opened her eyes and stared at me,' Nell said. 'I'd been in such turmoil; in pain, angry, scared of making a mess of it – just plain scared. And then suddenly I felt tender and calm and loving all at once!'

'Magic,' Elly said. 'You did well to achieve a natural birth. It's not something I even considered. How did Rob do?'

'He was brilliant. I couldn't have managed it without him.'

'Lucky you.'

'I must go,' Nell said. 'Lottie wants feeding.'

She sat dreamily suckling the child, so aware of the

tongue curled under her nipple and the jaws pressed firmly on to her, sucking strongly as she had from the very beginning. Nell still had in her mind the vision of her newborn baby alert on her stomach, the cord still pulsating, the little body streaked with blood and white vernix, the grey eyes watchful. She had managed to do it all without drugs, and without the necessity for stitches. She felt jubilant.

She found herself asking Rob about his first two; wanting to compare herself with the Mad Cow.

'Oh, Cassie didn't want to know when Josh was born,' Rob said. 'It was a very difficult birth and she was drugged up to the eyeballs. Love at first sight it wasn't.'

'Poor thing,' Nell found herself saying, 'and poor Josh.' She discovered that this was not a time for one-upmanship. She actually felt sorry for Cassie.

After a few days the euphoria slipped away and Nell began to feel different. Tears came to her eyes for no real reason, and she became fearful of every possible hazard that might potentially harm the baby. She wanted Rob to instal a smoke alarm but he pointed out that the wood-burner would set it off all the time. So then she worried about its effect on the baby's lungs, and about whether, in spite of Rob's best efforts, there was still too much residual damp downstairs. And then about the possible consequences of future, bigger, floods. She was even concerned about Rob's habit of driving off and shutting the Land Rover door afterwards. But above all, she fretted about Cassie's decision to stay in the West Country.

Rob on the other hand seemed even more laid-back than usual, and able to get enough sleep despite the interruptions in the night, plus all the work he'd had to do in clearing the flood damage. His very confidence undermined Nell, as it pointed up her own lack of it. He seemed to think that by going on as usual, she would take her cue from him, and all would be well. And then he didn't seem to notice when it wasn't.

Elly came to see the baby, and they sat together in the sitting room by a log fire with their feet on the bare floorboards. Everything had been dried out with hot-air blowers, and the room was almost back to normal.

'Hello, my beautiful,' Elly crooned, taking the baby and holding her on her lap. 'Who's a bonny babe then? How much did she weigh?'

'Seven pounds five ounces.'

'Oh, look at the soles of her little feet. They're covered in creases like tissue paper that's been scrunched up, and then smoothed out!'

'I think they're like poppy petals or butterfly wings – when they first emerge and before they're properly pumped up.' Nell had examined with fascination every possible aspect of Lottie.

'Have you tried drawing her?'

'Haven't had time!'

'Anyway, photos are so good, aren't they?'

Nell's eyes overflowed suddenly with tears, and she fumbled for a tissue to stem the flow.

'Whatever is it?' Elly asked, reaching out over the baby to comfort her. 'Tell me.'

Nell mopped her eyes. 'I wanted a picture of Lottie in her little perspex cot in the hospital, but Rob forgot to bring his camera.'

'But he's taken some since?'

'Oh, yes. I know it's silly, but he took ones of Josh and Rosie in their cots. I know, because I saw them at Cassie's.'

'Well, maybe that's because she wasn't very *compos mentis* and needed a reminder,' Elly said diplomatically. 'I mean, you'll never forget the picture in your mind's eye, will you?'

'No,' Nell sniffed. 'I keep doing this,' she said, 'bursting into tears. I can't seem to help it. It's so stupid.'

'Nonsense!' Elly said. 'Your hormones are all of a turmoil. Happens to us all.'

'I somehow get the feeling that Rob thinks I've had it easy, so he doesn't have to try very hard now it's all over. Maybe I should have made more fuss.'

'No. You just need to be able to ask for what you need. He's not a mind-reader.'

'You can say that again!' Nell smiled shakily.

'Is there anything else?'

'Yes . . . but you'll think it's silly . . .'

'I'm sure I won't.'

'Well, it's just that now Cassie isn't moving away after all, I suppose I'm worried that Josh and Rosie will become rôle models for Lottie, and somehow . . . contaminate her.'

Elly looked taken aback. 'That's a bit extreme, isn't it? I'm not sure I understand.'

Nell felt misjudged. 'I'm worried about their bad up-bringing and rudeness, and dishonesty and . . . constant quarrelling and Cassie's influence . . . that sort of thing. I mean, I want to bring Lottie up in my own way, with different values and attitudes from theirs.'

'Well, there's not much any of us can do about that,' Elly said practically. 'I tried to do it my way with my two. Everyone does. But they're far more influenced by their peers and television than ever they are by their parents.'

'Yes, but I'm talking about the first five years,' Nell said earnestly. 'That's when children are most vulnerable to emotional damage.'

'Oh, I think you'll find that Rosie and Josh will grow up as good as anybody,' Elly said. 'You worry too much.'

'Here's the midwife now,' Rob announced loudly above the crying of the baby. 'Shall I take her, so's you can get your tummy checked?' He went to the door and let the woman in, and then lifted Lottie from her mother. Nell looked harassed.

'Morning all,' the midwife shouted cheerfully. 'Having a bit of a bawl, are we?'

'I don't know what's wrong,' Nell said anxiously. 'She started and now she won't stop.'

'Course she will,' Rob said imperturbably, rubbing the baby's back and jogging her up and down. 'She's just a little colicky, aren't you?'

'But why?' Nell asked, as she had her blood pressure taken.

'Could be something you ate,' the midwife said, 'that's got across into your milk.'

'Well, I had Brussels sprouts . . . for the iron.'

'That'll be it. Good, your uterus has shrunk back to normal now. Shan't need to come and see you MUCH LONGER.' Her last words sounded deafening. Lottie had abruptly stopped crying. 'There you are,' she said in normal tones. 'She just wanted her daddy, didn't you, precious?'

'The little cord stump dropped off,' Nell reported, rather shortly.

'Good. And is she feeding well?'

'Yes.'

'And how's the bathing going?'

'They have baths together,' Rob explained. 'Nell feels safer that way.' He smiled across at her, but she glared at him. What have I said? he thought, aggrieved.

He waited until the midwife had completed all her examinations and left before he asked Nell, 'What's wrong?'

'You know.'

'No, I don't, really.'

'Well, you ought to,' Nell said. 'You showed me up; made me look pathetic and inadequate. As soon as you took Lottie from me she stopped crying, and then you had to go and tell her about us in the bath.'

'She didn't mind.'

'That's not the *point*!'

'I'm sorry,' Rob said. 'I don't understand.'

'Well, you ought to.' Nell burst into tears. 'It's easy for you. You've done all this before. You make me feel second rate and *useless*.'

'Come on, Nell, you know that isn't true.'

'I bet you weren't like this with Cassie.' Nell sniffed loudly and bit her lip.

'Here, have Lottie back again.' Rob put the baby on her lap, and she lay there waving her arms contentedly.

'Well?' Nell demanded.

'Obviously not with Josh. I was as inexperienced as she was.'

'Exactly!'

'Fancy a cup of tea?' He hadn't a clue what she was on about.

Nell snorted. 'That's your answer to everything, isn't it?'

'Well, I want one.' He went over and put the kettle on.

'Everything's going wrong,' Nell lamented to Sibyl the next day when Rob was out.

'Since when?' Sibyl asked, holding the baby in capable arms and cooing at her.

'Since Lottie was in the middle of being born and Rob wasn't a bit worried, and I *wanted* him to be!'

'But why?'

'So I wouldn't have to imagine he was thinking: I've done all this before; what's one more? – which is what kept going through my head.'

'I'm sure he wasn't thinking that.'

'But it wasn't a novelty for him, was it? He *has* done it all before. Nobody seems to understand how I feel.' Nell looked beseechingly at Sibyl.

The baby had caught hold of the end of her floaty scarf and was clutching it. 'I can see you're feeling insecure,'

Sibyl said, extracting it gently, 'and I think I understand why, but you've got Lottie and this lovely cottage, and Rob's a good enough man, isn't he?'

'Yes,' Nell admitted. 'Poor Rob. I seem to take it out on him all the time these days. It's Cassie and the children who are the real problem, now that they're not moving away after all.'

'But you seemed much happier before Christmas,' Sibyl said. 'You were getting on so well with the kids then, weren't you?'

'Yes, but that was before I knew they were staying.'

'So it isn't their presence that upsets you so much. It's more your perception of what their presence symbolises?'

Nell frowned. 'Sorry?'

'It seems to me,' Sibyl explained, 'that it's not what happens that matters so much as your *attitude* to what happens. I mean, the kids never left, but you were happy – so there's no reason why you can't be happy again, is there?'

'Well . . . if you put it like that . . .'

'Things change all the time,' Sibyl said, 'so we have to live in the present moment.'

'I've never been very good at that,' Nell confessed. 'I've always lived for the future.'

'And now,' Sibyl said, smiling at the baby, 'that future has arrived!'

Chapter Twenty-Six

In April Josh was soon to be eight, and Rosie was almost six. Cassie swallowed her pride and went round to Mic's flat to make peace.

'Well, well,' Mic said at her door, cigarette in hand. 'You still 'ere?' Her hair was now two-tone, blonde in front and ginger behind. She looked very fit and well.

'Can I come in for a moment?'

'S'pose so.'

'You've been decorating,' Cassie said, looking about her at the bright clean walls.

'Yeah. I'm good at that. Remember?'

'Look, Mic, I've come to apologise.' Cassie made a supreme effort to be humble. 'I've treated you badly. I recognise that now, and I'm sorry.'

'Telly didn't snap you up, huh?'

'That's none of your b –' She took a deep breath. 'I didn't even try. It wouldn't have worked out anyway. I see that now. I just want you to know that I'd like to be friends again, and put the past behind us.'

'Mmm.' Mic looked sceptical.

'You don't believe me?' Cassie was hurt.

'Nah, it's not that so much. It's just a niggly feeling I get wot makes me fink – What's she after now? – Course, I might be wrong . . .' Mic raised an eyebrow.

Cassie had the grace to blush. 'Well, there was something specific I had in mind,' she said, '. . . as a treat for Gavin.'

'Oh yeah?'

'Yes. It's Josh's birthday next week, and I wondered –'

'Oh, Gav'd love to come. He's a reg'lar party animal.'

'Well, that's not quite what I –'

'Oh, I get it,' Mic said. 'You wants me to organise it, don't you? Definitely no way!'

'Not organise as such,' Cassie said floundering. 'I thought you and Gavin could both come as guests. You're so good at games, and the children are so fond of you. Rosie has missed you dreadfully.'

'Arm-twisting, eh?' Mic observed. 'You oughter know by now that won't get you nowhere. 'Swater off a duck's arse wif me.'

'Well, of course I'd pay you extra,' Cassie said. 'Special rates for a special occasion, naturally.'

Mic looked fleetingly interested, and then carefully neutral again. 'An' I s'pose you'll be getting all the nosh in, and sending out the invites and stuff?' she asked casually.

'Yes, of course.' I can always buy ready-made party food, Cassie thought.

'And it's on Sat'day, right?'

'Three o'clock on Saturday afternoon. I thought we'd make it a joint party for Rosie as well, as it's her birthday on the twenty-sixth.'

'I've missed her, an' all,' Mic said. 'So's Gav.'

'So, you'll do it?'

'We comes, we plays games, eats tea, goes home, and gets three times the normal rate,' Mic stipulated. 'No more, no less. Right?'

'Oh, Mic, you're a treasure,' Cassie said, reaching out to hug her.

'Mind me fag!' Mic exclaimed, extracting herself awkwardly. 'Don't want to burn 'oles in yer cashmere cardie, do we?'

'I'll look forward to seeing you on Saturday then,' Cassie said, gracious with relief. 'Maybe you could come at two o'clock to be there to welcome the children as they arrive?'

'That's anuvver hour,' Mic pointed out.

'*Please*, Mic.'

'Oh, what the hell,' Mic said, acquiescing. 'We could do wif the dosh. Gav needs a new Man United strip.'

In Tesco, as she was being comforted after a touch of colic, Lottie was sick all over the shoulder of her mother's favourite multi-coloured cardigan. Nell, cross with herself for wearing it in the first place, complained to Rob when they got home.

'What if it won't wash out? It's so special.'

'Was it that expensive?' Rob asked absent-mindedly.

'No. It's its sentimental value that matters to me. I wore it that first Christmas we spent together, don't you remember?'

'Did you?' Rob was vague.

'Quite honestly I don't believe you actually *see* me at all,' Nell flashed at him irritably.

'Cassie used to say that too,' Rob observed, but without any obvious signs of self-reproach.

Once again Nell felt an unwilling rapport with the Mad Cow, and frowned at her own disloyalty.

'That reminds me,' Rob went on, 'she phoned while you were out. She wants us to have the children for a few days extra this Easter because she had to have them back early at Christmas.'

'What extraordinarily twisted logic is that?' Nell exclaimed, all fellow feeling for the sisterhood evaporating instantly. 'They're children, not some inanimate debit and credit system. And anyway, Christmas was an emergency, for God's sake!'

'Yes, well, that's how her tiny mind works,' Rob said. 'And I'm happy to have them, so who cares?'

'I do,' Nell said.

'You what?' Rob looked puzzled.

'Well, where are they going to sleep?'

'In their usual room, of course, where else?'

'And what about Lottie?'

'She can sleep in there too. There's room for her cot.'

'No,' Nell said positively. 'They'll wake her up, and I don't want her upset.'

'She's far more likely to wake *them* up,' Rob pointed out practically. 'And anyway, why can't she sleep in our room like she does at visiting weekends?'

'I want her to have her own room,' Nell persisted obstinately. 'Why should she always be the one who has to move? I don't want her all confused when she wakes up. She needs continuity and security, not regular disruption.'

'I'm sure she'll be entirely happy in with us.'

'That's not the point! I don't want her to grow up depending upon us being in the same room. It's a *bad* idea.' Nell felt passionate about this.

'Well, I'm afraid it's a case of three into two won't go. We've only got two bedrooms. You surely aren't suggesting that we move house?'

'No, of course not. But why can't we build a bit on to the cottage; extend it into the turnaround?'

'It would face north-east.'

'So?'

'And it would cost the earth.'

'But you've got some money left over from me buying the cottage from you, haven't you? It didn't all go into Cassie's lump-sum thing . . . clean-break settlement, surely?'

'Well, no,' Rob said cautiously, 'but that's the only money I've got for future emergencies. It would need thinking about.'

He doesn't want to put *his* money into *my* cottage, Nell thought, silenced. Perhaps he doesn't see our relationship as permanent? What if he were to leave? How could I manage here with Lottie, without him?

'At least Cassie is doing the birthday party,' Rob said, changing the subject.

'Mmm.'

'I never thought she'd ever put herself out to that extent – far too much like hard work!' He was clearly impressed.

'I bet she isn't doing the food?' Nell scoffed.

'Oh, but she is.'

'She's doing the whole party herself?' Nell was amazed.

'Steady on,' Rob smiled. 'Let's not descend into the realms of fantasy here. No, it seems she's conned that Mic female into being MC.'

'I hope she knows what she's doing.'

'Apparently they've discussed exactly who does what in advance.'

'She should get it in writing,' Nell said.

'Cassie?'

'No, silly. Mic!'

Mic and Gavin arrived at Cassie's house at ten past two on Saturday afternoon.

'You're late!' she accused them, looking at her watch.

'*Hello, Mic, hello, Gav. How nice to see you,*' Mic said sarcastically. ' 'Snot much of a welcome, is it?'

'Children make me nervous,' Cassie excused herself. 'You'll have to bear with me.'

'So what's new?' Mic muttered under her breath and winked at Gavin, who chortled loudly.

'The food's in the kitchen,' Cassie said, and it was.

'Coo . . . er!' Mic said, eyes wide. 'You've bin to a lotta trouble.'

'There's this lovely little man I know,' Cassie said, quite unabashed, 'Brilliant caterer. I can recommend him.'

'Fancy prices an' all?'

'Well, naturally he's not cheap. Paws off, Gavin! Wait until the guests arrive.'

'You mean the *other* guests,' Mic corrected her.

'Yes . . . well . . . Now what about the furniture in the sitting room? Do you think we should rearrange this?'

'Where's Rosie 'n' Josh?' Gavin demanded.

'Oh, they'll be back soon. They're at a friend's house.' She turned to Mic. 'I needed some quiet space to get this all arranged, as you can imagine. They'll be here at three o'clock with all the others.'

Guests at their own bleedin' party! Mic thought, but took hold of the end of the sofa Cassie was indicating, and helped her to move it back against the wall.

By the time three o'clock arrived, Cassie had wound herself up into a frenzy of apprehension. Mic watched her, fascinated.

'No Ribena,' she was saying. 'I can't risk any stains on this beautiful carpet. Do you think I should cover it with something? Dust sheets, perhaps?'

'Mighta bin safer in the town hall,' Mic said, deadpan. 'Where there's bare walls and floors, an' the ceiling's too high to frow one of them canopy fings.'

'Canapé,' Cassie corrected her. 'Not funny. Oh God! There's somebody at the door . . . Will you go, Mic? I simply haven't had a moment to redo my lipstick.'

Josh, Rosie and fourteen other six-to-eight-year-olds arrived more or less en masse, and burst into the sitting room in a noisy gaggle. Rosie had Mic by the hand and was demanding attention. Mic waved off their parents, and then gave her a bear hug.

''Ow's my girl then? Aren't you getting' tall? Look, there's Gav. He's bin waiting to see you fer ages, to –'

'Mic?' Cassie interrupted, coming in freshly made up and smiling brightly – too brightly. 'I think everyone's here now, so you can start. Their parents will be back around five to collect them, OK?'

''Ang on,' Mic objected, raising her voice to be heard above the general racket. 'Where d'you fink you're off to?'

'I've just got to slip out for a hair appointment. My stylist couldn't fit me in at any other time, I'm afraid. Won't be long.'

Mic caught her arm. 'Oh no,' she said. 'No, you don't!' That weren't part of our agreement.'

'I think you'll find,' Cassie said, at her most supercilious, 'if you think back, it wasn't actually specified that I had to be here the whole time.'

'Right,' Mic said briskly, blocking her exit. 'I'm off. Gav! Get yer coat.'

'Oh *no*!' Gavin whined, trailing over reluctantly. 'Me an' Rosie's playin' a game, an' there's all that food wot you *promised* me, an' I haven't et.'

'You can't do this, Mic,' Cassie insisted. 'You gave me your word!'

'*Please*, Mum,' Gavin pleaded.

'OK,' Mic conceded, thinking quickly. 'You can stay, Gav, an' I'll be back at five for you, yeah?'

'Yesss!' Gavin punched the air and was gone.

'Don't you worry,' Mic said to the increasingly frantic Cassie. 'You'll be well pleased wif my Gav. He knows all the party games, an' wos more, he only charges double time!'

It seems like no time at all since she was born,' Elly said, holding Lottie in the sitting room at Bottom Cottage, and getting her to smile. 'Her eyes are really brown now, aren't they? Just like Rob's. And her mouth is exactly like yours.' She made kissing noises at the baby. 'Lovely little Lottie . . . mmmmmm . . .'

'Goo goo, goo goo,' teased Will, making a face at Sam. 'You're not thinking of having another one, are you, Mum?'

'I do hope not,' Sam said, 'unless it's a girl too.'

'Why don't you two boys pop out for a bit of a walk?' Elly suggested. 'But be back in an hour with dry feet, OK?'

'C'mon, Sam,' Will said. 'I sense there's a whole lot more boring baby talk to come.'

'You're not feeling broody, are you?' Nell asked, when they had gone.

'Well . . . just a little.'

'Are you and Kipper . . .?'

'*Keith* and I are together, yes.'

'Already? How did you manage that?'

'That's not very flattering, Nell! If you must know, I told him how wonderful I am, and he believed me. But of course I did it in an artfully understated way, so he believes he convinced me. Subtlety is my middle name.'

'Huh!' Nell snorted fondly, 'you're about as subtle as . . .' she looked out into the garden for inspiration, '. . . as subtle as a dandelion!'

Elly accepted this with equanimity. She looked as happy as Nell had ever seen her.

'Who'd have predicted that we'd be where we are now?' Nell said. 'It's as though it was only yesterday when I was single and lonely, and you were happily married, and then it all reversed itself, and now it's sort of doing it again.'

'Are you unhappy, Nell?'

'Well, I shouldn't be. I know that.'

'Let's have less of the "shouldn't". What do you actually feel?'

Lottie began to get restless, so Nell took her back again, hitching up her jersey to feed her. Then she settled back comfortably and prepared to be honest. 'It's just that I love Lottie so much. I hadn't realised how passionate I'd feel – how I'd die to protect her – absolutely!'

'Of course.'

'But I'm never going to love Josh and Rosie that way; if at all.'

'Why should you? Other people's children can't be the same as your own.'

317

'No, but I think Rob assumes that I think of them in the same way he does, and it makes me feel bad . . . and cut off from him.'

'Do you two actually communicate at all?' Elly asked.

'Of course we do!'

'Seems to me you're both assuming things about each other.'

'Well, it's difficult,' Nell explained. 'Rob has such a battle with the Mad Cow all the time, he can really do without me making a fuss as well. But every so often I suddenly understand things from Cassie's point of view, and then I feel disloyal. For some reason he doesn't seem to have learnt anything from their breakup – he just goes on being the same old Rob, and it infuriates me too!'

'But no one is all good or all bad, are they?' Elly put in. 'Everyone gets fed up with their man sometimes, and I'm sure Cassie has her points. It must have been very hard for her in this godforsaken place in the winter with two small children. She would have felt so isolated, and maybe Rob wasn't very understanding.'

'No,' agreed Nell. 'He often isn't. But when I begin to think that way, I feel as though I'm taking sides with the enemy.'

'I predict,' Elly said confidently, 'that in another fifteen years or so, when the children are grown up, you and Rob and Cassie will all have a perfectly amicable relationship. Yes, it's difficult now, but it will work itself out eventually.'

'And you and Paul and Anna too?' Nell teased.

'Good heavens no!' Elly exclaimed in horror. 'That's totally different.' And they both laughed.

Rob worried about Nell. She wasn't her usual bouncy self, and it didn't seem to him that this change in her was caused simply by the exhaustion of new motherhood. She looked sad when she thought he wasn't looking at her, and when he was, she put on a brittle show of cheerfulness that didn't convince him at all. He feared she might go the same way downhill as Cassie had gone when she'd had her children, and he didn't even know how to broach the subject with her, let alone prevent it. He was afraid that she might be having second thoughts, and that quite possibly she would turf him out of Bottom Cottage, on the grounds that it wasn't big enough for him and his children too.

He sensed deep down that Rosie and Josh were a problem to her, but he never allowed those thoughts to surface, because he didn't know how to deal with them. His usual method of coping was to let events run their course and hope for the best. This time, however, he felt the need to take action, but something still held him back. He didn't want to analyse it. He wouldn't admit even to himself that it might be the fear of rejection.

He waited until the evening before Rosie and Josh were due to arrive for their ten-day Easter holiday, and then realised he couldn't put it off any longer. Nell was sitting on the sofa feeding the baby. She looked relaxed and beautiful in the soft light from the standard lamp. Rob went and got his Nikon, and banged off a few photographs.

'Nell?' he asked suddenly, his face half hidden by the camera. 'Will you marry me?'

'Why?' Now she looked astonished. He took another photograph.

'Well . . .' He put the camera down, feeling discomfited. 'For all the usual reasons, I suppose.'

'No,' she insisted. 'I need to know why.'

'Because . . . because I love you.'

Tears ran from the corners of her eyes. 'Why didn't you tell me that *years* ago?' She held out one hand to him over the baby.

Rob was nonplussed. 'I dunno . . . I suppose I always assumed you knew.'

'Come here.' She was smiling and crying at the same time.

'Well, will you?'

'Yes, of course I will.'

So he went across to her, took her hand and kissed it.

Epilogue

During the year since our wedding, Nell thought, I suppose we should have been *living happily ever after*. I wonder why traditional stories always used to end with marriage, just at the time when life's real difficulties begin? I suppose it's obvious really – it's the only chance for a fairy-tale ending. And everyone needs hope.

She, who had always had such difficulty living in the present, now found it impossible to imagine the future. Commonplace worries held her down, and the grindingly boring everyday chores overpowered her to such an extent that she had stopped painting altogether. There simply wasn't the time, or the space.

Of course there were good times – when Lottie did all the things that babies do to the delight of their parents. Nell recorded each milestone lovingly in her diary, and tried to hang on to that joy whenever she felt down. When she was depressed these days she kept it to herself, not confiding even in Sibyl. I'm very lucky. I ought to be happy, she reminded herself constantly. And if I'm not, then it's my own fault.

Rob was his usual laid-back self, going off to work with a cheery wave through the open door of the Land Rover. His only complaints were about the man with whom he had to share an office, and his only nostalgia was for the days when he worked from home.

Josh was now nine and Rosie seven, and they visited only every other weekend, sometimes separately, with schoolfriends for company. One Saturday when Nell had arranged to escape with Lottie to Sibyl's house for a treat, she overheard Josh explaining on the phone, 'My stepmum's going out, so the food won't be as good but we'll have more fun!'

She and Sibyl laughed about it together. 'I take it Rob's an indulgent dad?' Sibyl asked.

'He's the ultimate Mr Nice Guy,' Nell agreed. 'I get lumbered with enforcing all the discipline. I sometimes feel it's Rob and the three children versus me!'

Sibyl smiled. 'But then, you never did like aggressive macho men.'

'I thought I didn't.'

'And how are the other two? I can see Lottie's blooming.'

'Oh, they're pretty good really. Rob's been teaching them to play chess, and Josh is learning – with great difficulty – to lose gracefully. And lately I've been having to go upstairs and kiss them both good night after Rob has read them a story.' She smiled at the thought.

'That's nice. So they're not jealous of Lottie?'

'Rosie's sometimes resentful about not being the youngest any more, then the next day she's all over her. They both seem to be irritated by her and affectionate in turns.'

'Sounds normal,' Sibyl said.

But I can't trust them, Nell thought to herself. And I can't be honest about how I feel, or vent my spleen. And every time they come I feel *invaded*. And Rob doesn't support me enough, so our rôles are unfairly unequal, and I feel second best all the time, and I'm fed up with him being so easy-going and so *weak* . . .

But all she said was, 'Yes, I suppose it is.'

That evening, when she came downstairs after putting Lottie to bed for the night, she found the kitchen full of smoke and rushed to open all the windows.

'The bloody stove needs its sodding chimney cleaning out again!' she shouted at Rob, who was in the sitting room watching *Blind Date* on television with avid contempt.

'I know,' he said, not moving.

'Well, if Lottie dies of lung cancer it will be all your fault!'

'I'll do it later. Stop nagging!'

'I've never nagged in my life – before I met you. You'd make a saint nag!'

'Cassie used to –'

'And shut up about fucking Cassie! Hasn't it occurred to you that she might have had a point? Hasn't it ever entered your minute brain that there could be lots of reasons why your first marriage failed, and that they might not *all* be down to her?'

'Calm down, Nell. There's no need to yell.'

'I'm utterly pissed off with you!' Nell shouted louder. 'I'm sick to death of being taken for granted and always being second best. I've had it up to here with doing my duty, and having to cook your endless bloody meals, and shifting Lottie from room to room all the time to accommodate your horrible bloody ungrateful children!' And she stormed upstairs and lay on her bed and wept. Then, when her anger had subsided, she felt ashamed of herself and cried some more with self-reproach.

She was only roused when Lottie began to wail next door, and she had to get up to go and attend to her. She took her downstairs for moral support, hiding her face behind the warm pudgy body. Rob was still watching television, but he turned the sound off as they came in.

'Now she's upset too,' Nell said.

'Come to Daddy,' Rob said, taking the child from her and making silly faces. Lottie chuckled delightedly.

'I'm sorry,' Nell mumbled. 'I shouldn't have said any of that.'

'Perhaps it needed saying?' Rob suggested. 'Sounds to

me as though you've been bottling things up, and that's always a bad idea.'

'Mmm.'

'Look,' he offered, 'tomorrow's Sunday and the weather forecast is good. Why don't we walk down to the sea and have a picnic lunch, and talk things over?'

'But you never discuss feelings?'

'Well, perhaps I should make an effort. You look worn out, Nell. Go to bed. We'll sort it out tomorrow.' He reached out and patted her arm awkwardly.

Sunday was as bright and dry as predicted. Rob called Nell over to the bedroom window first thing to see a roe doe with her new-born faun on the small meadow on the opposite bank of the river. Nell watched the faun hopping beside its mother, like a hare, and focused her binoculars on the small pale head and ears and the darker back with its white stripes. The doe was a warm ginger colour in her summer coat. She stood there, calm and undisturbed in a ray of morning sun, and then turned with her youngster and disappeared amongst the darker trees.

Oh! Nell thought. I really needed that – something beautiful first thing to raise my spirits. The May garden was lush and scented with lilac. The swallows were back, and there would be a cuckoo any day now. She felt a little heartened.

At noon as they were setting off for their picnic, Rob discovered a cockchafer trapped in the rain gauge. The water was halfway up its abdomen, and it was waving its feet feebly. He fished it out with a twig and held it up for Lottie to see. She was getting fractious and beginning to struggle in his arms. 'Big Maybug beetle. Look!'

'They're actually quite handsome,' Nell said grudgingly.

'Lovely feathery antennae,' Rob smiled. 'Good thing it went in bum first!'

This is all very well, Nell thought, but he can't distract

me as easily as he does Lottie. We do have to *talk*.

They walked along the coast path as far as the first stile, and Nell held Lottie as Rob lifted her pushchair over it. Then they set off again, Rob pushing and striding out.

'The thing is,' Nell was desperate to begin. 'You see . . . I don't love your children.' She'd said it!

'Why should you?' Rob appeared unruffled. 'I probably wouldn't love anyone else's either. But you do a very good job with them.'

'You really mean that?'

'Of course I do.'

Nell skipped to get in step with him, and took his arm. 'I thought you'd be upset.'

'No. I know it's not easy,' Rob squeezed her hand with his forearm. 'You do your best, and it's a very good best. But there's something I should have done, and much earlier too.'

'What?'

'Well, the cottage is clearly unworkable as it is, and last night forced me to think about it properly. So I think we should build that extension, then Lottie can have her own room.'

'Oh *yes*!' Nell stopped in her tracks and turned to him.

'And, if you agree, I'd like an office too, so that I can work from home again. What d'you think?'

'Why not? I'd like that.'

'There's more.'

'What?'

'We need to upgrade our river defences, so I thought we could strengthen the wall and make it go right round the garden, and maybe rebuild the jetty and get ourselves a dinghy.'

'I've always wanted a boat!'

'So you think it's a good idea?'

'I think it's terrific.'

'Listen!' Rob put up a hand. Above them, carrying

distinctly through the clear air, came a strange rippling titter of a cry, repeated several times. Rob searched the sky with his binoculars and then pointed out half a dozen birds with slightly down-curved beaks, flying purposefully overhead. 'Whimbrel,' he said with satisfaction, 'on passage.' He looked at Nell and smiled.

'Seven whistlers, Lottie,' Nell said, bending down to the child in the pushchair. 'Up there, look! We usually see a few at this time of year, but they never seem to stop.'

'Reminds me of an old proverb,' Rob said. 'Persian in origin, I believe.'

'Tell me.'

'You can't stop the birds of sorrow from flying over your head, but you can prevent them from nesting in your hair,' Rob quoted. 'I realise now that I should have spent more time helping you to shoo them away. I will in future.'

That night, when they went to bed they lay there, talking.

'I've decided we ought to make sure you have a studio too in this extension of ours,' Rob said, 'so that you can paint again. You've got such talent, and it's a horrible waste not to use it.'

'That would be wonderful,' Nell said. 'I never realised you thought that much of my painting.'

'I suppose I never said.'

'True.'

'Well, I do. I'm very proud of you altogether. It's not the sort of thing I'm good at expressing, but I promise to try harder.' Nell reached to kiss him, and he rolled over to face her. 'I love you,' he said.

'So do I,' Nell said, 'love you. It's really very painless to say, isn't it?'

'After the first time, yes. I can't think why it took me so long.'

'Maybe you're a late starter.'

'But not an early finisher, I hope.' He rolled on top of

her and began kissing her neck. Nell put both arms around him and ran her hands down his back to the little furry bit at the base of his spine that she specially cherished.

Sometime later, she realised with satisfaction that she hadn't had to say 'Up a bit' or 'Down a bit' once. They lay silently on their backs, apart again, hot and drowsy and utterly contented. Lottie was quietly asleep in the next room. The river was flowing steadily past their garden wall. The night air was motionless and fragrant in an anticyclonic calm. All was peaceful. Nell, on the verge of sleep, fancied she could hear something hopeful – maybe from somewhere in the future. She closed her eyes, the better to concentrate, and there it was again: the faint, hesitant sound of a pig – singing.